THE TRAITORS OF
Amaryllis

CASSANDRA RIOS

PROLOGUE

Connor snaps out of his deep sleep at the intense sound of the alarm going off. It's been a while since they've had an emergency. Still, it's engraved in his body to be alert as soon as he hears that familiar ringing.

He jumps out of his twin bed, and hurriedly puts on his suit. It consists of long pants that taper at the base of the ankle and a narrow long sleeve shirt. It is made of a tough, heavy, dark gray material that takes effort to get on. He loops his gear belt through the waist of his pants and runs to Headquarters to see what's going on. He rounds the corner to the Intelligence room which is surprisingly barren, given the circumstances.

There are only five Intelligence agents occupying the monitors that cover the room. Besides them and Connor, Colonel Finch is the only other person here.

Damian and Shrina arrive within minutes of him. The other soldiers must be out on mission, as these three are the youngest soldiers able to deploy. They are very capable soldiers for their ages of sixteen- Connor and Shrina- and seventeen- Damian. Soldiers begin training at twelve years old and are released into the field as young as fifteen, depending on their skill level.

Colonel Finch begins debriefing them immediately.

"There are Necromancers casting evil spells in an attempt to destroy the Veil," Finch says sternly, her mouth hard and nostrils flared.

"But doesn't that mean-" Shrina starts asking the question that's stirring in all of their minds.

"That the humans would be able to see everything, yes. It would complicate the borders. It would mean the amount of human deaths would increase substantially and it would threaten our entire system of order and regulation. These Necromancers have someone on the inside. Otherwise, we would've seen it coming long before they got to this point."

"What's the assignment?" Connor asks cautiously, hoping the answer is different than he suspects.

"There are at least three people involved. Two of which are the Necromancers destroying the Veil. The third is the contact who most likely won't be on the scene, but is expected to be surveilling the situation. We have no idea if they have back-up, but according to Intelligence, this is a small disturbance."

"Let's get to it, then," Damian starts.

"This is not to be taken lightly, Soldiers. However small the group might be, it is a powerful one and you all need to be cautious. An Intelligence team will be deployed with you to try to detect and then block any surveillance from the Traitor. The ideal result is to take the Necromancers into custody. However, if this is not possible before the Veil is destroyed, you take them down by whatever means necessary. Am I understood?" The face Finch is wearing is not a familiar one, and it makes the hair on Connor's neck stand straight up.

"Yes Colonel," the soldiers say in unison.

"Gear up. You deploy in five," Finch commands and then turns back to the monitors, barking demands at the Intelligence agents who scurry to find the location of the disturbance.

The soldiers load onto the aircraft, their gear belts stocked with enchanted weapons, armor and Intelligence devices. The flight doesn't take more than 15 minutes, which means the disturbance is relatively close to Headquarters. Connor wondered why they weren't taking a ground vehicle but if the Necromancers are successful in taking down the veil, Headquarters will be visible to every creature and therefore vulnerable to attack. If Headquarters goes down, thousands upon thousands of other people will be at risk.

Before deploying, the Headquarter Necromancers enchant the soldiers and their weapons. The magic being used to take down the Veil is dark, though, and they can only hope the Headquarter Necromancers know how to counteract it.

The soldiers' suits are surprisingly movable despite being bullet, venom and magic-proof. The boots are extremely quiet on the forest floor, leaving every twig unsnapped as they move swiftly towards the disturbance area. It's a foggy night, not uncommon for the city this time of year, but unsettling for the mission they are now on. It could be the Necromancers' attempt at hiding themselves.

The Intelligence team circles the three soldiers, increasing the diameter with each step in order to cover as much area as possible in search of a signal.

Their earpieces remain quiet for what feels like an hour before Headquarters spits out the information "Intelligence has picked up a strong magic signal South East."

The soldiers simultaneously change direction and move even faster towards the Intelligence team that they can barely see in the distance. They catch up within minutes and realize the team's pace has slowed. Four of them have strong signals pulled up on their scanners.

Damian, Shrina and Connor briefly make eye contact before advancing between the Intelligence agents. Connor's heart rate picks up as they get closer. There is a dull glow not sixty meters from where they are.

"Connor, flank right. Damian, take left." Finch orders from the earpiece.

Their pace slows as they move forward, trying to block themselves from the Necromancers' views. Connor can make out two figures. The one on the left is male and the one on the right is female. They are both heavy set and look very strong, their sturdy arms moving quickly and their lips forming quick sentences- spells- when Connor notices a small shadow-

He stops dead in his tracks and presses the button on his earpiece to notify Headquarters of what he sees. Damian and Shrina slow to a stop to his left as they too see the small girl standing very still next to the Necromancers, facing away from them. They look at each other while the command "Continue your mission, soldiers," sounds in their headpiece.

Connor grows increasingly uneasy as he tries to come to terms with the fact that this otherwise peaceful night is about to turn into a bloodbath with multiple casualties. If the Necromancers are attempting something this dangerous and stupid, they are not going to back down. The three soldiers form a large triangle around the two Necromancers and child, closing the space between peace and violence in quick strides.

"Intelligence needs sound."

They are within two meters now and Connor throws a microphone towards the Necromancers. It levitates in the air, in an attempt to record the chants and verify the spell they're using is forbidden.

He looks quickly to the Intelligence soldier that is closest to him and he nods his head, confirming that this is the disturbance they were sent to eliminate.

"Move in."

Damian and Connor move quickly behind each of the Necromancers, while Shrina inches towards the small girl. When they're close enough, they look at each other and nod.

"You are under arrest by Headquarters for using illegal magic, do not resist," Damian and Connor shout in unison, surrounding the small group. "Place your hands behind your backs and lower yourselves to your knees."

There is a brief silence as the Necromancers pause their chant, look at each other and then strike. Connor instantly brings his left forearm up with a fist, barely activating his shield before a burst of light smashes against it. He knew this wasn't going to be a peaceful surrender. They continue moving in and he takes out his sword with his right hand. "Surrender now, before it gets ugly!"

The Necromancers disregard the orders. They are attacking quickly and in every direction, hitting the shields of everyone in sight. Connor is close enough to strike but where his sword should have made contact with the Necromancer in front of him, there is only air. He steps back and sees she's now to his right. He doesn't have time to adjust his shield before a string of magic hits his chest. It burns, despite his suit covering the area.

Shrina throws her knife and it meets the stomach of the Necromancer, burying itself in a pool of red liquid. The Necromancer grunts and snaps her arm in Shrina's direction, but not fast enough. The ball of light crashes against Shrina's shield and a spark hits the little girl that still hasn't moved an inch. Her eyes are open and unmoving.

The spark lands on her back and scorches it as Connor's Necromancer screams out. The male Necromancer halts his fight against Damian, snaps his head around, and throws a spell towards the little girl. Her back immediately stops burning, but his actions give Damian enough time to shove his sword through his chest.

Connor runs over to his Necromancer who is now on the ground, motionless, but still alive. "Roll onto your stomach and put your hands behind your back." His voice is firm and deep, making him seem a lot older than he is.

Nothing about this could possibly be humorous, yet the Necromancer spits out a laugh that quickly turns into a wicked cough. Connor pushes her stomach with his boot and holds her firmly there as he reaches for his handcuffs. They glimmer in his hand. He's putting one end on the Necromancer's wrist as she starts whispering under her breath. He's about to tell her to shut up when she seizes violently and then stops moving altogether. He reaches down to look for a pulse but there is none.

He looks over his shoulder to the rest of the group and suddenly the little girl, who can't be more than six years old, blinks for the first time. Her eyes open wide as she takes in the scene around her.

"Mama!" she cries out and runs to the Necromancer that lies at Connor's knees, lifeless. The spell holding the little girl must have broken with the Necromancer's death. The little girl's green eyes fill with tears and she sobs, clutching at the arms of what was her mother.

Connor grabs her hand in an attempt to draw her attention away from the horror she's experiencing.

"What's your name?" He tries to be as soothing as he can, while knowing full well that the actions of the people in that forest, including her parents, just ruined her life. He wondered what kind of parents would put their child in such a devastating situation.

What spell did they put on her and what did it have to do with their breaking down the Veil? How will we ever get the information we need now that they're both dead?

She whispers softly and holds tightly to Connor's finger.

"Wrap this up and head back," the voice on the headpiece is less demanding now and sounds more tired than anything.

Connor looks up just as Damian points his gun towards the little girl's back and pulls the trigger.

ONE

Lila

I stop paying attention to class the minute Professor Thort puts my graded test on my desk. I text my roommates, Rachel and Cindy, a picture of the score.

Cindy: Ouch.

Rachel: Oh Lila! I'm so sorryy…

Me: I'm never getting out of this stupid class.

Rachel: When will Philosophy ever help you as an artist anyway?

Me: It won't. It's useless just like the rest of my general classes.

Cindy: For real. Let's go out tonight, blow off some steam.

Rachel: Could be fun!

Me: I should probably stay in and study tonight, for obvious reasons…

Cindy: Boring. At least come for a little while, the guys want to go out tonight and Warren is dying to see you!!

Me: LOL. I'll let you know.

Class finally ends and I mosey back to my apartment, avoiding eye contact with anyone who might try to talk to me. Now is not the time.

Luckily nobody else is home yet so I hurry to my bedroom, throw on some headphones, and turn up the volume to my music.

I've got my nose in my sketchbook when I hear the apartment door open. Several voices, all of which are way too cheerful for comfort, spill into the living room. Great. I can hear Cindy's loud laugh almost immediately, after one of the guys says something to her.

Cindy is a great roommate to have- very social, helps us all make friends and find fun things to do- but she's a little… superficial? That word may be a little too strong. Though, it is sometimes hard to tell when the facade stops and her true bubbly personality begins. Drama follows her like a dog on a short leash.

Rachel, on the other hand, is very genuine. She shares my room. She's studying business, which surprised me at first, given her soft features and calm voice. She may be the kindest person I've ever met. Don't let that fool you into thinking she's anything close to boring, though. Rachel really knows how to let loose and have a great time or when to be completely serious and hardcore.

Suddenly my bedroom door swings open and Cindy gasps at the sight of me in bed.

"No, no, no." She's shaking her head and doesn't even try to hide her disappointment. "No sulking! Get out of bed, put on something cute and come out with us!" She's pulling me by my arms and clearly is not going to give up this time. If only Rachel were here to save me.

I comply and make my way to the closet, glaring at Cindy the whole time. She grins and closes my door again, allowing some privacy for me to 'put on something cute.' I scan my limited wardrobe in search of anything at all decent to wear. I have nothing that even compares to the bright yellow dress Cindy has paired with her hot pink stilettos and dramatic eyelashes. Only she could pull off looking like a highlighter.

I groan and pull my black dress shirt off its hanger. It's been a while since I've put it on, but it still fits nicely. Maybe a little better even, since my chest now fills out the top. It's got short, flowy sleeves and a v-neck opening that sits right above my cleavage. It fits very snug until the smallest part of my waist, where it then flows out in waves, matching the sleeves.

I pair it with my best blue jeans- the only ones not stained with ink or paint- and some delicate hoop earrings. I sigh to myself in the mirror as I try to prepare myself to go outside, knowing that Cindy will most likely tell me exactly what she thinks of my outfit before I even say hello to the rest of the group. I grab my black booties and head to the living room.

Warren is the first to spot me, since he's lingering behind the rest of the group. Cindy is occupying everyone else with an exaggerated story, giving Warren time to approach me.

"Are you coming out tonight?" He tries to sound casual but everyone with a clue can tell how much he thinks he likes me. Desperation is not attractive, but Warren is a nice guy. Tall and probably strong, with long dark hair and brown eyes.

"Yeah, I guess so," I try not to give him anything to read into. He hasn't made a real move yet, so I'd like to imagine that he's decent at reading social cues, but it may be wishful thinking. His face lights up and Cindy squeals across the room.

"Yay! You look hot. Let's go!" She grabs my wrist as she bounces toward the door. The guys follow closely behind her, pushing each other playfully as they fight for her attention. I feel Warren's eyes burn into me from behind as I let Cindy drag me along.

The disco is dark and stuffy as hundreds of people ranging from teenagers to thirty-something year olds push around each other, dancing to the music that's playing loudly through the speakers. Cindy takes turns entertaining each of the three guys that came with us, occasionally making room for a random disco guy here and there. She plays them so effortlessly, winning each of them over by strategic moves of jealousy, hope and flirtation. It's kind of entertaining to watch.

I push towards the bar and ask for a soda as I whip out my phone and text Rachel.

Me: WHERE ARE YOU!!?!?

Rachel: Sorry, got hung up with a group project.

Me: Seriously? On Friday night?

Rachel: "Welcome to the reality of the business world" - Professor Buttface

Me: Come save me.

Rachel: I'll let you know when I head out. I've still got to get home and get changed…

Me: Kill me now.

I hear my phone buzz once more but my attention turns to the hand that was just placed on my shoulder. I spin around to none other than Warren Blake smiling at me and standing a little too close to me. At least he smells good.

"One beer and a margarita, please," he shouts at the bartender. He's still smiling as he leans down and talks closer to my ear. "Bored already?"

"This isn't really my scene," I start to explain as the bartender places the drinks on the bar in front of us. Warren slides the margarita to me and takes a swig of his beer. "Oh, that's okay, thanks. I didn't really want to drink tonight. I have lots of studying to do tomorrow."

"Come on, it's on me. Take a break, you're so serious all the time."

I take a sip or two until Warren stops looking so expectantly down at me. He's probably right, I am kind of serious every time he's around. This group always puts me on edge. I wish Rachel were here. She would've been dancing too, but unlike Cindy, she would only be dancing for herself.

Warren eventually sits down and is talking about school or something boring until I check my phone. 11:26 PM, not nearly late enough to call it a night by Cindy's standards. No other messages from Rachel, besides the "LOL" she sent earlier.

"Am I boring you?" Warren still wears a smile but it falters a little as he asks the question that should have an obvious answer.

"Sorry, I'd like to make it home early tonight so I can have a productive day tomorrow," I feel embarrassed even saying the words out loud. Warren looks back at me skeptically. Then he takes my hand and leans close to my ear again.

"Let's get out of here, I'll walk you home."

"Oh, Warren, it's really okay. I don't mind walking alone-"

"It's late on a Friday night, in a college town, Lila. I'll get you home before curfew, don't worry." He laughs a little under his breath and gets down from his barstool, slaps some cash on the bar and pulls at my hand lightly.

"Alright. Let me tell Cindy I'm leaving."

He nods once and releases my hand, gesturing towards her. It's not hard to find her bright colors in the midst of dark tops and jeans. I have to shout into her ear three times before she really hears me.

"I'm going home, Warren is taking me." Cindy nods in understanding, finally. She winks at me, then smiles towards Warren, making my stomach turn. I don't have time to clarify before someone pulls her back to the dance floor.

It's a bit chilly outside as we make our way towards my apartment. I try to act casual though, as not to give Warren any funny ideas. His pace is slow and he takes the long way back, passing through a courtyard. He slows to a stop and I turn around to face him. I immediately regret it and a shiver runs up my spine. I can see the wheels turning in his head and I'm afraid that beer made him a little too confident.

"Are you cold?" My shiver distracted him from whatever he was about to say.

I begin shaking my head but he takes his jacket off anyway and wraps it around me. Great, now he's way too close. His face turns serious when he moves his attention to my lips.

"Warren," I say quietly and step back slowly. His face twists into something like embarrassment and maybe a little frustration and I'm very aware now that we are alone, still about a quarter mile or so from my apartment.

"What?" He asks abruptly, clearly feeling awkward from my subtle rejection.

"I'd just really like to get home-"

"Are you serious?" He laughs, but it comes across sour.

"What do you mean? That's what I told you when you offered to walk me." I try to sound innocent but I was afraid something might happen.

I don't feel the same as Warren but he's persistent and maybe I enjoy the attention a little bit. It's been a long time since I've been romantic with anyone.

"Oh, come on, Lila. We both know what that means. Is it because you're embarrassed to be seen with me? Did you want me to wait until we got to your apartment?" His questions sound genuine and I begin to think I gave him too much credit.

"What?" I scoff. "Warren, I didn't let you take me home so you would kiss me or-" I don't know how to finish the sentence without giving him any more ideas. "I just want to get some sleep so I can study tomorrow before my shift. I can make it from here, you should go back to the club and have some fun."

"Don't be such a prude. You should be glad someone is actually willing to give you a shot." He moves close again, grabbing both sides of his jacket that's wrapped around my shoulders and moves in yet again.

"I believe she said no." It's not a familiar voice, but I have heard it before. Before I can place it, he comes into view. I see him around all the time. He lives in my building and maybe even has a couple classes with me, but I can't remember his name- Riley? Rodney?

"This is none of your business, creep," Warren spits in the guy's direction. He keeps his eyes on me as he turns me around to face our apartment building. He moves his tight grip down to my left hand and starts walking me forward. "I'm just taking her home."

"I don't care what you're doing, she doesn't want it. Leave her alone." His voice is stern and I'm surprised but grateful. Where did he come from? Could he see us from his window? Maybe Rachel is home and will look outside-

"Shut up, prick. You don't know her or what she wants." Warren is getting angry.

As we get closer to him. I can start to make out some of his features. Brown hair, very strong, medium height, probably a little shorter than Warren but not by much.

"Ryker? Is that you? Oh come on, man. You really had me going there for a minute."

Ryker, that's right. His name is Ryker Johnson. His hands are casually in his pockets and he's leaning against one of the pillars on the edge of the courtyard, right where we need to pass in order to get to my apartment.

"Warren, don't make this harder than it needs to be. Let her go, she's not interested. Go back to your jock friends and find a different chick to gross out. Preferably one who gives consent." He's smiling but it doesn't reach his eyes. It seems I've managed to put myself in the middle of a pissing war. Wonderful.

Warren keeps his grip on me and I look up at his hard features. Usually his face is so pleasant but he is obviously angry right now and my stomach is a rock as he pulls me past where Ryker is standing.

"You're such an idiot." Ryker is behind Warren and before I know it, I get shoved to the ground, forcefully. I hear fist meet face mixed with grunting but I don't see who hit who before I hit my head, hard, against a rock.

❖❖❖

I wake up as a ray of sunshine cuts through my window and straight to my eyes. I hurry to cover my face with my pillow as I groan. Why does my head hurt so bad?

"Oh, thank you for waking up," Rachel says with a deep sigh. "I was starting to think you were dead and really didn't know what I was going to do."

I lift the pillow only enough to squint towards her direction. In this moment, I'm grateful for how expressive my face is as Rachel nods in understanding of my utter confusion.

"You're wondering why the room is so bright and why your head hurts so bad?"

I barely nod my head, and regret it the moment a sharp pain smacks my skull.

"Ouch."

"Yeah you probably shouldn't move until I get you some pain meds or something. You went to the disco - sorry I didn't come in time, by the way." She shoots me an apologetic glance before continuing. "But I guess Warren was walking you home and somehow you ended up with him in the courtyard, which is the opposite direction but anyway-" She pauses as I sit up and adjust my pillows so I can lean against them. "Warren tried to…"

"He tried to kiss me." The memories start coming back to me, slowly, as Rachel describes what happened. Did I really drink that much? Why does my head hurt and why are my memories foggy, did Warren slip me something?

"Yes, and you said no. He didn't take it as a no, though, and he tried again." Rachel's voice is full of regret, and I'm scared to ask her, but I need to know exactly what happened last night.

"Were you there? Did Warren drug me? Why does my head hurt so bad?"

She shakes her head slowly and then resumes the story.

"No. That hot guy stepped in the second time and told Warren to piss off. Warren got upset and started dragging you to the apartment, so HottieMcBody went to stop him and…" Rachel looks at me expectantly, her hands open as if she wants me to finish the story but I'm completely dumbfounded.

"What 'hot guy'?" As soon as I ask the question, the memory of a shadow near the edge of the courtyard pops into my head.

"He said that when he went for Warren, Warren pushed you out of the way and you tripped and hit your head on the stone. Then he took care of Warren-" she adds with finger quotes- "and brought you back here. He said to look for signs of a concussion and make sure you don't choke on your vomit." She smiles timidly, relieved that the story is over.

"Ryker." I remember him, but not well.

"Is that his name? I'd rather call him HottieMcBody." The amused look on her face makes me immediately want to crawl into a deep, dark hole and live there until all this stupid drama passes.

"So much for doing schoolwork today," I mumble and sink back into my bed. "Now that you know I'm not dead, can you close the blinds?"

The preoccupied wrinkles return to Rachel's face as she nods slowly, stands up from her position on her bed, and closes the blinds of the window. She walks past me to leave the room, avoiding eye contact. I reach out and grab her arm before she goes through the door.

"Rach." She hesitates before meeting my eyes. "It is not your fault that Warren tried to kiss me. He probably would've found a way to get me alone even if you were there. You're a great friend and I'm lucky to have you."

She smiles at that, the alleviation finally reaching her eyes as she hears the words. She squeezes my hand once before going through the door and closing it softly behind her. It's quiet outside the bedroom and I embrace the rare opportunity to rest.

TWO

Ryker

My stomach is tender as I lift her up and carry her to her apartment. Warren got in a punch or two before I knocked him clean out. What an ass.

I knock on the door loudly and wait for a response. It's got to be around twelve forty by now and I'm sincerely hoping someone is home.

For the first time tonight, I realize I've never been this close to her before. I wish it were under more pleasant circumstances, but I'm sure she won't remember much about me regardless.

She has very light skin, though some of that may have to do with being knocked out, and the contrast of the dark blood framing her otherwise flawless face. There is something so natural about holding her in my arms, yet she is barely more than a stranger to me. I'm secretly grateful for the opportunity to study her features without blowing my cover completely.

I knock again and it's interrupted by the door swinging open.

"Shhhh! It's the middle of the night what do you-" the girl on the other side of the door- Rachel- gasps as she finally takes in the scene in front of her. Some random guy, holding her roommate in his arms, completely passed out. "Lila?! What happened?"

"Warren was trying to make a move, she said no, he didn't listen."

"So he hit her?!" She's yelling now and typing frantically on her phone.

"No. Where's her bed?" I ask her, annoyed that she's staring at her phone at a time like this.

"What the hell-" she finally looks up.

"Your roommate's passed out in my arms and although I am pretty strong, I will drop her at some point. Where is her bed?" I ask again, more demanding this time.

Her mouth closes abruptly and she leads me to what must be Lila's room and opens the door. She points toward the messy bed covered in black and purple and I set Lila down gently. I roll her to her side and turn back towards Rachel.

"She's going to be fine. Let her rest, but keep her on her side. I think she may have had a drink or two. I don't see any signs of a concussion but if she acts weird tomorrow she should probably go to a doctor." I make my way towards the door but she jumps in front of me and sticks her hand out to my chest.

"You're not going anywhere until you tell me exactly what happened, unless you want me to call 9-1-1 right now." She went from sleepy to fierce in a matter of seconds. Her hair is tangled and she is wearing mismatched pajamas.

"Warren was walking her home, he tried to make a move, she said no. He didn't listen, I stepped in, he got pissed, pushed Lila out of the way and then she hit her head on a stone and I took care of him. Any other questions?" I am slightly bothered as I say the events out loud. Warren is such an idiot.

"Thank you," She says genuinely, calmer now that she knows what happened. "I'm Rachel, Lila's roommate. I was supposed to go out with her but I fell asleep..." she glances over to the bedroom, regret on her face.

"It's not your fault. Warren's been trying to get with her for months. He should be leaving her alone from now on. Have a good night." I walk past her now, not in the mood for any more chatting, and make my way back through the front door.

She takes the cue and closes the door behind me without another word. I hear the lock turn and I smile to myself, glad that at least one of her roommates isn't a complete ditz.

I walk back over to Warren, who is still passed out on the cold stone floor of the corridor that leads to the courtyard. This definitely wasn't the quickest way from the disco. Warren took the scenic route, trying to charm his way into Lila's pants. What an idiot.

I try not to think about her while I carry Warren's limp body back to his bed. I don't share his room, for which I am especially thankful tonight, but I am unfortunate enough to live in the same apartment as him. He's been non-stop talking about Lila for what feels like an eternity. When I overheard his loud conversation earlier with Chris and Brady, I knew he would probably pull something stupid tonight.

The rest of them are hooked on Cindy. In a way, I almost respected that Warren at least had enough sense to be more interested in Lila than Cindy. That is, until he pulled the line 'You should be glad someone is actually willing to give you a shot,' tonight. Asshole.

I begin to write my report of the incident but I can't get the idea of her out of my head long enough to focus. She looked nice tonight until he made her feel terrible about herself. Until he made her scared. I try to keep my thoughts in check before I get heated again and kill Warren in his sleep.

That's not the assignment, Ryker, focus.

But I can't help but wonder what she thought of me being there. Will she remember anything that happened tonight or will she wake up with a blasting headache and just forget it? Will she remember what Warren did or am I going to have to follow him around and make sure he doesn't go all terrorist on her? Will she remember that I was there? Will she think it's *weird* I was there? Does she even know who I am? Will she think I'm a stalker, that now she has to be wary of two men on a daily basis?

My assignment is to be invisible and I've got to admit, up until tonight, I have absolutely succeeded. I was surprised Warren even knew my name. Though it probably has more to do with the shit my roommates talk about me when I'm not around than actually knowing who I am or anything about me. I keep my head down in class, wear bland clothing so I don't stand out in a crowd, rarely talk to anyone and only when necessary.

I know I'm not going to get anything else done tonight so I take a shower. As I undress in the bathroom, I notice bruises starting to form on my abdomen from where Warren punched me. He did better than I had thought. He's not a small guy, after all. I grab an ice pack from the freezer and wrap it around my waist once I get back to my bedroom. I'm very glad Chris and Brady aren't here tonight. I'm sure they're out with Cindy, probably where Warren and Lila had been coming from.

I lock down my phone and computer before changing my towel for shorts and a tee shirt and settling into my bed. I usually don't stay up this late but then again, neither does she.

Warren either doesn't remember the events of last night or he feels like an absolute douchebag for how he was acting because he avoids making eye contact with me all day. It's pretty great, actually.

Chris and Brady got home late. They were totally wasted and are still sleeping when I leave for work. I don't make too much of an effort to be quiet, fairly certain that nothing could wake them up at this point. This is routine for them and I honestly don't understand the appeal of not being aware of your surroundings or even your own actions.

I've been drunk maybe once in my life and have never wanted to repeat it. Majority of our time as Soldiers is spent training, and there isn't an abundance of partying going on. Occasionally, the Soldiers will go out for a few drinks after a big mission and there are always a few who get plastered, but the rest of us usually just want to blow off steam with a good game of pool or throwing some darts.

I finish brushing my teeth, throw on a sweatshirt and my

sneakers, and head out the door. I pass Lila's apartment on my way to the library and briefly consider knocking, seeing if she's okay. The thought passes quickly, though, as I glance down at my watch and realize I'm going to be late. I rush past the housing buildings and towards campus.

I make it in time to put my things in my locker and clock in at one fifty-nine PM. This job helps me stay invisible since most people don't come to the library on a social quest. It's easy work, putting books on their respective shelves after the students return them.

Time passes slowly today as I think about how Lila's doing and worry if I made a mess of my situation by the way I handled things last night. If she got hurt then the entire situation was pointless and will make it harder to get things back to normal. The way Warren acted today, though, makes me hopeful that all will be forgotten soon.

I feel buzzing in my pocket and set the stack of books that are in my hands on the step ladder. I pull my phone out and answer immediately.

"This is Jordan," I say with a hushed tone. Anyone here knows me as Ryker Johnson, but my phone will only ring for Headquarters.

"What the hell are you doing out there, bro?" My obnoxious brother, Liam snarks into the phone.

"What do you mean?" It's been so long since I've heard from him, I can't tell if he's pissed or amused at whatever he's talking about.

"There's talk that your mission is going south. You made a scene and now people are starting to notice you. What are you doing, man?" He may be mocking me, but there is definitely a hint of concern in his voice.

Heat rises from my chest up to my face as I grasp the meaning behind what Liam is saying. If he's heard about it all the way back out in the field then I really might be in trouble.

"Are you messing with me, Liam?" I ask a little too harshly.

"No, Ryker, they're saying you punched a civilian. Are you good?" He almost sounds anxious on the other side of the call.

"I'll handle it, it wasn't a big deal. Thanks for letting me know. Hey, put in a good word for me, will ya? Don't want this to reach the wrong ears and all." Liam knows exactly who I'm referring to.

"No prob big bro. Get it cleaned up so they don't take you out of there. That would be bad for all of us."

"On it. See you."

"See you."

I have a hard time focusing at work after the conversation I had with Liam. Him having heard about last night means this is a bigger deal than I originally thought and I need to find a way to clean it up. Luckily, the job isn't very demanding. I mindlessly carry books from the huge return pile to the carts and stack them in their rightful shelves.

Close to the end of my shift, Krystal approaches me.

"Why do you look like that?" She looks me straight in the eyes, clearly displeased about something. Subtlety is not her forte.

I look down at my clothes before looking back at her with a shrug.

"Not your clothes, dummy. Why do you look so serious today?"

"Oh. Uh, just family stuff." I know it won't satisfy her but what else am I supposed to say? Yeah I'm on a secret mission and I may have just blown it and brought disgrace to the Jordan name?

"Boring. You look better when you're tired. I have an assignment that I forgot is due tonight so could you watch the counter for me for an hour?" Krystal gestures her hand impatiently towards the front desk of the library.

"Yeah, no problem."

"Thanks. See you later, then."

"Later."

The rest of the shift passes quickly, regardless of the fact that I stay later than normal to cover Krystal. When she returns, I dismiss myself and walk quickly back to my apartment, relieved to be done for the day.

Now that word is going around, I take my report a lot more seriously. As soon as I get home, I type it up as simply as I can and send it in. Not ten minutes go by before I receive a call from my commanding officer, John Hansley.

"Soldier," Hansley usually greets me as Ryker or sometimes Jordan but Soldier is pretty formal and my heart rate spikes a little at the sound of it. "I hope you understand the severity of your mission."

"Yes, Captain." I don't get the chance to proceed.

"There is talk that you may get switched out, given the circumstances. This call is a courtesy to make you aware that you are on thin ice."

"Captain, I admit that I could've acted with a bit more discretion, but did I not fulfill my mission?" It may be too forward but I'm failing to see my incompetence here.

"Ryker, you knocked someone out in the middle of a courtyard and then relayed the story. Not only did you cause a scene, you spread the word of it as well, and for what?" His tone is stern, which isn't out of the ordinary but it has a hushed edge, indicating to me that maybe he's not supposed to be communicating with me.

"'*For what?*' Was I not sent here to keep an eye on things and to step in if things escalated? What, was I supposed to just let-" I'm definitely starting to get defensive, which probably isn't going to end well with Hansley.

"You are supposed to be invisible Ryker, there are Traitors near you, who else would've reported you? This is a delicate case and you should know that by now. Every step you take is being watched and you better make sure that stops. Be forgettable, be invisible, and do it now."

"I-"

"It's not a question, Soldier, it's an order from your commanding Officer." His voice leaves no room for discussion.

"I understood, Sir."

Hansley ends the call and I punch my bed, breaking several springs beyond repair. I would've much rather punched a hole in the wall but then my idiotic roommates would probably trade the gossip for a chance to look at Cindy's ass.

THREE

Lila

I wake up to a dark room and silent apartment, which is more than rare. I sit up in a panic and check my phone for the time.

9:47 PM

Well, that explains it. Who would be home at nine forty-seven PM on a Saturday night? Why am *I* home and *in bed* at nine forty-seven PM on Saturday night? It dawns on me slowly at first and then all at once. Holy shit.

I jump out of bed and scarcely make it to the toilet before emptying my stomach, which, by the looks of it, has been devoid of food for quite some time. I rinse my mouth and head to the fridge.

There's absolutely nothing edible so I stomp to my bedroom and pull on some sweatpants and a sweatshirt. I throw my hair in a messy bun, grab my keys off my desk and pull my sneakers on. I hesitate before opening the front door. I know that nobody is behind it, since I've checked the peephole four times. But I'm scared of who I could run into while I'm out there.

Eventually, I muster up the courage and get to the campus diner to order myself a spicy chicken sandwich with a strawberry milkshake. I stay for a while, bopping my head along to the beat of each song on the alternate playlist that plays in my headphones as I eat. I'm looking out the window, staring at the night sky when something- or rather, some*one*- walks past my view.

He doesn't see me, he's focused only on the ground in front of him. His stride is quick and each step he takes would probably make up five of my own. He's walking towards the complex, so he must've been either studying or working.

Does he have a job? I've never thought twice about the guy until today. It's funny how much one night can forever change your perspective.

I finish my food and swipe my meal card at the counter before heading to the Campus library, hoping they store public information about students and staff members. If I hope to run into Ryker, I need to know where I can find him.

Thirty minutes into my research and I still come up dry. The only thing I find is a mostly-clear picture of Ryker. No age, no address, no job title, no social media. I guess I should be glad that the school doesn't just have its students' personal information on display, but I start to get frustrated by the lack of answers I come across.

I'm back staring blankly at the computer in front of me with Ryker's face and name pulled up when I hear someone come up behind me. My heart speeds up as I race to close the tabs I have open.

"He's hot, isn't he?" I turn around at the sound of her voice. She's got an employee badge with the name 'Krystal' typed on it. She's nothing like what I'd expect a library employee to look like. She has bright colorful hair, dark makeup and way too much jewelry.

"What? No I was just-" My voice sounds overly-defensive and I give up trying to get myself out of this one.

"Don't worry about it, you're not the only one swooning, babe." She smiles as she pulls out the chair next to me and sits. I don't like pet names in general, but especially not from strange girls I just spoke to for the first time. "Spill."

This girl is out of her mind! Who talks to a stranger like this? I look at her incredulously and I'm sure she can read my thoughts. My face is way too expressive to hide what I feel.

"Tell me why you're stalking my coworker or I'll tell him you're creeping!" She threatens with a smile and then looks at me expectantly.

"I'm not stalking- wait did you say coworker? Does he work at this library?" I raise my head and look around frantically.

"Oh wow, you've got it bad. He's not here dummy, he just got off an hour or so ago." Oh, duh. I just saw him walking home. Why am I so nervous? Probably because I don't know what he did to Warren and I don't know if he had a good reason to do whatever he did to Warren.

"I don't have it bad. I'm just trying to find him so I can thank him. I don't know him very well but he helped me out last night and I want to tell him how grateful I am, that's all. Get your head out of the gutter, you don't even know me." Yep, way too defensive.

"Damn. What'd he do, blow your mind in the bedroom?" Krystal is enjoying this way too much.

"Oh my g- you know what? Forget it," I stand up and gather my things. "Don't tell him I said anything and stop sneaking up on customers, it's bad for business." I'm embarrassed by how very not clever that just sounded and I don't give her another opportunity to humiliate me.

I'm huffing all the way home, frustrated and embarrassed that this Krystal girl just saw me searching Ryker's name and what probably looked to her like obsessively staring at his picture.

I throw my things on the floor, grab my sketchbook and sit comfortably on my bed, taking a deep breath. I sketch out the scene that plays in my head on replay: Ryker, standing with his hands in his pockets, leaning against the stone pillar of the courtyard. His stance was so casual yet his mere presence was enough to change the entire atmosphere that night.

The scene is black and white in my sketchbook and it makes shivers run through my body. If he's supposed to be the hero of my story, why do I feel so intimidated by him? He feels so cold to me in this memory and I don't understand why him being there to come to my rescue has me feeling so unsettled.

I run through what Rachel told me this morning and try to piece my memories back together, one by one. I remember Warren putting his coat around me, I remember stepping away from him and then feeling daunted by the fact that it was late on a Friday night and that nobody knew we were there. I remember feeling his anger at my rejection.

Something sticks out to me as I sketch the fragments from that night. Warren had said 'Ryker, is that you?' as if he knew Ryker personally. If he did, how come he never mentioned the name? Why did Ryker never join us when we went out as a group? How did he know where to bring me after I hit my head? Why was he there in the first place?

If he's the shy and quiet guy that sits in the back corner of my Biology and Communications classes, then why did he have the guts to stand up to a guy like Warren? What did he do to Warren and how? He's not obviously bigger than Warren in height or weight but maybe he's stronger. Maybe he's the type of nerd to do Taekwondo or Jiu Jitsu growing up and Warren just never saw it coming. Why do they know each other?

My head starts to swirl as I remain empty-handed when it comes to answers to my growing number of questions. Eventually, I tire of not knowing. I take some more pain meds and get cozy in bed, flipping on a good RomCom to drift off to.

I don't know how long concussions are supposed to last, but I didn't think I'd be excused from class without a doctor's note or something. Especially considering how much school I've managed to miss this semester. Now that we're almost two-thirds of the way through, I've re-committed myself to taking school seriously.

When I was younger, I promised myself that I would pursue art. In order to fulfill that promise, I have to keep my scholarships, which entails keeping my grades up, or at least passing. Somehow, I manage to drag myself out of bed in time to make it to Biology class.

It's harder to focus than normal, my hands are itching to draw Ryker's stern face. He's one part terrifying and two parts intriguing. I can't get his face right in any of my attempts and I realize I've never actually been face-to-face with him before. Some of the sketches nag at my head, begging me to remember, but what am I forgetting?

Majority of Biology class goes by with me sketching. As the professor wraps up the useless lesson about something to do with cells that I'm going to have to study later, I realize that this is one of the classes I share with Ryker. I quickly look around at the spaces in front of me and start to relax as my eyes don't find my subject to land on. Class ends and I close my sketchbook and gather my things.

When I stand up and turn to exit the auditorium, I notice an olive-toned man in the back of the room, walking out the door. My feet stop dead in their tracks. Was I seriously just drawing a man who was sitting several feet behind me for an hour and a half? What are the chances that he didn't see that? I'm going to have to jump out my window tonight.

Right now, however, I have to genuinely focus on Philosophy. Starting by getting to class.

For the first time in a long time, I actually understood what Professor Thort was talking about. Well, more than half of his lecture, which is more than I can say for any other day I've attended his class. My hand scribbles the last of the notes before packing up and going to work. I called in sick on Saturday and Sunday and am not particularly keen on going in today but working is a necessity.

I got hired as a secretary at a law firm- no, I don't know why they chose me- the week before I moved here for school. I actually enjoy it quite a bit. The job consists mostly of coffee runs, printing random documents, walking case files from one lawyer's office to the next, organizing paperwork, etc.

It's mindless but still doing some good in the world. Although, to be fair, we could be helping the worst people in the world stay out of prison to continue doing the worst things imaginable and I would be utterly oblivious to it.

The firm is off campus, so there is a significant amount of walking involved, but I don't hate it. It's nice to get out every once in a while.

The best part about the job is the hours. The firm is open 12-7PM every day. They are flexible with my school schedule, and I usually come in from 2-7PM, giving me enough time to get home from class, eat, and change clothes. It's a great company to work for and, though I have no qualifications to be here, they treat me as though I'm the key to their success.

Two of the lawyers took on some really big cases recently, so today I've got my work cut out for me. I won't have any time to worry about roommate drama, bad grades, or guy troubles. I run documents to get signed, take them to the post office, get coffee for everyone, and help the paralegals with their workloads a bit so they don't end up staying all night.

We wrap up for the day a few minutes after seven, when the CEO tells everyone to call it a night so we can start back up fresh tomorrow. Though the work isn't too taxing, I'm grateful to be done for the day. My head started throbbing about an hour ago and I'm ready to get home and decompress, maybe even work on my sketches in the privacy of my room.

The sun is setting behind the skyline but the night stays illuminated until I get to the apartment. I hear the voices from inside as soon as I twist the doorknob and dread floods every part of me. I peek my head inside and make a beeline for my bedroom, not quite swift enough to avoid being spotted.

"Lila!" Cindy squeals from the living room and comes racing

towards me.

I'm scared that if I turn around, I'll see Warren in the corner and- yep, there he is. Eyeing me hard from where he stands, always just shy of isolating himself from the group completely. Creepy certainly isn't a word I would use to describe Warren, but his presence in my apartment right now is anything but comforting.

I don't remember Friday night well enough to know how I should proceed. Was it just a misunderstanding? Was I scared about hurting his feelings or was I scared of him? His face is still brown and purple from Ryker's fist, I assume. I kind of hope it hurts and that he feels embarrassed.

Cindy hugs me tight while whispering carefully into my hair. "He wants to talk to you alone. I think he's probably harmless, but let me know if you need anything."

I nod and she pulls away from me, eyeing me carefully. I feel bad for kind of expecting Cindy to be on his side. Maybe I don't give her as much credit as she deserves. She might be a little crazy and we definitely have our differences but she's pretty great in her own way.

I'm being sincere when I say, "Thank you."

She releases me and goes back to being the center of the group's attention. Besides Warren, Chris, and Brady, there are three unfamiliar faces. On another night, I might have introduced myself but I don't have it in me. I turn awkwardly away from everyone and head to my bedroom.

I put my bags down on the floor and I'm disappointed to see that Rachel is nowhere in sight. I was hoping we could hole up here together. She always knows exactly what I need. I waste as much time as I can until the unwelcome sound of Warren knocking on my door leaves me with a choice I'm not yet prepared to make.

FOUR

Ryker

I wake up feeling sluggish and a little pissed off. How could Liam and Hansley doubt my abilities to carry out my mission? It's not even a very difficult one. If only stupid girls would make better decisions in regards to who they spend their time with, this whole thing could have been avoided.

It's Sunday, which means laundry and housework day. I'm really the only one who keeps the apartment clean and I blame it on my training. Back at Headquarters, we are expected to keep our things in order. Not only as discipline training, but we also never know when we'll be expected to pick up and move.

I was the first in my age group to get sent out on a solo mission. When I found out what the mission was and that I would be undercover for years at a time, I was totally stoked. The guys threw me a huge party and I knew they were all jealous, despite trying to hide it.

But then I got out here and well, it kind of blows. It's mundane, my job is literally to blend in with civilians so well that the same civilians don't even notice me. Sometimes I forget I'm even on a mission and that my life isn't completely pointless.

I start with the kitchen since Chris is still sleeping in our shared room. It doesn't take me more than eight songs on my playlist to finish the task. After an impromptu run around campus and a hot shower, I lose my patience and go to my room to remove my hamper. Warren is there speaking in a low voice to Chris and doesn't look up the entire time I'm in there.

I pass him casually, change into a clean outfit and get my

hamper, detergent, and dryer sheets before leaving. What a baby. I'd probably kill him if it wasn't for this piece of shit mission.

I finish folding and hanging up the remainder of my laundry and head to work early, wanting to avoid my roommates before I accidentally snap one of their necks.

Usually, I handle day-to-day civilian life rather well without thinking about the reality of it all too much. Today, I can't stop thinking about how stupid this mission is and how much I want out of it. I stopped a moron from almost-kissing some girl, woop-dee-doo. And then I got reprimanded for it from my commanding officer. Kill me now.

There are only four of us working at the Library the rest of the night, which is alright considering Sunday evenings are relatively slow. There are plenty of books to shelve, though, since most are due on Mondays and students are notorious procrastinators.

Not an hour into my six-hour shift, Krystal pops her head out from around the corner of the bookshelf I'm stocking and starts with her drama. Normally, she bothers everyone else and leaves me alone, but I guess this weekend's events may have given off the impression that I'm more than just a boring loner.

"She was asking about you, you know." She looks excited to finally have something in common with me. Except that she heard wrong and I'm not the guy she's looking for.

"What?" Don't ask me why I even bothered. I thought maybe if I could quickly help Krystal come to the realization that I *am* just a boring, drama-less guy who's super uninterested in gossip, that she'd never try to speak to me again. It was a rookie mistake.

"The girl you screwed this weekend. She came in here asking about you."

"I didn't screw any girl, you must be mistaken."

"Oh my- are you GAY?! Wow it makes so much sense and yet how did I not see that?" Her eyes are wide and I think she's more upset that her gaydar is broken than coming to the made-up conclusion that I'm gay. Civilians are annoying and I hate this mission more with each passing moment.

"Are you on crack, Krystal? I'm not gay and I didn't screw anyone this weekend. What do you need?" I snap.

Her snake smile returns as she picks up where she left off before going off on her random tangent.

"Oh, yes you did. The small one with green eyes and wavy brown hair? You changed her whole perspective of sex. Are you really that good, by the way, or is she just new at it?" She twirls a piece of her hair as her eyes drag over me.

Small one with green eyes and wavy brown hair? I didn't drink this weekend did I? My face obviously conveys my confusion because she backs down after several seconds of silence on my part.

"She told me not to say anything and I thought she was just embarrassed but," she frowns at me, clearly dissatisfied with my depressing sex life. "You seriously didn't sleep with anyone? She was researching you and said she wanted to thank you-"

"Who are you talking about?" Am I being pranked? Someone was stalking me? Wanting to thank me?

"I didn't ask her name, Ryker. If I had a dollar for everytime I caught a girl looking at you, I wouldn't need this shitty job. Damn, I thought you were actually becoming an interesting part of society." She's bored now and about turns to walk away but then retreats and asks "What did you do to her, if it wasn't something in the bedroom? She said she needed to thank you for Friday night."

The small girl with the wavy brown hair. Friday night. She doesn't mean-

"Are you talking about Lila?"

"Ugh, pay attention, dammit. I told you I don't know her name. I'm bored now, I'll see you later." She waves a hand limply and heads over to Bridget, another coworker, who probably has much more scandalous news to share.

Lila came to the library asking about me? Maybe Hansley was right, maybe I really did make a mess big enough to cause concern. I was sure she wouldn't remember me, and I didn't think Rachel knew who I was enough to tell Lila when she came to. I made sure not to tell her my name and I was in and out of there in a matter of five minutes, maximum.

Stupid, stupid girl. She just made this situation ten times worse and now I'm even more pissed than before. She's going to cost me my job, not to mention several of my close relationships that depend on this mission. I never should've gotten involved with her and Warren. It's not my job to protect her from her own stupid decisions and I won't make the same mistake twice.

The entire time I'm at work I think about Lila. I wonder why she was asking Krystal about me. I think about the fact that throughout the full length of the Biology class we have in common, she was drawing me over and over again, none of them quite right. What is her problem? Why is she so curious about someone who was just trying to help? I have to get her off my back one way or another.

I stop by the diner on the way home, since it's the only place open 24 hours on campus. As soon as I make my way to the counter, Miguel shouts my way. "The regular?"

"Please," I say with a chuckle.

Before this past weekend, the chef at the diner was the only person who knew anything about me personally: my food order. I've never gotten anything else from the diner and I don't plan to broaden my horizons anytime soon. Two Chicken Patty Melts, extra pickles, swiss cheese and a side of steak fries, to go.

I have eaten in the restaurant before, but I prefer to eat outside, if it's nice. If I work a long shift and get a lunch break, I'll eat in the library breakroom. Otherwise, I always take it to my apartment.

While I do somewhat enjoy the diner's ambiance, I don't know if I would stay invisible here. The building isn't very big and is full of booths and then the bar.

I could take a booth and possibly get left alone by most of the staff and customers, but each booth connects to a full window spreading from the tile up to the ceiling. I think it would make me feel like a zoo animal if anyone decided to pay attention to me, the loser, taking up an entire booth to ensure my loneliness.

The waiter hands me my order in a brown paper bag and I put the cash in her delicate hand. She's in what I can only assume is traditional diner attire, with her hair styled big and fluffy, a pink collared shirt and a delicate white apron tied around her waist even though she's not doing any of the cooking. She's wearing bright red lipstick that sticks to her front teeth when she smiles at me and thanks me for visiting.

I take my time as I stroll back to my apartment, never sure what I'll find when I arrive.

The climate has been so pleasant lately. Cool nights and perfectly warm days are pretty much year-round with some exceptions here and there. Summer is creeping up on us, though, and now I don't even wear a jacket most nights. The afternoons are a few degrees warmer and barely noticeable. I snack on some of my fries before opening the apartment building door and heading down the corridor.

Our apartment is nearly on the far end of the hall and it normally takes about a minute to walk down from the front doors. Tonight, it takes about a minute and a half.

My fingers are warm and salty from the french fries I'm still snacking on by the time I get to the door. I sigh with relief when I notice all the lights are turned off and the only thing making sound inside this apartment is the refrigerator humming its usual tune.

I set the paper bag on my desk and stow my backpack in my corner of the bedroom, right where it always is. Consistency played a huge part in my training and I like to know where everything is at all times, but particularly my bag that is full of essentials, should I ever need to leave in a hurry.

Being a student is a very handy cover sometimes. It's a good thing colleges don't take up the habit of checking what's inside their students' backpacks.

I'm not halfway through my sandwich when I hear the door to the apartment open. Ugh, there goes my peace and quiet. I'm annoyed, but it isn't until I hear the second voice that the pace of my heart spikes and heat rises through my chest and up to my face.

"I just want to show you-" Warren claims innocently, as if he could never betray someone's trust.

"Warren. I am not going any further," she says firmly. Good.

"Come on, Lila, I thought we were good. I told you I'm sorry for the other night-" the way he is begging is so pathetic and he is such an *idiot*.

"Yeah you *told* me a lot of things on Friday too. Go get whatever it is you want to show me, I can wait right here." I almost want to give her credit for standing up for herself, but she wouldn't have to if she weren't so *stupid*. I hate these people.

I hear Warren as he steps across the apartment and goes into his room. I take the opportunity to leave before I kill someone, attempt to run from the law, and then end up in prison. Or worse.

I grab my trusty backpack and I go to head out the door. Lila's face changes rapidly from discouraged to surprised to relieved when she recognizes me.

Here's my chance to right my wrong, to get her off my trail and go back to being invisible. Clearly my trying to help a damsel in distress was wasted on a nitwit who doesn't deserve to be saved again.

"Hey you're the guy who-" she starts as I begin to pass her on my way out.

"And you're way more stupid than I gave you credit for the first time around. Have a good night, you two deserve each other." I finish with a sarcastic head nod, wave my paper bag in her direction, and walk out the door. I bump her a little through the frame, though it's not my fault she refused to move. She's clearly got nothing going on up in that pretty little head of hers.

"Excuse me?" Lila scoffs at me. I've got to admit, I wasn't expecting a reply. I thought my honest comment would hurt her delicate- and readily manipulated- feelings to keep her away from me and maybe, hopefully, even Warren for the rest of time.

I just chuckle under my breath and continue my mic-drop-worthy walk down the corridor. Where the hell am I even going? It's close to midnight on a Monday night.

Am I going to go back to the diner that I just ordered to-go from? Am I going to eat in a parking lot or on the cold stone ground outside the building? I should've thought it through a tad more, but I don't regret getting out from under the same roof as Warren and Lila who are otherwise alone together in our apartment.

I don't want to hear the shit Warren says to someone in bed, especially her. I've already lost all respect for him and I don't need more ammo to fuel the rapidly growing hatred I feel towards him.

FIVE

Lila

Ryker's words hurt more than I ever would have anticipated. I don't even know the guy so I am unsure as to why, but the fact that he replied so quickly and ended his snarky comeback with 'you two deserve each other' makes it very clear that he regrets helping me escape Warren's drunk advances on Friday.

I haven't forgiven Warren and I'm still not sure I want to, but Ryker acting like I'm the world's biggest idiot is making me second guess hearing him out at all. Maybe he's right, I am now alone with Warren, yet again, and there is nobody in sight to help me if he tries to make a move on me again.

My eyes sting as he makes his way out of his room and meets me back at the front door. He's got something small and fluffy in his hands.

"Lila? What happened?" He notices my face as he closes the gap between us, careful to not come to close, and his goofy smile fades quickly. His hand lifts as if to touch my face but then he drops it suddenly before making contact with any part of me.

"Nothing." How am I supposed to explain that the roommate that beat him up just days ago, who left him with a bruised face and a healing split down his bottom lip, just called me stupid for talking to him again?

"Hey…" Warren moves his head, gesturing for me to look at him. "Is it something I said? I word vomit sometimes, Lila, I certainly didn't mean to make you upset. Here, look. This is what I wanted to show you." He smiles softly and hands the fluffy object to me. I turn it around and my face lights up when I recognize my favorite animal staring back at me.

"You remembered." It's really more like a whisper when it leaves my mouth. Over two months ago, we were all playing some stupid game where we had to choose an animal. I chose a kangaroo and everyone laughed it off for being so random. Except for Warren. Instead, he came up to me afterward and asked why I had chosen it.

I was hesitant to share with him that one of the foster homes I lived in had once told me that my parents were from Australia. I told him how since that day, I had loved everything Australia-related. I don't even know if there was any truth to it, maybe I was annoying the poor older lady and she just wanted me to shut up. Either way, I had believed it and wanted so bad for it to be true that I told everyone I was from there. Warren was so genuinely interested that I ended up telling him the whole story.

I'm not all that surprised that he remembered my favorite animal. He does spend a lot of time trying to get to know me, despite my efforts to blow him off. What did surprise me is that he actually saw a stuffed kangaroo, thought of me, and decided that he would get it for me.

"Of course I remembered. Lila-" he sighs a little and I'm suddenly nervous about what he's going to say next. "I'm really sorry for treating you the way I did. I shouldn't have had three beers before walking you home and I should've been more considerate about how you were feeling that night. But I'm even more sorry that I made you feel like I don't care about you.

"We all know I've been into you since the moment I saw you, but I didn't know how you felt. I don't regret trying to make a move, just the way that I did it. I tried and you rejected me, and I get it now, and it won't happen again. I would still like to be friends and get to know you, but it's your decision. Just let me know, okay? The ball is in your court."

I'm speechless by his response. I had forgotten how good of a guy he really is during these last couple of days. He wouldn't hurt me on purpose. For all I know, Ryker attacked him and Warren pushed me out of the way so I wouldn't get hurt. I remember Warren trying to kiss me and not exactly respecting my reaction, but maybe I wasn't clear enough and he didn't know I was rejecting him.

I don't want to assume, though. I want to be sure he's not going to do anything like it again, and I won't trust him again until he proves he's worthy of it.

"Thank you, Warren." I don't give him any more. I take a step outside, motioning to him that he can come back to my apartment to hang out with the rest of the group now. He follows my lead.

"You'll have to make the next move if you end up falling for me." He grins a little to let me know he's joking. When I laugh and roll my eyes back, he puts on his big goofy smile and we walk the rest of the way in silence.

"There you are, I was starting to get worried!" Rachel huffs, loud enough for Warren to hear. He backs off and joins his friends while we converse.

"Sorry, Rach. Thanks for looking out for me. I'm okay, he just wanted to apologize." I avoid meeting her eyes in an attempt to dodge her judgy glare.

"Did you forgive him? Oh, Lila, please don't tell me that you forgave him. That stuffed animal probably has a camera in it or something." She pinches it with her pointer finger and thumb and throws it to the sofa.

"Relax. I haven't forgiven him or forgotten what he did, I just gave him an opportunity to apologize and explain. I'm sure the kangaroo is clean but I'll be happy to let you search it for bugs later." I grab Rachel's hand and pull her towards the group. "Now come on, let's have some fun." She rolls her eyes but ultimately follows me in.

I've seen *him* a couple of times in the last couple of weeks, but only briefly and in passing. I notice that he hurries to his room the minute we enter his apartment. I see his pace pick up walking to and from class after spotting me.

Tonight's the first time I've been around him for longer than three minutes and I feel like I swallowed a rock. I don't know why his presence makes me so uneasy. Maybe the fact that he swiftly took out a big guy like Warren and left without so much as a scratch. Or that he told me how stupid he thinks I am and I'm still doing the very thing that made him call me stupid to begin with.

Why does he make me feel so small? And who the hell gave him the right to do so? My anger increases by the minute and I hate Rachel for suggesting he stay. Not that she should've known not to, I never told her anything that happened with him.

He refuses to look at or speak to myself or Warren directly, sending the not-so-subtle message to the rest of the group how he feels about us being friends. Though he ignores me, I see his jaw clench every time Warren touches me. I don't know why I pay attention to it. I can't seem to focus on anything else without addressing the big, strong, and tan elephant in the room.

Cindy looks a little uncomfortable as well and it does anything but settle my nerves. The rest of the guys couldn't be more oblivious to the tension and I'm not convinced Warren is aware of it either.

I'm pissed off now, and I want to punch Ryker's big stupid face for making me doubt myself and my decisions. Warren has done nothing but keep his promise and treat me with respect the last couple weeks and Ryker can't just come in here and destroy all of that. He doesn't even know Warren- or me!

I do the only thing I can think of to really get his attention. I squeeze Warren's hand and whisper in his ear, "let's go get milkshakes from the diner." I don't want Warren to think too much into it, but I whisper quietly enough so that nobody else can hear what I actually said.

He only sees me whisper in Warren's ear and then leave with

him alone. It definitely did the trick, Ryker's eyes are filled with fire as I close the door behind us.

❖❖❖

Luckily, Warren, oblivious as he is, did not read into the milkshake request. He walks casually to the diner, talking the whole way about how funny Chris's joke was. I give him a courtesy laugh as my head spins.

Right before we sit down, and as nonchalantly as I can, I ask him about Ryker.

"So the roommate that never comes out of his room is kind of creepy and ominous, huh?" I keep steady eye contact with my milkshake as I sit across the booth from him.

"Uh, yeah, I guess so."

"What is he studying? 'How to become a serial killer' or something?" I make a face as if I'm not really curious and just making fun of someone- which is not something I typically do. Warren knows me too well. He squints with his response.

"I've never asked him. Chris thinks he might be military though."

"He doesn't wear a uniform," I'm still trying to sound like I don't care but the more answers Warren doesn't have, the more intrigued I am.

He shrugs. "I'm not very close with him, Lila. If you haven't noticed."

"Sore subject, then? Sorry, let's talk about something else." I look away, trying to think of something, anything besides Ryker Johnson.

"It's not a big deal, Lil, I just don't know him very well. Chris says he's OCD about his stuff and he cleans the whole apartment like once a week, and that's all I've got. You should ask Rachel, I bet she's learning all kinds of things about him." He laughs at the last part.

"What do you mean?" I prod, hoping my face isn't saying too much.

"Seriously, Lil? Were you not there? She was practically sitting on his lap by the time we left! I'll be surprised if she doesn't stick her tongue down his throat by the end of the night. I'm just hoping they find somewhere else to do it." He rolls his eyes with a smile, as if the thought is entertaining him. The rock in my stomach sinks further. Warren notices. "Don't worry Lila, he's harmless. I've never even seen him talk to a girl before tonight. Maybe getting laid will help him chill out."

I can't listen to this anymore without giving some kind of reaction. I sip my shake and try to think of something else that Warren can blabber about. "So how's your statistics class going? Do you still think you want to be a nerd when you grow up?" I tease.

He immediately drops the previous subject- he's so consistent- and fills the rest of the time we sit at the diner talking about how many statistics we encounter on a daily basis as I zone out, nodding and smiling occasionally in order to keep the facade.

We're not at the diner for more than a total of thirty minutes before I ask Warren to take me home. He does, without any kind of guilt trip. It is late, after all, and I have class and work tomorrow.

"Thanks," I say to him quickly when we get to the door. I know he probably wants more, but I'm not ready, especially not tonight. He nods and I smile politely while closing the door behind me.

I head to the bathroom to wash my face and brush my teeth. I can't remember the last time I was this desperate to go to bed. It takes me several moments to realize that Rachel is not in our room. I check the bathroom, the living room, the kitchen, and still nothing.

I knock lightly on Cindy and Fara's room and open the door when someone says "Come in!"

They're both in their beds, so they've been home for at least a few minutes longer than I have, but they're wide awake still. "Hey guys, do you know where Rachel is? I haven't seen her since-" Oh, hell.

Cindy gives me a look that I've never seen before, a mixture of disgust and pride, a combination I never thought possible. "She took Ryker to his room about twenty minutes ago."

"Wait, what?" No, no, no, no!

"I know you're like a virgin, Lila, but come on. They're doing it, obviously." She's half annoyed with me. I have no words to give in response.

I don't know what I'm feeling but I'm positive it's not good. The rock in my stomach grows somehow and I feel sick.

SIX

Ryker

Two weeks go by before I hear from Captain Hansley again.

"I don't know what you did, Ryker, but it worked. The higher-ups are pleased with your dedication and are keeping you on the mission." He is a lot happier than the last time we spoke and it takes a weight off my shoulders.

"Glad to hear it, Sir. It's important to me to stay on this case."

"I know it is, son. Keep up the good work. Have you found any leads? Has anything of importance happened with the subject?" Hansley is not normally a curious man and I wonder if he's been worried since our conversation weeks ago.

"No, Sir. Everything is very mundane here. I don't believe she is involved with Traitors. Not knowingly, anyway. I am looking into a few suspects but don't have anything concrete yet." I don't want to disappoint him, but it's the truth. There haven't been many instances at all but especially none that make me suspicious.

"Well, keep at it. I will let you know if we receive any tips or see anything out of the ordinary here. Try to get insider information if you can but be smart, lay low and be discrete. A small lead won't be worth getting caught. Someone else is watching her just as closely as you are, keep that in mind. She's the key to bringing this whole thing down. Whether she's on our side when it happens, that's what matters."

There's nothing new about my civilian grind. I wake up, go to class, go to work, go to bed, repeat. It's boring but I'm glad that things have calmed down again. I still have to watch my temper every time I see Lila with Warren, which is almost every day now.

She hasn't made her move yet, but it's only a matter of time. I just hope I'm not within earshot when it happens. Warren is like a love-sick puppy and I don't even want to imagine the blasphemous sounds and declarations that would leave his mouth if she were to do anything more than hold his hand.

Rachel is still suspicious of him which makes her the only decent one of the bunch. I hear her trying to reason with Lila every chance she gets.

The group started hanging out at our place more often, though I have no clue as to why. It only ever gets clean when I decide to do it, and the decor is way better at the girls' apartment. At least now I can work from the comfort of my bedroom. Stay invisible and get the inside scoop.

Work at the library is the same, though I've been taking less hours. Krystal still hates me for 'leading her on' about being an interesting person. We never really talked before the night Lila talked to her about me and I never cared to try. She's the worst of them all, maybe even worse than Cindy.

Cindy is at least somewhat worth the hype. She's definitely beautiful, in a Barbie kind of way. She's got a decent sense of humor, she's full of energy and seems to make everyone have a good time. Krystal sucks the life out of people. She's cold and dark and nobody should be that involved in the drama of other people's lives.

I'm still at a loss for what to pick up in all the free time I've been accruing lately. I've attempted a few video games but the fighting doesn't even compare to reality. I keep what Hansley said in the back of my mind as I weed through classmates, coworkers, and people who live in my building. Most of them are in her life coincidentally. At least one was put there strategically, though.

I make my way home and try to organize my thoughts. I write out names of people that have caught my attention and I compile evidence little by little, for hours on end. My laptop's battery declines rapidly and I decide to bite the bullet and get my charger from the kitchen.

Every one of my roommates plus the four girls from Cindy's apartment- including Fara, who almost never leaves her room- have been in our living room for almost two hours. I made it almost two hours without needing to come in contact with any of them. I usually prepare for hibernation better, in an attempt to avoid them until they leave. It seems the cards are not in my favor tonight.

As I leave my room, I bump into Warren and Lila. They are walking in the direction of his bedroom. Warren stops in his tracks and the smile drains from his face as I stand firm in his way. I can see Lila looking to me and then Warren and back to me.

"Excuse me," Warren says, with an edge to his voice.

"You're excused." I shrug my shoulders at him and move a few inches to my right, now cutting off Lila's path. My hands are in tight fists at my side as I try to control my anger. She looks up at me with a scowl but I keep my eyes pinned on Warren, which makes him both irritated and nervous.

"Hey, hottie," Rachel calls from the living room "Ryker, is it? You should come join us."

Warren lets out with a chuckle under his breath. "Yeah right-"

"You know what?" I cut him off. "I think I just might. Thanks for the invite." I don't know where it comes from but I'm not sure I'm happy about it.

I push Warren's shoulder playfully and smile at Lila before moving to sit next to Rachel. Lila's face is completely unreadable. Warren swallows hard and then resumes his path to his bedroom. He turns when he realizes Lila's not following him yet, because she's still looking straight at me.

I know she did it just for me because she looked at me before and after whispering to Warren to take her home. What a brat. Maybe I shouldn't care so much but she's being so stupid. Why would she want to be alone with Warren after what he pulled on Friday night? Is she really that delusional about the guy?

Lila and Warren had been gone for ten minutes when Rachel slid herself on to my lap. I had been paying more attention to Lila and Warren and hadn't realized Rachel was flirting with me until she was sitting on my lap.

We continued playing with Cindy, Fara and the guys for a few minutes and I was zoned out until Rachel kissed the skin under my ear and muttered "Take me to your room, Soldier. We need to chat."

I was so taken aback by being called 'Soldier', that I snapped my mouth shut, nodded, and led her by the hand to my bedroom. "What did you just say?" I turn to her as soon as the door is closed.

"I know I shouldn't be talking to you, but I think we could work better as a team. I've got a pretty good lead and you just helped me get a lot closer to exposing it." She is very serious right now. I've only ever seen her laid-back and giggly, and this new demanding tone she's using confuses me even more.

"What the hell are you talking about-"

"Ugh, come on Jordan, did you think they would only send one Soldier to do this kind of mission? You can't live with her or follow her around everywhere without her noticing. You've had to back off several times, did you really think that seeing her in class would be enough?" She looks at me disappointed in my being oblivious and then reaches out a firm hand. "Rachel Brooks, fellow Headquarter Soldier."

I shake my head slowly in return, with absolutely no idea how to respond. This could be the Traitor, this could be the very downfall of the entire mission. She's right, she has way more access to the subject than I do and if she's part of the rebellion, the mission has already failed.

She pulls out her phone and gives a keyword that opens her Headquarters access and calls someone. "Captain, it's me, Brooks. I'm here with Jordan and I need you to verify-" She stops suddenly as the voice on the other end of the phone- Hansley- speaks firmly, maybe even angrily at her. "Yes sir, I understand. Our working together has just become vital, sir. We have a lead but we need each other."

There is silence for several seconds and then she hands the phone to me. "Captain? What the hell-"

"Jordan, I'm sorry you found out this way. I was not given authority to advise you about other Soldiers involved. They were supposed to stay undercover, even from you." A long sigh sounds from the phone. "Brooks is with us, okay? You need to be careful because if anyone suspects you two are working together, we're all screwed. I hope you've come up with a good cover. She knows everything that you do, and possibly more. I technically can't give you permission to disclose information to her or I will be off the case. Just do what needs to be done to figure this out. She's with us." There's a sound of a door in the background and Captain Hansley disconnects the call.

"That doesn't prove anything. You could be-"

"The Traitor? Ha! Get over yourself, Ryker. You seriously almost screwed everything by getting between Warren and Lila. I just saved your ass by including you tonight. I'm glad you followed suit and made nice with Warren. You still need to lighten up around the two of them, I need you to get closer to Warren."

"What are you talking about?" My thoughts are racing as I try to connect all of the dots. Of course Headquarters would want someone else on the inside. Otherwise, she's right, my assignment would have been to monitor the subject twenty-four seven and it would be too obvious, too easy for the moles to pick up on. How did I never think of that?

"Focus, Jordan. I don't know how much time we have tonight." She looks at me sternly until I gather my composure.

"What's the plan?"

"Warren. He's got to be a part of it. He made a mistake trying to kiss her that night. He overstepped and he almost lost his in. But then he came up with a whole sob story and wiggled his way back into her life. They're not romantic yet, as far as I can tell, but it may only be a matter of time. I need you to get close with him. Our cover is that we were jealous but then we found each other and now we're happy for them. He's involved, Ryker, I can feel it."

Rachel's right. He was too persistent, too much of an ass and he lost her. Then he changes his demeanor so she learns to trust him again. He's not in love with her, he's trying to get her on his side. I really did almost mess it up, then. I didn't like him from the start, but now it makes sense. "He has help. He's not alone, either."

"I'm afraid not. I've been trying to track him, but I can't get close enough. He knows I don't approve of Lila's decision to forgive him. He'd be suspicious but if y'all made up? You could be bros, you could get details, you can find out what he knows and who he works with."

"Genius. Good call."

"I'm not bad. But we have to keep up a good cover, Jordan. That's the only way this will work. We need to be obsessed with each other, and we need everyone to believe it. If Lila and Warren start dating, we will go on double dates. If they're in the living room, we are in the next closest bedroom."

"Agreed. This is too perfect of an opportunity to pass up. Are there others?"

"Soldier, I cannot discuss classified information with you." She gives me the warning with furrowed brows.

"So there are." I grin. "Who are they, where are they stationed?"

"Back down," She tries to remain serious but there's an annoyed smile lingering on her lips.

"We cover home, school, and extracurriculars. So there's

someone at her job, then?"

She rolls her eyes and changes the subject. "You need to suck on my lip and give me a hickey on my neck or something."

I shake my head again, sure I didn't hear her correctly. "What?!"

"We've been in your room for almost half an hour. I can't go back without some sort of evidence!"

"You're crazy."

"Don't be such a baby! Just do it quickly so I can go find Lila." She gestures for me to move in.

"Fine, but I'm warning you right now, you're going to have to try really hard not to fall in love with me." I raise an eyebrow at her and I'm grateful to have someone to work with. I've been alone at this for so long.

"I promise," Her voice is steady. "This is purely business." I pretend to be offended by how sure she is and she hits me playfully on the arm to tell me to knock it off. We are going to have fun.

She's tall enough that I don't have to bend down too far to reach her mouth. I chew on her lip until it's red. She looks in her phone camera and nods her approval. I move to her neck and leave a dark crimson spot four inches from her right collarbone, where it will be fairly visible.

We shake hands and Rachel hooks part of her shirt in her bra to look like it was pushed up at some point. Damn, she's good.

She leaves my room just as Warren is getting back. He blinks several times at her before muttering "'Night," and scuttling to his room.

SEVEN

Lila

Only a few minutes have gone by but my mind has managed to find the worst possible case scenarios about my whole situation.

I can't even articulate why I'm upset that Rachel and Ryker might be all over each other right now. I don't have the right to be hurt. But Ryker basically told me that he regretted saving me from drunk Warren and now Rachel is into him? I know she wasn't there when he said it, but she personally witnessed the way Ryker acted in the hallway right before she invited him to hang out. Am I making something out of nothing? Was he being funny and I couldn't read it because I was so on edge in his presence?

She's still not home. Is she staying overnight? She's definitely not the type to sleep with a guy she just barely met. Or maybe she likes him more than anyone else I've ever seen her with. I usually take my frustration out on paper, but as soon as I open my sketchbook I see ten versions of Ryker's face and slam it shut. Could this night get any worse?

The front door opens then closes and I brace myself for Rachel to walk in. She does, without any hesitation.

"There you are, Lila! Where did y'all go? Were y'all here alone?" She looks at me while putting her bag down. I'm too stunned by her appearance to respond. Her shirt is still stuck in her bra, so her shirt came off while Ryker was sucking on her face- and her neck, apparently.

"Lila? Are you okay?" Rachel turns her full attention to me now.

"I just…" What do I even say to a good friend that I'm angry at for no good reason at all? "I'm just a little confused."

"About what?"

"Where were you? I got home ten minutes ago and everyone else was here already." I'm not sure why I ask the question when I already know the answer, but I certainly don't want to talk about Warren right now.

"Oh, I was still with the guys..." She looks bashful all of a sudden. "Look, Lila, I'm sorry I was so rude to you about Warren before. I didn't get it, but I do now. Ryker is amazing and such a good kisser and I get it now and I'm sorry for being so judgemental."

"What do you mean?"

"I was jealous of what you and Warren have and I'm sorry if I made you feel bad about wanting to spend time with him or date him or whatever you guys are doing. It's totally not my place to make those decisions for you. I think I really like Ryker and I want you to be happy for me, so I'll be happy for you and Warren no matter what you decide." She leans over my bed and hugs me then.

"Oh." I don't even know what else to say. Rachel likes Ryker? She's happy for Warren and I? What alternate universe did I just stumble across?

"Well? What do you think?" She pulls away from me, putting some space between us, and looks at me eagerly.

"About what?" I struggle to match her energy.

"Lila? Did you even hear anything I said?" Rachel's smile falters and disappointment seeps into the big eyes staring back at me.

It's not fair to make her feel bad for something she's excited about. Ryker did call me stupid but maybe it was the heat of the moment. He did have to step in a few days before when I was alone with Warren and he was probably still frustrated with him.

Besides, none of that has anything to do with Rachel and I doubt she even knows about it. She likes him and even though he's blunt and maybe even a little rude, he does seem like a decent guy, protective of people he doesn't even know.

"I'm sorry, Rach. Yes, I was listening. I'm just tired and it's taking me a minute to process everything. I'm glad you had fun with Ryker. I would love to hear about it later, but I'm pretty beat right now and really just need to sleep. It's been a long few days." I don't say it with nearly enough enthusiasm but I can tell it makes her feel better and I'm glad I can say it genuinely.

"Sure, no problem." It seems I sobered her up with my negative attitude. She moves off my bed, changes into her pajamas, turns off the lights, and climbs into her own bed. "Good night," she says softly, turning towards her wall.

"Good night, Rach." I turn over and try to sleep, too. I really am tired, and it has been a long week, but I still can't calm my mind enough to sleep. Everything has changed in such a small amount of time and it's kind of hard to come to terms with my current reality.

I'm half-dating someone that I'm not sure I want to be, but don't have the guts to end it in case it really is something good.

My "hero" hates me and thinks I deserve the worst parts of the guy I'm half-dating, without even knowing the full story.

My best friend is crazy about the "hero" who hates me, and is now supportive of my half-relationship with the guy that doesn't always treat me well.

I don't know if I'm more upset at myself for being bothered by what others may think of Warren and I or if I'm more upset at the people for hating him and then turning around and telling me I deserve him.

Maybe they just got to know him a little better tonight and now they approve. Or maybe they're blinded by their own love that they no longer care about anyone else's well being. Maybe I just need to decide how I feel about Warren without letting outside influences affect my feelings.

❖❖❖

Rachel is still asleep when I leave for class. I can't remember the logic behind my decision to take early-morning classes, but it is now irrelevant and stupid. I don't even put makeup on before I head to class.

My sketching class comes first, energizing my morning. It's a three hour long class where we talk about different techniques, art history and then draw for the rest of the time.

I love learning about art, but I love creating art even more. It's been a part of me for as long as I can remember.

I had it pretty good for a foster kid. A lot of other people have it way worse than I ever did. But that didn't stop me from feeling pretty lonely on occasion. Art and music were always my way of escaping those feelings.

I don't have a very big imagination, so I usually stick to more realism. I would draw the old houses I was fond of, or the people who made me feel the most at home, the friends I made.

Lately, I've drawn a lot more people, since we usually have models in this class instead of objects. I've drawn my roommates a few times, Fara being the hardest to capture since I don't know much about her.

Sketching has become my favorite medium, as it's the most reliable. There will always be some kind of paper and drawing utensil to use whereas oil or acrylics are harder to get without going to an art store.

Thirty minutes remain of class when the professor makes the announcement to start working on our self portraits. I had completely forgotten that he was talking about self portraits last week and although I don't recall him giving the assignment, he did teach about them. That usually means we can expect to be working on them shortly after. I must've been distracted last Thursday.

I start to panic, as I don't have a picture to work off of. Our homework was probably to take a self portrait photo over the weekend so we could start sketching this week. Whoops.

"Don't worry, I know artists rarely ever want to be the subjects and I assumed some of you would conveniently forget to take portraits over the weekend. Kaylie will go around and take pictures and print them for whoever needs one. You will need to work on this outside of class since we're almost done for the day and it's due the beginning of class on Tuesday. Dig deep, make it special."

Sure enough, Kaylie does come by at some point, take several pictures of me and print them out. I will have to choose which one I'm going to blow up and draw but, luckily, class has only five minutes left by the time she gets to me, so I'll be able to choose at home. I shove all of my work along with the six prints of my head into my folder and then gather the rest of my things.

The communications lecture room is only about two-thirds of the way full, which makes his sitting next to me even more remarkable.

"Hey, Lila." I turn slowly to face him and see a big grin stretching across his face.

"Um, hey," I choke out after a few solid and uncomfortable seconds of silence.

"How've you been?"

"Why are you smiling like that?" I ask bluntly.

"Like what?" His face turns into an amused and curious one, but the smile lingers.

"It's just that I can count on one hand the number of times I've seen you smile and it's always right before a storm. It's unsettling."

Now the smile melts into a discouraged frown, reaction to my words and somewhat harsh tone. I'm still annoyed with him. He doesn't get to just come sit by me and pretend we're friends.

As if he's just read my thoughts, he stops the charming act and turns into a real person for a minute.

"Lila, I know I haven't been easy to get close to but you're Rachel's best friend, as far as I know, and I'd like to start over if you'll let me." He looks sincere, but he can't be, right? This is Ryker Johnson, after all.

"You're trying to play nice to get into Rachel's pants? Well to be honest I'm not sure that's necessary considering how much time she spent in your bedroom the other night." I say it sarcastically on purpose but with probably a little too much poison.

"Wow." He glares down at me like a disappointed father- or what I would expect one to look like. It causes something inside my body to tingle.

"Wow, what?!" I snap.

"I thought you two were close. Guess it's just one-sided." His eyelids drop halfway.

"It is not one-sided," I start, but Ryker doesn't let me finish.

"She would never say something like that about you, Lila. Even though your relationship decisions have been exponentially more stupid and thoughtless than hers." He's sticking up for Rachel, which shouldn't be surprising given his record, but it's sweet. My only regret is being a person he needs to defend Rachel from.

"My what?"

"Look, I don't know Warren all that well, but I think we both learned a lot about him that night in the courtyard. To put yourself in that position again by inviting him to your bedroom, I mean that's pretty stupid." He laughs but he sounds more irritated than humored.

"Warren is not a bad guy. That night is a little bit foggy still but I know he crossed a line, and I didn't forgive him easily for that. But he's been trying to prove himself ever since, which is more than I can say for you." I look away from him again and pretend to pay attention as the professor starts the lecture.

"I don't need to prove myself to you, Lila." His voice has taken on a different tone, daring me to meet his dangerously captivating eyes. "Actions speak louder than words. If you don't want to be friends, that's fine. I didn't come sit by you to call you stupid again. If you want to be with Warren then you do that, I'll stay out of it. But don't judge Rachel for being interested in someone too, even if she shows it a different way."

Why do I feel winded? "I'm not trying to judge Rachel, I just don't know how I feel about you yet and I don't want you to hurt her."

"I will not hurt her, and I think you know that. But you're welcome to hang out with us some more and see for yourself. I bet she'd really like your support. I know I don't know her very well yet, but I can tell you're important to her." He breaks eye contact this time and takes out his notebook, turning his attention to the professor.

I don't know what else to say, so I leave it at that. I try to focus on the lesson, but I'm distracted by Ryker's proximity to me and the conversation we just had.

How did I get into this position? How am I the bad guy here?

EIGHT

Ryker

I had never noticed the color of her eyes before. I'd seen pictures of her before coming here, I've been keeping an eye on her from afar, and even been face to face with her a couple of times, but I'd never looked into them so intently. They are an outstanding mixture of emerald, gold, and amber.

Her eyes stick out compared to her fair skin and coffee brown hair. She has naturally pink lips that are bigger than I thought. She can't be shorter than a meter and seventy but she looked small sitting next to me.

I said goodbye to her before leaving, but she just looked at me until I turned around and left the class. She's not hard to read. I could tell I had made her uncomfortable, but I didn't really know why. She was definitely frustrated with me but I don't know if it's from calling her dumb a few weeks ago or if she's upset about Rachel and I. Why would she be? Probably because I called her stupid and she's still not over it.

I'm clueless as to how I'm supposed to make it up to her. I usually don't get along with girls unless they're badass soldiers like Rachel. Tough, but with a good sense of humor. Someone whose feelings aren't fragile as an eggshell.

Hopefully the mission doesn't depend on me getting to a place where I can listen to Lila cry and tell me about what her boyfriend or roommate said that made her sad.

I head over to the library and spend a few hours working. The manager, Hannah, called me right when I got home from class to see if I could cover the last few hours of Bridget's shift. She didn't say why over the phone and I didn't care to ask. When I get there, Krystal takes it upon herself to fill me in anyway.

"She's totally pregnant." She starts every conversation as if we had been talking about the topic already instead of it being completely random.

"Hmm?" I'm shoving my things into my locker as she continues.

"Bridget, she's got to be pregnant, right?" Krystal asks impatiently.

"Why's that?" I try to sound as uninterested as I truly feel but it doesn't work. I'm not surprised, though, Krystal has never before let my lack of intrigue stop her from talking to me.

"She's totally gaining weight and she just threw up for like the third time in the last week. I've heard her cry in the bathroom too- sometimes I just sit in there to get out of working- and she was crying over nothing. I bet that low-life boyfriend of hers got her knocked up. I'd cry too if he were my baby daddy." Her eyebrows raise and lips purse as she judges Bridget behind her back.

What is it with girls judging their friends without giving them a chance to defend themselves?

I turn my attention to her finally and it surprises her. "Krystal, isn't Bridget your friend?"

"Um, yeah?" She looks back at me.

"Well then, why don't you just ask her?" It's a genuine question so I'm not sure why she reacts the way she does. Her body stiffens and her eyes narrow.

"What?" Her arms cross over her large chest and she looks at me pointedly, as if I'm in trouble and she's waiting for me to admit my wrongdoing. What is in the air today that's making these girls act so weird? And why do I keep talking to them?

"If Bridget really is pregnant, and her boyfriend really is as bad as you say, then maybe she needs support from her friends. Maybe she's all alone in this and, instead of talking about it behind her back, you could help her through it." I'm tired now and turn to leave the locker room, but not before seeing the completely baffled look on Krystal's face.

I'm not sure I've ever seen her like that. I hope it means something good and not that she's going to follow me around for the rest of the shift chastising me for talking to her that way or telling me about what kind of friendship she and Bridget have and why she can't talk to her about it.

Luckily it's the former, and she doesn't say a word to me the rest of the time I'm there. I should probably make sure I didn't hurt her feelings or something, since apparently I'm pretty good at that today, but I can't bring myself to do it. I'm no better at apologizing to girls than I am at trying to have a meaningful conversation without offending them. I head back to Housing before talking to her again.

"I might've messed everything up," I confess hesitantly as Rachel opens the door. She makes a face as I step into the apartment.

"What? What did you do?" Rachel demands.

"Well I was trying to make nice with Lila. Turns out, she is not my biggest fan and she's not thrilled you're starting to hang out with me." I avoid eye contact and walk into her room, closing the door behind me.

"When did you talk to her?"

"In class. I sat next to her. I thought it would be a good way to prove that I'm into you by trying to be friends with your friends and all that."

"Oh, that's not a bad idea. She'll come around. She's got a tough exterior but a heart of gold." Rachel speaks of Lila the way an aunt would about her mischievous niece.

"Yeah no kidding. I mean, maybe it went well, I did make her speechless… I just don't know if it was in a good way or not." I rub the back of my neck with my palm instinctively.

"Don't worry about it too much. I'm the one that needs to get through to her. I have to figure out a way to be supportive of her and Warren without pushing them together too much. I don't want her to be suspicious."

Rachel sits down on her bed, pushing herself back until she's leaning against the wall, deep in thought. I remain standing and pull out my notebook in an attempt to look less awkward. "Any news on Warren?"

"Not really. I apologized somewhat and asked him how it's going with Lila and he said 'Good' and then didn't want to expand much on the subject so I started talking about Statistics."

"Statistics?" Rachel snaps out of her daze.

"Yeah, he's a major nerd." I chuckle a little at the thought. "I put GPS on him and I'm watching his location. He's just been in class." I turn on my device, unlock it with the security code, and turn the screen towards Rachel. Warren's dot still shows that he's on campus. He's either really good at this cover or we have the wrong guy.

"Good, keep an eye on him. He's got to be working with someone and we need to be careful. The red dot?" Rachel points to the screen.

"Lila. She's at work."

"Nice. Well we'd better make the most of the time we have, then."

We're halfway through plotting when there's a knock on the front door. Rachel and I look at each other suddenly, dropping our conversation quickly.

"Is anyone else home?" I whisper to her.

"I don't think so-" She gets cut off when the creaking door opens and we hear footsteps coming from inside the apartment. Did someone just break in?

"What do you need, Warren?" An unfamiliar voice asks, definitely female, but doesn't sound like anyone I know. As soon as I hear his name, I look at the GPS. Yep, Warren is here.

"I just don't understand what exactly it is that you want me to be doing," he complains, clearly on edge about something. I guess it's good that we didn't leave the room. They think the apartment is empty and that means we're getting much needed information. But why are they here? Why aren't they meeting at our apartment?

"I just need you to stay close to Lila. You like her, don't you?" The voice is agitated and it confuses me even more.

"Yes, of course I do. That's why I feel weird stalking her like this. If she doesn't want to be with me I can't force it!" He sounds uptight. *What the hell?* I mouth to Rachel and she shrugs, motioning that she's just as confused as I am.

"Look, moron. I'm paying your tuition to get close to a girl. Stop asking questions. I just need the information that you can give me, and that's it."

"What kind of information are you looking for? Maybe I could just ask her whatever you need to know and then we can just be done with it." Warren pleads with the stern-voice person.

"Know your place. You do not want to cross me. Just report anything you find out. That's all I need from you, and if you turn out to be more work than you're worth, you're not going to like what I do to you. Any more questions?" Damn, we really need to figure out who's on the other side of this door.

"No. Sorry."

Feet shuffle across the floor. Then the front door closes loudly and it's quiet again. Rachel and I look at each other, not sure if it's safe to talk out loud. We wait several minutes before we dare make a sound.

"You think we're safe?" I whisper to Rachel. She's sitting on the edge of her bed now, close enough to me to hear my question even though it was nearly inaudible.

She opens her mouth as if to respond but then closes it quickly as the front door audibly opens back up. Her eyes widen as a voice speaks out in the front hallway.

"Hey, Fara. How are you?" Lila asks politely. I'm so focused on the fact that she said Fara's name that I temporarily forget that we have a cover to keep with Lila.

Rachel jumps into action, pulling off her shirt and then bringing my mouth to hers just in time for Lila to open the door. What a brilliant woman.

"Oh my- sorry I didn't expect-" She scrambles and her white cheeks flush with a rosy pink pigment.

"Lila! Hey, no worries. I wasn't expecting you to be home but I guess I haven't been looking at the clock." Rachel laughs as she pulls on her shirt. "We were just-"

"I'll study somewhere else!" Lila starts back towards the hallway but Rachel kicks me subtly.

"Lila," I call after her and she stops in her tracks. "I was just leaving, really. Stay. It's your room, after all." She turns around slowly, avoiding eye contact all together. I step back towards Rachel, lean to her ear, and whisper, "Keep an eye on Fara. Contact me if anything happens."

Rachel nods and smiles at me as if I had just said something romantic and I turn and walk out of the room. Lila waits at the door until I leave before going back inside.

NINE

Lila

It took several minutes for me to stop feeling uncomfortable once Ryker left. Rachel started talking to me immediately, as if nothing had just happened. She's acting so out of character and I don't know if this is just how she acts when she dates people or if she feels awkward because I haven't been supportive about her and Ryker.

"I thought maybe you'd be out with Warren tonight after work. How are things going with him?" Rachel asks it casually but it still agitates me.

"Just because you're dating someone now doesn't mean everyone else wants to." Too harsh? Probably.

Something flashes across her face but she quickly covers it. "Why are you angry with me?" I could almost applaud her for being so blunt. It's admirable and even though it's frustrating right now, this is actually the quality that really sets her apart from everyone else.

"I don't even know, Rachel. I'm annoyed that you're with Ryker. You barely even know him and I've never seen you act that way towards anyone and now that you are dating or whatever you're doing, you keep talking about Warren like he's my boyfriend when a few weeks ago you hated the guy's guts. What is that about?" I ask desperately.

"Wow, I didn't know you felt like that. Can we talk about it or do you want me to leave you alone?"

I hesitate before I answer, not sure whether or not I want to talk about it. Then I decide it beats being angry all the time. "Sure."

"Are you annoyed that I'm dating someone or are you annoyed that I'm dating Ryker?" Straight for the kill.

"Look, I don't expect you to know this and I know I can't hold something against you that you don't even know about, but he's kind of been a jerk to me."

"Really? I thought you didn't really remember that night in the courtyard? And I thought he was… saving you?" Rachel winces as she says it, making an effort not to say the wrong thing. It's appreciated.

"It was really more after. I was talking with Warren, you know, that night he apologized and gave me that kangaroo?" I wait for Rachel to nod along. "Well, he took me over to his apartment to get it and I was there for less than three minutes but Ryker left when he heard us and I wanted to thank him, for you know, for helping me out… and well, he called me stupid for talking to Warren and told me I deserved him." I have to fight back tears while I tell her, and I have no idea why. I still don't know why Ryker's words cut me to my core that night.

"Oh Lila, I had no idea," Rachel says softly as her eyebrows come together.

"It's so dumb, I don't even know why it matters-"

"Lila, it's not dumb. That night was probably pretty traumatic and without knowing exactly what happened, I'm sure it's been hard to know how to move forward. But you and I both know you deserve way better than Warren!" She comes over and sits on my bed, positioning herself directly in front of me and holding my shoulders until I look up at her. "I was just trying to be supportive because I thought maybe you liked Warren and I didn't want you to feel isolated if y'all started dating."

"Really?" She's an angel. How could I have possibly let myself think that she was completely indifferent to how I was feeling?

"Of course! I don't necessarily hate him, but I'm certainly not fond of Warren and I think you deserve much better." She says it as though it's something she's thought about a lot and I appreciate that she's tried so hard to get on board with something she doesn't agree with, just to make sure I wasn't alone.

She breaks eye contact briefly before she returns to the other concern I voiced. "I'm sorry about what Ryker said to you. He's anything but subtle, and he really doesn't like Warren all that much. He doesn't trust him after what happened and I guess there was some locker room talk going on before Warren tried to kiss you. Anyway, I told him that he has to deal with it if it's going to work with us. I'm sure he'll be very glad to know where you stand. Screw Warren!"

A laugh bubbles out of me, surprising us both. We continue chatting and giggling about boys and it doesn't bother me when she talks about Ryker and how good of a kisser he is. We laugh about how stupid the drama has been and how much of a dork Warren actually is. What started as a very awkward evening has turned into a much-needed girls' night.

The next several days are pretty uneventful. It's been a while since I've seen Warren. I'm not exactly ignoring him, but it's been easier to avoid him than I had thought it would be. I almost feel bad, since he probably doesn't even know why, but I try to remind myself that it's okay for me to set boundaries and that Warren will be just fine.

After talking with Rachel, I realized that I wasn't hanging out with him for myself. I was doing it to try to make him feel better. I'm not angry or upset with him anymore, and I almost pity the guy. He doesn't have a lot of friends and he's not doing great in the romance department. At least he loves what he's studying.

I see a lot more of Ryker and instead of booking it each time I arrive, Rachel's been asking him to stay and the three of us end up hanging out. He's not as bad as I had thought. He's kind of serious and a lot of mine and Rachel's jokes go over his head, which makes them that much funnier.

He's very strong and, when I'm not focused on how offensively blunt he is, I can tell he's handsome. He has olive skin that tans very well, and blue-green eyes that pierce into your soul. His hair is brown but not dark like mine. It's closer to Rachel's cinnamon brown but Ryker's is still a shade or two lighter.

School has actually been okay, now that I'm doing better. Ryker has helped me in Communications and Biology, sitting next to me in class and working on homework together occasionally

My philosophy grade has improved drastically and I attribute it to Rachel. She's constantly asking me stupid philosophical questions and then we banter back and forth until we come to a conclusion. She points out what kind of argument we each use in the middle of each discussion and we usually end up laughing off any contention that happened during our lovely debates.

My self-portrait is almost complete. It's been really hard to focus so closely on my own face. Of course, I've had to do self portraits in grade school art class, but I've never had to blow up the proportions and dive into each flaw. Though it has been difficult, I feel like it could also be a form of therapy. Being forced to see myself as a piece of art, something beautiful that needs to be captured by a pencil on paper, it's almost a healing process.

I haven't let anyone see it, outside of my art peers and professor, but I am hoping to finish soon and maybe show Rachel. Sometimes I wish I had a family member that I could show it to who would tell me how proud they are of me and hang up all of my art on their wall. Instead, my dream is to own a studio where I can show off my work to the select few I choose to invite.

Work has been boring since the lawyers have been in a slump, not receiving any new cases. But there are always plenty of legal documents to keep me busy when this happens. Time slows down when there aren't exciting cases, late nights or big potlucks going on, though. So while I'm busy, I am still incredibly bored.

Very occasionally, they'll give me a day off or let me leave early if I get caught up on my tasks. Tomorrow Rachel, Ryker, and I were planning to go to a karaoke night at the pub so, in hopes of getting off early tomorrow, I'm working late tonight. It's quarter to nine by the time the security guard, Hank, kicks me out of the building.

Goosebumps cover any skin exposed to the brisk air. Since it's dark, I walk without my earbuds so I can pay close attention to my surroundings.

As I turn the corner of the apartment complex, I see a slender figure standing in the trees near the front doors. I widen my path to put space between the shadow and myself but then he steps out into the light- Warren. It takes me less than a few seconds to realize he's lost a lot of weight. He was skinny before, but now his features are angular and unhealthy.

"Warren? What are you doing out here? Are you okay?" I walk towards him, mindfully keeping several feet in the middle of us. I'm overtly aware that there isn't another person in view.

"Lila, you have to help me." His eyes are dark and he stumbles as he walks slowly to close the gap.

"Warren, you're scaring me. What's going on?"

"I need information. I need to know what you're hiding, Lila. If I don't tell her what you know, she's going to kill me," Warren pleads.

I thought I was scared with Warren in the courtyard, but this fear is so much more tangible than that night. Something is wrong with him, he doesn't look or sound like Warren. He's not threatening, he looks threaten*ed*, beat, maybe tortured.

"What are you talking about? Let's go inside, I can get you some water or something." I try to walk past him but he grips my wrist, hard.

"Lila, no! We can't go in there, I need you to tell me everything you know right now or they're going to kill me. Please, you have to help me. I promise I won't hurt you or anything like that, I just need some information to give them." He sounds so desperate.

"Give who, Warren? Are you high or something? What information are you talking about?" I try to make eye contact to calm him down, to try to understand what he's talking about. "Are you mad at me for not hanging out with you lately?"

I'm not sure why, but my question makes him laugh. It's a pathetic laugh, almost like he's about to give up. What could possibly make him look and sound like this?

"You have no idea, do you? You have no idea how many people are watching you?" His smile drains quickly as he sees something behind me.

Warren pulls me to him with one arm, quickly turning me around so that my back is against his chest, his other hand bringing a pointed object to my side. He faces me toward the scene that made him act so quickly.

Ryker and Rachel are standing about twenty feet away from us, they must have just exited the apartment building. They hold their hands up so they're even with their shoulders, a sign for Warren that they are not a threat to him. I'm in shock, I think, and I can't make out whether it's good or bad that they're here with me.

"Get the hell out of here. You do not want to mess with me right now, I will kill her!" Warren is shouting like someone who is angry would, but his voice is thick with emotion. "If you take one more step-"

I automatically let out a yelp when the pointed object, a knife I'm guessing, presses harder into my oblique and a drizzle of warm liquid runs down my side. My eyes widen and I look back and forth from Rachel to Ryker. They are so calm I start to wonder if I'm hallucinating the whole situation.

The Ryker hallucination speaks first, taking a small step towards us. "Warren, I know you don't think you could take me down, we've been there before. So why don't you tell us what's actually going on here?"

"Get back!"

"Warren, I know someone has put you up to this, why don't you tell me who it is and I can help you? We can stop them together." Ryker's tone is firm but friendly, coercive, and he continues slowly in our direction.

"No! You don't know anything! Nobody can help me except for Lila, I need her to help me." Warren is hysterical now, his voice fluctuating quickly between frustration and hope, all still seeping with desperation.

"Warren, we can help you, we know a lot more than you think. Lila's innocent, she doesn't know anything but we have information, Warren, we can help get you out of this." Rachel's hallucination sounds exactly like real-life Rachel. Her voice is soft and angelic even though she's giving out commands.

"Bullshit! I'm tired of everyone screwing with my head! Just leave us alone and I promise I won't hurt her."

"It's Fara, right?" Ryker-hallucination is close now. I'm not sure when he moved toward us.

The edges of my vision blur as the knife continues deeper into my side with every move Warren makes. I have a hard time focusing on the conversation. If this is a hallucination, it feels very realistic. And if it's not, then what the hell is going on?

Warren is shaking behind me now. "Get back, Ryker!"

"Lila, stay with us," Ryker says calmly. "Rach? Do you have it?"

"Yep." She's still calm. I can see her holding something…

"What do you mean?" Warren barks, moving quickly to face back towards Rachel. The knife slips out of my side when he does, and a rush of blood comes out with it. I can't see it, but I feel the warmth of it flow down my leg as my vision blackens.

"She's going to kill you if you don't let Lila go. Give her to me, Warren. I know you never wanted to be involved in this. I know Fara has been threatening you to get information from Lila but she doesn't know anything. If Fara did it herself, she would have realized that. We can protect you if you just give her to me." I know it's a hallucination because Ryker never sounds this reasonable. He's angry, short-tempered, and always too physical.

The knife pokes me again and I see a flash of red light before everything turns black.

TEN

Ryker

Once Lila's magic exploded, we knew we had to get her out of there as soon as possible. There would be no way to repair our covers enough to keep everyone at bay, especially Lila. She doesn't let anything go.

We had to move quickly, before Fara or any other Traitor entities could figure out what had happened. Rachel called Headquarters for evacuation while I carried Lila to the closest car. I reach in my backpack and grab my multitool, opening the universal key to unlock whoever's car this is and start the engine.

Rachel starts strapping in and I go back for Warren. I'm not sure what the protocol is going to be here but I can't just leave a body in the middle of the sidewalk. I don't even know if he's dead or alive, I just pick him up, run him to the car, push him inside and hop in the driver's seat.

Rachel is wedged between the two unconscious bodies, all of her attention split between the phone call with Headquarters and trying to stop Lila's bleeding. "Damn it."

"Give me that," I shout back, reaching my hand for her device. She puts it in my hand without hesitation and then turns her focus back to Lila, using tools from her pack to hold pressure where Warren stabbed her. I hadn't thought he'd got his knife so deep but the blood is there to prove it.

"This is Jordan. I need coordinates now. We have the subject, severely injured and she just let out magic before passing out. It's only a matter of time before someone finds us."

"We're on it soldier, you will get encrypted coordinates for the nearest portal. Wait there for it to be activated and then walk through all together. It will close immediately after the first passing so if you hesitate, you will be left behind. Make sure the subject gets through no matter what. Understood?" Colonel Finch commands through the phone.

"Understood Colonel." I hang up the phone and wait for the coordinates to come to the device. "How's she doing, Rach?"

"There's a lot of blood Ryker. I hope we're close, I don't know how long she'll-"

We both fall silent as the device buzzes and I pull up the directions to the portal. "We're only seven minutes out, Rach. Just put as much pressure on it as possible."

Neither of us talks for the next six minutes. Though you could cut the tension in the air with a knife.

"Damn it, Ryk-" Rachel curses as I turn off the road into some rocky forest and slam on the breaks.

"Sorry," I give a quick apologetic glance into the rearview mirror. "I didn't want to miss it." I move quickly out of the car to help Rachel with Lila.

"You gotta hold the wound-" Rachel snaps.

"I got it, just get the moron out of the car please." I situate Lila in my arms so that her neck is on one arm and her thighs on the other. I hold her tightly, trying to hold pressure to the wound that is pushed up against my core.

"What am I supposed to do with him?" Rachel grunts as she drags Warren out of the car.

"Just drop him on the ground and drag him over here."

"Are you sure the portal will be on that side?"

"You wanna check? Go ahead, pull your device out of my pocket and see for yourself," I bark.

"Okay, okay, I get it. You know what you're talking about."

I can feel Lila's blood spreading down my abdomen as we wait for the portal to open. The worry makes each breath that much harder.

Finally, a bright light sparks and then spreads into a large circle, a portal to home. "You ready?" I glance at Rachel. With the nod of her head, we simultaneously step into the light.

It's been months since I've been home and it takes me a few minutes to orient myself. We portaled into the Infirmary, not coincidentally, I assume. There are medics rushing around, getting beds and medicines ready.

In the midst of all the chaos is Colonel Finch. Her face is hard and expressionless. I would love to know why she's not more relieved but there isn't enough time.

I walk over to a stretcher and brief the medical team. "Stab wound to the right abdomen, she's lost a lot of blood. She's been unconscious for about 15 minutes after releasing a whole lot of magic." They nod and promptly cut the clothing surrounding the wound and get to work.

I start to relax before I notice someone pulling on my arm. "Soldier," I finally snap out of my daze and turn my attention to the medic. "Soldier, please sit down."

She's pointing at the next bed and I shake my head in confusion, unable to grasp what's going on. A male medic approaches me. His mouth is moving, but I can't understand anything that comes out of his mouth.

I get one more glance of Colonel Flinch, who is still tight and unreadable, and Rachel, who is painted with worry, before I get pushed onto the bed and poked with needles.

I sit up straight and take in my surroundings. I am in the Infirmary, as a patient. I have needles in my arms and monitors on my chest. It's quiet though, the chaos is nowhere to be heard, which must mean I've been unconscious for at least an hour. Nobody is in the room. Lila is no longer in the bed next to me.

I stand up quickly and pull the equipment off of me. I throw on the clothes that are folded next to my bed and I rush out of the Infirmary without knowing exactly what I'm looking for.

I hide in the doorway when I hear medics turn down the corridor and wait for them to leave. As soon as it's quiet again, I hurry down the stairs and out of the building. Wow, it feels good to be outside. It feels even better to be home. I continue on my way to the main building on my search for anyone and everyone.

As soon as I walk through the doors, I hear what sounds like a million voices. I walk down the hall and find that the noise is coming from the Cafeteria. I should've known to check there first. I walk in and look for Rachel, Lila, or hell, I'd even be happy to see Warren at this point. I just need to know what is going on and where everyone is.

I get more anxious the more faces I don't recognize. I bump into people as I move throughout the large room, focused and distracted all at the same time. After what feels like an hour, I hear my name shouted a few rows over.

"Ryker!" I turn around quickly and see Rachel waving me over. I let out a breath of air I didn't even realize I was holding.

"Rachel." I make my way towards her, ignoring every person I pass. She's sitting on the bench across the table but I'm too tired to go all the way around the row. "I'm relieved to see you. What the hell happened? Fill me in."

"Were you discharged? You don't look very good. You should eat something. Here." She passes me her leftover potato chips and an apple as I sit down in front of her. She finally meets my eye. "You were out for a few days."

"A few *days*?" I stop eating and start the interrogation. "Why? And what do you mean by *out*? What the hell happened? Where are-"

"Ryker, take a deep breath and eat your food. Perhaps we can talk about everything else in more of a.. private setting." Rachel shoots me a look, warning me to let it go for now. I do, but I make an effort to eat as much food in as little time as possible without making too much of a scene.

We walk silently back toward the female sleeping quarters and find a vacant room to sit in. Rachel sits down and gestures for me to do the same but my nerves don't allow me. Instead, I lean against the closed door and fold my arms across each other.

"I think it was Lila's magic that wore you out. Honestly, I'm not even sure how you got us all here safely." She looked at me, still amazed by the experience, but her face quickly faded when she noticed the tension surrounding me. "Well, anyway, you did. You got us all here and within minutes you fainted, I guess. I mean, you were right next to her when she.. went off like that."

"Okay so I passed out? For three days?"

"I guess so, yeah. They didn't tell you any of this when you woke up?"

"Must've been distracted," I brush off the question and continue investigating. "So what happened after? What did the Colonel have to say about all of it?"

"I bet you could imagine how thrilled she was," Rachel responds sarcastically. "She was surprised and wanted detailed reports of everything, of course. She will probably come talk to you, but I was hoping to get to you first."

"What happened to..." My voice trails off, but Rachel anticipates what I am looking for.

"She's safe. They're trying to ease her into everything so she's been a little bit..."

"A little bit what?"

"Well, she's been a little bit.. isolated." She looks away when the word finally gets out.

My body stiffens as my heart rate spikes. "Where is she?"

"Ryker, just-" Rachel sighs as she stands up and moves to block the door with her body.

"What aren't you telling me Rachel?" My head is spinning now. I'm not sure if it's from sleeping for three days straight or if I was hooked up to some strong meds in the Infirmary.

I can see Rachel contemplating whether telling me will improve or worsen the situation. I take a seat as a way to convince her that I do have self control.

If I'm being honest with myself, I'm not sure what has me so strung up. Other than the gut-sinking possibility that my first solo mission may have been the biggest failure in the history of my community.

Rachel remains calm and seemingly composed, but there is something unsettling under the surface. "They have her in a cell, Ryker." The words take several seconds to register in my overloaded brain.

As soon as they do, though, my body moves faster than I can control.

ELEVEN

Lila

Without any clue as to how I got here, I find myself in a large field. It's beautiful and quiet and I have it all to myself. I run and spin and dance in this open space of bright wildflowers and tall grass. I've never felt so peaceful and free.

Within several minutes of spinning and twirling, I get dizzy and fall to the ground, laughing hysterically. I don't even realize I'm falling until I hit the plush grass and flower beds that surround me. I attempt to stand up and fall right back over, still giggling like a toddler experiencing dizziness for the first time ever.

Off in the distance, I notice a vibrant green forest and I make my way to it once my vision stops spiraling.

I'm not ten feet into the forest before the green begins to fade and I realize I have been here before. The feeling of peace and joy gets thinner the further in I go. I pause and look back to the beautiful field, but it's no longer in sight. I move in the direction I came from, reaching out for my haven, when I hear my name.

"Lila." It comes as a whisper at first. I can't decipher from which direction it comes, but I know somehow that I need to find it.

"Lila!" It's a shout now, and I don't have enough time to reach it before my eyelids fly open. My blissful dream slips away as I come back to reality. The reality wherein I live in a cell.

It's not an entirely unpleasant cell, it's actually more comfortable and larger than the room I shared with Rachel at college. This place isn't nearly as cute, though. The color scheme throughout the entire institution is greyscale, however they almost make up for it with the beautiful and aesthetic architecture.

It's less like a jail and more similar to a room at a psychiatric hospital. Plain and void of any dangerous objects that I could use to escape or hurt myself.

"Lila!" I panic as I realize that the voice yelling out for me wasn't part of my dream after all.

Before they can say it again, I hear more voices shouting and what sounds like chaos. You would think that in any kind of building with locked cells, chaos is the norm, but this place is more organized than anywhere I've ever been.

"Let me in there right now," the shouting voice demands.

"You know you have to get clearance, Jordan. Don't make things more difficult." I recognize the second voice as one of the three guards that has been taking shifts outside my door for the past few days.

There's a commotion followed by the sound of keys jiggling in the lock which echoes through my room. Before I know it, I'm face to face with him again.

"Ryker?" Seeing him here catches me completely off guard. I haven't seen him since University and I don't know how to react.

His expression softens and his body noticeably relaxes as he takes in my environment. "I'm glad you're okay," he pauses and the concern slips back into his face. "I mean- are you? Are you okay?"

"Um," I stutter as I try to figure out what to say. "H-how did you find me?"

He blinks at the question and I see something that resembles guilt flash across his face. Something is wrong. "Have they not told you?"

"Told me what? I've been accused of hurting Warren and they've been holding me here until they investigate or something."

"Well that's bullshit, though I wish you would've killed the asshole. Have you talked to Rachel?"

"Rachel? Wait I don't understand, were you in a cell too?"

Ryker's hesitation is interrupted by increased shouting and the sound of boots hitting the hallway outside my cell. I fear that I am going to be in more trouble now and I start to wish Ryker never found me.

"We have to go right now, Lila. I need you to trust me." He extends his hand out to me. When I don't take it, Ryker closes the gap between us, coming further into the room. "I know you don't know what's going on and I'm sure you're feeling confused on who to trust, but I promise you can trust me Lila."

"I don't want to get in more trouble and I don't want to drag anyone down with me, Ryker. You need to go, I can't leave," I shrug and glance down to the bracelets that are locked around wrists. My head shakes as I continue. "I don't know what they do, but I was told that they would hurt if I attempted to leave the cell with them on."

The warning is confirmed when Ryker sees them and the color drains from his face. "What the hell?" His voice is angrier than I've ever heard it. He's been angry in front of me before- at me, actually- but this time it's a very intentional anger. He is not reacting solely in the heat of the moment, his words and actions are controlled and confident. There is something big going on and he is not okay with it.

"Ryker!" Rachel's voice is both panicked and frustrated as she shouts his name and stumbles into the room. She stops just inside the door. Ryker's focus on me doesn't leave upon hearing her voice. How did they both know where to find me?

"Rachel?! What is going on?" I look back and forth between the two. Ryker is still looking at me, a regretful expression on his face. Rachel avoids my eye and keeps her attention pinned to Ryker's back.

"Ryker, you need to get out of here right now. It won't help anything to get yourself and her deeper into this shit." I've given up on following the conversation and instead turn my attention to the body language. Rachel shifts out of the way as someone pushes past her.

A tall, skinny, woman with silver hair and harsh features makes her way into the room. Two large men are behind her in the hall. This room doesn't feel as spacious with four bodies in it. The woman's broad shoulders are tight with tension and her expression unchanging as she looks at Rachel, glances past me, and she fixes her gaze to Ryker.

He is still standing away from the door, away from my other cell guests, watching me closely. He's even closer now, and I think he must be trying to shield me from the inevitable fate that awaits us.

"Brooks, you are dismissed," the woman commands, barely parting her lips. Rachel salutes the woman before scurrying out of the cell. Ryker's body stiffens noticeably at the sound of this woman's voice. She obviously holds a position of power here.

"Stand down, Jordan." I meet Ryker's gaze as the woman makes her second demand. He holds the same anger in his eyes as before but with less determination. "Jordan."

He finally spins around to look at her. His voice comes out calmer and more respectful than I anticipate. "Colonel Finch, with all due respect-"

"With all due respect, Soldier, I am your superior and you were just given an order to stand down. I will not ask so nicely the second time." Her voice is unwavering and becomes more severe with each word. The two large men take an intentional step forward, their eyes firm on Ryker's. They must be her manpower.

Ryker gives in and stands at attention, watching the woman carefully. He is no longer paying attention to me, but he maintains his position in the room.

The woman, supposedly Colonel Finch, satisfied from Ryker's obedience, turns and softens her demeanor before addressing me. "Lila, I am terribly sorry for this outburst. It will not happen again. Excuse us."

I nod in return, utterly speechless. She steps to the side of the door, implicitly dismissing Ryker before leaving herself. He steals one last glance before the door locks closed behind them, and I am left alone again.

❖❖❖

It takes me over an hour to compose myself and gather the courage to decipher what had just occurred in my cell. Once I do, I get a notebook and pen and write as much as I can remember down onto paper. I start from when I woke up in this place until now, dumping every piece of information I have into the cheap lined sheets of the notebook.

I woke up in a hospital room, alone, with no recollection of why I would've been there. I could tell they had me on heavy medications because I couldn't fully concentrate on my surroundings.

At some point, the doctors came in and asked me about what had happened. I don't know if I was able to answer them. I've had a lot of time to myself since then, and I've been able to piece together a few things.

Warren stabbed me. I don't really remember why, but I remember Ryker and Rachel being there too. It's possible they were hallucinations from the blood loss.

The officers that interrogated me told me that I injured Warren, once I was conscious enough. I don't recall doing any such thing, but honestly, I would be proud of myself if I had hurt him after he *stabbed* me in the stomach.

They asked question after question, each one harder to answer than the last. I tried to tell them that I couldn't remember and that I didn't hurt anyone intentionally. I asked them how they knew about the incident, who they were, and if Ryker and Rachel really had been there.

They didn't give me anything to go off of, but I think I may have just found my answer. Ryker was shocked that I said they accused me of hurting Warren, so maybe he doesn't know. There is no way

Rachel is out of the loop, though. She knows exactly what is going on here.

Since I 'refused to comply,' the officers decided to put me in a cell until they could 'investigate' the situation more thoroughly. I asked for a lawyer, told them I knew my rights and they couldn't keep me here but they ignored me.

At first I was mortified, I had never really been in any kind of trouble before, but after hours and days of being here, it has become more relaxing than scary.

I don't have to worry about being anywhere on time, I don't have chores or work or school to do. I just get to sit and relax. I can't remember ever having a day all to myself, to sit and read, take a nap, or doodle in a notebook. I'm not sure it'll feel as peaceful now that I know Ryker and Rachel are outside of my cell and at least one of them is trying to break me out.

I jot down everything that Ryker said. I note that they kept calling him 'Jordan' instead of his name. I write about how angry but collected he was, and how glad he seemed to see me.

I write that Rachel didn't look at or speak to me once. That she was worried about Ryker being there, but didn't care that I was.

I make note of the woman, Colonel Finch, who knew my name and spoke as if we were neighbors and her dog had run into my yard, 'I'm so sorry, it won't happen again, excuse us.' I acknowledge Rachel submitted to her immediately while Ryker stood up to her boldly.

Another half hour goes by before I realize the most important detail of all. Colonel Finch, Rachel, and Ryker- they all had the same uniform as the guards outside my door.

TWELVE

Ryker

We walk in silence back to Colonel Finch's office. There is a guard on each side of me, but I have no plans of running or being aggressive. I want to meet with Finch as much as she probably wants to meet with me.

I have a million questions for her and I'm only hoping the walk to her office gives me enough time to really calm down and handle this professionally. If there is one thing Finch responds poorly to, it is overly emotional Soldiers.

When we get through the doors, Finch positions herself behind her desk and dismisses the guards. Both of us remain standing.

"You should've come to see me as soon as you were discharged. You ought to have known that I would want your report," Finch says directly.

"Yes ma'am, I was a little disoriented."

"Yes, well, you should have let the Medics assess you first."

"Yes, ma'am."

"Soldier, take a seat. I reckon we're going to be here a while." I do as she says and take the seat that sits most directly in front of her. She sits down, too, and sighs deeply. "What is your report?"

"Brooks and I were working together, trying to have eyes on Li- the subject- at all times. Brooks let me know that the subject would be en route to the living quarters. I was watching the GPS until Brooks had eyes on her. I saw the subject arrive at the living quarters but I didn't hear from Brooks, which set off a little warning for me. I waited a few more minutes and then decided to contact Brooks. She hadn't seen the subject yet. I checked the other individuals we were tracking at the time and noticed Warren's GPS was stalled at the same location. I called Brooks and we went out to assess the situation together.

"When we arrived, we agreed that it was a hostile situation that needed interference. As soon as he saw us, he pulled the subject into a headlock and held a knife to her side. We attempted to talk him down, get him to admit that Fara was pulling the strings. Warren escalated pretty quickly and stabbed the subject.

"Before passing out, the subject released a large amount of magic, knocking us all on our asses. Warren got the brunt of it, and became unconscious. We then packed everyone into a vehicle and called Headquarters." I wait patiently for several minutes before Finch speaks to me again.

"Could this incident have been avoided?" She asks.

"Yes ma'am."

My quick response intrigues her. "How so?"

"Had I been debriefed with all of the information, made aware of my allies, I could have narrowed in on possible threats ahead of time and worked with allies to make sure Lila was being observed around the clock. With my limited information and orders, I was not able to protect the subject as well as I would've liked." I remain as dispassionate as possible to avoid confrontation with the Colonel.

"Do you believe another Soldier could have done better with the information you were provided?" Her frankness starts to rub me wrong and I force myself to take a subtle breath.

"While there is always a chance that someone could have done better, I believe I performed well with what I was given. I was quick to react, I followed orders, and I did find a Traitor and get the subject back to Headquarters safely.

"With all due respect, Colonel, you gave me a job and I did succeed at it, even if it wasn't as neat and tidy as I would've liked it to be." My confidence impresses her, though she barely shows it and would never admit it out loud.

"Very well, then. Thank you for your report, it will be submitted into the investigation." Colonel Finch ends the recording and closes the case folders.

"Ma'am, if I may, I need to ask a few questions."

She doesn't respond but she nods her head once, allowing me to continue.

"Why is she being held like a criminal? You know, as well as I do, that she didn't mean to hurt anyone. She isn't part of this. Surely you know that by now."

"It's not entirely up to me, Jordan. You should know *that* by now. The others think I am too close, they don't trust my opinion. They want a full investigation after. The subject used magic again-"

"'Used magic again'? Colonel you know she didn't mean to do that, we don't even know if she remembers what happened." As the conversation goes on, the more expressive I become. But it's just the two of us and I know she's on my side.

"The officers feel as if she is withholding information, not being totally truthful."

"And you can't do anything about it? If she's got those bracelets on, she won't be able to hurt anyone. Let her out of the cell. Let me try to talk to her, she may open up to me or Brooks. There's no reason to lock her up-"

"She has been well taken care of. Maybe for the first time in her life." There is passion behind her words now and I know I struck a chord.

"Colonel, I am not implying that you are mistreating her," I sigh and sit back in my chair. "I'm just saying… she didn't do anything wrong. If she was involved, we would've found evidence of that by now. She's not going to trust or choose us if we keep her locked up and feed her lies."

"Damn it, Jordan. You're a pain in my ass." Finch leans forward, putting her elbows on her desk and clasping her hands hard together-her down-to-business sitting position. "What do you propose?"

"We need to figure out how much to tell her. We'll need to let her out of her cell, give her a room over by female sleeping quarters, give her access to the facilities and cafeteria. We may need to provide her some protection as well- I'm sure some will not be pleased with her walking around freely."

"No, I predict they won't." The Colonel's attitude has changed drastically over the last hour. What started as pure rage has now become hopeful consideration. "Do you really think she could trust us after all that's happened?"

I have to think about it before I can truthfully answer. She has to trust us after we saved her life. But maybe she doesn't know that. I've personally saved her twice now, and that's got to count for something.

She's lost everyone in her life except for Rachel and I. While I don't know if she'll trust us right away, especially as we start to explain the truth to her, I hope she can learn to. "I don't think she has much of a choice."

I run as fast as I can back to the Penitentiary. The guard on duty is an old friend of my brother's.

"Hey James, what's up man?" I wanted to sound cool and casual, but it comes out more breathy from the run down here.

"Ryker, what the hell are you doing back here?" He gets up out of his chair and steps close to me, obviously attempting an intimidation routine.

"Funny that you ask, actually. I'm uh- I'm here to take Lila off your hands." I grin widely at him, knowing full-well that it won't help the situation. He reacts almost immediately so I jump in again before he knocks me out. "Yeah, you should've received a memo from Colonel Finch. She is dismissing the subject from lock-up and into my custody."

James scoffs at what he assumes is a lame second attempt to

break Lila out of her cell. "You are so full of sh-"

"Humor me." I cut him off, anxious to get the door open. I'm not sure why. There's a fifty-fifty chance that Lila will be the one to knock me out.

Finally, James checks his device and sees a new memo. He looks at me suspiciously before reading on. His stance shifts, he exhales dramatically, then shoves his device back in its carrier. "I don't know how you pulled that off, man." If I didn't know James better, I would venture to say he might be a little impressed. He unhooks the keys from his waistband and unlocks the door.

My lungs skip a breath in anticipation as James swings the door open. I'm surprised to see Lila in bed. She sits up as the door opens and pulls her blanket up with her. I guess the bolt being unlocked wasn't warning enough. Her eyes are wide open and her face is drained of color.

"Pack up, outlaw," James attempts a joke. He's never been good at reading the room.

"James, can you give us a moment?" I keep my tone friendly but also put enough emphasis in it to let him know to back off. Luckily, this time he does get the hint.

When I turn back, Lila's eyes are still locked on me. She sits up even more in her bed, getting more nervous with each passing moment. "Hi."

"What's going on?" She still has the deer in the headlights look on her face and I start to worry that maybe Colonel Finch should've assigned her a different Soldier.

"I've been assigned to your case. You are being released from here and you'll be given a room near the living quarters. It's not safe for you to be with the rest of the females, but it's not safe for you to be completely alone, so you will have a bodyguard for a little while."

"Let me just get this straight: you burst in here trying to get me to go with you, knocking out the guard outside my door and getting us both further incriminated. I don't hear from you or anyone for several hours, and then you come back here, civilly, and you want me to leave with you, again. Without any context or information on why you have a guard uniform or who you went to for permission to let me out or be my bodyguard. Do I have this right?" The fear that I saw in her face a minute ago has vanished and been replaced with resentment.

I am totally speechless as I contemplate which part to dissect first. Why did I think she would trust me? "Yeah, when you put it like that, it sounds really bad," I admit and look down at my feet.

"Turn around," Lila demands.

"What-" I start but don't get the chance to finish.

"I thought I was going to bed, alone, like every other night I've been in here, and I'm not entirely dressed. Turn around so I can get some clothes on." Lila leaves no room for protest and I don't try. I throw my hands up in surrender and turn my back towards her.

It takes only two minutes for her to put all of her belongings together and get ready to leave with me. She avoids eye contact with me while we leave Headquarters, walk through the small courtyard, and enter the living quarters. We head up the stairs and make our way towards the female rooms.

I want to make small talk, but I have a feeling it will lead to big questions that I won't be able to answer right now, so we walk in silence.

We get to the door of her new room and I unlock it with my copy of the key. Lila pushes it open, walking directly in front of me. I am about to speak to her to explain how her key works when she spins around, now only inches from my chest.

She looks up at me and I wonder if she's trying to seem intimidating. "So, what then? You saved me from one cell just to put me in another cell?"

I am totally perplexed by her question, probably apparent in my facial expression. "Lila, this isn't a cell. It's just a room, you're right next to all the other females." I point down the corridor, where the rest of the rooms are.

"Bed, shelves, void of decoration that I could use to break out, big hefty lock on the door… I'm not seeing much of a difference." Her face is blank now, hard to read.

"Well, here is your key." I hold out a closed fist, facing down waiting for her to open her hand to me so I can drop her room key in it. After a few seconds of internal debate, she finally does. "I promise it's not a cell. It's just a room so you can have some privacy and stay safe and all that."

"So I'm in danger?"

"I didn't say that. You're not in danger, yet. It's just a precaution in case anything were to happen."

"What would happen? What aren't you telling me, Ryker? Is that even your name?" She rolls her eyes at the question. She's still so frustrated with me, and I don't want to be insensitive, but I can't protect her if she refuses to trust me.

"Yes, it is." I attempt to reassure her by taking her hand but she pulls away immediately. I shake my head, wondering why the hell I thought this was going to go well. "Look, I'm trying to make everything right by you. I may not be doing it in the most conventional way, but I'm trying to make the right choices that benefit everyone involved. Right now, there are a lot more people involved than you can imagine, and that complicates things.

"I've always tried to protect you and I haven't always done it the best way, perhaps, but you're still alive. That has to count for something. You don't have to confide in me, tell me your deep dark secrets, I'm just asking that you trust me enough to let me do my job."

Lila softens her body language along with her tone. "What is your job exactly?"

"I'm a Soldier," I report proudly.

"But a Soldier of what? What kind of place is this?"

I have to calculate my answer before responding to make sure I don't tell her too much. "Well, it's a kind of government, I suppose. We regulate the population, make sure everyone is following the laws. When they're not, well we- the Soldiers- are assigned to either eliminate the threat, or," I wave towards Lila, "we're sent to protect a potential victim of such activities."

Lila's eyes light up with an emotion I can't quite read. She opens her mouth twice as if to speak but instead snaps it back shut both times. She looks down, breaking eye contact or the first time in minutes.

The increasing silence makes me nervous. "Lila," I start but I'm not sure how to finish. Am I seeing sadness, fury, or relief in her eyes? Should I try to comfort her or should I be honest with her?

"I'm pretty tired, Ryker." She glances at me quickly and then looks down at her hands, which are fiddling with the key I gave her. "Can you fill me in later?"

I stumble over my thoughts for a few seconds, not sure what the right call is. I guess she would know what she needs most right now. "Yeah, sure."

"Thanks," She says quietly and reaches to close the door.

"Wait, uh, Lila?" I ask hesitantly, unintentionally stopping the door with my hand.

She opens the door about halfway until my hand falls off. "Yeah?"

"Keep your door shut and locked until I get here in the morning, okay?" I'm nervous that being so ominous is going to stress her out again but she just nods in return and shuts the door completely.

THIRTEEN

Lila

I toss and turn all night. I'm unable to turn my brain off after Ryker supposedly rescued me and told me that he's been protecting me from some kind of crime against whatever government I'm inadvertently involved with.

Obviously it had something to do with Warren since Ryker did indeed have to save me from him twice. What was it that Warren wanted from me that night? He was asking for information but I can't remember if he specified what he needed, I only know that I couldn't provide him with whatever it was and he was not accepting that reality well. He was afraid of something though.

I guess I haven't put too much thought into what, or who, he was afraid of. I wonder if Ryker knows. It's not adding up, though. The fact that he was afraid of something bigger than him and he needed me to do something that I couldn't do and then stabbed me for it- it doesn't make sense.

And on top of that, this government was accusing me of hurting Warren? The very people sent to protect me from people like him questioned me and then held me in a cell for days after he stabbed me. I can't make sense of it.

Eventually I drift off because I wake up to a loud knock on the door, followed by a familiar voice. "Lila, it's me, Ryker. Are you up?" *I am now, dummy.*

I roll my eyes and lay back down in my new bed. It may be the most comfortable bed I've ever slept in, and while that is not the only reason I do not want to leave it, it is still a pretty good one.

Another set of knocks echoes through my ten square-foot room.

Without thinking much about it, I roll out of bed and snap the door open, with an irritated "What?"

Ryker's eyes pop open and he stands up straight. He must have been leaning on the door. "Why do you look so surprised? You are the one knocking at my door."

"Um, I'm not surprised to see you, I was just taken a little off guard by the-" He points a loose finger down at my clothes and I gasp as I realize what I'm wearing and slam the door shut. I really can't believe I just opened the door without pants on.

As I look in the mirror, I'm relieved to see that my big tee shirt covers everything important. "There should be something to wear in your closet," Ryker calls out from behind the closed door. He maintains his professionalism, but I swear I can hear him smile.

For the first time, I look around the room and notice two additional doors. I go to the one nearest to my bed first, finding the closet. It is maybe the first walk-in closet I've ever seen and, though it is nearly empty, I get excited at the idea that someday it could be full. I bring myself back to reality too soon though, remembering that I am a half-prisoner in this place and I doubt they'll let me go shopping with the company credit card anytime soon.

I grab the single outfit that hangs in the closet and try it on. It fits fine. There is excess room in the shoulders and the pants run too long, but the fit is overall impressive, since I have no idea how long this has been sitting in here for.

It's the same bland grayish color that I saw Ryker and Rachel wearing yesterday but the material is much more comfortable than I had assumed. It's lightweight but not at all see through and the fabric stays in place, making it look stiff even though it isn't.

Once I'm dressed, I open the second door and find myself in a beautiful master-sized bathroom. It is simply designed, matching the aesthetic of every room I've seen here so far. There is a large bathtub next to a standing shower with glass doors and black tile. There is a geometric gold-framed mirror above the marble countertop sink, which has a gold faucet to match. I walk three steps further and find the toilet hidden behind a door of its own.

Three more knocks sound on the bedroom door. "Everything okay in there? We're going to miss breakfast." I guess the luxurious bath will have to wait. I use the restroom quickly, washing my hands with the potent floral soap afterwards, and take a look in the mirror.

I've definitely looked better but considering I was stabbed a few days ago, I'd say I'm doing alright. I put my hair into a bun on top of my head and walk back to the room.

I take one last deep breath before opening the door again to Ryker. "No room service then, huh?" I ask sarcastically.

He chuckles at my taunting, probably just glad I'm not as grumpy as before. "I wish, but no. You're not in Kansas anymore." He looks at me when the last word leaves his mouth, watching my response to see if he needs to be more careful of what he says.

He is constantly studying my nonverbal queues and it makes me nervous. I've never had someone pay such close attention to what I am saying under the surface and I feel exposed by it.

"No, I suppose I'm not," I let him off the hook, not ready to get into the carefully calculated deep discussions yet. I need caffeine and something in my stomach before trying to understand the weird reality I am now in.

Ryker looks relieved by my answer and moves his hand to the right, gesturing for me to go that way.

"Where exactly are we going for breakfast?" I ask as I start towards the indicated direction.

"The Dining Hall," Ryker answers plainly.

"With, like, other people?" I suddenly feel the urge to vomit.

Ryker must sense it because he slows his stride, barely, and changes the subject. "So I was thinking after breakfast, maybe we could see about doing a little bit of exploring, what would you think about that? Get some fresh air and whatever."

"Fresh air sounds nice," I answer quietly.

Neither one of us feels the need to carry on the conversation as we walk through the sky-lit corridors and make our way back down the same stairs we came up last night. If I remember correctly, there are three floors.

Before getting even halfway down, the first floor's door opens and voices from what I assume is the cafeteria bounce off the walls of the stairwell. Anxiety eats away at my stomach again and I get queasy. I squeeze the railing with a white fist.

When Ryker realizes that I'm no longer walking he snaps his head back toward me. "What is it?"

I close my eyes and shake my head slowly, unable to communicate the emotion I'm feeling.

"Okay, let's sit down for a minute." He grabs my forearm and helps me lower until I'm sitting on the edge of a stair. Someone walks past us without so much as a word. But Ryker doesn't flinch, so I try not to worry about how stupid and juvenile I probably look. "Take a deep breath, Lila, you're not breathing."

I do what I'm told and continue focusing on my breath until Ryker speaks again.

"How's your incision?" I'm not sure I hear him right so I open my eyes and look at him with furrowed brows. His face remains serious as he touches his side with the tips of his fingers. Oh, yeah, I got stabbed.

I lift up my shirt slightly to get a look. I still have a bandage so I pull one side off, revealing a colorful gash just under my ribs, bedazzled with staples that hold the skin together.

"It's probably infected. We can go to the Infirmary after breakfast."

My head moves way too quickly, a dead giveaway for how I'm feeling.

"Ah." Ryker nods once in understanding.

"I just- Is there anywhere else we can get food?" I ask, embracing the humility of my situation.

"Lila, you're going to be fine. I know I must not be your favorite person right now, but it is my job to protect you and I won't let anything happen to you."

I look back down, pretending to fix my bandage while I consider what he says. Ryker quite literally is the only person I have right now. That doesn't make him my favorite, but he might as well be. He is the only one who took the initiative to get me out of incarceration. I don't know how long Rachel knew I was there but I'm not sure I want to.

I reluctantly agree with a quick shrug. Ryker helps me carefully back onto my feet and we finish our descent. I take a quiet breath before Ryker walks through the door, holding it open for me to follow. We don't make it ten feet into the cafeteria before the voices start to hush into a nerve wracking lull. Ryker guides me towards the buffet lines, standing between me and the hundreds of people seated at the picnic-style tables. It almost looks like a rich person's high school cafeteria room.

I'm grateful that Ryker blocks my view and acts as if nothing out of the ordinary is happening. I guess this may be *his* ordinary. Once we start picking out food, the whispers slowly grow back into their normal volume and it's easier to pretend that eyes aren't staring into the back of my head.

I quickly assemble a fancy omelet, adding in vegetables I have never seen in my life. When I finish, Ryker leads me to the closest empty table, right on the corner.

We sit facing each other, my back against the crowd and Ryker across from me. I'm not sure if he does this for safety reasons or to make me feel less nervous, but I appreciate it nonetheless.

Minutes later, the kitchen staff comes out to clean up the buffet, and most of the people eating have finished. As the crowd starts to dwindle, I finally relax enough to taste the omelet I've been mindlessly eating. I'm pleasantly surprised by the amount of flavor it has. In a community of grayscale, I didn't expect to find such diverse food.

When I finish eating, Ryker stands up and begins cleaning the space. He grabs my trash and we walk over to the garbage can.

"Ready to go to the Infirmary?" He holds his hand out, the same way he did when he did when we 'pointed' me towards breakfast. It's kind of funny that he does it. I guess it's a formality thing but it really just makes him look like an usher. I follow his lead anyway.

Before exiting the cafeteria, though, I feel a pair of eyes on me and can't help but look back. Across the large room, a man is staring at me blankly. Meeting his eyes sends a shiver up my body. Next to him is a young woman. He mumbles something under his breath and the woman turns to face me- Rachel.

The nurse finishes dressing my wound, giving me instructions on how to clean it and when to take the antibiotics the doctor prescribed. "Two times a day, with food, unless you want to throw it up. Two times, morning and night. Got it?"

"Yes, sir," I respond sheepishly.

"She's decent, Jordan," he calls over his shoulder and hands me the medication. He gives Ryker a sort of respectful bow of the head when he passes. It makes me wonder if he's a pretty big deal around here. It would explain why the Colonel didn't arrest him when he mauled down a guard and broke into a cell of a supposed criminal. Now I really get why Rachel likes him.

"Ready to go?" I can't tell if he's actually this friendly or if he's the stone-cold soldier that will destroy you if you get in his way like Warren and the cell guard did. Either way, I do know that he is keeping the truth from me. A portion, at least.

"Wearing this? I look like one of you." I click my dark gray combat boots together.

He chuckles. "Is that so terrible?"

"Maybe," I tease, but I'm not sure if I mean it. "But I mean, won't people take me for one of you? Couldn't that be bad?"

Ryker shrugs slightly. "It's not a problem. There aren't many options for clothes around here."

"Let's go, then." I give him a half-hearted smile and hop off the bed and go out the door. He follows half a step behind me. I think I make him uncomfortable.

As soon as we step out of the building, all the anxiety and stress that was suppressed inside of me leaves my body and I finally can take a deep breath. I turn my face up to the sun and soak its rays into my skin. I wonder how long it's been since I've been outside.

Technically, we were outside for a few minutes on the night of my 'arrest' while walking between buildings and again last night, but I don't look back on those moments fondly.

"Lila?" His voice brings me back down to earth, and I'm not ready for it. I squeeze my eyes harder and try to will myself back to life, back to freedom.

His hands come to my shoulders and shake me softly. "Lila, what's wrong?" I open my eyes reluctantly and find a worried Ryker for the second time today. I don't move otherwise and I hold his gaze until he drops his hands from off of my shoulders and takes a step back, contemplating his next move.

He very clearly doesn't know what to do. I'm a little confused as to why he is concerned but I also don't have enough energy to guess. I feel depleted by reality and want to pretend I'm free to go wherever I please.

"Do you want to go back to your room?"

I shake my head violently at the question. "Of course not, why would you think that?"

He points at me but I still don't get it. "You started crying as soon as we stepped outside."

I reach up and touch my cheeks. Yep, they're soaked with tears. If I wasn't so frustrated at him, I would feel so bad for Ryker right now. He's dealt with a lot of crazy in the last twenty-four hours and I have a feeling he's felt this way for as long as he's been assigned to my case.

"I'm sorry." I attempt a chuckle but it sounds kind of pathetic. "I just haven't felt the sun on my skin for a while. I guess you don't realize how much you need it until you don't have it, ya know?"

He looks away from me when I say it, and I start to feel like a complete lunatic. He types something into what looks like a smartphone and then raises it to his ear. Oh no, he's going to send me back to my padded cell.

I can't make out what he says but he mumbles something into the phone, turns it off, shoves it back in his pocket, and turns to face me. "Come on."

FOURTEEN

Ryker

I take Lila to the train station so I can take her to Amaryllis. I know it's not going to fix anything, but I can tell that being here is a nightmare for her. I thought that if I could get her out of the cell that she would be fine, but I've never been very great at nurturing people.

"Do you like big cities?" I ask her randomly as we wait for the train.

It must have been longer than I thought since we had talked last because I think my voice startled her. She looks away, then back to me. "I'm not sure."

"You haven't been to one?" I turn my head towards her.

She shakes her head, still avoiding my eyes.

My mind goes blank, unable to entertain her. I've never been great at entertaining or keeping conversation, but it's never really mattered in my line of work.

Our train finally arrives at the station and we board it wordlessly. I notice Lila staring at the destination for the first several minutes of the train ride and I use this opportunity to strike up a conversation again.

"Amaryllis is the name of our main city. The train only takes about fifteen minutes from Headquarters, which is where we just came from." There aren't very many others on the train with us, but I keep my voice down still so as to not draw more attention to ourselves. Everyone in our community knows very well what Amaryllis is.

"Where does that name come from?" Curiosity sparkles in her

eyes again. It's familiar to me, though I'm not sure when I would've seen it before.

"It's a Greek name but it stems from the Greek word 'amarysso' which means 'to sparkle,'" I've never actually had to explain it to anyone before. Everyone I grew up with learned about our history at the same time I did.

"Well, does it sparkle? Do all of the buildings look like the Eiffel Tower at night?" Lila continues.

I chuckle as I try to imagine the picture she has in her head and how it will compare with the real city. "Hardly at all. It's more of a 'diamond in the rough' kind of definition. Do you know much about Greek mythology?"

"Not really," She admits sheepishly.

"Well, as it goes, there was a woman, Amaryllis, who loved a man, Alteo. She went to his house every day for thirty days, piercing her heart with a golden arrow and leaving her blood for Alteo. On the last night, a flower grew from her blood and won Alteo over."

"That's..." Lila's eyes widen as she processes the story. "Interesting."

I smile at her confusion. "The name Amaryllis signifies determination, perseverance, and love. For us, our city represents the same. It took a lot of time, war, patience, and love to create this city and government. We are very proud of what it has become."

"Wars against who?"

I know that the more I tell her, the more questions she will have. It makes me nervous but I don't know how to get around it. I need to finish this mission out strong for my family, get the information we need and then leave Lila back in her world without a scratch.

"It's complicated-" The train comes to a screeching stop, saving me from the question. "We're here."

Lila raises her eyebrows and follows me out of the train.

❖❖❖

We are more than an hour into our stroll around Amaryllis and I have yet to see Lila blink once. She is soaking in everything she sees, asking me for details about every building. I often don't have the answers to her many questions, though she doesn't let my lack of knowledge interrupt her enthusiasm. She is shy about it, trying to bury her excitement, but I'm starting to hope again that maybe we'll be okay.

I often wonder if she would open up to me if I told her why I need to be assigned to her case. Would she trust me finally or would she hate us all forever? It's a delicate case, with too many factors and people involved and I don't know how I'm going to make everyone happy.

"What about this one?" Lila points to a small antique building with vines growing up both sides.

I shake my head, indicating yet again that I don't know. "Unfortunately, I haven't actually spent very much time here."

"Really?"

"Nope."

"But why not? It is so beautiful," She states, clearly amazed.

"It is," I nod my head. "I'm always training. There isn't much freetime at Headquarters, I guess. When there was, I would hang out with friends or visit my family." I stay very aware of our surroundings as we walk, maintaining a meter-wide radius between anyone else on the street.

"You have a family?" Lila asks, bewildered by the idea. Her shock makes me laugh under my breath.

"Yes, even the devil has a family," I tease.

"I guess that's true." She smiles and looks down at her feet. "What's your family like?"

"A little complicated." I struggle to think of what to say. "I have two brothers, both older than me. My parents died in a train accident when I was pretty young."

Lila nods her head slowly and I know she truly does understand. "Where do your brothers live?" She looks back up at me.

"Well, the oldest is actually at Headquarters. The younger of the two is on a mission in England."

"Is that far from Amaryllis?"

"Yeah, you could say that." It would be difficult to try to explain the geography of Amaryllis to her, so I'm relieved when she drops it.

"And your brother at Headquarters? Do you see him often?"

"Before my assignment we saw each other a couple times a week, mostly during meals."

"And now?"

"I haven't gotten the chance to see him since I've been back."

"Why not?"

"A certain someone has kept me pretty busy," I throw her a pointed look and she smirks.

"Why are you on my case, anyway? Is it for Rachel?"

Her question catches me off guard. "Rachel?"

"Yeah, did you offer to be on my case and save me or whatever because Rachel asked you to?"

"Why do you ask that?"

"Well since she was my roommate and best friend and she's your girlfriend and all," She looks away from me again, focusing on her moving feet. "I just thought maybe she had asked you to do it."

"Ah," I press my lips together, thinking of what to say. "We're not dating, Rachel and I."

"You broke up? Is that why she was acting so weird to me?"

"Not quite," I sigh quietly, bracing myself for the worst. "Rachel and I met on the mission. We were both assigned to protect you, and I assume maybe there were others as well. I thought I was the only one until that night she brought me aside and wanted to team up."

"What? When was that?"

"That game night or whatever." I watch her expression carefully before continuing. "After you left with Warren." It comes out more accusatory than I had planned.

I can tell my statement affects her but she brushes it off and continues her interrogation. "So all those times when you and Rachel were…"

"It was a cover," I confirm. "Don't get me wrong, Rachel is very talented and obviously sexy. We just don't feel that way about each other. Just had to work together to get the job done."

"So Rachel screwed you to keep me safe," Lila lets out a laugh but it's fueled with fire.

"Well-" I try to stop the thought before it spirals but I fail.

"She was never my friend. That's what you're saying, right? I was just a job for her and as soon as it was over, she just packed up and moved on?"

"Lila, it's not that simple-"

"Why the hell are you still around? If it's not to make your girlfriend happy then why are you still trying to take care of me? You got me out of danger, right? You saved me from Warren or whatever- which, might I add, you did a terrible job with since he *stabbed me in the stomach* while the two of you just watched." Her sarcastic tone has escalated into a furious shout and heads start to turn.

"But now I'm here and being treated like a child so, yeah, mission accomplished. Go hang out with your brother and let me rot in this hell-"

I grab her arm and pull her towards an alleyway to hopefully get her out of view of the city.

"Get off of me!" She smacks me across my face with a lot more force than I would've expected her to have.

It leaves me speechless long enough for Lila to attempt an escape. I snap back into reality fast, though, grabbing her firmly by both arms this time.

"Lila."

She resists relentlessly and I end up pinning her to the side of the brick building that lines the alley. She grunts and kicks and refuses to settle down.

"Stop moving!" I shout, my mouth close to her right ear.

She winces at the volume of my words and finally relaxes her body. Her teeth are still gritted when she looks up at me and spits, "Let me go."

"You know I can't do that. I know you don't understand, and it must be so frustrating for you to hear the truth, but you honestly don't even know the half of it," I spit back. "Maybe you can't handle it. I must have overestimated you."

She pushes back on my hands again and I let her go, half expecting her to hit me again or take off in a sprint. Instead, she looks down at the ground and takes a deep breath.

When she meets my eyes again, hers are filled with tears. "You have no idea how I'm feeling. Looking out for me for a few weeks doesn't mean you know anything about me."

I focus on her then, not sure how to communicate with her. She's the most frustrating person I've ever met and yet I know she has every reason to be. Her life is so complicated and she is unable to choose anything for herself. "I know you much better than you might like."

She wipes the tears from her cheeks- a useless effort since they never stop falling- and then puts her hands firmly on my forearms. "Am I ever getting out of here?"

"What do you mean?"

"I want to go home, Ryker," she pleads breathlessly.

"It's so complicated, Lila. I can't tell you everything or you'll never be able to trust me. I promise you I won't let anything bad happen to you, we just need some time to get used to each other."

She laughs and brushes more tears off her face. "Easier said than done."

I let out a breath of relief. "You have no idea how difficult I can be, I'm really going to test your patience."

"Well as long as you act this chill every time I cry, we might be able to make something work," I dig through my bag and find a tissue for her to use. "Thanks."

"Anytime," I say quietly. "Hey, are you hungry?"

"Starving." She smiles again and we share a small moment of peace before I guide her to my favorite restaurant in the city.

It's dark by the time we leave the restaurant, and the city lights start to come on. The restaurant, Amore, turned on the sparkling lights on their outdoor seating patio, pulling a gasp out of Lila.

"Amaryllis," she whispers, full of wonder.

I smile to myself before turning back into my security guard alter ego. "Right this way, ma'am."

Lila shakes her head. "You're such a dork."

We take our time on our way back to the train station, mostly because I'm nervous how Lila is going to feel once we're back. I don't think Colonel Finch and the rest of the Council is going to let her go to town every day. I'm not sure what they have planned for her, but I know they need her to give them information that I doubt she has.

"Hey, I'm sorry about Rachel. If it makes you feel better, she does care about you. We're not really supposed to get attached in this line of work, but it's inevitable." I continue to look forward as we walk, checking our surroundings and avoiding eye contact with Lila.

"It would be very hard for me not to get emotionally attached," she says softly. "But I'm not sure I agree about Rachel. She's pretended I don't exist since being at Headquarters. Even if she hadn't known where I was until you showed up, she didn't try to protect me. And based on her reaction, I think it's safe to say she knew."

"The mission is over, it's not her job anymore. Her job was to protect you in the field. The last thing we wanted was to have to bring you here, but this is where you're safest. She doesn't think she needs to protect you here." I don't realize until after her next question that I'm putting my foot right back in my mouth.

"And now we're back to where we started," Lila slows her steps to a stop and looks at me directly. "Why are you still involved? Why do you need to protect me if I'm safe here? What are you getting out of it, Ryker?"

"Yeah, I really walked right into that one, didn't I?" Lila smirks and I let out a sigh. "I don't want to upset you again."

"I can handle it," she says confidently. I shoot her a pointed look and she rolls her eyes. "I can."

I let out another short sigh. "For Rachel, it was always just a mission. She cares about you, we often have some emotional connection to the subject of a mission, but she could get in a lot of trouble for defending you from Headquarters post-mission."

"Why doesn't that apply to you?" Lila shakes her head, confused.

"That's the complicated part. First of all, I did get reprimanded, as you saw. But it's different for me. This mission was always a little personal and that's the reason they wanted me on your case."

"I'm asking you *why*, Ryker. Why is it personal to you?"

"Because we have a history, Lila," Something resembling disgust crosses her face and I take it upon myself to clarify. "Not like that, not me and you," I sigh again, louder this time. "My family has a history with you, a history of trying to take care of you."

"What do you mean?"

"It's a lot to explain right now and I'd much rather be at Headquarters to do it." I wave my hand at the scene ahead of us. "It's dark, people are starting to celebrate and drink and I don't want you out here for that."

"Fine." Lila turns and starts walking again.

The rest of the trip is silent except for me giving her directions on what to do and where to go. Once we're back on the train, I get on first, scan the crowd, and then have Lila sit in a chair close to the door. I stand next to her for a few moments until the doors close and we start to move.

"Sit down, you look creepy," Lila whispers to me.

I take a seat next to her but still keep my eyes busy, watching everyone that looks at or comes near Lila. There is a noisy group of teenagers in the back of the train but they seem to mostly keep to themselves.

I notice an older woman looking at Lila. She then looks me in the eyes and pointed subtly at her wrist. I nod in understanding and tell Lila to cover the bracelets with her sleeves.

The rest of the ride goes smoothly and I make sure to thank the woman as we get off the train. We walk past Headquarters and head for the Living Quarters again.

"So?" Lila asks expectantly.

"Man, you just do not give up, do you?"

"No, I don't. Come on, Ryker, if I had information about you and refused to tell you, it would drive you crazy. You would probably beat the information out of me, you should just be grateful that I'm not a fighter."

"I wouldn't beat the information out of you!"

"Ryker," she warns.

"Okay, okay." I grimace. "My brother was one of the first ones to be assigned to you. The mission didn't really go as planned and he has never really recovered."

I squeeze the back of my neck. "When they were assigning people to your case, I volunteered and they chose me because they knew I would do a good job to make my brother proud."

"So I've met one of your brothers?"

"Yes."

Her eyes go wide as she considers the information she is hearing. "How long have you guys been watching me?" I realize now how scared she is and I try to console her.

"Lila, we've been protecting you for a long time."

"Protecting me from what? Warren? I've only known him for

like a year." She shakes her head defensively.

"No, not just Warren," I sigh, knowing that giving her this information is not going to go very well. "Are you sure you want to-"

"Yes, I'm sure. I need to know what kind of place I'm in."

I turn to her and grab hold of her arm closest to me. "Lila, you can't run. You have to promise me you won't try to leave. You will not get away and they will lock you up indefinitely for that kind of attempt."

She contemplates for a moment and then accepts my terms. "I will not run away from you. I don't know if I can promise that I won't get away from this government as soon as I hear what you have to say, but I won't run away from *you*."

"Lila, I am a Soldier of the government, that's not a promise at all-"

"I promised I won't run away from you, and that's all you're going to get!"

My life would've been so much simpler without her. She's a lot calmer than she was at Amaryllis, though, so I carefully give more information as we climb the stairs to get back to her room. I watch her face carefully as I speak. "Our government protects regular humans from… misused magic."

Her head spins around faster than I can anticipate. "*What*?"

I confirm with a slight nod of my head.

"Come on, Ryker, just tell me the truth."

"That is the truth," I argue. She rolls her eyes. "Lila, what do you think those bracelets are for?"

She looks down at her wrists, running her fingers softly over one of the metal restraints. She covers it up with her sleeve and turns her attention back to me, a scowl on her face. "I'm not stupid, Ryker."

"I knew you wouldn't want to hear the truth." I shake my head, irritated at the situation. "That's why they detained you. Do you remember what happened when Warren attacked you?"

"You were trying to talk to him and he stabbed me. Then I woke up in a hospital bed." She shrugs.

"I didn't stop Warren. I was going to, but I couldn't get close enough before he pushed the blade in. *You* stopped him."

"H-how?" she stutters. Her brows are furrowed in confusion and I can tell she's trying to remember.

We come to a halt at her door and I turn to face her. "With your magic."

"That's impossible," she defends quickly.

I look at her intently, trying to understand what I could say or do to help her make sense of this information. How do you tell someone information about themselves that they don't know?

"Look, it's been a long day. I think maybe we should talk about this more tomorrow so you can rest. You've heard a lot of information today and I think you may need time to process it. Tomorrow, if you'd like, we could go talk to Colonel Finch and maybe she can give you more details on your case."

I wait for a response but instead, Lila just leans against the door frame, rubbing her head with her fingers and closing her eyes.

"Lila?" I barely make contact with her arm before her posture straightens and her eyes shoot open. I take my hand off of her. "Sorry. Um, do you want to go to bed?"

She looks at me with a blank stare for a few seconds before responding with a quiet "Okay."

"Do you need me to get you something to drink? You look a little pale."

"No." She finally blinks after what feels like twenty minutes. "No, I'll be fine. You're right, I just need to sleep for a little while. Thank you, for um-" she brakes off mid-sentence.

"Lila, are you okay?"

"Yes, sorry, I'm fine. Just tired, I guess." I can see the moment she snaps back to the present conversation. "Thank you for today. Amaryllis is a beautiful city and it was really nice to get out. Thank you."

"You're welcome-"

Lila steps inside her room and turns to close the door. "Good night, Ryker."

"Um," Her quick change in awareness catches me off guard. "Good night." And with that, the door closes shut.

I shake my head and get back to work. I make sure Lila's door is closed and locked and then go to my own room. I remove my gear and sit down at the desk, getting ready to notate my report of the day when my device rings. I open it and answer the call from Colonel Finch.

"This is Jordan."

"Ryker, I'm glad to hear your voice. I've been anxious all day. How is Lila doing? Are you back from Amaryllis?" I can't remember the last time I heard the Colonel speak this way.

"Yes, ma'am. It was a long day but she is back and there haven't been any issues with citizens or Soldiers today."

"Very good," Finch affirms.

"She was asking a lot of questions, Colonel. I'm not sure I handled them all correctly. I think it would be good if you could meet with her soon."

"Yes, well," There is a pause on her end of the line.

"I know that may be complicated and difficult, ma'am but I'm afraid there really is no other way."

"Very well. I will contact you tomorrow when we can meet." Finch says decidedly.

"Yes ma'am, I will wait for further directions then."

"Goodnight, Soldier."

"Goodnight, Ma'am." The call clicks off and I put my device down.

My mind is racing too much to write my report so I hop in the shower first. The water feels so refreshing on my skin and I'm so grateful to have a room to myself. I take my time, letting myself enjoy this moment without a single thought of the day.

At last, my shower comes to an end and I work myself up to write the report. I keep it short and sweet, explaining where we went and giving brief summaries of the conversations Lila and I had throughout the day.

I finish up, organizing my things before getting into bed. I drift off as soon as my head hits my pillow, but it doesn't last long. A few hours into the night, I am woken up by Lila's screaming.

FIFTEEN

Lila

I am in the forest again, running fast as I try to escape back to the beautiful field I had previously been in. The light from the sky dims the farther I run.

My panic grows and I start to feel claustrophobic in the dark, thickening trees. I collapse to my hands and knees on the forest floor, gasping for air.

As I catch my breath, I notice a small glow in the distance. I struggle into a stance and stumble towards the faint glisten of yellow and green light. It's a mysterious glimmer and I slow my pace as I creep up on the scene.

There are six people that I can make out. One must be a child because it is much smaller than the rest of them. Before I know it, I'm witnessing what looks like a murder.

Three of them hold weapons, using them to knock down the remaining two adults. Light shoots across the scene until both of the adults lay lifeless on the forest floor. One of the remaining individuals holds up a gun, pointing at the child.

"Stop!" I yell out as loud as I can but nobody hears me. I squeeze my eyes shut and continue to scream as waterfalls of tears flow down my face.

I am alone in my agony for several minutes before I hear banging and footsteps approach me. I refuse to open my eyes. Someone grabs hold of my shoulders and I thrash, fighting off whoever is trying to take me.

"Lila," the person grabbing me shouts. "Open your eyes."

But I'm not going down without a fight.

"Ow!" The voice yelps as my elbow connects with something hard. "Lila, open your damn eyes! It's me." The dots start to connect and though I can't remember who the voice belongs to, I know it's not someone who is trying to hurt me.

I give in to the pressure that battles to restrain me. I let my eyes flutter open and I give myself a moment to take in my surroundings. It is still dark, but I am not in a forest.

Ryker is halfway on top of me, holding my arms with his large hands and pinning down my legs with his torso. Past him, treetops have been replaced with a white, barely textured ceiling. It is almost completely silent besides the pounding of my heart and Ryker's panting.

I look around to see I am in my bedroom and can feel, now, the comfort of my new bed. My eyes land back on Ryker's face and can barely see he is looking back at me in this light.

"You're okay. You're safe. Can I let you go now?" Ryker asks in the most genuine and peaceful voice I've ever heard him use.

I nod slightly and he releases his hold on me with a quiet breath. He sits down in the chair across from my bed and runs a hand through his hair. I always thought his hair was short until we got here. Now I see that it is very long for a Soldier.

I roll onto my side so that I'm facing him and pull my sheets up to my chin. "Sorry," I offer up timidly.

"No need to apologize," he responds genuinely. "I thought someone was hurting you. Where were you?"

I blink at the question, briefly worried that he might think I'm crazy, but then quickly get over it since I know he's seen much worse from me already. "I was in a forest. I've been there before, just the other night, actually. I was in a field and then I saw a forest and I went in. I went too far and couldn't get out. I woke up when you broke the door down to my cell." I glance at Ryker and notice his distressed expression has taken on a deeper, disturbed demeanor.

I continue relaying my nightmare to him, intentionally observing his reaction. "Tonight I was in the forest again, trying to get out, but the more I walked, the darker it got until I saw some sort of glimmer of light." Something that looks a lot like fear creeps into Ryker's eyes, giving me goosebumps.

"I followed the light and-" My voice cuts out then, making it impossible to go on.

We sit in silence for a long time before Ryker gets out of the chair, puts a hand on my shoulder and says quietly "I'm glad you're safe now." I attempt a smile but it doesn't fool him. "Are you going to be okay?"

"Could you actually stay in here for a little while maybe?" I'm embarrassed to even ask, but I'm more afraid of reliving that nightmare.

"Okay," he says calmly and retakes his seat. "No problem."

We look at each other for a few minutes, unsure of how to fill the silence.

Today is the first time I feel like I am seeing slivers of who Ryker Jordan really is. I can tell he is loyal to his core. Family and where he comes from mean a lot to him and I'm almost jealous.

He is much more impressive than I had originally thought. It's hard to find him endearing, though, when I know that he's holding back information from me.

"You know something about my nightmares, don't you?" I ask him directly, still keeping eye contact.

He fixes on his hands which are intertwined in his lap. "I believe so."

"What do they mean? Do I want to know?" I ask cautiously.

"Probably not. I'm not sure I'm the one who should explain them to you." He looks briefly up at the ceiling, shaking his head.

He glances back at me before getting up and beginning a slow pace from the closet door to the bedroom door and back. "I hate this, Lila. I hope you know that I hate knowing more about you than you do. Not knowing what to tell you and what will hurt you, it's torture."

I sit up on the bed with my back against the wall, still facing him. "Imagine being on the receiving end, Ryker. You think it's frustrating for you? Meanwhile, I have to rely on you, a stranger, to tell me about my own life. You can't even compare the two." I don't want to be harsh, but I do think it's within my rights to be angry. In fact, I should probably be angrier than I am.

"I know, I didn't mean it like that, I just…" He exhales loudly, pulls the chair closer to my bed, finally sitting back down.

"I don't want to lie to you, I don't want to keep things from you." He runs his fingers through his hair again. "But I know the truth will hurt you. My job is to keep you from getting hurt. How am I supposed to balance the two?"

My patience is running thin but I know he's trying to be considerate and I do want the information that he has, so I take a deep breath and calm my thoughts. "I can't be the one to help you navigate that, Ryker. I need to know what has happened to me to get me to where I am now. If you can't provide that, then I either need someone who can or I need to get out of here."

His posture somehow becomes even more severe. "Lila, you promised me you won't leave. We both have too much riding on this for that."

"That's the thing, Ryk! I don't even know what I have 'riding on this.' Don't you see?" My rage threatens to overflow into my words. "I have nothing to lose by leaving this place and never coming back because I don't know what dangers you're talking about.

"Warren is taken care of. I'm fine. What I'm seeing now is that I'm being held hostage by my captors and I'm being lied to about my 'safety' so that I'm too afraid to leave." My voice is firm and I am proud that I am sticking up for myself.

"We're going to meet with someone tomorrow who can tell you more," Ryker says quietly.

"That's not good enough. I need some answers." I'm proud of myself for demanding my needs.

"Warren wasn't the real threat, Lila. He was a pawn." Ryker pinches and rubs his temple while he explains. "We think Fara was threatening him to get information out of you. We don't know why, but we believe she's part of a terrorist group of sorts."

"Fara? My roommate?" I ask incredulously. He's lost his mind.

"Yes. We believe they want something with your…magic." He looks at me warily.

"You've got to be joking-" I breathe out an exasperated laugh.

"Look, you can talk to Finch tomorrow and she'll explain more." He crosses his muscular arms across his broad chest, finalizing his decision.

Unfortunately for him, I'm not willing to accept so little. "You can't ask me to go back to sleep knowing what's waiting for me in my subconscious. Tell me what my nightmare means," I demand.

"It's not a nightmare, Lila," Ryker responds remorsefully. "It's a memory."

"A memory of what?"

"You remember how I told you that our government protects humans from evil magic?" I roll my eyes but he continues regardless. "We live in harmony with Necromancers, people who use magic. But we are responsible for keeping them in check. There are some Necromancers that believe in dark magic, and their intentions are to mix humans with magic to create monsters.

"There is a boundary up around all of Amaryllis that controls the magic they are able to use, and it prohibits dark magic. The rebel Necromancers need to break that barrier before they can use that kind of magic." He waits for me to confirm that I'm following along.

"So, I'm a Necromancer?"

He hesitates before bowing his head.

I catch my breath. I barely know how to ask the daunting question that takes up most of the space in my brain. "Doesn't that mean like killing rituals and conjuring dead people?"

"Oh." The question totally derails Ryker's plan for this conversation. "Um, that's kind of the history, yes. I guess those types of things fall into the 'dark magic' territory. But they are not regularly practiced, and definitely not within Amaryllis boundaries. Necromancy is broader than some humans believe. It is used for a lot of good, too."

"So, what are they trying to do by mixing magic and humans? Is that bad magic or good magic?"

"They are trying to create half-breeds, which are very dangerous. They can take on many forms and are very difficult to… manage."

"What does that mean?" I question, doubtful of the narrative I am being told.

"You've heard of werewolves, vampires, fairies, I assume?" I nod. "Well, similar to that. Mixing dark magic with humans can create half-breeds that we haven't had for many years. We don't know what kind of effect they could have on our society but imagine what that could do to the human race."

"Woah." I search for a better response but come up empty-handed. I have to give credit where it's due. They may be helping people after all. If what he tells me is true, that is. "Wait, so if a magic person and a regular person… you know… do it… would it create-"

Ryker's serious expression cracks with his laugh when he realizes what I'm asking. "No, no it's not from procreating." He laughs again. "Mixed children simply either get the magic gene or don't."

The smile slips off his face as he explains further. "Half-breeds are created by a ritual where the magic works as a sort of parasite or cancer, changing the nature of the cells. The half-breeds then become obedient to the owner of the magic used during the ritual."

Ryker was right, there is a lot more at stake behind the scenes. "That sounds awful, but what does it have to do with my nightmare?" I refocus the conversation.

"It's a memory of a mission." Ryker pauses, suddenly uncomfortable again. "The group that you saw was a rebel group- terrorists- trying to take down the barrier."

"A memory? You mean that I was there?"

"Yes. That was the first time we came into contact with you." Ryker's tone has changed again and the combination of his voice with the words he is saying makes me feel uneasy.

"Were you there, too?"

"No. I was too young."

"Then how do you know?" I accuse.

"There are records from several accounts- the Soldiers, Headquarters- but my brother was there, Lila. It was very traumatic for both of you and while your memory was wiped, Connor has re-lived that night every single day of his life. I heard the story several times a day until they took him away."

"Why did they wipe my memory? What does that even mean? What did they do to me?"

"I honestly don't know the specifics, but there are Necromancers that work here at Headquarters and I was told they did some kind of spell to make you forget that night. It sounds like it's wearing off, though, which I didn't think was possible."

"So the people that got murdered in my nightmare?" My eyes gloss over with tears and I attempt to blink them away.

Ryker groans, an outward expression of the internal conflict he's battling. It's hard to sympathize with him, but I try to understand what this experience feels like from his perspective. It's ugly on both sides. "We think they might have been-" His voice trembles with emotion and makes it harder for me to breathe. "Your parents."

I was expecting it, but somehow it still punches me in the gut. I double over in pain and try to breathe as the tears spill over my face aggressively.

"Lila," he laments. The pain in his voice makes me wonder if he's crying, but it's the least of my concerns right now. "I'm so sorry. That's all I know."

When I finally catch my breath, I hop off the bed and make it to the bathroom barely in time to throw up in the toilet. Little comes out and I dry heave for what feels like half an hour but must have been only a few minutes.

I pull myself up by the counter and splash my face with the coldest water the sink will muster. I still have water in my eyes when I hear soft footsteps on the tile floor of the bathroom.

"Lila?"

Neither of us say a word until I dry my eyes. It takes me another minute to gather the courage to meet Ryker's eyes in the mirror. "Get out."

My quiet but confident demand seems to appall him. His eyes grow big and his face pales. It might've been satisfying to see him like this if it weren't under such devastating circumstances. I am an orphan because of these people. My parents broke their rules and got murdered for it.

"What? No, I-"

"Get. Out." I repeat with more severity.

He still doesn't process what I'm saying because he stays where he is, shaking his head ever so slightly, unable to speak, or move, apparently. I stare at him for a second longer and then look back at the sink. "Lila, please, you have to understand-"

I cut him off by shoving him hard in the chest, causing him to finally take a step backward. "Get out." I shove him again, gaining another step.

He looks hurt, but he no longer makes an effort to persuade me otherwise. "Get out." I give him one more push until we're at the hallway door. He is still facing me, remaining quiet and not making any attempts to open the door. I reach past him and open it myself. "Get out!"

Ryker steps backward through the doorway, his eyes pleading that I don't shut him out. I hesitate half a second before slamming the door in his face and locking it behind him. I know it won't make a difference, but I push the chair up against the door handle, giving myself an extra barrier.

Time warps as I drift off, repeat my nightmare memory, wake up, and repeat. I don't understand why this memory decided to come back now, and I'm not particularly grateful for it.

Part of me hopes there is something embedded in the nightmare that will help me digest everything I've learned today but it's so horrible that I can't bring myself to find out.

I stay awake as long as I can, but I always end up falling asleep. There are no clocks or windows in my room, giving me no way to tell how long I've been in here. There have been no attempts to enter on Ryker's behalf and I'm glad to have the time and space to myself.

At some point, I turn on the shower and end up sitting on the shower floor, unable to stand for long. I let the water fall on me like rain as I try to understand what I'm supposed to do.

I run through the events of my life, assuming that this place is the reason I ended up in foster care. I can't understand how they could kill my parents and then drop me off at an orphanage. Why couldn't I stay here? Why couldn't they raise me as one of their own or have the Necromancers take care of me? If my parents are Necromancers then so am I. How has that never come up?

Is my magic dangerous? Is that why I have to wear these stupid bracelets? Apparently I hurt Warren with it, so I must have some kind of access to it. Maybe magic is the reason I'm remembering that night in the woods.

After what must be more than an hour, I feel brave enough to dive in deeper to find answers. I let myself go back again, quiet my mind and return back to the memory hoping to notice something new this time.

I am running in the forest, trying to catch fireflies and giggling each time one escapes me. The man and the woman take turns yelling for me, telling me to come near them and to stop playing. They call me daughter but there is a darkness that surrounds them as they come into my view.

They tell me to stand still as they work together, casting a spell. I don't know how I know it's a spell, but I recognize it as a dangerous one. I start to feel nervous, telling my parents I do not want to play this game.

The father slaps his open hand across my face and tells me in our language that he does not want me to be selfish. I want to cry but I know I will be punished.

I pretend I am a statue and stay as quiet as possible. The girl's parents begin their chant again, humming and stringing words of a foreign language together.

Within a few minutes, they both turn to face her- me- while they chant, the words becoming louder and more powerful. A familiar green light glimmers against the dark forest, floating in between the three of us.

Without warning, the adults throw their hands forward simultaneously and the light follows the command, knocking the breath out of me.

SIXTEEN

Ryker

As soon as morning hits, I gear up and wait outside Lila's door. I'm unsure of what to do, given the events of last night. I don't blame her for making me leave and I don't blame her for ignoring the knocks on her door.

I regret telling her about her parents last night, I didn't want to overwhelm her with information. She wasn't going to trust me if I didn't tell her. Now she trusts me even less.

After a while, I take a seat on the floor, leaning my back and head against the wall next to Lila's door. I give patience an honest try but don't make it more than an hour before I knock again. No answer.

I'm not sure how I can make this right. I wish I had told her that the purpose of the mission was originally to arrest the Necromancers, not to kill them. I wish I'd told her that they attacked the soldiers and that the soldiers were just trying to defend themselves. I still could explain that if she would open the damn door.

I consider forcing my way in several times but I know that won't help the situation. I need to tell her that we are not her enemy, that we want to help, that's all we've ever wanted.

Her parents were using extremely dangerous magic and there's no telling what they would've done if they'd had the chance to finish. Lila would be in a much worse situation now if we hadn't intervened.

My eyes start to flutter closed after hours of waiting and I stand up to keep myself from drifting asleep. I pace back and forth in front of the door, do some push ups, knock on the door again, pace some more.

After several hours of waiting, head bobbing, door knocking, and pacing, Lila finally opens the door. I shoot up from my position on the floor and wait for her to speak.

"I want to talk to Colonel Finch." She looks at me straight on, expressionless, giving me absolutely no indication on where we stand. Maybe she wants to request a new bodyguard.

"Okay. Do you want some food firs-"

"No," she cuts me off, remaining eerily calm.

Instead of forcing a conversation, I step to the side, bringing my arm up in the direction of Finch's office. She hesitates for half a second, unnoticeable to someone not paying attention. It passes quickly, though, and Lila walks past my arm, toward the stairs.

We walk in silence, and I let Lila take the lead, hovering behind her like a child. While it's embarrassing, I'm trying to stay out of her way as much as I can. At each fork in the road, I silently point her where to go.

The halls are almost barren, as most people ought to be at dinner by now. There are a few stragglers but luckily nobody gives us much attention. As we step into the corridor leading to Finch's office, my chest tightens a fraction more and my breath shallows.

We come to a stop in front of her door and Lila looks at me. I knock on the door and Finch's assistant, Margaret, opens it.

"Yes, how may I help you?" she asks expectantly.

"We would like to meet with Colonel Finch, please."

"My apologies, Soldier, but the Colonel is not available at the moment and I do not have an appointment on the calendar," she starts. Lila looks at me sternly. "Would you like to make an appointment for a later time?"

"No, ma'am. I know there isn't an appointment on the schedule, but Colonel Finch is expecting us." I tell Margaret politely. Lila takes her laser vision off of me and gives Margaret a supportive smile.

"Well, I'll have to check-" Margaret seems a little baffled and is not sure how to proceed.

"If you'd like, I could get her on the phone to confirm," I offer confidently.

"That's alright, I can call her and let her know you are here. Please take a seat."

I nod my head triumphantly and direct Lila towards the waiting room chairs. She takes the seat closest to the door we came through. I take the seat next to her, closest to Finch's door. Margaret dials a few numbers and speaks into her phone with a hushed voice.

Before she finishes, Finch opens her door looking past me and landing her stressed glare on Lila. I feel Lila's posture stiffen beside me and I stand up.

"Colonel Finch." I salute her and wait for her salute to release me but she is still focused on Lila. "Ma'am."

She blinks, then, and salutes me. "Soldier," she says, finally acknowledging my presence. "We discussed that I would call you when I was ready-"

"I wanted to see you now," Lila demands. Considering how nervous she seemed just minutes ago, I am impressed with the force her voice contains now.

"Yes, well," Colonel Finch says, switching her attention back to Lila. "I suppose you must have some questions for me."

"An understatement," Lila retorts shamelessly. "But yes, I do."

"Right this way." Finch steps into her office and holds the door open until we walk through. "Please, sit down." Lila chooses to sit directly in front of Finch, the same chair I sat in a few nights ago when I met with her about Lila. I follow suit and sit next to her, pulling the chair out several inches to put space between us.

There is a long silence, overflowing with a cocktail of emotions, mostly negative. I feel out of place, almost guilty, as if I were eavesdropping at the door. Lila is almost bursting with anticipation to learn about her roots and our imposition on her life.

Finch is motionless, making her appear calm from the outside, but I know her well enough to see the underlying anxiety she has about this conversation finally happening after all these years.

Finch is first to break the silence. "What would you like to know?"

"Everything," Lila says sincerely, somewhat taken off guard by the question. "I'm a Necromancer?"

"Yes," Finch responds quickly, very matter-of-fact.

"And my parents are- were- Necromancers?"

"Yes."

"And I've used magic before, then."

"Yes."

"Have I killed anyone?"

A flash of concern flashes across her face, a clear indication that she had no idea that Lila was having questions like this one. I guess I hadn't either, but I was more prepared for it than she was. "No."

Lila is visibly relieved by the answer. "What happened after my parents were killed?"

Finch is surprised by this question as well and she makes a point to look at me before attempting an answer. "Lila, you-"

"Don't lie to me. I want to know why you kept me, why not just leave me in the forest? What did you do to me?"

"I don't think it's appropriate to discuss-"

Lila cuts her off again, her anger growing with each word. "It's my life. I deserve to know the truth, despite how uncomfortable it might make you-"

"Let me finish," Finch barks. Lila closes her mouth and sits back slightly in her chair. "It is not appropriate to discuss this in front of

Ryker. If I am going to discuss classified information, it needs to be cleared. With you, I may be able to bend the rules a bit, if you can keep it confidential. However, I cannot justify disclosing classified information about previous or ongoing missions to Soldiers without clearance." Finch keeps her attention focused on Lila.

Lila turns to me with an intense expression on her face. "Am I safe here?" she asks me. When I don't immediately respond she tries again. "Ryker. Is she going to hurt me or can I trust her?"

I look at Finch and then back to Lila. "You can trust her. She won't hurt you." My jaw tightens with the words.

"Okay." Lila touches my shoulder to make sure I hear her next request. "Then please leave so I can get the truth."

Her words hit me like a punch to the gut, but I understand the assignment. I stand up from my chair and walk out of the room, closing the door behind me. I'm too proud- or hurt- to look back at either of them.

I hesitate outside the door for a few seconds. Should I wait for her? Or have I been dismissed from this mission? Does Lila no longer need someone to protect her or will she ask for a new soldier? It doesn't take me long to decide what to do.

SEVENTEEN

Lila

"It sounds like you've received some information." I feel like a teenager again, getting caught with something I'm not supposed to, as if my life's history isn't my business.

"Not nearly enough." It comes out barely louder than a whisper.

"Lila, they weren't your parents. I'm sorry that you were told that before I had the chance to give you the truth. Ryker doesn't know very much about your case, though his family knows more than most others, because of what happened to Connor."

"What? What are you talking about?"

"Let's start from the beginning, yes?"

I can't force any words out so I nod instead.

"Our history is full of devastating battles between Necromancers and humans. Necromancers used to have no governing power, nobody to guide or restrict the magic they used. They created monsters, they killed, they controlled. Our people fought valiantly against them, and many died, but eventually we won the war. Enough honorable Necromancers joined our movement and we've governed both sides since then. Necromancers get the same privileges and rights as the rest of us as long as they keep their magic aligned with the law.

"It hasn't been all smooth, though, as the occasional rebellious Necromancers will attempt to overthrow our government. We have withstood a lot in our time. This particular group had been taking children from their Necromancers parents, stealing them with magic that we could not trace, and disappearing with them. We calculated about twenty children that had gone missing. The night that you speak of, we detected evil magic being used, and we sent out Soldiers to investigate. Once they verified that there was illegal, and very dangerous, magic being used, I gave the order of arrest. The adult Necromancers did not back down and I cleared the soldiers to take them down by whatever means necessary.

"When the soldiers took them down, you were released from some sort of spell they had you in. You moved and spoke for the first time. You called out to them as your parents, so we assumed you were their daughter. One of the soldiers on the mission knocked you out and they brought you back to Headquarters."

Colonel Finch takes a deep breath, seemingly reliving the events of that night. "You woke up after a few hours and you were very afraid and confused. You couldn't give us any information, you were too young. So, we decided to use magic to access your memories. We got information dating back to your birth and we realized that the Necromancers killed in the forest were not your parents. They had taken you a few years prior to the incident. We don't know what happened to your parents because you were asleep when they took you and it wasn't in your memories. We decided to remove the painful memories and give you a shot at a normal life. The Headquarter Necromancers erased your memory and we gave you a human life."

"You got rid of me," I say quietly, unable to express the complicated emotions that swirl inside.

"We did what was best for you."

"How do you figure that? How was handing me over to abusive people 'doing what's best for me'? How did never telling me who I was or what had happened to me help me?"

"Lila, we did not drop you off and leave you. We kept tabs on you, we've always looked out for you." She's starting to sound defensive and I recover my fire from earlier.

"What?" I spit the question with so much hatred that it startles Finch. "You mean to tell me that you watched what happened to me and you left me in those situations knowingly?" I stand up from my chair before she has time to react. "It sucked when I thought I was abandoned by my parents- the two people in the world who are supposed to care for and love me unconditionally. But I forgave them, gave them the benefit of the doubt- they thought it would be better for me and all that."

I scoff at the thought of it now. "But then I find out that my parents wanted me, I was kidnapped from them, then my kidnappers were killed. Instead of returning me back to my parents, y'all kept me hostage. You put me in foster care, you let all those people do those terrible things-" Tears prickle the corner of my eyes and my voice threatens to fail me.

I compose myself and sit back down. "You're going to be honest with me about why."

As I walk out of Finch's office, I notice Ryker's nowhere to be seen. Finch exits behind me and it doesn't take her long to notice either.

"Margaret, get Mr. Ryker Jordan down here right now to escort Miss Lila back to her room."

"Yes ma'am!" Margaret shoots into action, picking up her phone and dialing a short number.

"Good night, Lila. I look forward to speaking with you again shortly."

"Likewise," I dismiss her and she returns to her office, closing the door behind her. I turn and glance at Margaret, who is fidgeting with things on her desk as she pretends I'm not there. I don't know if I make her nervous because I'm a Necromancer, or if her job truly keeps her on her toes, but she is surrounded by a weird energy. I take a seat and try to stay out of her line of sight.

Within about ten minutes, Ryker comes in with a cautious expression on his face. He doesn't say anything and barely looks me in the eye before he does his typical 'go-this-way' hand motion. I chuckle to myself and exit the room.

"Were we in there that long?" I ask him as we step into the corridor.

"Huh?" He asks, still avoiding eye contact. He keeps several feet of distance between us.

"Were we in there for a long time?"

"Oh, I'm not sure," he says shortly.

"Then why did you leave?"

He's quiet for several seconds. "You asked me to."

"You were offended?" I slow my pace and eventually he matches it.

"You asked me to leave, so I did. I don't understand what you're getting at." He's being evasive and immature.

I stop walking and turn my body to face him. I wait for him to do the same. He stops walking when he notices, but he stays facing forward.

"Ryker," I keep my voice calm and try to be understanding. "You really need to learn how to express yourself."

"Just drop it, Lila. I'm back, what's the problem?"

"I don't know the problem because you won't tell me, dummy."

"I don't have a problem. Let's just get back-"

"Ryker, something is bothering you and I'm not going anywhere until you tell me what it is."

He glances at me briefly. "I could always force you," he mumbles.

"Something made you leave and I'm guessing it's the same thing that is making it hard for you to look at me."

He chuckles and starts back toward the sleeping quarters.

"How am I supposed to trust you if you don't trust me? Trust is supposed to be a two-way street."

His head snaps in my direction, brows furrowed and eyes dark. "I have been very honest with you. I've answered every question you've ever asked me-"

"Then ask me a question!" I raise my voice this time.

"Why didn't you want me there?" he shouts back, turning and closing the gap between us. His voice hints more of hurt than anger.

"What do you mean? She said she couldn't tell me if you were there."

He steps closer so he can tell it to my face. "That's bullshit and you know it. If you had told her you wanted me there, she would've listened."

I look him in the eyes and try to show him that I'm being genuine. "I'm sorry."

He chuckles breathily and shakes his head, starting to turn away. I grab at him firmly.

"No, Ryker, I mean it. I'm sorry. I didn't mean to kick you out."

He meets my eyes shortly before looking past me again. At least he doesn't turn away again.

"Hey." I step closer to him and wait to continue until he returns his gaze back to my face. It feels like several tense minutes, but when he finally does, it sends a jolt through my body. "I'm sorry that I hurt your feelings. That honestly wasn't my intention. I just desperately needed to know the truth about my life."

I put my hands on each of his forearms, trying to settle his mixed emotions of betrayal and rejection. "I got my answers, Ryker. Thank you for bringing me here."

He must hear my sincerity. "I always wanted you to have the truth."

"I know, Ryker. I know that now, more than ever. Thank you."

Before he has time to turn away from me again or brush off the conversation, I pull him down into a hug. Because of his height, I'm sure most would hug around his waist, but I wrap both arms around his neck and hold tightly. Halfway through, he relaxes his posture and hugs me back. It feels like this may be the first hug he's had in a very long time.

When he lets go, I back up a step and offer him a shy smile. He grins back at me and I try to take mental note of this shared moment. I look down at my feet and turn back towards the opening of the corridor to the floor lobby, suddenly feeling exposed somehow.

He follows my lead and starts walking slowly, waiting for me to set the pace. I realize all of a sudden that it's dark outside, and there isn't another soul in sight. I must have been in there longer than I had thought. I feel slightly odd knowing that we are completely alone.

After a few minutes of silence, I get anxious to change the attention from what had just happened. "Guess what we're doing tomorrow," I say playfully.

"What's that?" He plays along as we start up the stairs of the Living Quarters building.

"We get to train." I move my eyebrows up and down at him.

Ryker laughs like it's the most ridiculous thing he's ever heard. "What?"

"I'm serious!" I nudge him with my shoulder.

"How in the hell did you get her to agree to that?" He nudges me back.

"As it turns out, I am valuable to 'the cause,'" I put air quotes around the words to exaggerate. "Finch wants me on 'this side of history' and all that. So, I told her that I need to learn combat skills and, after several minutes of arguing, she agreed. But you-" I stick a finger at Ryker- "have to be the one to train me."

"Oh, goodie." He smirks.

"Oh, come on." I bump his arm, "I know you're excited."

"Ha!" He snorts. "Excited to finally have an excuse to knock you on your know-it-all ass, maybe."

"I'm going to humble you in front of all your Soldier friends."

"Is that right?" He asks doubtfully.

"Hey, I'm stronger than I look."

The smirk fades away before he replies. "Oh, I know." He turns to me as we arrive at my room. He looks at me with so much sincerity that it sends a twirl through my stomach.

I refuse to acknowledge the change in energy and instead decide to lighten the mood. "I'm starving. Did we miss dinner?"

Ryker clears his throat and straightens his posture. I didn't realize how relaxed he had been until he wasn't. "Yeah, the dining hall is closed by now."

He looks around deliberately. "Go in your room, lock the door. I'll be back in a few minutes."

"What are you going to do?"

"I'm going to get you some food. Don't open your door for anyone, okay?" He waits for me to agree and close the door before he takes off down the hall.

I hear someone come through the door while I'm finishing my shower. I haven't broken a sweat today and yet this is my second shower of the day. Though, I'm not sure how many hours have passed since the first one. I dry off, leaving my towel wrapped around my hair, and slip on my boring baggy gray pajama outfit.

My heart's beats increase their volume in my ears as I move my hand to push the bathroom door the rest of the way open. Ryker is sitting very still at the desk, intentionally looking straight at the snacks he has in his hands.

"What's wrong?" I ask cautiously.

When his eyes meet mine it sends a shiver up my spine. "Are you cold?" He stands up, uncertain of how to help.

I shake my head. "I'm fine." I close the gap between us and peek around him. "What'd you find?"

He doesn't move or attempt an answer for several seconds. I look up at him and he lingers a second longer then turns back towards the desk. He clears his throat and blinks his eyes.

"I'm not sure it's enough." He spreads them out so I can see them as he tells me. "Just some protein bars and some cracker things."

I laugh and grab the crackers, my arm brushing past his firm waist. He stiffens when my arm touches him, causing me to pull back quickly. I back off, hopping up onto the bed to eat my snack.

"You should eat one of these protein bars first."

"*You* should eat one. I assume you haven't eaten all day either?" I accuse.

"It's your fault," he teases, sitting back down in the desk chair. He grabs one of the bars anyway and starts to eat it.

I laugh again. "You want to get into it?"

"No." He laughs back, diminishing any tense feelings that existed just seconds ago. "I guess not."

When we both finish eating, Ryker stands up and dismisses himself. "Make sure-"

"To lock the door, I know." I smile at him from my side of the doorway. "I will."

"Am I that predictable?"

"Yes! Yes, you are."

He chuckles. "Well-" he leans his hand against the wall just to the side of the outside of my door- "better safe than sorry, Right?"

"Definitely."

"Good night, Lila."

"Good night, Ryker."

I rest my forehead against the door as I secure the lock. Today ended very differently than how it started. This morning I never wanted to see Ryker's face again. Now, I'm excited to see him again tomorrow. How bizarre.

EIGHTEEN

Ryker

I'm awake before my alarm but wait until it sounds to get out of bed and get ready for the day. I shower and put my suit on quicker than ever before and rush to Lila's door. I knock three times and wait for a sign of life from the other side.

It doesn't take long. Lila swings the door open, revealing that she has been up probably as long- or longer- than I have. She's completely ready to go. "Hey coach, ready to train?" Her eyes are bright with excitement.

I chuckle. "Hold on, now."

"What?" The enthusiasm drains from her face.

"Don't worry, we're still going to train." I gesture for her to come out of her room. "You just need to eat first."

She visibly relaxes upon hearing my answer. "Yeah, I'm starving!"

Today marks day two of us walking not in awkward silence. We talk the whole way to the dining hall.

"How are you sleeping? Are you still having those..." I pause, unsure of how to classify her horrific memories. "Flashback nightmares?"

She considers my question thoughtfully. "No, actually. I didn't have any last night."

"Huh." I'm relieved. "That's good."

"I think they were a little warped. I was a child after all, and I couldn't understand everything that had happened back then." She shakes her head, trying to brush off the conversation. "How about you?"

"What about me?" I ask curiously.

"How are you sleeping?"

"Um, good, I suppose." I shrug, not sure what else to say. I feel so boring when I talk with Lila. She is so fascinating, she has a complicated history and regardless of her past, she has so many facets to her. She's intriguing, interesting to get to know. And then there's me. I've lived a very simple life, one that is not all that deep.

"You came over really fast the other night. Do you stay outside of my room for a while after I go to bed?"

"Not really, no."

"Then how did you know when I was screaming in my sleep?" She is more curious than concerned and it worries me. It really is time for her to be trained.

"My room is right next to yours."

"It is?" She's surprised.

"Yeah," I respond casually. "You should've been more bothered if you thought I was creeping outside your door like that."

"I didn't necessarily think that you were *creeping outside my door*-" She cuts herself off to circle back to my previous answer. "I thought those sleeping quarters were female-only."

"Well, they are." I wave my hand at the silly line of questioning. "But I'm assigned to protect you, and I can't do that from across the building. And bodyguards need sleep, too, dork."

"Fair enough." Lila shrugs.

"So did Colonel Finch mention some kind of training routine, or is it totally up to me to decide your fate?" I smirk at her mischievously.

"It's all you." She raises her eyebrows at me.

"Oh, this is going to be fun," I say, taunting her as we turn the corner to the Dining Hall. There are less people here than last time and I'm relieved. Before we even step into the large space, I am scanning for open tables, possible threats, and exits.

"It smells so good! What is that?"

"That," I emphasize. "Is fresh sweet bread. It tastes even better than it smells."

Her smile stretches even wider and she picks up her pace towards the food bars. I step quickly behind her. By now, rumors must have spread about her because more heads are turning today than when we were last here. I stay alert while we get food, find a place to sit, and eat.

"Oh," she moans. The sound temporarily distracts me. Luckily for me, she's totally oblivious of her surroundings and doesn't catch the look on my face. "Oh, wow."

"It's good, huh?"

"Who knew this place would have the best food in the world."

Her comment makes me laugh. "You are only surprised because Americans have very disgusting food in their cafeterias."

"Well, yeah, probably." Lila shrugs and continues her meal. By the time we leave, she's finished about four servings of sweet bread on top of the fruit cup, omelet, and juice she had.

It only takes a couple minutes to get from the cafeteria to the Training building. Lila lets out a small gasp as we walk through the doors. This is my second home but even I am slightly taken aback by the space. It's been a long time since I was last here.

The entrance opens into a large room with thirty-foot-tall walls that hold up a glass ceiling. There are machines of all kinds spread around the room, but most of the space is taken up by padded flooring for combat training. There are hallways on the opposite side of the entryway that lead to the locker rooms and armory.

Lila spins in awe, taking in the impressive space with an eager smile.

"You ready for this?" I ask her, suddenly a little nervous.

She looks at me and I can see the anticipation in her body language.

"Okay, here's what we're going to do. We're going to start out with some machines, and then I'll teach you some basic self defense moves."

"Okay." She gives me a forced smile.

"Let's start with some basic strength and conditioning. Here, follow me." I lead her to a leg machine and set her up on it. "Let's see what you got!"

We spend about an hour using different machines so I can get an idea of Lila's current strength and the areas we need to work on most. I have trained a lot of soldiers in this very building before, so I do have an idea of what to do. This is a little different, though, as Lila did not grow up training and being physical.

She talks a lot while we go through different machines and I assume it's due to nervousness. I reassure her that she's doing fine and that she doesn't need to feel awkward or embarrassed, explaining that I just need to know where to start and that I'm not judging.

When I get all the information I need to start putting together a training schedule, I let Lila rest while I write it up. She has strong legs and her core has potential, but her upper body strength and endurance need quite a bit of work.

I sit down on the bench by the door and Lila joins me, panting from her workout. I plan out our training on a blank piece of paper, choosing my words carefully as I go, since Lila keeps glancing over my shoulder. She'll probably ask for a copy anyway, so it works out.

As I scribble, she looks rapidly from my hand to my face, trying to follow along but getting more anxious as I go. I smirk a little at the fact that I get to choose what she has to do for the next several weeks.

Luckily for her, I have no intentions to make her suffer. I am actually eager to get her trained effectively, since she has such a knack for getting herself into dangerous situations.

Lila DEFENSE TRAINING PLAN

GOALS:
- resistance + endurance
- upper body strength
- core strength

WEEK ONE
- core conditioning
- body weight exercises
- upper body strength building
- weights & machines, build up to body weight
- defensive training basics
- learn punches and kicks, practice them

WEEK TWO
- practice defensive moves
- fluidity between moves, partner work
- leg strengthening
- incremental weight training
- endurance training
- distance run

WEEK THREE
- partner work, kickboxing and self defense
- continued full body conditioning

"That looks like a lot of exercise," Lila gulps.

"What did you think training entailed?" I tease.

"I don't know." She blinks. "I guess I thought I'd get to punch you today." She relaxes after saying it.

"Ah, well-" I put my pen down and look up at her. "If that's what you came for then I'd like to see you try."

Her eyes sparkle as she imagines it. Does she still hate me? Man, I'm much worse at reading people than I thought. "Okay, then."

"I'm not going easy on you, though."

"Wouldn't dream of it," she challenges. She's way too confident. This is going to be hilarious.

I get Lila's hands and wrists all wrapped up and get some gloves on her before putting on my own. We walk over to the floor mats and I show her the basics.

I push her a little from behind until she puts a foot out to catch herself. "Good. Keep your feet in that position so you don't topple each time you get hit or try to throw a punch."

I move around to face her. "Keep your hands up in front of your face like this." I demonstrate with my own hands so she can reflect it. "Never put them down."

"Okay." She's very concentrated as she listens closely to and follows my directions.

"When you go to punch, use your core."

She tries to apply it but I can tell that part didn't click.

"Hold on."

I move around to her side and position her arm for a right hook, holding my hand out in front of her. "Okay try punching my hand by only extending your arm and not moving anything else."

She does and I can barely feel the contact through my glove. She chuckles a little at the face I make.

"You see?"

She nods with a grin on her face.

"Okay, now…" I move her back to her starting position. "Now try by only moving your waist."

She twists her torso slowly before trusting the process. Once she sees the potential, she starts over and twists hard, connecting firmly with my hand. She smiles on contact.

"Better?"

"Much."

"When you hit with your other hand, you may need to shift your weight or put your other foot forward. You gotta stay on your feet and keep your hands up to cover your face."

"Okay." She practices a few swings with their steps until she starts getting cocky. "When can I knock you on your ass?"

"I'd like to see the day."

"Stop flirting and get your hands up then." She points her chin up at me, trying her very hardest to appear intimidating, but failing miserably at it. There's no doubt in my mind that she's tough, but she's not intimidating in the slightest. Not as an opponent, at least.

I indulge her anyway and stand ready for a fight. She stumbles as I slowly dodge her first attempt. I give her a tap on the stomach, showing her where I would have made contact in a real fight.

It gives her enough fire to try again and when she misses, I tap the fist of my glove against her cheek, pointing out that she dropped her hands from her face. It takes her off guard and she takes a step back to resume her fight position.

"Quit playing around, let's go," I groan, trying to get under her skin so she'll fight harder. It's a tricky balance between pumping her up and pissing her off.

She winds up again and starts moving in a slow circle around me. I don't know whether I should keep humbling her or actually give her a clean shot and hope she rises to the occasion. She throws another punch and lets out a big huff when I side step it.

"Do you want me to let you hit me?"

"No," Lila spits. "I can do it myself."

"That's the thing, though-"

She attempts again and I casually block her by raising my hand a few inches.

"Lila, I have been fighting forever. You cannot beat me."

She grunts as she takes another swing.

"You'll get there if we keep practicing, but I'm a lot more skilled than you right now," I keep reasoning as she takes her shots and fails to hit me time and time again.

"Do you want me to let you hit me?"

"No!" She swings again. Miss.

"Lila."

"No!" Swing and a miss.

People start looking over to us the more she yells and I start to worry about how many people will start to notice her poor combat skills and maybe recognize who she is or see the rings around her wrists when she takes her gloves off.

"Lila, stop." I grab her wrist and step closer. I want her to look me in the eye so she can see how serious I am but instead, she takes the opportunity to strike again. I act faster than I can think and I grab the arm she tries to hit me with and pull hard.

If this were a fair fight, I'd let my companion fall to the ground. Luckily, I think to catch her before taking it that far.

She gasps as she falls into my left arm. She stays there for just a minute as she catches her breath. I help her get up and she lets out a big puff of air, throwing her gloves to the ground and walking away from me. If only it was safe to give her some space.

I quickly step in place behind her as she makes her way toward the locker rooms.

"Hey," I grab at her wrist and she snaps it back towards her chest, spinning around to glare at me. "I can tell you're frustrated-"

"Oh you can, huh? Wow, Ryker, the know-it-all, knows exactly how I feel. Isn't that wonderful?"

"Lila, I can't let you go in there," I continue, despite her spoiled attitude.

"I need to shower!" she snaps.

"You'll have to do it in your room."

"You've got to be kidding me-" She shakes her head with a bitter smile.

"You know I like to joke, but not about your safety. I can't protect you in there and clearly you can't protect yourself." She shoots me a sharp glare and I ignore it. "Let's get back to the room, you can rinse off and then you can choose what we do next."

The walk back is silent but not peaceful. Man, I'm not sure I'll ever understand this woman. I am used to Soldiers, who use their logic instead of emotion. Of course, every Soldier will act emotionally from time to time, but mostly they listen to commands and decide by reasoning what to do.

A young trained Soldier may have had the courage and confidence to try to fight me, but unlike Lila, they would have been trained for years already and would probably know when to back down. One of the cocky ones might have needed a punch to the gut to get there.

She is so complicated and I can never fully anticipate how she's going to feel about any certain thing. She was the one who wanted to fight me and I warned her I wasn't going to go easy on her. Is she upset with me because I didn't let her punch me? I offered several times.

I'm starting to get frustrated by the fact that every time we start to get along, somehow I mess it up and we're back to where we started.

We get to her door and she pushes past me into her room, shoving the door closed behind her. Luckily, I have quick reflexes. I slip my foot in the door frame right in time.

"What the-"

"I'm tired of this, Lila." I'm almost too exhausted to have this conversation.

"Get out-"

I push my way into the room. "I'm not leaving until we find a solution."

"A solution? For what?"

"I'm tired of you being angry at me every time I do my job."

She lacks a comeback for once in her life.

"We pretty much have two options," I sigh as I lean back against the wall behind me. "You start to trust me." I hold a finger up for each option. "Or, you find another body guard that you can trust."

Lila looks at me the same way she did when I tapped on her exposed face during our 'fight'. "You don't want to work with me anymore?"

"It's not that I don't want to." I've never talked this much to anyone in my life and I have to put a lot of effort forward to keep my cool. "You don't seem to want me around much. I keep thinking we're getting to a good spot where you trust me and then some shit happens and you get pissed again. I can't keep up with it and if I'm making you miserable then maybe you should get someone else who doesn't."

She looks down at her feet for several minutes, defeated by what I said. Somehow, this frustrates me even more and I don't know what else to do. I stand up and turn for the door. A delicate hand tugs at my forearm and I exhale loudly, not ready to turn around and face her. But her gesture is enough to stop me from leaving.

"Ryker, I'm sorry." Her voice sounds thick with emotion and I dread the tears that are about to follow. "It's not that I don't trust you or that I'm angry with you-"

I unwillingly turn around to reassure her. "It's fine, please don't cry."

"I don't really know what I'm supposed to do with myself," she says quietly, ignoring my comment. She stares at her hand that remains on my forearm while she talks. It makes me even more uncomfortable and I don't know what to do except listen.

"I'm all alone, Ryker." Tears start to fall down her face like dying stars and I can't bring myself to look at her.

"I'm just starting to learn the truth about my past and the complicated future that lays ahead of me. I don't belong to my world anymore and I definitely don't belong to this one. I'm so broken and damaged and I'm just trying to find a way out of it." She's sobbing too much to finish.

I begrudgingly pull her into my arms and hold her tightly. She sobs into my chest for minutes while I worry about how to console her.

Lila takes a long deep breath. "I know I need to trust you more, and I promise I will work on it. With one condition." She pulls away from me and waits for a response.

"Yeah? What's that?"

"Please don't hand me off to someone else. You're the only person I've got right now. I know it's going to take a lot of patience for you to stick around-"

"Deal." I stick my hand out for a hand shake. She takes it and doesn't let go. If it were anyone else, a handshake this long would make me uncomfortable.

NINETEEN

Lila

This is probably the fastest shower I've ever taken. I hurry to dry off and when I step into my room, I notice a new suit neatly folded on the bed. I smile to myself then get dressed quickly and knock on the hallway door to let Ryker know I'm decent.

He's the only other one with a key- though I'm sure they have copies locked up somewhere- so he told me to never open the door until he comes to get me. I wait for a few seconds, but when I don't hear anything outside, I shout for him.

"Ryker? I'm ready," I call out. There is at least a minute of silence before I start to get a little anxious. I'm stuck in here until he comes to get me. Maybe he's in his room showering or he's gone to get food. I sit on my bed and wait. I pull out my sketchbook and start to scribble my memory of Amaryllis onto paper.

After several minutes, I hear a knock on the door. I sit up straight in my bed and wait for Ryker to say something so I know it's him.

"Who is it?" I ask loudly.

"It's me." His voice sounds different, but it still sounds like Ryker. I hop off the bed and open the door. When I see him, I'm stuck in place, unable to move quick enough.

When he takes a step forward, I snap back into action, and slam the door, but he reaches it first. He is very big and strong and my heart rate hits its new personal high. "Ryker!" I scream out.

"No, it's okay, I'm not going to hurt you. I'm here to protect you." The man smiles politely. He's familiar to me, but I can't place it for a few moments.

"I'm only supposed to be with Ryker Jordan," I demand.

"It's okay, Lila, I'm his brother." That's it. This is Connor, the one from my dreams.

I barely recognize him, he looks so different now. His body is muscular and in very good shape, making me wonder if he's a bodybuilder.

His face is dark and sunken in, though, almost as if he were sick. "Don't worry, Lila. I know you, you're going to be alright. It's my job to look after you. Someone was trying to get in here but I took care of it. You're safe now."

What he says makes a little bit of sense, of course Ryker wouldn't trust me with any random Soldier. But I know Ryker, and he would've told me ahead of time, especially after the talk we just had. Plus, he hasn't even seen Connor since getting back to Headquarters and I'm pretty sure it had to do with keeping me away from him.

"Perfect, then you can guard the door and I'll wait in here until Ryker gets back." I go to close the door again, calmly this time, but he stops it again.

"You don't understand, you're too little. I won't let anything happen to you." He steps into my room, looking around rapidly, as if he is checking for potential dangers. His massive body takes up about fifty percent of the room.

I slowly back up and jump in my skin when I bump into my bed. "Take a seat." I gesture towards the desk chair while I try to think what to do.

Ryker would be so mad at me right now. Where the hell is he? This is the exact case scenario he warned me about, I just hadn't thought it would happen. He'd be so angry that I opened the door in the first place. He'd get me out of this mess by joking around with Connor, asking him to leave me alone, and then beating the crap out of him when he refused. But what would he tell me to do?

Connor locks the door and then sits in the chair I offered. He smiles and it makes him look so kind and innocent.

I feel smaller and smaller the longer he's in here. "What's your name?" I try to play along with his game, stalling until I figure out how to get out of this situation.

"I'm Connor. What's your name?"

I hop up on the bed, trying to get more space between the two of us. "I'm Lila," I respond softly. He smiles for a second before something snaps behind his eyes.

"NO!" He yells and knocks me back on my bed. "You can't shoot her!"

"Connor-"

His eyes get dark again but he doesn't say anything. His face is twisted with emotion and I know I need to tread lightly.

"It's okay, Connor, we're not there anymore," I gesture for him to take my hand and he does. "We're safe now, Connor. You saved us."

He must still have a lot of trauma from that night because he is lost in his head, unable to stay focused on the fact that we're both okay. His facial expression changes rapidly as he tries to understand everything that's going on up there. I make an effort to stay calm and not make any sudden movements.

"Connor?" He looks up at me like he'd forgotten I was here. "I'm starving. Do you think we could get some lunch?"

His face changes again and I can't read it. He stands up quickly and his chest rises and falls rapidly. "I can't let you go, Lila. I can't let them hurt you."

I hop off the bed and put my hands on his biceps, though I can barely reach them. "Hey, hey, it's okay. We're safe here."

"They're trying to shoot you, Lila. They're trying to take you away. It's not your fault. I know you didn't do anything wrong." He's starting to pace, but my room doesn't allow for much space to do so. It reminds me of the way Ryker paced nervously just days ago. The difference between the two experiences is disturbing.

"Connor, we're okay. That's all over, nobody is going to hurt me anymore. I'm safe now."

"No!" He pushes me out of the way, hard, and my hip whacks against the bed frame. I clap my hand around my mouth to keep from yelling. I need to act quickly before this giant accidentally hurts me while thinking he's the only one who can protect me from his delusion.

"Connor," I have to say it firmly to get his attention. Then I act like the scared little girl he thinks I am. "I think I heard something in the bathroom. Can you check for me?"

He responds to my crybaby voice. "Okay, stay here."

As soon as he gets far enough into the bathroom, I close the door. I run to the bedroom door, unlock it and run into the hallway. I scream for help and bang on Ryker's door.

It doesn't take long for Connor to get out and there are only a few feet between us. I can hear someone yelling and footsteps slapping the floor but I don't have enough time to figure out whose. I run as fast as I can the opposite way from Connor.

He catches up to me in a matter of seconds and grabs me hard. He is full of anger now, and I think he must see someone else as he looks into my eyes.

"How could you do this to her?" He spits in my face as he pins me to the wall with his massive hand around my throat, cutting off my air supply.

I kick and hit him as much as I can, remembering what Ryker had just started teaching me about an hour ago.

"Lila! Connor!" I hear our names being called but the voice is muffled as he suffocates me. "Shit! Ryker! Someone, help!"

I throw one more punch before my arm goes limp to my side. My vision goes from fuzzy to black.

I come to in the Infirmary, waking up in a panic. Two nurses rush to me, one on each side, to hold me down and reassure me that I am okay now. I try to calm my breathing as they put a mask around my nose and mouth.

"This will help you breathe," the nurse says. "Deep breaths. In. Out. Very good."

I hear yelling nearby and my heart starts to race again.

"You need to stay out here, Soldier!"

Ryker comes busting through the curtains to where I am. He looks absolutely horrible. His face is bruised and he has a large gash across his cheek that is still gushing blood. His lip is split near the corner and he looks like he's going to get a gnarly black eye.

"Lila, are you okay?" He sounds more panicked than I am.

I shake my head. "What happened to you?"

"I am so sorry." His voice is heavy with regret and betrayal.

"Ryker," I sit up and hold my hands out for him to come closer. He walks to me and takes my hands, but only for a split moment. As soon as he gets close, he sees my neck and reaches up to touch it. I flinch in response and his eyes grow very dark.

I've never seen him so angry and, based on his response, I'm not sure he's ever felt this much rage.

"Ryker, what happened to you?" I pull at his arm so he'll let me get a better look. When I do, I notice the rough and raw marks on his wrist. I look up at him and wait for an answer.

He is unable to stand still, as if he'd storm out and hunt down my attacker if his arm wasn't tethered to mine. I tug slightly and he relaxes enough to look at me. His eyes look me up and down, making me blush.

"He never should've been left alone to-"

"What did he do to you, Ryker?" It seems that every time I say his name, it anchors him back to me.

"He saw me leave your room after I left the clothes for you. I didn't see him fast enough. He thought I was a threat or something." He shakes his head at the thought. "I punched him, which only made things worse. I blocked the first blow but he's strong. He punched me and I fell down. He knocked me over the head with something and I blacked out. I woke up when you banged on my door and yelled for me. I tried to get up but he had tied me up, I couldn't get out fast enough."

"I don't understand why-" I can't even finish my thought. I'm relieved when Ryker understands what I'm trying to say and offers an answer.

"He's not well, Lila. He has some issues, he has since that night he met you. When they shot you with a tranquilizer, in Connor's head, they killed you. He never could get past it. He was just a kid, after all."

"That must be really hard. For all of you." I rub my thumb on his hand. "Do you know who saved me?"

"No, they just barely got me out and I wanted to see if you were alright." He looks down at my hand and I blush again. I hope he doesn't notice.

"I'm okay," I say reassuringly. "I'm sorry, Ryker."

"No," he shuts me down quickly.

"I shouldn't have opened that damn door. You've told me so many times."

He shakes his head but doesn't say anything.

"I should've waited for you like you said-"

"He never should've been let out," he says angrily.

"What do you mean?"

"Connor is supposed to be under twenty-four hour surveillance. He's attacked me before, anytime I mention your name, really. It used to be really bad when I was younger. I think I reminded him of you because of my age. My dad always had to pull him off of me. When my parents died, they put him in Headquarters care. He's been better for the last several years, but it's unpredictable. He's only allowed to leave with Liam or myself, but I haven't gone to see him since we got back." There is a lot of regret behind his eyes and I don't understand why.

"I saw him in the cafeteria the first day after you got me out," I say quietly.

He snaps his head toward me. "What?"

"He was sitting with Rachel. I didn't recognize who it was yet."

"I need to meet with Colonel Finch-" He starts moving again.

"Ryker, please do not leave me alone again," I beg with a shaky voice.

My words sting him as if someone had punched him in the gut. He turns back to me and looks me in the eye. After just a moment, he takes a seat in the chair near my bed and he grabs my hand closest to him. "Never."

It doesn't take long for us to convince the Infirmary to let us go. We go directly to Colonel Finch's office and I listen to Ryker yell at her about Connor's release conditions and he points out mine and his marks as evidence that Connor cannot ever be left unsupervised again.

I sit quietly and let him speak his mind, as does Colonel Finch. When he's done, Finch assures him nothing like this will ever happen again, that she and her peers have it under control. Ryker continues to look at her like she's stupid until she agrees that he will be under twenty-four hour surveillance until they can find a better solution.

"I expect you to come to me before a final decision is made. He was watching Lila in the cafeteria the first day she was out of her cell. He knew where her room was. He's been watching us, probably since we got here. Take care of it," he demands. Finch nods in agreement. "One last thing."

"Soldier, don't forget your place."

"Who saved Lila?" He asks, ignoring her comment.

"Rachel Brooks did. She is one of the Soldiers who was assigned to your brother."

"So she didn't save anyone, she caused it?"

"Well that's not entirely fair-" I try to interrupt.

"You've already proven that it wasn't a good idea for him to be out like that. Brooks is a fine Soldier and you know that. We chose her because she has a way of calming Connor down when he gets… anxious."

Ryker scoffs.

"She is also the one that took Connor down before he squoze the life out of Lila and the one who got you out of the pickle you were in. She told the Officers to get into your room and she's also the one who brought Lila up to the Infirmary. You should be grateful instead of spiteful."

"I want her on our team." It shocks both me and Finch when the words leave his mouth.

"What? This is not a mission, Soldier, you cannot expect me to sacrifice two of my finest Soldiers to a civilian-"

"With respect, Colonel, that is uncalled for. Lila has a lot of potential to do good here, and we can't groom that potential if people keep trying to kill her. I want Brooks. I don't need her full-time but I want her available when we need her."

"When she is not working on something for me, you can have her. Now get out of my office, Jordan."

"Yes ma'am," he says, satisfied with the results of his rampage.

He gives a head nod to Margaret on the way out of the office. We turn the corner of the corridor and I realize I have no idea where we're headed.

"What are we going to do for the rest of the day?" I ask Ryker. He smiles and raises his eyebrow at me.

"Let's go blow off some steam."

TWENTY

Ryker

Over the next couple weeks, Lila takes her training very seriously. She only agrees to have Rachel around when she's partner training so she can try to hit her. Things have been a little rocky with the two of them and I do understand, but I definitely would've been past it by now.

Rachel has tried to talk to Lila a few times, to explain why she left her in the cell and all, but Lila wants almost nothing to do with her. I get to be the lucky mediator between the two, trying to keep both parties happy. Fortunately, Rachel can be pretty professional and do the job without acknowledging any of the drama. We don't socialize outside of the three of us, but I don't think any of us mind.

Lila trusts me more than ever. She's getting decent at defensive fighting, and she has become a lot more confident in herself and in our Headquarters way of life. I think the whole Connor incident really freaked her out and made her realize that she needs to get serious about learning self defense. She's gained muscle, strengthened her core, become proficient in defending herself in partner training, and she's built up a lot more endurance.

Since the incident with Connor, I've been staying in Lila's room until she falls asleep. She asked me that first night and I haven't made her ask again. She has nightmares every so often and I don't think they are always about Connor, but I can tell that they are sometimes.

We don't talk about it anymore but I know she thinks about it because I think about it almost daily. I think about how she must have felt- and then I have to stop myself before I march over and kill him.

We've gotten to know each other pretty well, though, over the last couple weeks. We don't get on each other's nerves quite as much as before. It's been refreshing.

Today, Rachel and I are training her more on attacking- which shots to take and when. I stand in front of Lila and let Rachel guide her on how to attack. I keep my eyes on Lila's trying to get her to focus on me so she doesn't punch Rachel in the face every time she directs her to move.

Lila gets a few punches to my hands and Rachel helps her dodge some of my half-hearted swings.

"Hey," Someone yells across the room. Rachel and I snap into action, defending Lila from both sides. "You're looking good. Any chance you want to practice with a different partner?" I barely recognize him. He's a fellow Soldier but not ranked very high, considering I've never worked with him.

"Ben! Long time no see," Rachel says warmly but doesn't move from her spot next to Lila.

"Rachel." He nods. "Who's your friend?"

Both girls look at me but I keep my eyes pinned on Ben. "Soldier in training," I say curtly.

"You got a name?" He asks Lila.

"I guess you don't know how to take a hint, but we're training here."

"Easy, Jordan," Ben's smug grin never leaves his face. "No need to get your panties in a wad. I'm talking to-"

"Lila," Lila blurts. "My name is Lila, you're Ben. What can we do for ya?"

Ben's smile grows an inch bigger. "Looking for a sparring partner. You interested?"

"I'd love to knock-" I start but can't finish before Lila interrupts again.

"Sure, why not?"

I look at her in disbelief but she seems to have forgotten my existence and the purpose thereof. Rachel raises her eyebrows at me. I move in front of Lila, blocking the space between her and Ben.

"Why in hell's name would you think I would let you do this?"

"Ryker, I need a partner who won't go easy on me."

"You're kidding yourself if you think he's actually interested in anything other than-"

"Ryker, just let her do it. We'll be right here the whole time," Rachel intercedes.

I look back at Lila and she shrugs at me. Damn them all.

"Keep your hands up in front of your face. Pay attention to his patterns and use them against him. Keep your feet firm and don't let him get you on the ground." She nods in understanding. I offer both fists and she fistbumps them with her own. "Give him hell."

Ben steps onto the mat, still ogling Lila like a schoolboy. As he gets closer, I realize he probably would be in Lila's height and weight class anyway. I hope she knocks him onto his tiny ass.

Rachel comes to stand by my side, matching my wide bodyguard stance, crossed arms and all. Lila doesn't hesitate to start warming up while Ben takes his chance at trying to flirt.

"How come I haven't met you yet?"

"That's classified," Lila responds quickly, taking her first step forward. Instead of being intimidated, Ben looks pleased. It throws Lila off a bit, which in turn makes me nervous.

She regroups quickly though, getting back into her stance and continuing her circle around him. I don't know where she learned to move around her opponent in a circle but it's entertaining to watch. I guess the rest of the Training building agrees, as stragglers watch from their machines and pause their routines.

"Well, I intend to learn a lot more than just your name, honey." Ben's fist swings and hits Lila in the obliques. It wasn't hard enough to hurt her, but it razzles her, as I'm sure it was intended to.

"Good luck with that." Lila gets her first hit in too, with a lot more force than Ben's. Her fist makes contact with his gut and it knocks some air out of him.

"Ooh," Ben laughs from the hit. "Good one. So what do I need to do to get you to go out with me tonight?"

"You'd have to kidnap me."

"Oh, don't tempt me."

Lila's fist connects with Ben's jaw and I've never been more proud. A small smile creeps onto my face and Rachel shakes her head at me, though she's wearing a smile of her own.

"Ouch. I was kidding."

"Guess I've got a bad sense of humor," Lila remarks. She swings again, but this time Ben catches her arm.

He twists her around so her back is to his chest and he wraps his free arm around her throat in a headlock. I talked to Lila about how to get out of a situation like this, but we haven't practiced it yet.

Ben is saying something in Lila's ear, but I can tell she's focused on how she's going to get out of his grasp. Instead of grabbing his arms and twisting her way out of it, Lila chooses the most difficult maneuver.

She takes a deep breath, positioning her feet. I barely have time to doubt her execution before she moves. She grabs a tight hold of Ben's arms and simultaneously jerks her hips back and upper body down, successfully flipping Ben across her back and onto the floor.

He lands on his back, hard, and looks as if he had just fallen off a cliff. Lila positions herself on top of him, pinning him down firmly. I wonder if I'll ever stop underestimating this woman.

After the initial shock of it all, Ben taps out and laughs-coughs as Lila releases him and helps him back up.

"Damn, girl." He holds out a hand and Lila shakes it proudly. "Same time tomorrow?"

She answers before I can jump in. "Sure," she says provocatively. "But next time I'm not going easy on you."

By this point, too many people are paying attention to Lila for my liking. I nudge Rachel to take her to the locker room to get cleaned up so we can leave.

"Well, I look forward to having you on top of me again."

Lila snorts and turns around, her eyes passing over me completely and landing on Rachel. She points her chin up at her as if to say she's ready to go now. This simple gesture is probably the most friendly thing Lila has offered to Rachel since being at Headquarters.

While I'm glad she's finally giving Rachel the time of day, I don't appreciate that she's ignoring me. Don't even get me started about her flirting with Ben. That shit is going to get annoying quick.

I wait until they enter the Ladies room before heading to the Men's room to freshen up.

"Hey," Lila says firmly. "Yoo-hoo!"

I look up then, suddenly aware of the fact that both her and Rachel are staring at me strangely.

"What?"

"The salt," Lila says, pointing at the salt sitting on the table to my left, just out of reach for her.

"Oh." I grab it and pass it to her, keeping my gaze on my hands.

"Where are you?"

I shake my head, trying to focus back on the present. I am pretty good about staying focused, especially on the job, but sometimes my head gets a little too crowded and I can't seem to push my thoughts away. I've been a little foggy since the gym, worrying about Connor and what to tell Liam when he gets home. Thinking about Lila and Ben.

I snap out of it when Margaret approaches us.

"There you are! Colonel Finch is requesting to see the both of you in her office." Her voice shakes slightly and I wonder if she is ever not nervous.

"Why?" Rachel asks.

"Unfortunately, I am not aware of the reasoning behind the meeting." Margaret turns back to me. "I was simply sent to summon you."

"Why didn't you just call?" I question curiously.

"The Colonel would like to see you right away," Margaret looks back and forth at Lila and myself. "I am not supposed to leave until you come."

I sigh and roll my eyes slightly, standing up begrudgingly from my spot at the table. Lila follows suit with a lot more concern and less attitude. Rachel and I stand on both sides of Lila as she stands up and follows Margaret.

We walk in silence, with Margaret occasionally looking back as if to make sure we are still following along. She seems more frantic than usual, but it may have more to do with leaving her office than anything else. I rarely see her outside of that room.

Lila and Rachel look up at me every so often, never at the same time, but I act as if I don't notice.

There isn't a particular reason for my mood, though I almost wish there was so I could move on from it. I think I might just need a night to myself. I'm not sure that'll be an option, especially if Colonel Finch wants to speak with us again. That typically entails something has gone wrong or that someone is being chastised.

We get to Margaret's office and she motions for us to go ahead of her to Finch's office. When I reach for the door handle, Margaret makes a noise.

"Ope!" She rushes over on her stocky legs. "You need to wait out here." She points at Rachel dramatically, almost poking her chest with an index finger.

"She's a part of our-" I begin to argue.

"Nope, uh-uh." Margaret shakes her head firmly. Man, this woman is eccentric. "Just the two of you were summoned." She wags her same index finger at Lila and I.

I roll my eyes again and turn to Rachel.

"It's fine." She waves it off. "Go. I'll be here when you're done."

Rachel turns and takes a seat on the chair closest to us and looks around the room, avoiding further discussion. I shrug and open the door.

Inside Finch's office, Finch is seated at her desk and she looks as if she's having a very serious conversation with a man sitting in one of her chairs that faces opposite of us. When we enter the room, Finch motions for us to come in without so much as lifting her eyes.

I close the door behind us and I quickly look at Lila, who looks alarmed and confused. I gently move her forward, barely touching the lower part of her back in an effort to put her at ease. We both look at the man as we walk towards them, wondering who it will be, and hoping that whoever it is will give us an answer as to why we are here at all.

They seem to finish the private part of their conversation because as we step up to the chairs, they both turn to look at us for the first time.

"Thank you for coming on such short notice," Finch says politely.

"It's not a problem." I keep my attention on the man sitting in front of us, unable to pinpoint why he looks so familiar to me. He has dark hair, dark eyes, and tan skin. He is thin but his features aren't nearly as pointy as Finch's.

Finch catches on quickly. "Ryker, Lila, this is Lorenzo Sosa."

Lorenzo nods his head curtly and extends his hand out to both of us. I'm not sure if she does it intentionally, but after shaking his hand, Lila backs up until her back and shoulder touch my stomach and chest. She doesn't move and I don't make her, knowing how nervous she was just a moment ago.

"Lorenzo is a member of our Necromancer Branch of Headquarters," Finch continues. I can feel Lila flinch next to me.

"Ah, yes." I acknowledge, finally connecting the dots of how I know him. "You were one of the Necromancers who briefed me before I went into the field."

"That's right." Lorenzo nods again. A man of many words, it seems.

"Well, let's get started, then. Shall we?" Finch motions for us all to sit and she follows suit. "Lorenzo is well aware of the situation at hand and I've asked him here to speak with you, Lila, about a few things. Would you prefer that Jordan remained with Rachel outside?"

"What? No!" Lila defends quickly.

"That's fine, dear, he can stay if you'd like."

"Please."

"Very well. Lorenzo, go ahead."

I don't want to interrupt or make the situation uncomfortable, so I subtly move my foot over until my shoe touches Lila's. I'm not sure she notices but I keep it there anyway as the conversation goes on.

"Miss Lila, it is a pleasure to speak with you directly. We have been carefully watching your magic over the years. I assume you've discussed what happened the first night we met you." He glances at Finch to confirm, which she does.

I don't know what exactly he is referring to but obviously everyone else in the room does. I brush off whatever emotion it is I'm feeling so I can hear the rest.

"Because you have so much power connected to you, we have had to monitor how much you have used or any time we suspect someone may pull from that power. We saw what happened with Warren."

Lila looks down at her hands guiltily and the urge to defend her rises to my throat. I struggle to push it back down.

"Lila, I do not mean to upset you. You are very powerful and I am glad that your power protected you from being seriously hurt," His accent makes it slightly hard to tell that he is being kind. "However, that amount of power wielded only by emotion is very dangerous."

I meet her eyes, and it is obvious that neither of us understand what he intends to say.

"Miss Lila," Lorenzo waits until Lila looks up at him to continue his proposal. "I would like to teach you how to use your magic responsibly."

Lila's posture straightens as the words leave his mouth. She looks to Finch, then back to Lorenzo, then Finch, then to me, Finch, and eventually settles back on Lorenzo. "Are- are you serious?"

"Yes, madam, I am very serious," he responds with a small smile.

"That's great!" Lila beams. She almost jumps out of her chair in excitement. She moves up in her seat to the corner closest to Lorenzo, leaving me and my foot behind. I almost wish I had left the room for this but I try to keep that desire hidden.

"Yes, I would love that! When can we start?"

Lila and Lorenzo spend the next hour discussing when, how, and where they are going to train her magic. Colonel Finch makes it a point to tell me that while Lorenzo can keep her safe, Lila must still have her bodyguard with her at all times. I think it is a little strange but don't give it much more thought than that.

Lila doesn't stop smiling the entire conversation. My energy drains as the time drags on and I feel almost empty by the time we are leaving. Lorenzo is dismissed first and we politely bid him adieu.

"Do you feel ready for this, Lila?" Finch asks once it's just the three of us.

"Yes, I didn't know if I'd ever be allowed to learn magic. I'm very pleased and excited to learn."

"Very well. You will need to be careful. At the beginning, we will keep your bracelets on in between sessions. As you learn how to control your magic and especially in connection to your emotions, we will explore the option of taking them off permanently."

"Yes ma'am."

"Good. Well, you will start tomorrow. You have a few hours left in the day, so go enjoy them. Make sure to get some rest afterward to be prepared for training. You will continue to train with Ryker and Rachel in the mornings after which you will have lunch and then head to train with Mr. Sosa in the afternoons."

"Yes ma'am."

"Very well. Have a good evening, you are dismissed."

"Thank you ma'am. You as well."

Finch nods in return and Lila and I get up simultaneously. However, when she turns to head for the door, I remain facing Finch.

"Yes, Soldier?"

"Ma'am I'd like to speak with you privately if I could." My voice is firm but not rude. Finch looks at me strangely then moves to Lila.

"Lila, please wait with Rachel outside my office."

I don't look at her but somehow I can sense the hesitation. I feel as if her eyes are burning a hole in the back of my head. The pressure lets up as I hear the door close behind her.

"What is this about, Ryker?"

"Do you really think that introducing magic is the best thing for her right now?"

"Yes, I do."

"Why?"

"Why not? She is a magical creature. One way or another, magic is going to be part of her life. She can either be scared of it and fall victim to it again, or she can learn to control it and use it to her advantage."

"It seems like an unnecessary risk." I don't even mean it, I just can't identify the real concern I have. Everything she said makes perfect sense. Of course I want Lila to be herself and to learn every tool she has to protect herself. I sit back down, suddenly feeling defeated.

"Is that really what's bothering you? You don't think having unlimited and uncontrollable magic is more dangerous than her learning to use the magic she has anyway in a safe way? Or is there something else on your mind?" Finch accuses.

"I need a break."

TWENTY-ONE

Lila

I sit in silence with Margaret and Rachel for only a few minutes before Margaret gets a call.

"Yes ma'am, will do," Margaret says before hanging up the phone. She swivels in her chair to see us around her monitors. "You girls are dismissed. Rachel, please take Lila to the next appointment or to her Living Quarters."

Rachel looks just as caught off by the news as I feel, but she covers it quickly by obeying the command without question. She gets up from her seat and moves to the door, waiting for me. I don't know what else to do, so I follow along.

Rachel and I haven't been alone since University and I was promised I wouldn't have to be alone with her at all. What could Ryker possibly need to discuss with Finch right now, privately, and for so long that we might as well leave? I'm not going to be able to relax until he's back and tells me what's going on.

It's still afternoon and I don't know what we're going to do all day to keep occupied. I really don't want to sit in my room for the rest of the afternoon, but I don't want to hang out with Rachel either. I follow her in frustrated and anxious silence.

"So," Rachel looks at me briefly. "What do you want to do?" Oh, kill me now.

I exhale, dramatically blowing air through my lips. "Is there anything to do here?"

"Sure there is. What do you usually do with Ryker?"

"Umm…" I'm annoyed by the question. Most of the time we just hang out and talk but I don't want to tell Rachel that. "We've gone to Amaryllis a few times."

"I'm not sure if I'm comfortable going to Amaryllis without him there."

"Fine."

"We could go see a movie?"

"I didn't realize movies existed here." I'm totally baffled by it.

"Well every Sunday they show a war movie from your world. I don't know if that would be something you'd want to do?"

A movie means Rachel can't try to talk to me and it wouldn't be a terrible idea to watch fighting techniques. "Sounds great."

The 'theater' is very small and probably used as a lecture or prep room of some kind. The screen is rather large, considering. The movie is fine. It's an old Korean film so I mostly read subtitles the whole time. Headquarters doesn't do all the frilly movie things like popcorn and candy so it was a pretty dry experience, but it ate up a lot of time, which is what we needed.

After it ends, we grab dinner- just before the cafeteria closes- and head to Living Quarters. The awkward tension builds up as we get to my door. I undo the lock and Rachel puts her hand on my shoulder.

"Let me check it first."

She checks under the bed and then waves me in from the hall. She goes on, checking the closet and bathroom.

"All clear." She lingers near the door and I dread what's about to come next. Dammit Ryker, where are you? "Lila, we haven't gotten the chance to really talk-"

"Rachel we've been over this. I do not want to talk to you about it."

"Lila, you need to hear it. You can still hate me afterward if you want and I'll accept that but I need you to hear my side."

I huff a big breath of air to make it clear I'm frustrated but then I hop up on my bed and try to listen to her.

"I was sent on a mission to protect you. I knew Ryker and a couple other Soldiers were deployed as well but I wasn't supposed to make contact with them." I scoff but she ignores it. "I was supposed to protect you. Being your friend was not part of the mission but I did need you to trust me so it all kind of worked out, I suppose.

"I couldn't figure out who was targeting you by myself and neither could any of the others. When Warren tried to kiss you, we all thought that was just a stupid mundane incident. Ryker didn't see it that way and he stepped in, which got him in a lot of trouble at the time, by the way. My Commanding Officer warned me not to break rules like he had.

"Anyway, Ryker and I teamed up but you still got *stabbed*, Lila. I know you're recovering fine and all that, but that should never have happened. I couldn't believe it and I definitely couldn't look you in the eyes after I had let that happen.

"I found out that they put you in a cell right before Ryker did. Unlike him, I did not want to get more involved. I trusted that the system would take care of you, like they always have. I wasn't briefed on your extensive history, Lila. I don't know your life story and I don't know what you've been through, here or otherwise, outside of what you told me in University.

"I never wanted you to get hurt. I was supposed to be there for you. I couldn't confront you about it. Then, with Connor, I just had to stay away from you. His obsession with you runs so deep. He carries so much guilt about you but in his mind, they killed you that night. I was assigned to him when they released him, and they didn't want Ryker to find out. I was supposed to keep him away from you, which meant I couldn't come talk to you. I'm glad Ryker wanted me on your case so I could be around you a bit more and..." she trails off, uncertain of how to finish her monologue.

I genuinely have no words for her. I do not know what to say to comfort her or to fill the heavy silence.

"I just wanted you to know that I loved being your friend but my job was to keep you safe and I failed. I didn't handle it well, and I'm sorry. I will do my best to make up for that by being here for you now, in any way you'd like me to be. I care about you."

Dumbfounded, I remain silent on my bed, cursing Ryker for letting this happen. I can't bring myself to forgive her and I know that's what she is seeking. After another uncomfortable minute, she realizes I'm not going to speak.

"Well, I'll let you rest. I will be outside, if you need anything. Good night."

It's the first night in weeks that I've had to be in my room alone. After she leaves, I do the only thing I know to do when I need to process. I take out my sketchbook and scribble away.

In the morning, I am disappointed when Rachel picks me up alone. I let her sit in my chair as I get ready in the bathroom. Once I have all my gear on, we head for breakfast, which is uneventful.

Both of us pretend that Rachel's speech last night never happened. There's a part of me that thinks we are both more relaxed with each other because of it, though.

When we get to the Training building, Ben is waiting for us on the mat.

"Ladies," He holds out his hands like a celebrity walking into a crowd of fans. He's immediately humbled by our lack of enthusiasm. "Wake up on the wrong side of the bed today?"

"I hope you're ready to get beat by a girl again," I mock. I could see us as friends, and I kind of hope we can be. This place is never going to stop feeling like jail until I can meet people.

He snickers and watches as Rachel helps me wrap my wrists and get my gloves on. We warm up a little and I hit her hands, practicing each of my swings.

"I'll warm you up, don't worry," Ben calls over Rachel's shoulder. It distracts me and I miss a punch from Rachel. It lands on my stomach and I stumble back a few steps.

"Sorry," Rachel and Ben say simultaneously.

I roll my eyes at both of them and regroup. We practice for a few more minutes and then Rachel tells me to do some jumping jacks to get my legs and core warmed up too.

Ben and I spar for about twenty minutes before we begin our 'match'. He tries to ask me get-to-know-you questions and I leave him hanging on almost every one.

"Is it true you came from a University?"

I perk my head at him. He's not supposed to know that.

"Yeah, okay, you caught me. I've been asking around about you."

The sentence runs a shiver up my spine. How much information did he get? "Ah, so you're the stalking kind of guy."

"I didn't follow you! I was just asking around to see if anyone knew you. They didn't. You're a hard person to get to know, especially with Jordan hanging around you." Ben pretends to look around, though it's obvious he already noticed Ryker isn't here. "Where is he, anyway?"

"I'm not his keeper." I shrug. "Not that I'd tell you if I were," I tease.

"What's all the mystery for? Why doesn't anyone know who you are?"

"Obviously someone does. Who gave you the information?"

"A magician never reveals his secrets."

"That saying doesn't even make sense here, you dork." A smirk sneaks its way onto my face without consent. "What about you, Ben the Soldier? What's your story?"

"You'll have to get some alcohol in me before I get into that."

"So you expect me to talk about my story without giving me anything on you? I've never met a hypocritical stalker before."

This makes Ben's smile grow brighter. "I will gladly tell you anything you want to know about me, if you go out with me tonight," he says quietly so Rachel can't hear. I raise my eyebrows at him.

"No need to whisper. If I go, Rachel comes with."

Rachel perks up from the opposite corner of the mat while Ben pouts.

"Are we going to fight or did you just come here to flirt with me?" I pretend to be annoyed.

"I came here to flirt, but we can fight, too."

TWENTY-TWO

Ryker

I leave as soon as I know Lila and Rachel are gone, heading straight for my room. I strip down to my underwear, planning to rest in bed for a few minutes, but end up falling asleep.

I don't remember the last time I've had the time or liberty to go to bed so early.

It takes me several minutes to orient myself upon waking up. I have to remind myself that I'm at Headquarters and though I technically do have a job, I don't have to worry about it today.

I didn't look at the time before passing out last night, but it's past ten o'clock now, which means I've missed breakfast. I check my device to make sure nobody has tried to contact me and, when it's void of any kind of notification, I let myself relax and take my time to get up and moving.

Typically, I shower with cold water for productivity and health reasons, but today I treat myself to a hot shower. It's a nice change but I won't make it a habit after how long it ends up being. Afterward, I get dressed and decide to visit an old friend.

"Hey, bro!" Connor greets me warmly. He looks depressed and sleep-deprived, which makes me feel guilty for insisting he stay in here. "I think you've grown again since I last saw you!"

"I'll be bigger than you someday." We start almost every conversation this same way when I come to see him. He chuckles everytime.

"Where's Liam?"

"He's on a mission. He should be coming back here in a few days, actually. I'm sure he'll be excited to see you."

"Good." He looks at me curiously. "What happened to you?"

"What do you mean?"

Connor draws a circle around his face with his pointer finger. Oh, right. I must still have a shadow of a black eye from his fist. Hopefully the rest of the wounds are mostly healed. I didn't pay much attention to them once the nurses stopped the bleeding. Someone else has been occupying my thoughts nonstop.

"Oh, this old thing?"

"Did you get assigned a new mission?"

It used to make me sad that I had to keep things from him, but I guess it kind of became second nature at some point. Keeping him sane was more important than telling him the truth. Maybe it's time for change.

"Connor, if I tell you the truth, will you promise to try to stay calm?" I meet his eyes and await his response.

"I did that to you, didn't I?" Shame fills his eyes.

"Connor, I've been on Lila Martin's detail."

"Oh." He blinks slowly and I fear I might have set him off. I subtly brace myself for impact.

"I wasn't sure if I should tell you or not." I fidget with my hands in my lap.

"Did you?"

"What?" I meet his eyes.

"Did you tell me? Is that why I hit you?"

"No, you saw me outside her room."

He's quiet for a moment while he tries to recall the events. "They told me I had an episode, but they didn't give me any details." He exhales a heavy breath. "Damn it, Ryker. I'm so sorry."

"It's not your fault," I say for the hundredth time. Sometimes it's hard for me to believe. I don't know how I can forgive him for what he did to Lila, but can I really hold it against him?

"Did I scare her?" There is so much going on behind his eyes, it makes me feel sad for him. He never asked for this, after all.

I'm not sure what I should tell him. My silence might be enough.

"Did I hurt her?" It's almost a whisper.

"She's okay now," I match his volume.

Connor hangs his head between his shaking shoulders. I wish Liam were here to console him. The ability to console and comfort has never come naturally to me.

"I should've told you before, maybe it would have helped." I reach out to put my hand on his shoulder.

"I'm so sorry," he cries.

"Hey." I squeeze his shoulder softly until he stops shaking. "We'll get through this together."

It takes him several minutes to compose himself. His eyes, red and puffy, finally meet mine. "Can I apologize to her?"

His question makes me hesitate. I don't know if I can trust him with her. "I'm not sure that's such a good idea-"

"Just ask her, please," he pleads.

"Connor, I don't think I want to put her in that position. She still can't sleep unless I'm in the room with her." My voice is way too expressive.

Something flashes across Connor's eyes and I have a feeling I'm about to find out what. "You're *sleeping with her*?"

"You knocked on her door, got into her bedroom and then *strangled* her. So yeah, I have to sit at her desk every night so she can fall asleep and calm her when that memory haunts her dreams."

Connor clasps both hands around his mouth in horror as I spit hateful words at him. *It's not his fault, Ryker.*

"I'm so sorry. Thank you for keeping her safe. I'm so sorry I hurt both of you." Connor gets up as if to leave, as if he had come to me. As if there was somewhere else he could go.

"No, I'm sorry." Regret cakes my voice. "I didn't mean to make you feel worse-"

"No, I get it. I'm sorry for implying-" He cuts himself off, rubbing his face hard with both hands. "If she's ever willing, I'd really like to apologize to her."

"I'll think about it. If she keeps going at the rate she is, she'll shake off the whole thing soon. If she does, I'll ask her about it and leave it up to her, okay?"

"Thank you, man."

"Not a problem."

Connor finally sits back down, putting me at ease. "Ryker?"

"Yeah?"

He looks up at me with a hopeful expression. "Is she still incredible?"

"Absolutely magical," I respond truthfully.

We're able to chat for several more hours, and it's so fulfilling. It's been a long time since I've been able to talk with Connor so candidly, and it might be the first time I've been able to do so without Liam playing referee.

By the time I leave, though, it still hurts to see the guards lock the door behind me. This can't be what's best for him.

At sunset, I take a train to Amaryllis and walk around the city aimlessly. I don't think I've ever been so adventurous in my life. I'd argue that the Soldier lifestyle doesn't really allow for it, but there are plenty of Soldiers who can let go and have a good time. I am more of a by-the-book kind of guy and, while I get teased about it by Liam and other peers, I don't see the benefit of getting wasted or sleeping around or doing anything unintentionally.

Tonight is different, though. I need to get out of my head and will do just about anything to achieve a quiet mind.

After an hour or two of roaming, I find myself in front of a club. For just a second, I think about how stupid this might be. I quickly push past it, though, and head in.

Once inside, I remember why I never do this. The loud music, the crowds of people, the smell. I don't know how to dance and it's way too noisy to have a real conversation with anyone. I choose the loner route and head to the bar upstairs, since the main level is over-populated.

I give one of the bartenders my order and take a seat at one of their tall tables that could barely fit two chairs. I think the point of these tables is so people can move around and stand at the table but I shamelessly sit on the tall skinny chair, turning it so that I'm looking over the crowd below. Hopefully making it so that nobody finds me approachable. Tonight is about getting buzzed and nothing else.

A waitress who looks way too young to be serving alcohol hands me my beer with a smile. I try to return the gesture, but can tell by her expression that it was probably more of a grimace. I take a swig of my drink, being painfully reminded of how much I hate beer. Regardless, I tip the cup to my mouth until more than half of it disappears.

Two girls come up to me before I finish my beer but I don't pay them any attention. Instead, I wait for another waiter to pass by. It doesn't take too long for the girls to give up and a waitress to take their place at my side.

"What are you having?" The bubbly waitress asks. This one looks even younger than the last. It takes effort not to roll my eyes at her, at myself, at the stupid decision to come here.

"Anything better than beer." I hand her my empty glass and she chuckles as she returns it to the bar.

A few minutes later, the girl returns with a clear drink in hand. I don't know my liquor well, but I'm positive this one is stronger. I try to block out the smell of it as I take a drink. I hope this one hits faster than the beer.

I sit around until I start to feel the buzz and as soon as it hits, I make my way through the ever-growing crowd towards the door. On my way down the stairs, I see a familiar face that stops me in my tracks.

Rachel is on the main level, near the bar. Why the hell is she out here when she's supposed to be watching Lila? Next I see Ben, the guy from the training building that was shamelessly flirting with Lila.

They don't look like they're here together since Ben is dancing with someone else, but what are the chances they're both here and it has nothing to do with-

My stomach drops when Ben's dancing partner turns around. Damn it, Lila. I push through the crowd to Rachel and give her a piece of my mind.

"What the hell, Rach?"

"Ryker?" She swings around.

"What was so hard about keeping Lila near Headquarters? She shouldn't be out here, especially late at night."

"She's fine, Ryker. She needed a night out of her 'cell' as she put it." Rachel inspects me closely. "Are you drunk?"

"No, I just had a couple drinks," I brush her off. "You need to-"

"Go home, Ryker. I got this. I'm watching her, I'm not drinking, I'll keep her safe. You are not sober and you'd probably cause more trouble than you'd diffuse. Go home, sleep it off. We'll see you when you're done taking time off."

It's hard to follow her advice when I feel so angry at her being here, but after what she said, I recognize that I am, in fact, a little buzzed and should just go back to my room. I swallow my pride and get outside.

The brisk fresh air helps me get back to reality. I walk straight towards the train station. Luckily, I've forgotten the brother drama I'd been worried about earlier. However, my Lila stress is occupying almost all of my thoughts. My brain is slowed down by the alcohol, but I try to go over the events in my head as I walk.

Why is Lila at a bar? Did she go with Ben or did he just happen to find her there? Does it matter? Obviously they found each other and are hanging out either way. Why does he bother me so much? I know Connor would say it's jealousy, but I have the same feeling I did with Warren and I was dead on about him. I just want to keep her safe, for her sake and for my family's.

By the time I get back to Living Quarters, my head is pounding. I hesitate as I pass Lila's door, unable to move past it. After several minutes of contemplating, I unlock the door and step inside.

TWENTY-THREE

Lila

My first lesson with Lorenzo is anticlimactic as he explains Necromancer history and goes over the basics of magic. Usually, I would've fallen asleep from boredom from learning about history, but this time is different. Learning about my ancestors for the first time in my life keeps me on the edge of my seat.

"Well, that's all the time we have today. Here, take this." Lorenzo hands me a book. "Read this in between our lessons when you're bored. It has a lot of information about the logistics of magic."

"Thank you for all of your help, Mr. Sosa."

"Please, call me Lorenzo."

"Thank you, Lorenzo. I'm sure you're busy and I just really appreciate all that you're doing for me here." I've always been a little awkward about expressing my feelings but especially with someone I don't know.

"You're welcome, mija. See you tomorrow, same time?"

"Yes, absolutely!"

Lorenzo reaches out his hand and I shake it.

"See you."

"See you!"

Rachel is sitting just outside the door, waiting for me. She is a lot less attentive than Ryker, which, I guess, is a good thing. She gets up when I walk out, and we head back to my room.

"We have some time to kill before dinner," Rachel states. "Do you mind hanging out here so I can get in a quick nap?"

"That's fine, no problem."

"Sweet, thanks. Keep the door locked, stay in-"

"Inside, don't open the door for anyone, I know. I'll wait for you to come get me."

"Great." She starts to turn.

"Rachel?"

"Yeah?" She turns back to face me.

"Just set an alarm so we don't miss dinner?"

Rachel laughs. "Will do. Get inside." She points to my room and waits until the door is closed and locked behind me.

I am in the middle of studying my sketch of Ryker when Rachel knocks on the door. I haven't figured out what about his portrait seems off to me yet, but I snap my sketchbook closed and sit up obviously straight in my bed when the door opens.

"You got dirty magazines in there or something?"

"Don't be gross."

"Why did you look like that when I opened the door?"

"Because I was relaxing and the door scared me!" I defend pitifully.

"Didn't you hear me knock?"

"I heard the knock-"

"Then why did it scare you when I walked in?"

"Can we just drop it? You're so annoying." I shove Rachel in the shoulder and she snickers. For a second it feels like we are friends again. I put the guard back up quickly though.

They serve a variety of chicken and vegetables at dinner. I get grilled chicken with mashed potatoes and gravy and some mixture of bell peppers, squash, eggplant, onion, and tomato. I'm not sure I'll ever get used to the fancy food they serve here.

My plate is as delicious as it is beautiful. I'm not halfway through it when I hear a familiar self-assured voice behind me.

"Hey, beautiful."

I turn around to find the owner of the voice.

"So you *are* stalking me!" I accuse sarcastically.

"I've been here way longer than you. Are you stalking me?" Ben flirts. "I mean, I know I'm irresistibly attractive, but-"

I punch him half-heartedly in the shoulder. "You wish."

Ben pushes his way into the seat next to me. "What do you have going on tonight?"

"What?"

"Do you have plans tonight?"

"Oh, yes, absolutely," I lie through my teeth.

"Liar."

"I am not!"

"What are you doing, then?"

"I'm not at liberty to say-"

"Come out with me."

"What?"

"Come out with me tonight. We'll get drinks, we'll dance, we'll talk and then you can walk me to my door."

"You're crazy-" I shake my head.

"I'm not! I'm interested in getting to know you, why is that crazy?"

That question digs deeper than I'm sure he intends. "Rachel and I are a package deal. You get both of us or neither of us," I say confidently.

Ben looks to Rachel to confirm, which she does with the nod of her head, then turns back to me with an outstretched hand. "Deal." When I take his hand to shake it, he holds onto it and kisses the top, as if he were greeting the Queen of England.

❖❖❖

During the train ride, Ben is a lot more personable and casual, easier to talk to. He tells me a little bit about his parents and sister, who live in Amaryllis and own a shoe store. He speaks very highly of them and it's admirable.

When he asks about my family I quickly change the subject, asking more about what he does at Headquarters and about his friends and family.

"Have you been on a solo mission before?"

"No," he answers timidly, hesitating briefly before explaining. "I'm not sure I'm cut out for that lifestyle."

"Why not?"

"Typically the Solo Soldiers are a lot bigger and stronger than I am." He looks away as if he's embarrassed. Maybe it's a shameful thing around here, but I'm not from here and it doesn't make a difference to me.

"So what kind of things do you do, then?" I ask innocently.

"I actually just got recruited for the Intelligence team." I don't have any idea what this means but I have a feeling if I were from here, I would. I panic slightly as I try to respond appropriately.

"Wow, that's great, Ben!" Rachel chimes in, saving me from the moment. I'll have to ask her what an Intelligence team is later. Ben turns around suddenly as if he had forgotten she was here. "I had no idea you were looking into that but that sounds perfect for you."

"Yeah, thanks." Ben smiles. "I'm pretty thrilled about it. I haven't told anyone, so-"

Rachel zips her mouth shut with her fingers and throws the pretend key across the train car. Ben turns back to me just as the train comes to a stop at Amaryllis. We all stand up and look out the glass door at the big city.

Rachel and I follow Ben to a club that he's supposedly fond of, chatting casually as we go. We can hear the music faintly from outside the building, but when someone opens the front doors, the sound floods the courtyard. Rachel and I exchange a wary glance.

Ben turns around as we approach the doors, his expression full of exhilaration. He grabs my hand boldly and pulls me into the crowd. I check to make sure Rachel is nearby and I'm relieved to find she's closer to me than Ben is.

None of the songs that are playing are familiar to me but they are phenomenal. The energy in this club is unlike any other I've ever experienced. There is a shared feeling of ecstasy throughout the entire building, as if there were happy pills being vaporized into the air.

Ben and I dance to our hearts' content to every song that comes on. Every once in a while, Ben or I will drag Rachel out to join us as well. It's funny to imagine what Ben must be thinking about this situation- Rachel standing at attention in the midst of a bunch of happy partiers. It makes me giggle any time I give it attention.

"What's so funny?" Ben shouts in my direction.

"Nothing," I lie obviously, still giggling.

Ben shakes his head and spins me around. My laugh catches in my throat as I see Ryker in the corner of my eye. Ben only sees my expression and stops me in my tracks. "Hey." He puts his hands on my shoulders. "Are you okay?"

I nod but don't convince him. I try to distract him when I see his eyes search for Rachel. "I think I need a drink. Would you get me one?"

It works. His search ends short and he moves his eyes back to me. "Sure. What'll you have?"

"Surprise me!"

As he makes his way to the bar, I push towards Rachel. Ryker is already gone.

"Hey," I get her attention. "What was that about?"

"It was nothing." Rachel waves away my question. "Are you alright?"

"Yeah." I wonder if it'll raise a flag if I press harder. "Is Ryker joining us?"

"No, he's headed home. He just wanted to make sure we were good."

"He looked angry," I say pointedly.

"He wasn't thrilled we're here but I told him he's got nothing to worry about. He agreed it's good for you to have a night out. Go enjoy it! I'll be here the whole time."

It bothers me that Ryker had the audacity to come here just to tell us we shouldn't be here and then leave. If he thought it was dangerous and Rachel couldn't handle it, why wouldn't he stay? And if he knew that Rachel is capable of protecting me then why bother come at all? I decide to take Rachel's advice and shake it off so I can enjoy the night.

Ben returns with my drink. It's a light blue color with a fruity scent and pink sugar around the rim of the martini glass. Ben offers his yellow drink up for a toast and we clink the glasses together with an obnoxious "Cheers!"

I don't drink often, so there's a chance I've just never known what to order, but I swear even the alcohol is different here. It feels lighter than I remember.

We dance for probably an hour longer before fatigue creeps its way in. It must be obvious because both Ben and Rachel suggest we leave when the buzz from my first drink wears off.

"I'm gonna get another drink," I tell Ben before moving towards the bar.

Rachel follows behind me. "I don't think that's a great idea, Lila. Let's call it a night. The crowd starts to change this time of night."

"I'm having fun!"

"Let's end on a good note. I can come up with an excuse for Ben if you want. It's time to go back."

I consider her words carefully. I want to stay out all night and make Ryker feel bad for missing out but is it worth my safety? No.

But Ben and Rachel can protect me. Rachel feels like it's best to go home, though, and I should listen to her. "Okay, if you think it's time to go, then we should go."

We find Ben again and Rachel shouts something in his ear. He nods and gestures for us to follow him. He politely pushes through the massive crowd of people and out of the club.

❖❖❖

"What a night!" I say as we exit the train for the last time.

Ben is calmer now, but still wears a smile on his face. "Glad you enjoyed it."

"I did! I didn't realize how much I needed a night out. Thanks for taking us." I wrap him in a bear hug that totally catches him by surprise. I don't think hugs are a normality here. Oh well.

He pats my back in response. "It was my pleasure."

We smile awkwardly at each other for just a moment before Rachel steps in. "Thanks Ben. Have a good night!"

"You both as well. See you."

Rachel looks at me sideways and I pretend I don't notice and start walking toward the Living Quarters.

"We're going to be walking the same way as him, aren't we?"

"Yep." Rachel chuckles.

Luckily Ben pretends we're not following him on his way back. Finally, he splits off on the second floor and we can walk the rest of the way alone. When I use the key to open my door, I notice a folded piece of paper on the table with my name on it. I quickly stand in the way of it as Rachel checks the room.

"All clear," she reports. "Sleep well."

"Thanks, you too."

I unfold the paper immediately after she leaves.

Lila,

I apologize but I am no longer going to be on your detail.

Keep up the great work, you are strong and very capable.

Good luck with everything.

Ryker

TWENTY-FOUR

Ryker

I am startled awake by the unfamiliar sound of pounding on my door. I quickly slip on my shirt and pants and open the door to stop the obnoxious knocking. I'm surprised to find Lila at the door. My head is aching and my vision is blurred.

"What's going on?" I mumble.

"What do you think you're doing, leaving this damn note on my desk and taking yourself off my case?" Lila shouts loudly while pushing her way into my room.

I close the door rapidly, nervous she's going to wake up the rest of the floor. I rub at my eyes as I try to process the situation at hand. Lila is upset about the letter I left in her room tonight, which happens to be crumpled in her white knuckled fists.

"Lila, it's nothing personal," I lie through my teeth. "Colonel Finch just thinks I should be focusing my attention elsewhere."

"Oh, bullshit!"

"What?" I ask defensively. I can count the number of times I've heard Lila swear on one hand. That, on top of screaming at me in the middle of the night, is crazy- even for her.

"*You* requested to meet with her and you're telling me that it was *her* idea?"

She got me there. "Lila, look-"

"You're the only one I can trust here, Ryker. You *promised* you wouldn't hand me off, you told me I could trust you!" Lila's voice catches as she starts to get emotional.

Damn it. Damn it, damn it, damn it. "I want what's best for you. I want you to be safe-"

"Then keep me safe! *You* are what's best for me!"

If she only knew how much I wish that statement were true.

"It's just not that simple." I let out a big breath. "I'm distracted, Lila, and I can't let that compromise your safety. We still don't know who is looking for you and your bodyguards can't be distracted."

Lila shakes her head slightly. "I don't understand."

"I'm sorry."

"What do you mean by distracted?"

I take a second to form a response. After all, I'm not even totally sure what's distracting me. This feeling of being incapable of finishing my mission is new. "I just have some stuff going on that I can't seem to figure out and I can't stop thinking about it," I answer vaguely.

"Come on, Ryk," Lila pleads.

What else am I supposed to tell her? "Stuff with my brothers, and you, and I don't want you to worry about it." I throw my hands up helplessly.

"I thought we agreed to be mutually vulnerable. Trust is a two-way street and all that."

"That was before-" I cut myself off.

"Before what?"

Before I started caring about you the way I do, I think to myself. "It's just different now."

"What's going on with your brothers?" She refocuses me.

"I just don't know what I'm supposed to do about Connor. How can I justify locking him up like an animal? How would I justify letting him go, knowing he's a threat to you? What is Liam going to think of me when he comes home and realizes I chose you over Connor?" I spiral.

"Oh, Ryker." She pulls me into a tight embrace. When she lets go, she pulls me toward the bed. "Sit down. Let's talk this through."

I reluctantly follow her lead and we sit together on my bed. I position myself so that my knees bend over the side of the bed, my body barely angled toward Lila at all. She sits sideways, facing me, with her legs loosely crossed in front of her. I struggle to look her in the eye as we speak.

"Ryker, I don't want to be a point of contention between you and your brothers. If you think Connor should be free, talk to Finch and tell her that. I really don't mind. I don't necessarily want to be around him, but you can help me stay at a safe distance. And if you need to visit him, Rachel or someone else can stay with me for the duration of your visit and you'll at least have eyes on him so you'll know I'm safe."

"Lila-"

"Maybe someday we can even meet together, ya know? In a controlled environment, to talk things over. That might really benefit him!"

The corners of my mouth turn up as she goes on.

"See? We can work these things out! I'm not only a liability, I can be helpful sometimes."

It makes me chuckle. "I never thought of you as a liability."

"Oh, I beg to differ! With Warren? That's exactly what you thought of me!" She laughs along with me.

"You were being stupid." I shake my head.

"Yeah, well…" She exhales. "I learned my lesson, didn't I?"

"I hope so," I mumble under my breath, regretting it as soon as it comes out.

Lila tilts her head at me. "What does that mean?" She's not upset yet, but I don't want to push her to that point again.

"Nothing." I wave my hand to reassure her, but with no luck.

"Are you referring to Ben?" She lowers her gaze from my eyes to my chest. "That's why you were so mad tonight?"

The question dumbfounds me.

"I saw you." Her majestic eyes meet back up with mine. "At the club. I saw you there tonight, talking to Rachel. You were mad that I was with Ben?"

"I didn't follow you there," I evade the accusation.

"You think he's dangerous?" She lifts both eyebrows, as if she really does want the answer.

"I feel the same way about him that I felt about Warren."

Lila appears taken aback by the comparison. "At the risk of you calling me stupid again, I don't think you have anything to worry about."

"You don't have the greatest track record with being a good judge of character."

She scoffs and I briefly worry that I took it too far. Though, if she gets angry enough with me, leaving this mission will be a lot easier. "I won't see him anymore."

I almost snap my neck turning to her. "What?"

"If you think he's dangerous, I will stay away from him."

Why is the world's most complicated woman making everything that I've been wracking my brain about for days seem like a children's puzzle? "You will?"

"Consider it done. What other excuses do you have to not work with me anymore?"

"I don't know," I attempt a smokescreen. But she waits patiently for me to offer up another reason. "I'm not sure about the whole magic thing. I know it's important, but I worry that it'll make you vulnerable to unknown forces."

Lila shrugs. "I'll be careful. You can stay in the room during my lessons and if you see or feel anything suspicious, we stop."

"Why the hell are you being so reasonable?"

"This is important to me, Ryk. *You* are important to me. I've never felt safer than when I'm with you. I trust you more than I've ever been able to trust anyone in my whole life. I know you want what's best for me, and you'll fight for it if you have to." She wraps her dainty hands in mine. "Please let me do the same for you."

I am at a complete loss for words. There is a surge of emotions- all of which are unrecognizable to me- running through my body. I never imagined someone would ever say anything so pure and powerful to me. Now I *really* can't go back to pretending like I don't feel something deeper for her.

"Ryker?"

I shake my head, not sure what else to do. What should I do? What can I say?

"Talk to me," Lila pleads. "What is it?" There is a fierceness in her eyes that I would be wise to fear.

I shake my head weakly. "You'll change your mind-"

"No, I won't. Hey, you're safe with me." She moves closer and we're only inches apart now, making it harder for me to focus. How can I possibly lie to her when she's been so honest with me? But if I tell her and lose her, what good will that do me? *Trust is a two-way street.*

"Lila," I exhale, trying to gather my racing thoughts. "I haven't been honest with you." *No, damn it, Ryker, that's not what you needed to say.*

"I mean," I let out a shaky breath. "All of my concerns are true, I didn't lie about any of that. Damn, I don't know what to say." I shake my head again, unwilling to torture either of us any longer.

"None of those concerns are valid reasons not to trust me," Lila repeats, squeezing my hands gently as she waits for me to say more.

I look to her vivid eyes for a solution to my complicated predicament. Something flickers in them and I suddenly feel more exposed. "I'll lose my job..." I trail off. How is this the most difficult thing I've ever said to someone? I've had to tell Lila a lot worse than this and yet I can't bring myself to do it.

"Ryker." Lila's eyes pierce through me and I try to look away but she holds my face in place. "Just say it." Her voice is quiet now, sending chills through me.

I take one more deep breath before I finally release the heavy words out of my head and into reality. "Since that night at University with Warren, since seeing you up close and touching you for the first time, I haven't been honest with myself. I don't know if I honestly only defended you for the mission. I felt something that I hadn't felt before, something possessive and…" I shake my head again.

"Anyway, when Warren turned out to be an actual threat, I let myself brush off whatever I felt as intuition. But when I saw you out with Ben, I don't know, it just made all those feelings resurface and I finally realized that I was jealous. I was jealous of Warren, it had nothing to do with intuition about your safety. I was jealous of him getting close to you, and angry when he didn't stop trying after you rejected him. Just like I'm jealous of Ben now. I can't think about what you did when you were together. I don't want to know if you go out again. I won't be able to handle it. I want you to be mine. I want to be selfish with you. I never want anyone else to even think of you again, not the way that I do."

The drum of my heart pounds in my ears as Lila stares blankly back at me. Her cheeks turn bright red and I wonder if I just committed the error of a lifetime.

TWENTY-FIVE

Lila

Before I have time to think it through, my left hand is reaching up to join my right hand in pulling Ryker's mouth to mine. His shock only lasts half a second, then his hand wraps around my right thigh and pulls me into his lap.

Holy crap.

I feel butterflies when his hands touch my back, then my waist, and rest on my hips. What are we doing? How did this happen so fast? I never would've imagined I'd be kissing Ryker Johnson from University. A million thoughts rush through my head, trying to distract me from the feeling of Ryker's lips against mine.

"Lila," he comes up for air.

I quickly close the gap by bringing my lips back to his, unable- or un*willing*- to stop just yet.

He kisses me back for a few more beautiful seconds, then his hands come back to my hips and he pushes me back slightly. It hardly moves me at all, but it's enough to get my attention.

"Lila, stop." The words seem to cause him physical pain.

I pull back quickly. Ryker's eyes are racked with torment, causing my stomach to swirl. What did I just do? The reality of it all hits me like a bus. "I'm so sorry." I quickly hop off the bed and turn towards the door.

"No!" Ryker shouts. I am unable to process the wave of emotion and hormones rolling through my system, freezing me in place.

Ryker is behind me before I can take a breath. "Lila, please, don't go." He gently takes my hand in his, tugging ever so slightly, encouraging me to turn toward him.

I do, slowly, and without making eye contact.

"I didn't mean-" He takes a deep breath.

Dread fills my body as I wait for the 'I didn't mean romantically jealous, I meant professionally jealous' clarification. The subtle rejection after I just stuck my tongue down his throat. So much for convincing him to stay on my team.

"I didn't mean that I wanted you to stop, I-" He stumbles over his words. My stomach starts to feel lighter, as if the boulder is being lifted off of it. *Spit it out, Ryker!* "You've had a few drinks and I just want to make sure you understand what I'm saying."

I finally meet his beautiful, irresistible eyes. "What do you mean?"

"They'll take me off your case as soon as they find out how I feel about you." The way he speaks with such sternness almost makes me laugh. I bite my lip, hard, to stifle it. "I don't want you to suffer the consequences of my-"

A tiny chuckle escapes my mouth. I slap a hand over my mouth.

"Are you laughing?" Ryker wears a puzzled expression that does nothing to help my outburst.

"No." I try to compose myself. "Definitely not."

"Lila, I'm serious!" He's almost smiling now, at my sudden laughter, but I know he really is concerned.

I put one hand on each side of his face. "Have you learned nothing tonight?" His eyebrows furrow together, telling me he has no idea what I'm referring to. "We are better together. We can figure this out- we *will* figure it out," I reassure him for the fourth time tonight.

He exhales and pulls me to him, wrapping his strong arms around my shoulders. The sound of his heart pumping against his chest is incomparable to anything I've ever experienced. I could stay like this forever. "You are something else, you know that? I've never met anyone like you before." He pulls back to look at me.

It feels like I've unlocked a new level of Ryker, a side to him I wasn't sure existed. It's surreal and I'm afraid if I blink I'll wake up and find it was just a silly dream. But I know my mind isn't capable of creating a kiss like that. I've imagined many times how kissing him might be, and I never got close to what I just felt.

"What's going on in that pretty little head of yours?" he interrupts my thoughts, brushing his thumb across my forehead.

"Just wondering if this is one of my hyper-realistic dreams." I smile at him innocently.

"I hope not." How is it that this side of him is so foreign to me, yet it feels familiar and natural? "We've got to get you back to your room without anyone noticing," he whispers.

"If you insist," I tease.

He pauses briefly, considering the alternative option I alluded to, before stepping back and moving toward the door. He gestures for me to stay back as he peeks outside, first to the left, where my room is, then to the right, making sure nobody is in the hall. It's late, so I'd be surprised if someone was out, but I'm sure some Soldiers like to have a good time.

He opens the door fully and motions for me to go through. He follows very closely behind me, making it hard for me to focus on the current objective. Eventually, I get my door open and step inside, not sure if he'll be joining me or not.

Ryker smiles and shakes his head slightly. "Good night, Lila." He goes to pull my door shut and I slip my foot in before it shuts. Luckily, he notices, and pushes the door back open until he can see my face.

"I'll see you tomorrow?" I ask, shameless of my desperation to see him very soon.

"Try and stop me," he confirms.

I remove my foot from the door frame and let Ryker pull the door closed.

It takes me only a few minutes to get ready and into bed, but sleeping is another story. Thoughts of Ryker's mouth and arms swirl around in my head for what feels like all night.

I suppose I dozed off at some point because I am being woken up by a knock at my door. When the brain fog dissipates a bit, I run to the bathroom, brush my teeth, pull my clothes on and rip the door open.

The thrill of a new day wears off when I see Rachel on the other side. My excitement deflates and I have to hurry to wipe my disappointment from my expression.

"Good morning," Rachel says cheerfully. "Ready for breakfast?"

"Um," I blink. "Yes, I'm starving."

"Well, let's go!"

Breakfast is hard to enjoy while doubt fogs my mind. Did I make it all up in my head? No, I know it happened. So why isn't Ryker here? Is he regretting last night? Is he still going to request to be taken off my case despite our conversation?

I didn't even say anything to acknowledge his super sincere confession. Maybe he thinks I don't feel the same? What kind of lunatic just sticks their tongue down someone's throat without telling them how they feel? Do *I* even know how I feel about him?

"What's wrong?" Rachel pulls my attention back to the cafeteria. I have no idea how long she's been watching me move my food around my plate with my fork. I wonder how expressive my face has been.

"Nothing," I attempt to brush off her concern. She doesn't buy it for a second, so I add, "I don't feel very well."

"You're probably hungover, you party animal. Food would help with that." Rachel pushes my plate towards me an inch.

My stomach churns as I force food down my throat. Once I start eating though, I realize how hungry I really am.

When we finish, we walk towards the Training building as we do everyday.

The conversation Ryker and I had about Ben slips my mind until I see him again. I have to tell him I can't practice or hang out with him anymore. How am I going to do that without raising Rachel's suspicion? One night I party with him, dancing the night away and the next day I never want to see him again?

He's talking to someone when we arrive, though, and barely acknowledges us. At the end of their conversation, he briefly nods his head at me and then walks the opposite direction. I look at Rachel who is already looking at me.

"What was that?" I ask her innocently.

"I was about to ask you the same. Did something happen while you were dancing last night?"

I shake my head. "Not that I know of."

"Weird." Rachel shrugs. "I'll talk to him later. Looks like it's my turn to spar with you!"

My heart skips a beat when the person at the other end of Ben's conversation turns around. I didn't recognize him from behind due to the hat on his head. Ryker smiles at me softly, sending a chill through my spine.

"Ladies," he says smoothly. "Glad to see you both in one piece after last night."

Right. According to everyone else, the last time we saw each other was at the club. I channel my inner drama queen. "Bold of you to show up today." I push past him with my shoulder on my way to get my gear that he already picked up.

I see him and Rachel share a glance in the reflection of the glass walls. Ryker throws a hand up and Rachel only shrugs in response. I gear up and turn back to face him.

"What'd you say to Ben?" I ask defensively.

"That I'd be training you today," he responds casually.

"Just like that? You leave for days, then just come back and interrupt our routine?" Ryker looks taken aback by the frustration in my voice. I wonder if I'm laying it on too thick. "Did you even tell Rach you'd be back today?"

He looks at me for a moment before finding the words to respond. "It's my mission, Lila. I don't report to Rachel. In fact, she reports to me."

I take a swing at him, which he barely dodges.

"Woah," he warns.

Rachel grins and makes her way over to where Ben is standing. Ryker readies himself for our sparring match.

If it were a true competition, we all know Ryker would kick my butt. He doesn't, though. He, of course, spares me, but I can tell he's impressed by how much progress I've made since the last time we fought.

Ryker only gets in a few relatively soft punches and the match doesn't end with me on the floor, so I'll count it as a win.

When we determine it's over, Rachel takes me to the locker room. She eyes me carefully, acting as if she has something to say but won't.

"What is it?" I ask directly.

She smirks. "I didn't say a word."

"Yeah," I concede. "But you want to."

"I just didn't realize how mad you were with him." She suggests cautiously.

"He's not being very fair."

"Lila, he needed a few personal days to work some stuff out." She shrugs. "I appreciate you trying to stand up for me and all, but he's right. He is my direct report on this. He's been watching over you for a long time, and no offense or anything, but it can take a toll. I was happy to help him and I'm actually grateful we had some time to ourselves," she adds timidly.

Her candor is unexpected. I was mostly acting but after Rachel's point, I appreciate Ryker even more than I did before. "I guess I didn't realize how much he is probably sacrificing for me."

"I'm not excusing his behavior either. I understand why you're frustrated. I'm just saying maybe there's more than meets the eye."

"Thank you. I'll try to cut him some slack."

We smile at each other as we finish up and leave the locker room. Ryker is waiting for us outside, trying too hard to look casual as he leans against the wall.

I roll my eyes, partly for the performance, and partly because I'm annoyed at how much the sight of him affects me. I've never had these gushy, nervous, excited feelings about anyone before, and I definitely wasn't expecting to experience it now, when life is at its messiest. But it is nice to have something else to focus on.

TWENTY-SIX

Ryker

It's harder than I expected to pretend like there is nothing between Lila and I. The events of last night play through my head non-stop. Not being able to talk to her, or touch her, how I want to kills me with every passing minute. I avoid looking at her so I don't give Rachel anything to notice.

Lila pretends to be holding a grudge and I consequently act as if I'm trying to be respectful and give her space. We play the part through lunch and up until we're headed to Lila's magic lesson with Lorenzo.

"Hey, Rachel, why don't you take a break. I can hold down the fort for a while."

Both girls look at me with the same hopeful expression. It's laughable, as they probably think they're hiding it well, too.

"Yeah, if you're sure?" Rachel asks.

"Definitely. Go relax, you deserve it."

"You'll let me know when you need me?"

"Yes ma'am," I confirm.

"Okay. See you, Lila." She puts her hand on Lila's forearm and leans in to whisper "go easy on him" not quietly enough to be out of my earshot. It makes me smile.

"Enjoy your burden-free afternoon." Lila waves her goodbye and then turns slowly back toward me. She doesn't look me in the eye and instead begins walking to our next destination.

I try to think of something to say, but find myself suddenly feeling very intimidated. I've been waiting to be alone with this girl for twelve hours and, now that I finally am, I can't think of anything to say to her.

She's quiet too. Maybe she really is mad at me still for leaving. Things were pretty intense last night and I don't remember ever resolving her frustration.

Has yesterday's professional problem solver returned to her complicated self? As much as I hate to admit it, it's kind of exciting not knowing which version I'm going to get at any given moment. More than ever, I want all versions of her.

I don't realize until we get to the door that I ended up not saying a word the whole walk over. *You are such an idiot.* Lila hesitates before reaching for the door. It's now or never.

I intercept her hand with mine and I could swear a spark flies into the air. She looks into my eyes for the first time since training this morning and it makes me nervous. "Is it still okay for me to come sit in during your session?"

I still have her hand in mine and she doesn't attempt to remove it. "Yes," she replies curtly.

"Thank you." I pause a few seconds longer and then let go of her hand, turning to open the door.

On the other side, Lorenzo is sitting in a sofa chair, reading a book. When he notices us, he swiftly removes his glasses, closing the book and standing up to greet us.

"Well, hello!" he welcomes us warmly. "I hope you know you don't have to be precisely on time."

"What?"

"I noticed you were outside for a minute. You don't have to wait until the time of our appointment. If you get here a few minutes early, you're welcome to come in."

Lila and I briefly make eye contact before my curiosity gets the best of me. "How did you know we were outside?"

"It's a Necromancer gift. We can feel people's energy, almost like hearing and recognizing someone's footsteps." Lorenzo smiles as if he knows the information slightly disturbs me.

"No way!" Lila chimes in. "How come I can't feel someone like that?"

The phrasing of her question invites a compilation of inappropriate thoughts into my mind. It takes a lot of effort to push them away. This is definitely not the time nor the place, *the guy just said he can read your energy.*

"Your magic has been suppressed for a very long time. You will learn to recognize energy with time. Did you bring your book?"

"Oh shoot." Lila throws her head back. "Day two and I've already forgotten everything from day one."

"No worries. Read it in your free time. Today we are going to learn about channeling magic through emotions. There is important material about this in your book, but I'd like to get a little hands on today." Lorenzo looks at me the second he says the words, anticipating they would trigger me.

Lila must also sense it, because she speaks before I can open my mouth. "Oh, Mr. So- I mean- Lorenzo, is it alright if Ryker sits in during our sessions?"

He takes his peculiar gaze off me to respond to her. "Of course, mija. Whatever makes you more comfortable."

I keep my eye on him throughout the whole session. I'm wary of everyone that goes out of their way to get to know Lila, but especially Necromancers.

I will say, Lorenzo does a pretty good job of convincing me he's one of the good guys. I can tell he cares about Lila, though it's unclear as to why.

He takes Lila's bracelets off her wrists and coaches her on how to recognize the energy she gets from emotions. It's quite fascinating, actually, and my attraction to her grows deeper as I watch her learn about her potential.

"You have to be very cautious with negative emotions. The last time you had a surge of magic was in an upsetting situation, yes?"

"I was being held hostage and then stabbed by a psychopath, so yeah you could say it was upsetting," Lila says flatly.

"Do you remember the incident?"

"Not the magic part, no."

"But you were there?" Lorenzo directs the question at me.

I feel like I've been caught eavesdropping. "Um, yes. I was there."

"Would you mind explaining what you remember about it?"

"Uh," I stammer and shift my weight from one foot to the other as I try to recall that night. "Well, Lila and Warren were having an escalating conversation when my partner and I arrived at the scene. We attempted several talk-down techniques and it only escalated him more. He poked Lila's side with a knife and put his other arm around her throat-"

"How was Lila feeling, what did she express?"

"I don't recall her saying much, but she was obviously distraught at the position she was in. When I got too close, Warren pushed his knife in further and that's when her magic- what did you call it?- surged."

"Was it something you saw, felt, heard?" Lorenzo continued his questioning. He is unphased by anything I've said so far, meaning he has probably seen much worse.

"It wasn't audible. There was a very bright flash of light and it felt as if an explosive had gone off. Warren immediately became unconscious and my partner and I were knocked down but still coherent."

"Mm," Lorenzo hums.

I try to push the image of Lila's crumpled and bloody body from that night out of my head. Instinctively, I look to make sure she is okay now. There is an intensity about her as she hears about that night for what I assume is the first time.

"Did it have a color?" Lorenzo interrupts my thoughts.

"Hm?" I ask, distracted. I look away from Lila so I can pay better attention to the question this time.

"Did the light have a color?"

"It was red at the center, but the explosion was just light, I'm not sure it was colored."

"I see." Lorenzo sets his hands face down on the table that fills the space between Lila and him. "You must have been angry and in pain at that moment, which could cause a red light, but-" He shakes his head.

"But what?" I ask, though I'm not sure it's my place to. Lila doesn't seem to mind.

"It sounds more like a protective response, which wouldn't make any sense if you were taken from your parents before the age of ten." Lorenzo shakes his head again, not sure how to make sense of my description.

"What does that mean?" Lila asks.

"Usually, when a Necromancer reaches the age of ten, there is a ritual in which they receive magical protection on their powers, called Aegis. Typically, they are 'enchanted' as babies, which provides them with protection until they turn ten. But this sounds more like Aegis than an enchantment. Do you remember what happened with the rebels?"

The question peaks my interest.

"No, not really. Colonel Finch just said that they put some kind of magic storage thing into me, whatever that means." She looks at me and I move my gaze to my feet. She didn't want me to know this and I can't help but feel like I don't belong in this conversation.

"May I?" Lorenzo puts his hands palm up on the table. "I might be able to feel something that will help us figure out what they did that might be affecting your magic outbursts."

Lila puts her hands on top of his and waits quietly as he closes his eyes and mumbles under his breath.

I take a deep breath and let go of whatever frustration I'm feeling about being left out of the loop. It's not a big deal and it doesn't change anything. I wonder what else Lila is carrying all by herself.

"Ah," Lorenzo says at last. "They are using you to store their magic. I am not able to access it but someone must be able to. I think we just discovered why they want you so bad."

Lila appears to be as speechless as I am.

"It doesn't explain why they wanted you in the first place, however. You were alone with the two Necromancers in the forest?"

Lila nods her head numbly.

"I will investigate this more. You need to be very careful who you trust. Be wary of other Necromancers, yes?"

She nods again. Lorenzo pats her hands comfortingly.

"Well." He stands up and pulls Lila up out of her chair as well. "This was a very productive session, I think. Read your book when you find time. Learn as much as you can. I do have to put these back on, for your safety." He holds the bracelets that impede her magic in the air.

Halfway through our silent walk to the dining hall, Lila pushes me into an empty room. It takes me completely by surprise. I search her face and find it full of panic.

"What's wrong?" I rush to her side. Is she hurt? Did I just totally miss a bloodbath going on in the hall? I move back toward the door and Lila grabs at my arm, hard.

"Were you in there?" she asks, exasperated by whatever battle she just escaped.

"Where?"

"Ryker!"

"Sorry, I'm trying to underst-"

"With Lorenzo! Did you hear what he said?"

"Of course I did," I respond, still unsure of the point she is trying to make. She's clearly worked up about something. "You mean about the magic being stored in you?"

"Yes! That I'm a target because of whatever it is? Why are you acting so casual about it?"

"Lila, I'm not casual about it. But we did know that there were people after you, that's why we're in our current position."

"I guess." Lila exhales finally. "Yeah, you're right. I guess I didn't understand the severity of my position until now."

It takes everything I have not to roll my eyes at her. Of course she didn't understand the severity of the situation. If she had, she wouldn't have been so careless about where she went and who she went with. "Nothing's changed except now we have more information as to why you're a target. That's a good thing."

I unconsciously reach up and rub her cheek with my thumb. I almost pull away when I realize what I'm doing, but Lila leans into it just in time. She knows she's safe with me.

I would do just about anything for this girl right here.

TWENTY-SEVEN

Lila

Tonight's dinner quickly becomes my favorite meal since being at Headquarters. Rachel, while not on duty, sees us in the cafeteria and comes to sit with us, bringing Ben and a few other friends with.

The food is fantastic. They serve some kind of pasta with a creamy light green sauce and I get grilled vegetables on the side. While tasty, the company is much more mentionable.

Ben and his friends keep us laughing for almost two hours, making jokes about everything under the sun. Many are specific to Amaryllis and Headquarters, meaning that some go way over my head, but for the most part, they reach the right crowd.

I love seeing Rachel in her natural element. She always fit into whatever scene she was in, but there was always something about her that made me feel she was too good for college, too good for stupid frat boys, obnoxious roommates, or business classes. She was always more mature than her peers and way too physically fit to just be a corporate sheep.

Ryker always seemed like a loner to me, and I suppose he still kind of is, in a way, but he is much more respected here, too. During dinner, he subtly touches me any chance he gets, making very calculated movements so that nobody would have a clue. He doesn't laugh nearly as much as Rachel and I, but each time a chuckle slips out is music to my ears. It's nice to see him enjoy himself for a change.

This afternoon's session with Lorenzo really took me by surprise but it seemed to have brought some kind of peace or resolution to Ryker. He no longer seems just like a bodyguard, he has become a person who goes out of his way to protect me. Though maybe it has more to do with last night than Lorenzo. Either way, I've never had anything like it in my life.

At last, the night comes to an end, and Ryker walks me quietly back to my room like the gentleman that he is. I open the door and step inside, expecting him to follow, but I turn and see him waiting awkwardly in the hall.

"Aren't you going to check the room?" I ask, offering him a logical excuse for why he should come in.

"Right," he mumbles. He swiftly moves from room to room, checking that I'm safe. I almost giggle as I watch him work faster than I've ever seen before.

It doesn't take long for the doubt to kick in and tell me that maybe he really is uncomfortable and doesn't want to be here at all.

I take off my shoes and hop onto my bed while he checks the bathroom. I sit on the edge so that he'll have to walk past me to get to the door.

"All clear," Ryker says as he leaves the bathroom. His pace slows significantly as he walks past me and makes his way to the door. "H-have a good night."

I let out a quiet sigh and drop my head in disappointment as he reaches for the door handle. "You too."

"Lila?"

"Hmm?" When I don't get a response, I raise my head again to see him. He doesn't move his body but I can see the muscle in his jaw jump as he tightens his jaw.

He drops his hand from the handle and his shoulders turn quickly to face me, his left foot following the motion. "I just want to make sure you're okay."

I'm not sure how to respond so I say "I'm okay."

A smile of relief quickly crosses his face, so fast that I would have missed it, had I blinked. "Tonight was fun."

"I thought so too," I respond breathily, growing increasingly self-conscious. I feel exposed under his gaze.

Ryker clears his throat and takes a step closer. "I never really got to thank you for last night." The bed is only a few feet from the door but tonight it feels like it's miles away.

"Oh yeah?" I wonder if he can audibly hear my heart pumping warm blood through my body.

He looks at me intently as he takes another step. "Yeah, I wanted to, but I-"

I have to force myself to look away from him in an attempt to lower my heart rate. Why am I so nervous? I grip the edge of my bed with my hands and try to focus on my breath.

"Today was just kind of crazy, you know? And I couldn't express myself in front of Rachel or anyone-"

"I understand." I barely slip the words out of my tight chest.

"Do you?" The question begs me to look him in the eyes and I comply.

His face is so serious, the brown in his eyes deeper than ever. He bites his bottom lip slightly as he decides what to say next, making my stomach tingle.

"Well." He stops in his tracks, now just a few inches away from me. "Thank you. Thank you for listening to me, consoling me, and reasoning with me. Thank you for letting me be vulnerable with you."

I swallow hard and hope he doesn't notice. I don't know how he couldn't, he's staring at me so intensely, I'd bet he can see everything from the breaths I take to the thoughts flying through my head.

I know I need to say something back but I can't possibly string a sentence together right now.

Ryker puts his hand halfway on my cheek and neck, leans forward, and plants a soft kiss on my forehead. The tingle in my stomach rises to my chest and then falls down through the rest of my body.

I still don't feel brave enough to move, but Ryker lingers and I know he wants to give me the chance to make a move. I swallow hard, again, and tilt my head up at him.

Relief visibly washes over him and he doesn't wait a second longer to close the gap of tension between us. He pulls me toward him at the same time he steps forward, causing our bodies to crash into each other. His lips are firm, then soft, then firm again.

I reach around his waist and hold him tightly to me, unable to get enough. His hands move desperately up and down my spine, sending sparks at every contact. A deep hum sounds in his throat as my legs wrap around him, making me want him so much more.

And just like that, his phone starts to ring.

"Damn it!" Ryker groans at the inconvenient interruption and straightens his posture. I chuckle at his apparent disappointment, which makes him smile and shake his head.

I look him straight in the eye as I retrieve his phone from his back pocket.

He sighs deeply and kisses me once more on the mouth before answering the call. "This is Jordan."

As he talks, I take his left hand from its place on my thigh and scribble in his palm with my pointer finger. He is focused on his conversation, but every few seconds, I look up at him and his expression softens. I wonder if anyone else has seen this side of Ryker Jordan. The thought makes me a little jealous and I selfishly hope the answer is no.

The call only lasts a few minutes and then Ryker's attention returns to me.

"Who was that?" I ask as I replace his hand to its rightful location.

"Colonel Finch," he responds quietly, distracted by the thigh he's holding.

"Well?" I nudge for more information.

"Shall we pick up where we left off?" Ryker sidesteps the question. He pretends to go in for a kiss and I push him off, making us both laugh.

"You're not going to tell me what she said?" I ask incredulously.

"I wouldn't want to ruin the mood," he teases.

I laugh again. "No, we certainly wouldn't want that." I move in front of his line of sight to hint that I really do want an answer.

"She wants to talk about your progress and decide what to do with you going forward." Ryker raises a playful eyebrow. "I told her I had some ideas of what *I* could do with you, but she didn't like them." He smirks at his dirty thoughts.

"You are much more mischievous than I ever could have imagined," I marvel. He smiles down at me with a big, goofy grin.

"She wants to meet with me about it tomorrow, so I'll have Rachel train with you. I'll try to get back in time for your lesson with Lorenzo."

"Why do you sound like you're saying goodbye?" I try not to let the disappointment seep into my voice.

"I should go," he says with a small bob of his head, as if he's trying to convince himself, too.

"You don't want to stay?"

"Hell yes I do!" He reassures me, cupping my face in his hands. "I have thought about it non-stop all day."

"Then stay!" I wrap myself around him again to persuade him.

"I can't." Ryker shakes his head and sighs.

"You stayed in here all night after Connor," I argue. "If anyone asks, just tell them I was scared again."

"Lila, you're killing me." He shakes his head again, as he tries to convince himself that I'm wrong. "No. No, I can't. I know it wouldn't necessarily raise any flags, but I don't trust myself to behave with you-"

"Who said anything about behaving?" I ask defensively.

He sighs. "Lila, please let me say no to this. I really want to do this right, but I am not strong enough to keep saying no to you." He ends his short and powerful argument with a sweet kiss on my lips.

"Okay," I relent, rolling my eyes. "You and your stupid honor code."

"Yeah?"

"Yeah."

"Thank you," Ryker says before kissing me again. He adds a little more passion this time, though not enough to get back into the same groove as earlier. "Okay, I'm going now." Another kiss.

"Okay, goodnight." Another kiss.

"Goodnight." Another kiss. We both laugh and then Ryker finally pulls away, leaving me alone in my room to think about him all night.

"I can't believe I didn't ask this earlier, but is there something between you and Ben?" I ask Rachel after training.

"What?" She acts like the question is out-of-this-world ridiculous.

"You like him, don't you?"

"I have no idea what you're talking about," she lies through her teeth.

"Fine, I'll drop it. But I've seen the way you talk and look at him, and I think y'all would make a cute couple."

She rolls her eyes.

"Wait, is there someone else?"

If looks could kill, Rachel's scowl would be my murder weapon.

I throw my hands up to surrender my point. But I proceed to make faces at her all throughout lunch with Ben.

Towards the end, Ryker joins us, sitting across from me. I play footsie with him under the table. He refuses to make eye contact, despite my several attempts. I can't tell if he's upset or just embarrassed that I'm touching him in public.

After a few minutes, I give in and decide I'll wait to let him tell me whatever it is.

TWENTY-EIGHT

Ryker

"What's going on between you and Lila?" Finch asks bluntly.

"Things are fine. She almost had me stumped when we sparred together yesterday-"

"That's not what I'm referring to," she says disapprovingly.

There's no way she knows about us, she can't know. "Okay, then what are you referring to?" I act confused by her interrogation, careful to not be too defensive.

"Lorenzo seems to believe Lila has romantic feelings for you," she says pointedly.

I laugh lightly at the accusation. "The guy who barely knows her? Sure, why wouldn't he know her deepest desires?"

"Necromancers are able to sense these things about other Necromancers, Ryker."

I shrug innocently. "Well, I'm not going to tell you what Necromancers can or cannot do. However, I have spent a significant time with Lila and I think I would have a clue if she had feelings for me. I can ask her if it's a big deal, but she's just barely begun to really trust me-"

"No." Finch exhales. "If she doesn't bring it up, then it shouldn't matter. We need her to continue to trust and listen to you and Rachel. I don't want to make an issue out of nothing."

"Understood."

"Well, how is she doing otherwise?"

I choose my words carefully now, making sure I don't give her any ideas about how *I* feel about Lila. "Her physical progress is outstanding considering she started with zero experience in self-defensive fighting. She makes an honest opponent out of Ben Whatever-his-last-name. I couldn't tell you how the magic stuff is coming along, but she seems to work well with Lorenzo."

"Very well. I would like to move her out from under your protection. I think it's time for us to let her blossom."

"What does that entail?"

"She needs to learn how to defend herself. You and Rachel won't always be there to do it for her. She needs to learn how to know who to trust. She needs to learn how to protect and use her magic wisely. She needs to learn how to control it." The amount of passion she has about the subject leads me to believe Finch knows more than she is letting on.

"She'll get there," I defend. "She's working on all of that right now. She's getting stronger and smarter, she just needs more time and practice."

"She needs to get there faster. She needs to be pushed harder." Finch doesn't leave much room for negotiation.

"What kind of push?"

"We need to put her in more dangerous situations," she says decidedly.

"Excuse me?" I'm being as agreeable as I can, but this is getting ridiculous.

"We've been too easy on her. She doesn't understand the danger she is in." Has she lost her damn mind?

"What the hell are you talking about?" I demand. "Either you're crazy or there's something you're not telling me."

Colonel Finch puts her head in her hands and sighs. "There are rumors of disturbances that are getting closer to the city. Small groups of Necromancers practicing dark magic. Three bodies have turned up, believed to be the missing Necromancers that were taken as children. No good can come if this, Ryker. They are going to come for her soon."

There is nothing that could have prepared me for what she was going to tell me. I have to sit down while I process the information. "How long have you known about this?"

Finch does not answer immediately, which only fuels my anger more. I bite my tongue hard to keep myself from lashing out. "The first incident was within the week of Lila's arrival-"

"Damn it, Finch. You didn't think I needed to know about it sooner? Why in the hell would you think that's a good idea?"

"It appeared random, a fluke. It was far from the city, looked like a bunch of kids playing with magic and took it too far." She shakes her head, like she's calling her own bullshit.

I run my hands through my short hair, rub my eyes, and scratch my chin, trying to figure out what to do with this news. "Okay." I stand up. "Okay, I'll take care of it. We'll train harder, I'll make her stronger. Her lessons with Lorenzo will be extended to the whole afternoon."

"Ryker." Finch tries to rein me back in.

"No. She's not getting hurt again because of you. You've done enough over the years, you all have. I'm taking over this case. I will get her where she needs to be and I'm not leaving her side from now on. I am one of the strongest soldiers here, I know what needs to be done, I will do it and nobody will get in my way. Do you understand?"

Lila looks as beautiful as ever. She's so happy today, probably the happiest I've ever seen her, and I'll have to be the one to ruin it. I can barely look at her during lunch. It's hard to be around her in public now. I just want to take her away from danger, wherever that is, and hold her all night and then spend everyday with her.

She touches my feet with hers under the table, which makes me nervous now that Finch thinks she's in love with me. I can't bring myself to make her stop, though, because everything about her makes me feel better.

After everyone finishes eating, Lila and I separate from Rachel and Ben. We're supposed to be headed to Lorenzo's office but instead I lead her out of the Headquarters building and into the training mountains, hoping they will be vacant.

"Ryker? What's the matter?" Lila struggles to keep up with my pace. "Where are we going?"

I don't stop and turn around until we're several feet into the mountain forest, out of anyone's view.

"Hey." Lila puts a hand on each of my arms. "Tell me what is going on."

"I can't lose you, Lila. I just got you and I barely have you, I can't lose you-"

"Hey, hey! You're not going to lose me. Talk to me, Ryker."

"Finch she- they're still after you, Lila. They're moving toward the city, they're coming for you. Finch should've told us earlier," I ramble on, not giving Lila a chance to catch up. "And Lorenzo knows about us. He told her. They're going to take you away from me and I'm not going to let that happen, I can't let-"

Out of nowhere, a hand slaps me across my face. I look at Lila, too stunned to speak. She holds the hand that slapped me with her other hand, as if to chastise it. "Sorry."

I frown and instinctively move my hand up to hold my face.

"I didn't know how else to shut you up."

"I can think of several nice ways," I mumble.

"Sorry," Lila repeats sheepishly. "You were stressing me out and I just- I don't know. Anyway, what do you mean they know about us?"

"Lorenzo can feel how you feel about me, apparently."

Lila's cheeks turn bright red. "H-how?"

"He's an emotion detector I guess, supposedly it's a Necromancer thing. He told Finch about it and now she's suspicious."

"So they know how *I* feel, not that it's mutual."

"Well, yeah-"

"Who cares? That's not a big deal. I'm sure a lot of people are attracted to you." Lila shrugs it off. "We'll be more careful and they won't find out, okay?"

I let out a sigh of relief. "Okay."

"Now tell me about who's after me and what Finch should've told us earlier," she requests, much more politely to me than I was with Finch.

"There are Necromancers using illegal magic, just like the time that Connor's mission found you. They started after you arrived back at Headquarters and they're getting closer to the city, closer to you, and more frequent. Something bad is coming."

Lila nods slowly as she takes in the information. "Well that's inconvenient," she says lightly.

"Finch wanted to put you in more dangerous situations so you'll be better prepared to defend yourself. I told her she was crazy and that I'm taking over your case and I'll decide how to best train you."

"Woah." Finally, an appropriate response from her. "How'd she take that?"

"She agreed silently. She's all freaked out about it so I don't know if she even heard me."

"So what are we going to do to get me ready?"

"Starting today, you're going to be working much more with Lorenzo, with focus on defensive magic first and then we can go from there. Starting tomorrow, our training plan goes out the window. I'm going to get you new opponents to fight with who will not go easy on you."

She nods again, definitively, then reaches for my hands. "We're going to be okay, Ryk."

Why in the world is *she* comforting *me* right now? "I can't lose you, Lila," I tell her again.

"You won't," she says confidently. "You're going to train me so that you'll never have to worry about that."

I read up on some of Lorenzo's magic textbooks during his and Lila's lesson. They are very interesting and I'm surprised they never made us learn half the stuff in these. Soldiers should know how much power Necromancers have so they know who they're up against.

Lorenzo spends the session trying to get Lila's magic to work. He gives her different scenarios to imagine so that she'll have emotional reactions to them and hopefully respond with magic, but to no avail.

"We need to try something else, this isn't working. I would like to create a situation with magic so that it feels more real. Then, we can try to get your magic going."

"How is that different from what you've been trying and failing to do all afternoon?" I blurt.

"Instead of telling her to imagine it, I'm going to make her see it. With my magic," Lorenzo replies, peeved by my lack of faith in him.

"You're going to make her hallucinate? No!" I stand up suddenly from the chair I've been reading in.

"Ryker." The way Lila looks at me stops me in my tracks. I swear I'd do almost anything for this girl. "He's trying to help, remember? I need to learn how to use my magic and Lorenzo knows how to teach me. I'll be fine."

Lorenzo keeps his focus on Lila, agitating me even more. I begrudgingly return to my seat and allow him to continue, closely watching his every move. His arms wave rapidly in the air, twisting at the wrist as he creates a scene. Everything looks the same to me, but I can tell by Lila's expression that she is seeing something different.

It bothers me that I don't know what she's seeing as she stands up and spins, looking around at her new surroundings. I watch as her faces turns from wonder to horror.

"Ryker?" she calls out as she stares into a wall.

"I'm right here," I tell her calmly.

"She cannot hear or see you," Lorenzo warns.

"Ryker! Watch out!" Lila starts running towards the wall. Luckily Lorenzo is paying enough attention to cast some sort of spell to keep her body in one place before she knocks herself out.

"Lila, use your magic. It's the only thing that can help him now." Lorenzo half whispers into her ear.

I struggle to keep my composure as Lila calls out for me, terrified of whatever is happening in her hallucination.

Lila lifts up her shaky hands and sparks fly between them. Tears well up in her eyes as she strains to save the imaginary me from whatever danger lies ahead.

"I can't do it!" she shouts desperately.

"Lorenzo-" I move towards them but he freezes me in place too.

"Focus, Lila," he tells her calmly. Why can she hear him and not me?

A few more sparks sprinkle the air between Lila's hands until finally a small purple flame catches. A small gasp escapes her throat as she keeps the flame steady.

I unintentionally hold my breath as she warps the flame with her hands and throws it against the wall, valiantly defending me from my fictional attacker. Lila's face relaxes and I'm filled with pride as I realize she won the battle.

"Ryker." She starts walking toward the wall again, a worried expression on her face. Before she can get to me, though, her head snaps around to the opposite direction. She's now facing Lorenzo's office door, horrified yet again. "No!"

TWENTY-NINE

Lila

Ryker strokes my hair as I lay on his chest, silent tears rolling down my face. I came straight back to my room after the extra long and painful lesson with Lorenzo today, Ryker following close behind me.

As soon as we got through the doorway, I crumbled on the floor. Within only a few seconds, Ryker picked me up like he would a small child throwing a temper tantrum, and placed me on his lap as he sat on my bed. As I calmed down, we stretched out until I got in my current position, with my whole body laying on top of Ryker's.

They're trying to make me stronger, I know, but I don't know if I can repeat today.

I see Ryker get on his phone but can't bring myself to care enough to find out why. The visual of him being attacked by that vicious monster while he lay helpless on the forest floor is hard to remove from my brain.

"Can you tell me a good story?" I whisper my request.

Ryker kisses the top of my head, warming my soul a couple of degrees. "There once was a princess who lived in a castle all alone. She was absolutely beautiful. Her body and mind were covered in scars that proved just how strong she was.

"Anytime she left her castle, the demons would come crawling. They came to torment and defeat her, and while they occasionally made a mark, they never won. She was mightier than any demon and the strongest of all warriors.

"After lots of time alone, the princess found a humble fellow. He was not a prince, he had no ties to royalty at all, but he loved the princess. He fought for her, and despite hundreds of princes, kings, and warriors also trying to get her attention, the princess ultimately chose the humble warrior."

"Was she happy?" I ask curiously.

"The happiest she'd ever been. The humble warrior became the princess's family. They fought side by side until the demons finally conceded. At last, the princess and humble warrior could live happily ever after in their beautiful castle."

"That *is* a good story," I say approvingly. I tilt my head up to look Ryker in the eyes.

"I think so." He smiles back at me, eyes sparkling more than ever. He slowly brings his lips to mine, kissing me softly. "Do you feel better?"

"I do, actually." I'm pleasantly surprised by the genuinity I can put into my voice. "I think I'd like to shower. That lesson was far more physically demanding than I expected. Will you stay?" I plead with my eyes.

He takes a small breath before he responds. "Maybe I should get Rachel to stay with you tonight."

Ouch, that came out of nowhere. "Seriously? Why?"

"Please don't be upset with me, Lila, okay?" He reaches for my hand.

"Do you feel like I'm pressuring you to-" I start defensively.

"No," Ryker responds quickly. "I just want to be respectful of you."

I carefully examine his face. He's being serious. "What does that mean? You're always respectful of me."

"I don't ever want to make you feel like I'm using you, or that I want you for... I want you to always feel safe with me. In order to accomplish that, we need to set boundaries, take things slow. You have a lot to deal with right now, and I don't want to complicate things anymore than they are now." He speaks as if he's not really saying what he wants to say.

Does he mean that he doesn't want to spend so much time with me? Or is he worried that I want to seduce him in my bedroom?

I'm sure I look silly and slow-witted as I think of how to respond. "In that case, do whatever you think is best. I'm going to rinse off and get ready for bed." His face mirrors my confusion and instead of trying to explain and ask for more expansion on where he's at, I just accept the awkwardness and push past him to get to the bathroom.

The hot water of the shower is exactly what I need to release the chaos that was today. I stand in its stream for longer than necessary, letting every negative thought roll off me and swirl down the drain.

As I dry myself off with my towel, I realize that I never fully closed the bathroom door. I guess I've gotten used to having my own room. I slap my forehead with my palm. *So much for convincing Ryker that you're not seducing him.*

When I finish getting dressed, though, I let myself off the hook, seeing as Ryker is nowhere in sight.

I snap my sketchbook shut at the faint sound of a knock on my door.

"It's me," a voice calls from the other side.

I've fallen for that before, so I just respond with, "Come in." Anyone who has a key is safe.

Ryker opens the door with one hand, the other full with two bags and a drink. Curiosity sits me upright on my bed, eager to learn why he's back and what he's brought with him.

He must know, because he drags it out longer than acceptable, practically making me beg for the reveal. I refuse to give him the satisfaction.

"Thought maybe you were gone for good when I came out and didn't see you."

"Just wanted to make sure you ate something." He turns around, revealing the contents of bag number one- a cheeseburger and fries.

A shame-worthy noise escapes my throat as I reach for the greasy food. It's been so long since I've eaten something so simple, it almost brings tears to my eyes.

Ryker's mouth stretches in a wide grin upon seeing- and hearing- my reaction. "You will not starve on my watch, Lila Martin."

He hands me the food and sticks close to watch me eat the first few bites. I didn't even realize how hungry I was.

Halfway through the burger, Ryker is satisfied enough to turn back to the rest of his belongings. My eyes fall down his spine and I'm not sure I look away fast enough when he turns back to me.

"This is also for you," he says, holding up a smaller, sleeker bag.

I finish off the last bite and wipe the excess grease and sauce off of my mouth, then clean my hands the best I can with the last napkin. I extend my hands and Ryker gently puts the bag in my open palms.

Inside, I find something that looks like a wristwatch, a replica of Ryker's phone, and some sort of... belt? Ryker is amused at my apparent ignorance.

"Are you going to clue me in or do you want me to just pretend I understand what's going on?"

He lets out a soft chuckle and moves to stand close to me. He picks up the belt first. "This is a utility belt of sorts. You can use it to store weapons, any magic-related instrument, assuming they exist. Anything you need to stay safe can be kept right here."

"Very handy," I remark.

The phone is next. "This is a device that can be used in a lot of ways, but primarily for making calls. I have already programmed myself, Rachel, and Finch into it, so you can contact us whenever you might need it. You open it by inputting a security code, face scan and fingerprint. Like most of our devices, these are individualized to your needs. We can set it up together."

I nod once to show that I understand and am still paying attention.

"Last but not least." Ryker holds up the watch. "This has GPS and a heart rate monitor. It can be useful for training, but I mostly want you to use it because if your heart rate spikes, it will notify me and send me your location. If I'm ever not with you and something happens, I will know and get to you as soon as I can," he promises.

I know he's being sincere and taking the necessary precautions to keep me safe, but I can't let the tension build too much. "I am *not* wearing that while we make out!"

He is mortified for only a second before he laughs and pushes my shoulder. "You are such a perv."

I'm glad to have lightened the mood, if only momentarily.

"Lila?" He avoids my eyes.

"Ryker?" I try to get him to look at me.

"I know you probably don't want to hear it, but I just need to apologize for earlier. My lack of self-control has nothing to do with you and I'm sorry if I made you feel responsible for any of my past, current, or future actions." He pauses and I wonder if he's done. "I will control myself because I want to be with you all the time. I never want to take my eye off you. I refuse to let anything happen to you."

I pull him in for a firm kiss to express everything I cannot put into words. I release him and he reluctantly lets me.

"I appreciate the sentiment, but you cannot protect me twenty-four seven." Ryker tries to argue but I cover his mouth with my hand. "That being said, I want to be with you as much as you'll let me."

I raise my eyebrows. "But I have to warn you, the more you talk about control and boundaries, the more I want to seduce you," I tease mercilessly.

Ryker rolls his eyes, but it seems more flirty than anything else.

We meditate first thing in the morning, per Ryker's request, in order to 'start our day with a good mindset' or whatnot. Honestly, he went on and on for so long that I just said yes so he'd stop talking about it.

Had I known how physically, mentally, and emotionally exhausting my day was going to end up, I would have taken it more seriously.

Instead, I roll my eyes, sigh here and there, and peek when I'm sure Ryker's eyes are closed. I'm sure he knows I wasn't doing it wholeheartedly, but he kept trying nonetheless. While I was pouting, Ryker was focused, reciting mantras and humming. Maybe that's why he's so grounded.

Breakfast goes about the same as usual, nothing out of the ordinary. But as soon as we finish, the day becomes a never-ending hell. Training is three times as long as usual and Ryker gets everyone in the Training Building to fight me. Okay, not *everyone*. But it feels like it.

I have to keep reminding myself that he's trying to protect me by making sure I'm prepared to defend myself when the time comes, in case something happens to him that separates us. By the end of training, it doesn't matter enough to keep me from being angry.

I stomp back to my room, ignoring Ryker's attempts to console me. When we reach the door, I turn back and demand he leave me alone. I can tell my words hurt him, but I don't care enough at the moment to do anything about it.

The reflection that looks back at me in the mirror surely cannot be my own. My lip is split in two different spots, both bleeding uncontrollably, making it near impossible to rid my mouth of the copper taste. My right eye is swelling and the discoloration of what are sure to be gnarly bruises are already forming on my fair skin.

My left eyebrow is also bloody and it takes some cleaning to realize half of the hair is completely gone. I lose the desire to inspect the rest of my tired body. Instead, I leave the bathroom and lay down on the hard carpet floor next to my bed.

I wouldn't normally care about my bedding getting dirty, but I don't know how the laundry situation works here. Ryker brings me fresh sheets and clean Soldier gear every few days, but the last time was yesterday, and I don't want to sleep on bloody sheets for two days.

Not enough time passes before Ryker knocks on my bedroom door.

"Lila? Can I please come in?" He sounds apologetic, but maybe he's just muted by the door.

Unfortunately for him, I'm in no mood for an apology. I stand up from my uncomfortable position on the floor and swish water in my bloody mouth one more time before stepping out into the hall.

I start towards the dining room, pushing past Ryker as if he were invisible.

Being able to use my magic is indescribably empowering. It seems to fill the spaces between the broken parts of myself, replacing the void with beauty and light. Lorenzo has helped me recognize the difference between good and evil magic and I can feel the evil magic stored inside of me like a heavy stone.

In movies and books, magic always requires a spell or a wand of some sort. It's been interesting to find out that's not always the case. Of course, there are certain spells that need to be recited, others warrant a wand or another instrument which facilitates magic. Mainly, though, magic feeds off of emotion.

While I wouldn't declare myself comfortable wielding all the power I have access to, I am proud of myself for how far I've come in such a short time.

I know how to channel the emotion I'm feeling into power. My energy shifts and I feel it throughout my whole being. I used to get punished for expressing what I felt. I was taught from a young age to suppress things that made me seem uncontrollable. Adults always told me it was hard to find a placement for a crazy girl. If only they could see me now, turning their weaknesses into my strength.

Today, Lorenzo starts me out with some exercises. I am expected to hit targets- first still targets, then moving targets- with bursts of magic. Each time I miss, I have to start over.

Eventually, we move onto the harder stuff. Lorenzo makes me pull magic from objects, which requires an immense amount of focus. Then, I practice blocking Lorenzo from drawing on my magic.

Drawing on objects for magic feels like getting plugged into a power source. Electricity and light floods into me, making every inch of my body tingle.

Someone else attempting to draw on me feels more like a limb falling asleep. It's numbing, and yet, I can still feel pins and needles. I can't imagine how it would feel if Lorenzo were successful.

The one thing that keeps me motivated is Ryker. I sneak glances at him in between exercises and we almost always make eye contact because he is always looking at me first.

His gaze of admiration makes me feel ten times more capable than I've ever felt on my own. I was worried that him seeing me use magic might make him change his mind about me. It was new to me and I was insecure about it from the beginning. Having to put all of my emotions on display for Lorenzo was one thing. But letting Ryker see the absolute rawest parts of me was terrifying.

I also knew there's a lot of history between Soldiers and Necromancers and I guess I wondered if it was against their nature to get along. Like maybe him seeing me this way would disgust him or scare him off.

While that hypothesis could still be proven at any point, the way Ryker is making the butterflies in my stomach go mad almost guarantees that if we ever split, it'll have nothing to do with nature.

THIRTY

Ryker

Lila leads the way back to her room without so much as a word or a glance in my direction. She hasn't said anything to me since this morning, unless you count after training when she told me to leave her alone.

If I told you I knew why she's ignoring me, I would be lying. Though, I do wonder if it has anything to do with how many times she's caught me looking at her today. I can't help myself, she's like a hurricane- beautiful and powerful, and while she might be dangerous, it's impossible to peel your eyes off her.

She must be exhausted after today. I trained her harder and longer than ever, and she barely had a break before Lorenzo did the same. I don't know if using magic is energizing or draining, but it seems Lila got a second wind during her lesson with Lorenzo.

I look at my watch and realize the dining hall is going to close for the day in less than half an hour. I hesitate before I mention it to Lila, but she's got to be hungry.

"Maybe we should get dinner first?" I brace for impact.

Lila checks the watch I gave to her last night and makes a sound. "Okay." She continues past her room, toward the dining hall.

I typically sit across from her so I can watch her back, unless Rachel is with us, but Lila intentionally sits next to me tonight. I don't budge, since dinner is almost over and most people have left, meaning there are few people to be wary about.

Besides, Lila's arm brushes mine each time she takes a bite of her food, and that's not something I'm willing to sacrifice right now.

Her pace slows on the way back to her room, and I match it so we are side by side as we walk. Lila scans the hallway, first in front of us, then where we just came from, making me nervous. Maybe she can sense something that I can't.

But when she faces forward again, she catches my hand, intertwining my fingers in hers.

My head spins embarrassingly fast, creating a smile on Lila's face. "Long day, huh?" she asks nonchalantly.

I pull her in for a headlock as she opens her door. She giggles at me, lighting up every part of my soul.

It's been way too long since I've heard her laugh. My new goal in life is to make her laugh every chance I get. Starting now.

As soon as the door is closed and locked behind us, I grab both of Lila's arms with my left hand, and use my right hand to tickle her mercilessly. She's hysterical as she attempts to escape my attack, which, of course, only encourages my behavior.

"Ryker!" She manages to scream in between gasps of air.

When I ignore her plea for freedom, she swings her knee into my crotch. My hands immediately release her and catch the ground as I fall to all fours. I hear Lila's voice but I can't focus on anything aside from the burning pain filling my groin.

I certainly didn't see that coming. If I weren't feeling so much pain, I'd be proud of Lila for being able to take on a man my size. She really has come a long way.

After several minutes of writhing, I feel Lila's fingers scratching my back soothingly.

"Are you okay?" She asks regretfully.

I slowly push myself to my knees, grunting quietly through the lingering ache. Once I'm up, I can see Lila is on her knees beside me, concern plaguing her face.

"Nice shot," I say through half-gritted teeth. My ego is not so fragile that I can't acknowledge her victory.

"I'm so sorry!" she laments, frantically flicking her eyes from my face to my pants, unsure of how to help.

"Lila." I wait for her to focus back on my eyes. "I'm fine."

I chuckle under my breath when her face remains serious. "That was a powerful hit, I'm truly impressed. I've trained you pretty well, but that was all you."

A smile sneaks onto her face. "Can I… do anything?"

Intrusive thoughts push to the forefront of my mind as I consider what to say. Eventually, the angel on my shoulder wins. "Nah, don't worry about it. I'll just sit while you do whatever you need to do." I wave my hand towards the bathroom.

"Sure." She helps me up into her desk chair. She goes through the bathroom door, runs water, then returns shortly after with a glass of water. "Here."

The gesture brings a small smile to my face. I can't remember the last time I was taken care of by someone else. "Thanks."

"I'm going to shower and change and everything… If you're sure you're okay?" Her eyebrows pull together once more.

"Go shower, you smell awful," I tease.

Lila pushes my shoulder before she spins around and enters the bathroom. I force myself to avert my eyes from the space of the open door. I briefly consider calling out to let her know that she forgot to close it all the way, but I don't want to embarrass her.

Instead, I'll do what I've done the last three times it's happened: pretend I don't notice and leave the room when I can't take it any longer.

The steam of the shower flows through the crack in the door and now I desperately need a distraction. Luckily, Lila's magic textbook is within reach. I open the book and a small yellow paper falls out. It has Lila's name at the top of one side but is otherwise blank. I'll have to ask her about it later.

I flip to the page of the book where the note was placed. Its title 'Locking Magic' grabs my attention. I skim through the next two pages, learning that there is a way to lock magic so that others cannot pull energy or power from someone else. Did Lorenzo specifically mark this for Lila? We talked about it during her first lesson, why would he be secretive about it?

In the midst of my investigation, I must've missed the sound of the shower being turned off. Lila walks through the door with only a towel wrapped around her body, covering the space between the top of her chest to the middle of her thighs. Just like that, I can't remember looking at anything other than her.

"Sorry," Lila says sheepishly. "I forgot my clothes." She tiptoes quickly to her closet, leaving a trail of water marks on the floor from her dripping hair and half-dried feet.

I know I need to look away, but I can't seem to get my eyes to follow along. *Blink, Ryker. Just blink and then keep your eyes closed.* Though I know she's all I'll see with my eyes closed anyway.

When she turns back toward me, her cheeks are bright red. She offers an awkward smile as she slips back into the bathroom. This time she closes the bathroom door tightly.

I'm absolutely screwed. I absentmindedly put Lila's book and note back on the desk and stand up to leave, only to realize- *oh shit.* I can't go anywhere like *this.* The bathroom door wriggles and I drop back down in the chair, covering myself with her textbook.

Lila's eyebrows wrinkle together as she witnesses the end of my embarrassing coverup. "What happened?" *Smooth, Ryker.*

"Uh, nothing, I was just-" *replaying the vision of you in a towel.* "Have you read this?" I point to the book in my lap.

"Not yet. Why?" Her eyes narrow but the rest of her hasn't moved from the doorway.

"I just saw this section about how you can hide your magical footprints from other mystical creatures-"

"Show me," she cuts me off, walking toward me.

I search for the page with clammy hands and a racing heartbeat. Of course I closed the book without the piece of paper in it. Lila lifts the book up into her hands, and while searching for the page, she plops diagonal onto my lap. I unconsciously bring my arms around her, as if to keep her from slipping off, causing her eyes to widen and the corners of her mouth to turn up.

She quickly buries her expression, though, and pretends to search for the pages that I'm not entirely sure exist anymore. Alarms are going off rapidly in my brain, making me overly aware that the same girl I just saw in a towel is sitting on my lap. And she smells fantastic. Clean and floral. Weird, since all the soap at Headquarters is the same and doesn't smell this sweet.

"This one?" Lila crashes my train of thought, shifting her shoulders so I can better view the book in her hands.

I intentionally hold very still and keep my voice low when I confirm, in an attempt to conceal my uneven breath. "Yep."

"That's weird," Lila says, confused.

"Hm?" I think I'm tipsy from being so close to her.

"The parts that are circled. It looks like a message of some sort." She's no longer flirting with me, she's skipping through the pages rapidly. "I don't understand."

Her words sober me up. "Wait, what circles?" I peer around her shoulder and just see regular pages. She points her fingers in three different spots. "I don't see anything."

The dots finally connect and I get the yellow paper from its spot on the desk. "What do you see on this?"

Lila makes a sound as my arm reaches around her waist and she sees the piece of paper for what must be the first time. "It's from Lorenzo. He's warning me…" She trails off.

That sentence does something weird to my stomach. "Warning you about what?"

Lila stashes the yellow paper in its original spot to mark the section then closes the book, shifting her weight on my legs until she is facing me. "I'll have to look into it a bit more, but don't worry." She leans in until her mouth is only an inch from mine.

"Stop trying to distract me," I accuse, leaning my forehead against hers to cut the building tension that hovers in the space between our lips.

This makes Lila laugh softly. "I *am* trying to distract you, as a matter of fact." She laughs again and brings her hands to each side of my face. "It's not something that you should worry about. I need you to trust me on this, please. Lorenzo is trying to tell *me* something and he did it this way for a reason. He doesn't want anyone else to know."

Her words do not ease my uncertainty in the least. I don't appreciate the secretiveness behind his messages, he could be trying to take advantage of the connection they have. What would he try to protect her from that he wouldn't want me, her bodyguard, to know about? I refuse to let it go, but there's not much to do about it tonight.

Lila asks me to sleep in her bed with her and I compromise by bringing the mattress from my room to her floor. I lay with her, scratching her back until she falls asleep. Then I slip out from under her and onto my own mattress. I'm glad I thought of it, because I wasn't sure I could take another night sleeping in her desk chair.

I'm determined to make morning meditation part of our training routine, even if Lila huffs and puffs through the entire attempt. At least she's improved since yesterday morning. Even still, she gets bored after only a few minutes and starts talking about random things.

What do I think they're going to serve for breakfast? How many countries have I been to? Am I sure I can beat her in a true match? And so on.

My time alone with Lila comes to an end way sooner than I'd like as we head out for the day. Breakfast and training seem to go by much faster than normal and I can't help but feel like time is running out. It scares me much more than I anticipated when I first accepted this mission. A lot has changed since then.

Lila and I haven't spoken much since leaving her bedroom this morning and I wonder if maybe she feels it, too. Rachel joins us for lunch and, unfortunately for me, Lila invites her to tag along the remainder of the day.

When we get to Lorenzo's door, Rachel takes a seat in the hallway. I move to open the door for Lila but she gets in my way.

"Ryker, I need you to get something for me." Her eyes move quickly, searching my face for some kind of reaction.

"What is it?"

"Something I left in my room. Will you go get it please?" The way she's asking makes me start to worry.

"I'll have Rachel get it-"

"No, I need *you* to get it." Her big eyes are trying to tell me something, but what?

"You're not going in there without me," I shut her down and move my hand toward the door handle. She intercepts me.

"Ryker." Her voice warrants attention. "Rachel, could you give us a minute please?" I don't even realize she's looking at us until Lila talks to her. She hurries around the corner, leaving Lila and I alone in the corridor.

Lila's eyes are fierce and her body language is firm, planted in front of the door. "Ryker, do you trust me?" The question is so intense that I dread whatever is coming next.

I can barely answer. "Of course I trust you, but-" I shake my head.

"I promise everything will be okay. It might not seem like that all the time but everything will be fine. I just really need you to trust me, okay?"

"Why does it sound like you're saying goodbye to me, Lila?" My question comes out frantic and angrier than I intended to speak to her, but I feel like I've lost all control in a matter of seconds.

"Ryker, look at me." She lifts her soft hands to my face, anchoring my attention to her magical eyes. "I promise I will be okay and I will see you soon."

She must see the distress in my expression because she pulls me down and gets on her toes to kiss me tenderly. Then she lifts her mouth to my ear and whispers quietly, "I need you to look at something in my magic book." When she pulls back, she stares intently into my eyes until I nod my head.

She releases her hold on me but watches me until I turn the corner toward her room.

Everything looks exactly the same as when we left this morning. I take a seat in her desk chair and try to dissect what just happened. Why would Lila tell me I can't go in with her when just yesterday we realized how much danger she is in.

The memory of last night plays through my head while I sit in this chair. I can't stop thinking about Lila being on my lap, her heartbeat pulsing through every part of her that came into contact with my body. But there is something else I'm supposed to remember.

I look at the contents of her desk. Everything is placed the same as last night, but the magic textbook draws my attention. She didn't get the chance to read it any more. So, she's either in danger and it's because I distracted her from this stupid book, or she understood more than she let on last night and she's trying to be brave.

My hands flip through the book again, unsure of what I'm searching for. Whatever messages are in here are still hidden from me. Lila's sketchbook is also on her desk. While it might be reasonable to go through it, I decide against invading her privacy until I have no other option.

What are you trying to tell me, Lila?

I hold her textbook upside down and flip through the pages. After only a few seconds, a note with my name on it falls to the desk.

I don't have enough time to fully digest and understand her words. My stomach sinks and I find myself running through the building. I don't know if it's my speed or the shock that makes me feel like I'm flying. *Please, no.*

Ryker,

I know how confused and frustrated you must feel. Please know that I do trust you and you can still trust me. I can't fill you in yet, mostly because I am not certain how things are going to play out. Know that I will be okay and I promise I will be back in your arms soon.

If anyone asks, tell them I asked you to leave me alone for my lesson with Lorenzo.

The truth is, the necromancers are going to take me. I know that sounds scary but Lorenzo has prepared me mentally and you have prepared me physically for this.

I am strong Ryker. The necromancers will most likely underestimate me.

Take care of yourself, Headquarters is not as safe as we thought. Be looking for my signal- you'll know it when you see it.

Be careful. See you soon.

Xoxo Lila

THIRTY-ONE

Lila

After Ryker leaves, I take a deep breath and enter Lorenzo's room. I'm surprised to see Lorenzo sitting down like any other day I've come to his office. I have a split second to relax before a shadow crosses behind him and the nerves return to my stomach in a knot.

The shadow is a woman with dark features. She's round despite being taller than average.

"Hello, Lila." She says my name as if she's said it a million times before. She wears a serious expression, surely meant to intimidate me, but it's not quite doing the job. Though, Lorenzo looks as if he's seen a ghost.

"Hello," I respond formally. "My apologies, I didn't know Lorenzo was going to have company." It's not entirely true though, Lorenzo warned me about this very situation. I wasn't necessarily expecting it so soon, but I could feel the difference in energy from outside his office.

"Do you call all your instructors by their first name?" The lady squints her tiny eyes at me, baffled by the idea. It would make me laugh under different circumstances.

"No," I say with a polite smile, trying to appear casual and collected. "Excuse me for interrupting." I begin to turn around, forcing the broad, over-confident woman to stop her charade and get to the point of her presence.

"I'd rather you stayed," she says plainly, regaining control. "I am not visiting Mr. Sosa, in fact, I have come to see you, Lila. I am

Mr. Sosa's superior, and your case has piqued my interest. Come, sit."

I'm not usually steps ahead of anyone else. Lately, I've been the last to know anything, including truths about my own life. But I know this woman is going to take me away from everyone that has become important to me. I know that she is a powerful Necromancer, with less than honorable intentions.

Unfortunately, I don't know where she is going to take me or what she is going to do with me, leaving me vulnerable to the element of surprise.

I approach the table and reach my hand out to her, "Nice to meet you, Miss…?" She may have an advantage, but so do I. I know more than I'm letting on and I'm stronger than she knows.

"Jaquelin Warner," she says as firmly as she shakes my hand. "I understand you have a complicated past with both Headquarters and magic." Her tight expression leaves no room for debate.

I chuckle softly to break the tension. "Yeah, I guess you could say that."

She isn't humored but she offers up a thin smile. "I'd like to see what you're made of."

My heart skips a beat. It's happening. My eyes unintentionally flicker to Lorenzo, whose expression confirms my suspicion. "Um, okay," I try to keep my voice light. "What would you like me to do?"

"I'd like you to come with me to Necromancer Homebase. We'll see where you're at with Necromancy and show you a few things."

"You don't trust Lorenzo to do a good job training me?" I try to keep my voice from shaking.

Jaquelin forces a tight and ingenuine smile. "I'm sure Mr. Sosa has done a fine job. But you are an anomaly. Most Necromancers start in Necromancy school at a young age. You, however, are behind in every possible way. This is a disservice to you, as well as to the rest of our Necromancer population. You need to be properly trained."

I swallow hard and wonder if it was loud enough for Jaquelin and Lorenzo to hear. There's no getting out of this. I can feel that truth in my bones. There is no escaping Jaquelin's grasp. I have two choices: fight and risk myself, Lorenzo, Rachel, and Ryker, or go in peace and trust that I can take care of myself. It's an easy choice.

Traveling through the portal was an extremely unique experience. I imagine drugs might be the only other thing that would affect the body in such a way. I could *feel* my body move through space and time for a short couple of seconds. Lights flash and my limbs tingle until we arrive at our destination- the building that Jaquelin calls Necromancer Homebase.

It's not run-down, per se, but it does feel like it should be found in a less than nice area of town. I play along as Jaquelin walks me through. Not a single person is in sight as I follow her from room to room, learning what they use each for.

Before Headquarters, I would've thought this was pretty big for an office building. But Headquarters has some of the biggest buildings I've ever seen. If this is the Necromancers' version, why would it be so small? Why wouldn't they get a building at Headquarters?

It's lit up but somehow still feels dark, as if all the light is artificial. There is light coming through the windows that sprinkle the building, but all of the glass is opaque.

"Do you remember it?" I don't notice Jaquelin looking at me until she asks.

I almost give myself whiplash turning my head toward her. Did I hear her correctly?

"Every Necromancer comes here as a child. Some even live here while they attend Necromancy school." Jaquelin watches me carefully as I listen. Lorenzo didn't tell me how much I should disclose.

I stay on the side of caution and return my attention to the building, scanning my brain for any memories of it. I have to force the frustration down when nothing comes up.

"Follow me," Jaquelin says from behind me. "I'd like to go over some history with you."

She leads me to an office with her name on the door and points to the single chair in front of her desk. I sit down as she takes her seat behind her desk and pulls a folder from her desk drawers.

"I assume you were given some information about our complicated history with Headquarters. However, there are two sides to every war. Even now, when we are on peaceful terms with them, we are never treated the same.

"Necromancers are naturally blessed with many skills that other races of *homo sapiens* do not possess. They tend to covet our abilities. Historically, they've hated us, even killed us, in an attempt to steal our Necromancy for themselves. Unfortunately for them, that's not how it works. When we die, our magic dies with us.

"Hundreds of years ago, we got dangerously close to being extinct. Then the Queen got sick and the King hunted down Necromancers to save her. To be clear, the King had never ordered Soldiers to kill Necromancers, they had simply taken it upon themselves. Because of this, our people were in hiding when the King was in need. They barely found a Necromancer in time to save the Queen, but because they did, the King made a law against killing us.

"Over time, we gained our rights to safety, to property, and eventually, to peace and love. Our people could finally produce offspring without fear of them being killed. Within only a decade or two, the rising number of Necromancers started to cause panic for the people of Amaryllis. They began to require that we bless the Soldiers of Amaryllis as babies, making them stronger to ensure we would not use our magic to overthrow the government again.

"In schools throughout Amaryllis and Headquarters, children of Soldiers and Necromancers learn about how dangerous Necromancy can be and why it needs to be controlled," Jaquelin says bitterly.

I try to take the information with a grain of salt, knowing full well that Jaquelin intends to turn me against Headquarters. I do wonder how much of what she is saying could be true. Why didn't Colonel Finch tell me any of this?

"Well it *is* dangerous. I know firsthand how much damage it can do," I interrupt boldly.

"Lila, you have no idea how much potential you have. Your Necromancy protected you from harm. It is not dangerous unless provoked."

Maybe I'm supposed to shut my mouth and agree, I'm sure that's what she'd like me to do, but unfortunately for her, that is not who I am.

"In the wrong hands, though, it can be fatal. Many people perceive 'being provoked' in different ways. If someone calls me stupid, that wouldn't give me the right to curse them."

She raises an eyebrow at me. "We are not speaking of silly arguments from your civilian life, Lila."

"You think my life was silly? That I wasn't in situations that could have warranted magic, had I been taught to use it when I felt I was treated poorly?" I retaliate.

Jaquelin's face twists briefly before returning to its stone-like expression. "Fair enough. But you could have protected yourself in those situations if Headquarters hadn't isolated you from us."

Her choice of words unsettles me. "What do you mean by 'us'?"

She eyes me carefully before answering. "Necromancers."

"Who were they supposed to give me to? You?" I accuse.

Something shines behind her eyes at the thought. "Perhaps. Or maybe they could have tried harder to find your parents."

"If my parents knew where I was, they would have fought to get me back," I say valiantly. The truth is, I don't know if they would have. Nobody has ever talked about my parents. I have no idea if they're the kind of people to fight for what's right.

"It's getting late, you should get some sleep. We have a lot to do tomorrow."

"What about my parents? What happened to them?"

Jaquelin takes a controlled breath. "They were killed when you were young. Though it was never determined who was responsible. Headquarters claimed it was a rebel group of Necromancers, and the Necromancers argued it was Headquarters who killed them."

My chest feels tight. "But why?"

"Once the rumors got out that you had been recovered from the rebel Necromancers by Headquarters, your parents did fight to get you back. Two agents from Headquarters brutally killed them for retaliating."

I don't know why it hurts so much to hear that they're dead, since I've thought that for as long as I can remember. But now it's final. I know for sure I'll never see them again, and it's painful.

"Let me take you to your room."

I can't even tell what time of day it is with the weird lighting in the halls. Given that they still aren't populated, I assume it's late.

The room Jaquelin takes me to is half the size of my room at Headquarters and not nearly as bright. Headquarters' detainment cells are nicer than this. The bed is only a foot and a half off the ground, and hard as a rock. The bathroom doesn't have a door and consists of only a toilet and small shower.

I'm not a snob when it comes to living situations. I've lived in much worse places. But it's missing more than just a sink and a closet. And I don't know how I'm going to sleep without him.

Lila, you cannot trust everyone at Headquarters. I hope the Soldiers in charge of your safety are honorable. There are some among us that work with the rebel group. Soldiers and Necromancers alike. I wish I had names for you, but pay special attention to anyone who tries too hard to get close to you. In this chapter, you will find information about safeguarding magic. I was wrong about you, Lila. You were not created by them. They took you because you're different.

Please be careful.

Lorenzo

I wake up drenched head-to-toe in sweat. I look rapidly around the room- yes, I'm still alone. So why do I feel like I'm being watched?

I have no idea what time it is but the opaque light from my window leads me to believe that it's morning. Or at least that's what they want me to think. I begin the day with meditation and a quick workout in the limited space the room has to offer. Something tells me I'm going to need to stay in shape while I'm here.

Even though in some ways I feel more a prisoner here than at Amaryllis Headquarters, I'm slightly excited by the idea that once I'm ready for the day, I can leave my room by myself.

I hope you're not too worried about me Ryker.

As Jaquelin takes me through the day, I focus closely on the words she chooses, and even closer on everything she doesn't say. She is trying to recruit me. Of course, I assumed this from the beginning, but I didn't realize how carefully thought out her plan was going to be.

She finishes telling me about Amaryllis-Necromancer history, carefully spinning the information in a way to persuade me to subconsciously distrust the Amaryllis government. She's very specific about her wording surrounding the group of rebel Necromancers, never taking a position contrary to what a leader of the group might believe.

Jaquelin tells me she wants me to stay here, to learn everything I need to know about Necromancy. She wants to 'teach me the truth' about Necromancy, and the correct ways to use it. And, of course, she doesn't want me to taint my experience by philandering with 'outside forces.' Or, in other words, I'm being cut off from anyone I know and trust. Anyone that might help me.

I follow her lead to a small room that resembles a garage that doubles as a home gym. This room is stuffy compared to the Training building with its short ceiling, cement floors, and windowless walls.

"This is Norman, he'll be your trainer for the time being," Jaquelin gestures as the man enters the room. It's been somewhere between twelve and twenty-four hours since I've seen someone other than Jaquelin.

I must look as strange as I feel because Jaquelin has to say my name before I snap into action. I take a stride forward and reach my hand out to the man. "Nice to meet you."

His grip is not very intimidating and I wonder what exactly he's going to teach me. He is probably in his mid-thirties and looks like someone's next-door neighbor who works as a software engineer and has three kids that stay home with his wife. His unremarkable presence makes me second guess my beliefs about this place.

I'm not going to be rattled by one person, though. Whoever is pulling the strings chose Norman for a reason.

"Well, I'll leave you to it, then," Jaquelin says cheerfully. She spins around and exits the door we came through, leaving Norman and I alone in the room.

I decide to take the confident route. "What's on the schedule for today, Norman?" I ask sunnily.

"Well, what do you know how to do?" He turns the question back on me. Clever.

"Um, not much," I admit. "I can barely make a spark between my fingers." I let out a breathy laugh.

Norman offers a small, doubtful smile. "I'd like to start with some basic information. Do you know what magic comes from?"

Lorenzo didn't tell me whether I should hide my knowledge of Necromancy from them. I should act less powerful than I am, I suppose, but to what degree?

"It's fueled by emotion."

"Well, it can be, yes. But magic comes from the universe. Only some are born with the power to wield it, but magic can be found in any living thing."

"Even humans?"

"Yes. A powerful Necromancer can draw on energy from humans, other Necromancers, even nature. But this aspect of Necromancy comes at a cost. A human or animal contains only enough energy to keep them alive and functioning. If you were to draw magic from a human, you would incapacitate them at the very least.

"A Necromancer, on the other hand, has an abundance of power. They possess more than enough energy for survival. It takes much more to dry them out."

"So I can draw on other Necromancers' power? Why would I want to do that?"

"It is very painful to the donor. Because of this, drawing on the magic of your peers is forbidden in Headquarters. Outside of the law, Necromancers use this type of magic when they are performing a large ritual or spell that requires more power."

"Why would someone need to perform a spell that would require them to hurt someone else?"

Norman hums without an answer. "Do you know any spells or incantations?"

It was a smooth transition, I will give him that. "I don't believe that I do." While technically untrue, I have an inkling that the spells I learned at Headquarters are going to greatly differ from the ones I will learn here.

"Let's get started, then," Norman says decidedly.

For the next several hours, he pushes me to my absolute limit. I perform spell after spell, recite incantation after incantation. Norman does not let me stop until I collapse on the training room floor.

When I wake up, I am back in my dull room, laying on the top of the bed. Sitting up is taxing on my overworked body. The spellbook that Norman gave me is at the foot of bed, probably because there is nowhere else to put it in here besides the floor.

It takes me a few minutes more than I'd like to get myself up and out of bed. The only time I've experienced this kind of exhaustion is when I woke up in the Headquarters Infirmary. It must be the price of magic. Maybe it gets better with time and practice.

The sound of unfamiliar voices echoes through the hall as I search for food. I peek around each corner, trying to locate the owners of the voices.

"How do they know it's actually her?" One voice asks skeptically.

"Apparently she *feels* different. More powerful or something," the second voice says enthusiastically. Are they talking about me? Surely not, I've got to be the weakest Necromancer to ever walk the earth.

"Does Anna know yet?"

"Not sure, but I hope she doesn't make a scene when she finds out."

Both of them hum softly.

Who is Anna? Why would it matter to her more than anyone else? More importantly: who is going to answer my questions?

I walk around the corner nonchalantly, as if I weren't just eavesdropping. The two women stop talking altogether as I come into their view. Both simultaneously widen their eyes as they take me in.

I'm surprised how young one of them is. I wonder if she was voice number one or two. She is probably just a couple years younger than me. She is tall and has a sturdy build.

The other is probably in her late thirties. She is a skinny little thing. She has a handful of gray hairs peppering her light brown hair.

I greet them with a small smile and a curt nod of my head. "Hi, I'm Lila." I reach my hand out. Instead of shaking it, they both bow.

"Enchantress," the younger one blurts incredulously. Her voice matches the first one I heard, the skeptic.

It takes me a minute to realize they're referring to me. "Excuse me?"

The older one's eyes are filled with wonder and maybe fear? "You're the Enchan-"

She's cut off by my captor. "Ladies, back to work," Jaquelin orders.

Just like that, they snap back to reality and scurry off, disappearing around the corner.

I unwillingly turn to face Jaquelin. "Why did you do that?"

"I needn't explain myself to you, dear, but they have things to get done." Jaquelin says matter-of-factly. "Come." She then spins on her foot and walks the direction she came from. I guess she was looking for me.

I take four quiet deep breaths as we walk. *You cannot freak out on her yet, Lila.*

She takes me to an office that contains one table, three chairs, and a 'window'. There is a single plate of rice, beans, and chicken on the table. She can't be serious. She does look the part, though. I'm going to force the words out of her.

Jaquelin looks back at me expectantly. "Well," she sighs, impatient. "Sit. Eat. I'm sure you're hungry."

I give her my back before I roll my eyes and take a seat. She sits across from me while I eat, tapping incessantly on a large device. It looks exactly like an iPad but I'm sure they have another word for it here.

"Why did those girls call me Enchantress?" I ask bluntly, tired of playing Jaquelin's stupid game. I want answers and I'm going to get them. What else is the point of being here?

"That is a very important question, Lila. With a very important answer." She doesn't bother to look up from whatever she's doing. "I'm not sure you're ready for the truth."

I unexpectedly burst into laughter. *That* gets her attention. Her cross expression makes me laugh even harder. "I'm sorry-" more laughter. "It's. just. so. funny." My core aches.

"Stop it this instant!" Jaquelin demands, severely unamused by my behavior.

Eventually my roar settles into a cackle, then a giggle.

When I am finally capable of inhaling and exhaling a full breath, I lock my eyes with Jaquelin's. "It's just so funny to me how you think you saved me from my Headquarters prison, just to lock me up here. I came here looking for answers. Maybe you think I'm stupid, naive. And that's fine, I understand why you would. But, despite what you may believe, you did not lure me here. I drew you in until you couldn't walk away. You know who I am. I know I'm powerful, I know you need me. Now I just want to know precisely why."

By the look on her face, I've been successful in channeling an intimidating aura about me. There is a physical spark inside me, igniting my determination. There is nobody to hide behind here. Ryker can't help me, Finch can't feed me lies. I will find the truth. And nobody will get in my way. Jaquelin feels it, too.

THIRTY-TWO

Ryker

"You little piece of shit!" Lorenzo's shirt collar is bunched in both of my fists as I pin him against his office wall.

Rachel is trying to calm me down from behind, to no avail. "Ryker! You have to let him go!"

"Am I the only damn person who gives a shit about her?" My voice rumbles through Lorenzo's office. I change my death glare from Lorenzo to Rachel and back.

"Of course not!" Lorenzo laments. He's only saying it to get out of my grasp.

I have never in my life been filled with this much spite and disgust for a person. *"Where the hell is she?"* The air in my lungs burns on its way out.

Rachel must realize the severity of the situation, because she ceases to impede my current objective.

"J-Jaquelin h-" Lorenzo chokes.

I loosen my grip on his collar to let him finish.

He takes an overly dramatic breath and I almost close my hand around his throat this time. "Jaquelin has her. You don't understand, I couldn't get in her way or they would rush their plan. Lila is ready for this, Soldier. We prepared her for this." He holds my gaze firmly.

My hands release Lorenzo and fall to my sides, still clenched in powerless fists. "What do you mean? What are they planning to do with her?" My voice is finally evening out as well.

"I don't know exactly, but I know they need Lila. I was wrong about her, Soldier." He says the last words in a hushed tone, glancing at Rachel suspiciously. I take the hint.

"Rachel, will you wait outside, please?" I call over my shoulder. Lorenzo nods his head slightly.

There is a tense silence for less than a minute before Rachel huffs a tiny breath and leaves the room, closing the door behind her.

Lorenzo and I never take our eyes off of each other. "Lila seems to trust you quite a lot, so I'm going to go out on a limb and hope she was right to."

He starts pacing around his miniature library of an office. "Each Necromancer has a gift specific to them, to their magic. These gifts need to be embraced and practiced to be of any use to us, but even out of practice, Necromancers have a footprint, a way for other Necromancers to detect each other. But it's just a feeling, not a piece of DNA that can be identified by just anyone. This is one reason why we haven't been able to find the Necromancers responsible for the Rebellion. We can only recognize a magical footprint- if you will- if we come in contact with that same magic again.

"Obviously, within the Necromancy community, we tend to ignore these footprints to keep our community safe from, well, you." He shoots me a short apologetic look. "Not all of them, of course. Typically, we only ignore footprints for kids that use harmless magic that happens to be against Headquarters law. Obviously, your people have caught on to this to some extent, for which you have bred Headquarter Necromancers.

"Well, the irony is that there really isn't such a thing as an unbiased agent of the law. There are snitches and there are pushovers. Would you rather be a traitor to your people or to a government that oppressed you? It's a hard thing to navigate. If you haven't noticed, Headquarters has been choosing their own Necromancers. We don't get to vote for who represents us. They pick based on scores, supposed loyalty to Amaryllis, and whoever will best serve their desires.

"All that being said, in the last few years they've changed the Headquarter Necromancers a number of times. The Council is very distrustful of our kind. But some Necromancers have studied their game, the criteria they use to choose us, and they've begun to manipulate it.

"Whoever can trick Headquarters into believing they are wholeheartedly loyal to them, truly rules over all other Necromancers. They have more power than any of us. If they say you're guilty, Headquarters takes their word for it. If they take part in a crime…" Lorenzo waits for me to finish his thought.

"They can ensure they never get caught," I conclude, pensive. He's totally right. We're blindsiding ourselves because the Council sees Necromancers as inferior. We're making it possible for them to destroy us, from the inside out.

Lorenzo nods, as if he hears and agrees with each of my thoughts. "But they still need one thing. The key to total dominion. They have small numbers, and many types of magic are not possible within Amaryllis. They need to break the barrier and create half-bloods, who will be unfalteringly devout to their Creator's demands."

I take in Lorenzo's every word. My mind races trying to keep up with the overload of information. "What did you mean that you were wrong about Lila?"

"She's not a storage unit for them. I was wrong, I didn't understand. I was reading up on some old, religious texts from our history. Therein lies the tale- or prophecy, really- of one they call The Enchantress. It is believed that a child will be born of Necromancer parents, but with a special capacity to *absorb* magic. Without harming other Necromancers. Every Necromancer can pull on others' powers, but it is painful and highly illegal here. This may not have much significance to you, but it means that this child would have begun absorbing traces of magic as an infant and continue throughout her life, making her the most powerful Necromancer in history."

THIRTY-THREE

Lila

Everything is different now that I know who I am. I feel different, invincible. Jaquelin treats me differently, too. She knows I know how much authority I hold. She's the one who told me, after all.

And, really, she knew all along. But her demeanor has morphed from domineering to submissive. She no longer runs the show.

I've been released from captivity, not for the first time in my life, and I'm now able to interact with other Necromancers.

The first time I step foot into the cafeteria, I'm overwhelmed with the amount of eyes on me. Silly little me had thought it was bad at Headquarters, but it was barely a moment of Soldiers seeing someone new for the first time. This is exponentially worse. Everyone here knows exactly who I am, hence the stretched out silence and mumbled prayers.

I hurry to grab my food and I sit by the women I met just yesterday. Their eyes are in danger of falling out of their faces as I start eating.

"Hi again," I try to sound casual.

The younger of the two is the first to speak after what feels like an eternity of chaotic silence. "Genevieve." She stretches her right hand out to me and I take it gratefully.

"Lila," I introduce myself with a relieved smile.

"Are you uncomfortable yet?" Genevieve asks sarcastically. She has hazel-colored eyes and the same colored hair that she wears in two dutch braids.

I respond with a laugh under my breath.

Genevieve doesn't break eye contact with me as she introduces the other woman. "This is Nonni."

Nonni seems very matronly. She is a natural beauty, in a very simple and innocent way. She smiles shyly at me from across the table. "It's nice to meet you," she says softly.

"Likewise," I try to match her sweet tone.

All three of us smile at each other once more and then turn our attention to our food, ignoring the ogling eyes that still surround us.

It takes less than three minutes for my curiosity to get the best of me. "Who is Anna?" I don't think much of it until both Genevieve and Nonni's lips separate slightly, a funny look in their eyes.

Again, Genevieve is the first to speak, but not without looking around to see if anyone else heard me. "W-why do you ask?"

Did she stutter or did I imagine it? "I just heard y'all say something about her the other day. I may have been eavesdropping a tiny bit," I confess bashfully.

Genevieve and Nonni regard each other. "It's probably best if you ask her yourself. I'll take you to see her after your meal."

"Anna?" Genevieve says softly as we walk into the room.

A woman is sitting at a large table using what looks like a sewing machine, her back to us. When she hears her name, she spins around.

She greets Genevieve with a warm smile and a kiss on the cheek. She moves to Nonni and does the same. When she makes her way to me, though, her eyes go wide.

"Anna, this is Lila-" Genevieve starts.

"My baby!" Tears well up in her round eyes.

I shake my head, unsure of how to react. "I think you may be confusing me for someone else-"

"I could never forget you, my sweet angel." Anna latches onto my shoulders. "You have no idea how much I've lost trying to get you back."

"I- I don't understand-"

"You're my daughter, sweetheart. I'm your mother."

I shake my head again. She's crazy. Or manipulative. Maybe both. "No-" I want to tell her she's wrong, but my ears ring in a familiar way and my vision turns white.

It's magic and it's coming from Anna.

I see flashes of a mother looking down at her newborn baby, watching her grow into a toddler. I see a toddler tell her mom she loves her for the first time. I feel the love they share.

The room we are in spins as the visions dissipate. Someone is holding up my limp body until I can stand up again. I squeeze my teary eyes shut until the swirling of my vision halts.

"Now do you see?" Anna asks earnestly. "You're my baby."

We embrace in a messy heap of tears, snot, and joy. The last time I imagined meeting my birth family was when I was about eight years old. Since then, I knew it wouldn't happen. Not even the government knew who they were or if they were alive. Any lingering hope was lost when Jaquelin told me they were all dead just days ago.

As soon as I find my voice, I ask Anna, "What about my father?"

She pulls back and gives me an apologetic look. "He was killed several years ago."

"Killed? By who?"

A darkness shades her eyes. "Necromancers. Though anyone you talk to here will claim it was Headquarters agents. But I was there. I saw Jaquelin's predecessor, Roman, kill both my Robert and the Jordans."

It's a lot to take in, but my body goes frigid upon hearing the last name. "Did you say the Jordans?"

Anna catches something in my expression. "Yes, dear. They were the Headquarters Agents that tried to help us escape from this hellhole. The Necromancers who brought us here told us that Roman could help us find our Lilabug." She holds my face soothingly. "But they were unaware of the evil of this place. It didn't take long for us to figure out that Roman was responsible for taking you in the first place. They wanted to use us to lure you here. To force you to be their Savior.

"Jaquelin has done an excellent job in blurring the line between fighting for the rights we should have as Necromancers and sedition. The people here are being misled. I've tried to spread the truth, but I tend to get myself into trouble." Anna shows me her arms, whose skin is covered in long and skinny scars, possibly from a whip. I immediately feel protective of her.

"These are two of the good ones." She gestures to Genevieve and Nonni. "They shouldn't be here anymore than I should. And that Teresa. I didn't get the chance to speak to many others before they locked me up in here and convinced everyone I had lost my mind."

"Why are you allowed to come in here? Won't that make you guilty by association?" I ask the other two women.

"Genevieve is one of Jaquelin's star students," Anna says mockingly.

I look at Genevieve and she rolls her eyes at the comment. "I tested really high in Necromancy school," she explains. "I'm good with my magic and my parents were part of the rebel group already. Jaquelin chose me as her sidekick. I'm sure she's skeptical of me being around Anna, but I just have to talk about how crazy she is once I return to Jaquelin. She can't risk losing me until she's sure I'm not on her side."

I know how that feels.

"Nonni here is too quiet to make any trouble. And she's got a family. According to the Leaders, she wouldn't do anything that might get them hurt."

Nonni confirms with the nod of her head.

"And who is Teresa?" I ask.

"Teresa is newer. We had the same shift as her a few weeks ago and she's starting to latch onto the truth. We think her husband is the real skeptic."

"Shift?"

"The women sew clothing, cook, and nurse the ill and injured. We take shifts."

Who knew this kind of lifestyle still existed? Or that it was even legal? "And the men?"

"Well, they protect, of course," Anna sneers. The other two chuckle and I figure it must be a running joke amongst the community. Sexism is still alive and well.

A bell chimes in the hall and Genevieve grabs hold of my arm. "We've got to get you back to Jaquelin before she finds you with Anna."

"I can't just leave-"

"Lila," Anna consoles me. "Baby, you've got to go. It'll be alright. We'll see each other soon, I promise." She kisses me on the cheek and wraps me in a tight hug.

And just like that, I'm saying goodbye to my mom.

Nobody could have prepared me for coming here, despite their efforts. Learning that I am not just an outsider, but a key figure in the strange world of Amaryllis is dizzying.

Nothing could have prepared me to meet my mother. It was so different than I had always imagined it would be. But I never could have known what laid beyond my simple human life.

Anna and I didn't have the pleasure of going for brunch and catching up, getting to know each other. She had taken the time to show how much she cares about me, and to warn me about Jaqueline.

An overwhelming sense of inadequacy pulses through me as I consider the position I've gotten myself into.

Within weeks, I had gone from a slightly too-old college student and orphan with one friend, to a helpless Necromancer in a sea of Soldiers learning to trust again, and now a powerful figure of some alternate reality who couldn't be more alone.

I knew I couldn't trust Jaquelin. I knew when I laid eyes on her in Lorenzo's office that she had been exactly the type of person his note warned about. She was using me. But for what?

Everyone wants me on their side. I'm being manipulated at every angle. Not that I think Anna and Genevieve are lying to me. But I also can't know who is taking advantage of me. I can't be certain everyone at Headquarters wasn't doing the same as Jaquelin or anyone else.

I know that I can trust Ryker, though. It isn't logical. Making me fall for him would be a great way to recruit me. Somehow, though, I know our moments were genuine. I wish he could be with me now, to help me decide who to trust.

Nevertheless, he is not. I am alone.

The only thing I can rely on now is my gut. Something tells me to trust Genevieve. And she trusts Anna.

Quickly, I throw a plan together of how to finish this with the good guys on top.

First, I need to find Jaquelin.

THIRTY-FOUR

Ryker

"The Council has declared Lila a Traitor of Amaryllis." My stomach sinks as the words leave Colonel Finch's mouth.

It takes a minute for the words to sink in deep enough. We have failed her. Once again, we've turned our backs on her, leaving her to fend for herself.

Then, the anger sets in and my body acts before my mind has time to catch up.

My arms effortlessly fling one of Finch's office chairs against the wall, making a large hole. A loud noise is coming from my throat as my hand picks up the second chair, giving the hole in the wall a friend.

Two of Finch's guards force their way into the room, despite Finch telling them to stay outside when we arrived. Maybe in the midst of my breakdown, she called for them.

I've lost sight of Rachel, I'm not even sure she's still here.

I throw a few punches before the guards are able to pin me down. Once they get the upper hand, I give in and let them haul me to Lila's old cell.

As soon as they leave me alone and lock the door, I lose any remaining control over my emotions.

THIRTY-FIVE

Lila

Once the hallways grow quiet, I channel the stealth that the sexy characters in spy movies always use to steal an artifact or escape from prison. My feet are silent against the hard floor as I make my way through the eerie Necromancer building, searching for clues.

My heart beats aggressively in my chest each time I enter a new door. It feels as if there are shadows all around me, but each time I swivel my head around, I am alone. I have yet to hear or see another Necromancer out and about.

Before long, I hear noises, muffled voices, coming from the opposite side of two very large industrious doors. I've never been to this part of Homebase before. The light on the ceiling flickers slightly as I lean my ear to the door on the right.

Even pushing myself flush against it, I'm unable to decipher the words being said. *Think, Lila, think. You are supposed to be the most powerful Necromancer in history and you're going to let a door stop you?*

I wrack my brain for any kind of spell that could help. It has to be somewhat concealed so the individuals beyond the door can't sense the energy.

It comes to me. I hold my hands out in front of me, palms open to each other and focus my thoughts. *Discretion. Hearing. Block detection.* Once I'm confident that I have my magic controlled, I press both palms against the cool door.

"She's not strong enough."

"Why does it matter-"

"We have one chance!" Someone shouts. "If she doesn't make it to the end of the ritual, that's it. You can kiss your dreams goodbye."

"Watch your tongue."

A sigh.

I can't pick out whose voices the harsh argument belongs to.

"Can we not channel her Necromancy while she's unconscious? We take what we need to bring the Veil down and be on our way."

"Don't be so daft, Jaquelin," someone barks.

Jaquelin.

"Enough, Roman. You do not get to speak to me this way."

Roman.

"The Enchantress will need to be coherent, as she will need to be the Necromancer who performs the ritual."

"How will we know when it's been completed?"

There is a brief silence.

"We believe there will be a large eruption of light and force. Anything within a thousand meter radius will simply cease to exist."

He can't possibly mean-

"And what of the Necromancers that are involved? What will happen to the Enchantress, Norman?"

Norman.

"Their bodies will implode on impact."

A gasp escapes me as my lungs desperately suck in air. I hadn't realized that I was holding my breath.

"What was that?"

Crunching leaves tip me off that one of them is approaching the double doors my hands are pushing against. I cast a spell I learned from Lorenzo at my feet so I can run silently through the halls.

It takes me about four minutes to find my way back to my bedroom, taking only two wrong turns in this maze of identical hallways. As far as I can tell, nobody has followed me.

My right hand reaches for the handle, but it doesn't budge.

My door is locked.

How, I do not know. I wasn't aware it could lock. Especially from the outside.

Logic takes the back seat as the door handle rattles excessively in my hand.

"Come on, come on, come *on*!"

Footsteps sound from around the corner. Before I have time to react, a hand reaches out and pulls me into my room.

The same hand clasps on my mouth, the owner shushing me as several people walk past my closed door.

My eyes strain as I try to make out who is in my dark room. I can feel the energy of a Necromancer using magic on the other side of the wall I'm pushed up against. The two eyes staring back at me get wider.

I nod, agreeing to be quiet as the hand leaves my mouth, moving instead to the door. Light emanates from the palm and it illuminates its owner's face.

Genevieve.

The pounding in my ears softens.

When we're sure Jaquelin and the others have left, Genevieve releases herself from her protection spell. I throw my arms around her neck and squeeze tightly. It catches her off guard, but she's quick to process and reciprocate the spontaneous embrace.

"How did you know I would need you?"

"I came looking for you. Jaquelin was discussing the ritual earlier and it sounded like they were going to move forward with it soon. What happened to you?"

"After talking with Anna I felt like I needed answers. I waited until the halls were quiet and then I left to… well I didn't really have a plan but I found out what I needed to know."

Her eyebrows pull together. "What do you mean?"

"I heard voices by those big metal doors- where do those lead by the way?"

"Those are the only doors to get outside. Very few people have been through them or even been near them when they're opened. Jaquelin decides who gets clearance."

There is a way out. "Would you be able to open them?"

"Maybe," she answers hesitantly.

"The ritual will kill me and whoever is within one thousand meters, including the Necromancers that I need to pull energy from."

"Oh, *Lila*."

"How soon are they going to do it, Genevieve?"

She shakes her head but doesn't say anything.

"Genevieve! When are they planning to do it?"

"Day after tomorrow."

My chest tightens. "We have to leave tomorrow, then. As soon as we can get that door open."

THIRTY-SIX

Ryker

No amount of time makes my reality any easier. Granted, I'm not sure how much time has passed since Lila left. I don't even know how long I've been in this room. I barely sleep, so my perception of time ought to be skewed.

Occasionally, a guard will bring in food and then come back hours later to remove the untouched plate. I think I fall asleep at least once a day, but I'm not sure how long or if I've slept through a full night here.

I just lay here and hope that someone will wake me up from this nightmare.

"Hey, bro," a familiar voice says. I lift my head and see Liam in the doorway. I'm too stunned to react right away. "Let's get ya out of here, okay?"

We travel together to Amaryllis without so much as a word between us. Liam occasionally steals a glance in my direction, clearly unsettled by my silence and uncharacteristic behavior. It's not until we get seated at a small pub in the outskirts of the city that Liam finally addresses me head on.

"So do you want to tell me what the hell is going on with you or do you want me to just start guessing?" He holds two fingers up as the waitress approaches the table and just like that, she spins back towards the bar. This must be one of his spots.

"There's not much to say." I push my back against the wooden booth seat, crossing my arms across my chest.

"Yeah, I figured as much." Liam scoffs and leans forward, intertwining his hands and placing them on the table. "Why did you attack Colonel Finch?"

The question baffles me. "I didn't!"

"You destroyed her office, Ryker. What would you have me call that?"

"I lost my cool for less than a minute. I never touched a hair on Finch's head, and I never intended to."

"Well, she had to call her security detail to come and detain you, so clearly, it wasn't that simple. What brought it on?" I can see worry in his eyes and I hate that I'm the one who put it there.

I have to look away before I can answer him. "They declared her a Traitor."

"Ah shit, Ryk." He runs his fingers through his hair. "It's not your fault, bro."

I shake my head but can't bring myself to respond. Liam means well but there is nothing he can do or say to change the situation I've got myself into.

"Is that what this is?" His question begs me to meet his eyes. "You blame yourself? Ryker, you couldn't control every decision she made-"

"What? Liam, you have no idea what you're talking about."

"She manipulated you, that's what they do-"

"Stop!" Liam's mouth snaps shut. "She's not a Traitor. They took her, Liam. I was supposed to keep her safe and I didn't. That's not anyone's fault but mine."

The waitress quickly drops off two large drinks at our table before scurrying off. Poor thing. She probably deals with a lot of angry men who think alcohol will help. Liam looks at me strangely and I take a sip of my drink to avoid his gaze. Unfortunately, it's beer.

"So if she was that helpless, why did you leave her at all?" Liam's voice is calm, understanding. He knows the answer to his question, he just needs me to say it out loud. He wants me to say that *Lila* left *me*.

"It's not her fault. She thinks she's being brave." My breath shakes as I exhale. "She's going to get herself killed unless I can stop her."

"How close did y'all get, exactly?" His eyes drop when I look at him.

He knows me too well.

"Damn," Liam whispers under his breath. His left hand runs through his hair again as his right hand brings his beer up to his mouth. He chugs half of the large glass before continuing his interrogation. "Does the Council know?"

I shake my head no.

"Who does?"

"Nobody but Lila," I admit, defeated.

"Okay." Liam nods his head slowly. "Okay, we can work with that." He takes another swig of his beer. "What's the plan?"

My stomach drops as a heart rate notification sounds on my device. I blink at it several times, unable to believe what I'm seeing. As soon as reality hits me, I'm running through the halls as fast as physics will allow.

I barge into Finch's office without so much as a thought. "I need to talk to you," I pant. "Now."

Something sparkles in Finch's eyes and she tells everyone in her office to leave, including her beefy bodyguards. They eye me suspiciously as they follow her order.

"She's alive," I blurt as soon as we're alone.

"Is she here?" I can't identify the emotion in Finch's voice, but it's more than I expected out of her after what happened. I never did understand her connection to Lila.

"Not yet. Her GPS just activated, we have to send a team out to get her," I demand.

Her face drops. "Ryker, you know we can't do that."

"Colonel, you know as well as I do that Lila's not a Traitor. She's sending me a message, we have to go help her! We have no idea how much danger she's in-"

"You know the Council will never allow a team to head into a possible ambush like this. They declared her a Traitor, it doesn't matter what we think. And there's no way to prove it's her sending you that location. My hands are tied." I notice that Finch never says Lila's name. She looks defeated and sad.

"What would happen to me if- hypothetically- I went without orders?" I ask boldly. I'm aware that even asking could get me into trouble, but I'm hoping Finch will keep this conversation to herself.

Relief is plain on her face but I know she's not able to endorse such an obviously disobedient plan. She chooses her words carefully. "The Council would simply not allow it. Anyone who assisted a Traitor would be sure to face consequences. And if the Council had any reason to believe that such an attempt was being planned, they would put a stop to it before its execution. Am I making myself clear?" Finch gives me a very intense, pointed look.

"Yes, ma'am." I nod my head once. "Apologies for the interruption." I bow my head slightly and turn toward her office door.

I barely hear the "be careful" she whispers as I exit the room.

I try not to draw much attention to myself on the way to the Armory to gather a few small items. Luckily I slip in and out pretty easily. I mostly gather small weapons that will fit in my utility belt.

As the door to the Armory closes behind me, I bump into Rachel.

"Hey, Ryker!" She has an edge to her voice. I wonder if it has anything to do with the fact that the last time she saw me, I freaked out and threw two chairs through a wall. "How are you?"

I really don't want to do anything other than find Lila right now, but I can't afford for anyone to be suspicious of me. "Good. You?"

She touches my arm then, with a regretful look on her face. "How are you really doing?" Pity. She's pitying me. I don't have the patience for it.

"I'm really fine, Rachel. I've gotta meet up with Liam, though, I'm kind of in a rush. See you later." I walk away before she can get in another word.

When I get back to my room, I hurry and pack all my things and get a map of Lila's location. Shit. I have no idea how I'm going to get to her. She's in the middle of nowhere, far away from any public transportation. I need someone who can teleport me.

I'm stunned to my core as I open my bedroom door and find Liam, Connor, and Rachel on the other side. "Hey, bro! What's going on?"

"What the hell?"

"We know you're not actually dumb enough to do what you're about to do, but we thought we'd come check on you anyway," Liam says kindly, pushing into the room. Connor and Rachel are soon to follow.

I blow out a long breath of air as my plan falls apart. "Seriously, guys, I do not have time for this-"

Connor and Liam push me until I'm seated on the edge of my bed. "Talk to us, moron." I don't know who made Liam the spokesperson of this group, but he's definitely the most direct out of them.

"I have nothing to talk about, I just have a meeting I need to get to-"

"Really? 'Cause you told Rachel you were meeting up with *me*." Liam shrugs. "I came as soon as I heard. Wouldn't want to miss a meeting with my second favorite brother." A goofy grin spreads across both his and Connor's face. Are they seriously enjoying this?

"Snitch." I point my chin at Rachel, who presses her lips together.

"Hey, it's not her fault that you're an asshat. What exactly is your plan?" Connor finally speaks.

"I need to go get her." My voice cracks as the words come out. I'm almost embarrassed by it, but I can't bring myself to care enough about what people are thinking of me right now.

Liam's voice is kinder now. "And you think you're just going to ride a bus to some random location, pick her up, and bring her back here?"

"I don't know, Liam," I raise my aching voice. "I just can't take it, not knowing if she's okay. She's been out there too long, everyone else has given up on her, and I just can't do that. I can't give up on her." I have to take a deep breath before my emotions take over.

Liam, Connor, and Rachel all look at each other for a few seconds. "Okay," Liam decides.

"Okay? Okay, what?" I meet his eyes.

"We're coming with you." All three of them have their eyes locked on mine.

Each of us takes on a task for our mission. Rachel gathers weapons. Liam is in charge of getting Connor cleared for the rest of the night and then the both of them have to find food. I've already finished my assignment- convincing a Necromancer to help us escape Headquarters- by the time I run into Liam and Connor.

"How'd you do it?"

"I sneak him out all the time. They practically handed him over to me as soon as they saw me," Liam brags.

Connor shoves him hard on the shoulder. "Only because you've slept with the whole staff."

Liam pushes him back but Connor's gigantic figure doesn't budge in the slightest. I shake my head at the ridiculousness of them both.

"How'd your assignment go?" Liam asks.

"Fine."

"Did you threaten him?"

I squint at him. "I didn't need to. Why are you asking me that?"

He shrugs. "Rachel seems to think you almost killed him the other day."

"Why are you and Rachel talking about me?"

Connor and I both eye him suspiciously until he holds up his hands in surrender. "Forget it."

"Go get the food, dumbass."

"Hide Connor in your room then, yeah?" He claps both of us on the shoulder at the same time and we simultaneously punch him in the gut. Not enough to actually hurt him, despite the award-worthy groans that leave him as he walks away.

"How are you feeling?" Connor asks, watching me closely as I open the door to my bedroom.

Huh, what a deep and difficult question to answer. "I'm... restless, overwhelmed, borderline hysterical." I laugh humorlessly. "I don't really know what to do with myself without her."

I can feel the blood rush to my face and up my ears at my confession. Discussing my emotions with Connor is a foreign concept. Especially since my feelings are about Lila.

"I'm sorry for what I said to you when you told me you were watching over her."

I gawk at him, the unwarranted apology catching me totally off guard.

"I didn't know how you felt about her. I would've been more sensitive."

My head is shaking before he even finishes. "Come on, man. Don't even worry about that. She's been a huge part of your life for two decades. I appreciate that you still want to look out for her. The only thing I care about is her safety."

"I know man, but I didn't have a right to question that. It's your job to protect her and obviously you're doing a much better job of it."

"Stop, Con. It's not about being better. It's just different. I didn't expect to fall for her like this. Tried ignoring it for weeks, until she confronted me. Then when we finally seemed to figure it out, she…" I trail off. There's a sadness hanging in the air now. We're both feeling like we failed at our job to keep Lila safe.

"We're going to get her back, Ryk. I'm not coming back here without her. In one piece. We're all going to be okay."

THIRTY-SEVEN

Lila

"Are you sure someone is coming? Maybe we should-" Anna starts. I can tell everyone is starting to wonder if they picked the wrong savior to believe in.

"He'll be here," I promise. *He has to be.*

"That thing will share your live location with him, right?" Genevieve verifies.

"Yes," I say a little too confidently.

"Okay, then it won't hurt us to keep moving forward, right? Let's try to get to the nearest city. Maybe we'll find someone who can help us." The other seven of us agree with Genevieve and we start moving forward. I make sure to keep my heart rate high so Ryker can find us.

For the first hour or so, we walk in almost complete silence. Finally, Tom begs his parents for something to eat.

Nonni and Fern are in charge of rationing our limited food. Teresa and her husband Javier are in charge of the map, and leading our valiant group. Anna walks just in front of Genevieve and I- the masterminds behind the operation. Now, our most important role is to keep everyone calm.

When it starts to get dark, Javier makes the call to rest for a few hours. Unfortunately, we had to leave Necromancer Homebase later in the day than we originally planned, in order to escape undetected.

We decide that two people need to stay awake at all times. Teresa and Genevieve take the first shift. It takes me a while to drift off. Every sound of the forest, the twinkle of every star, and each racing thought preoccupy my mind. But, eventually, I do.

It's still dark when I'm being shaken awake. My eyes split open to Anna's frightened face. I sit up quickly and look around. It's pitch black and it takes several seconds for my eyes to adjust. Seconds we apparently do not have. Anna pulls me up- surprising me with her strength- and pushes me forward through the forest.

I can see people running around us but I can't recognize any of them yet. Nobody is making a sound. I want to call out and make sure we're all still together, but I assume we're dashing silently for a reason?

Then I see it. Sparks of light litter the forest behind us. There are Necromancers chasing us. A blaze of purple shoots past my right shoulder and connects with a tree as I pass it.

Nonni and Fern are starting to slow down in front of us and I immediately feel responsible for keeping them safe. Tom doesn't need to experience that kind of loss right now. Definitely not because I dragged them out here without a plan.

As we come up on a thick line of trees, I tackle them to the ground. Anna and Genevieve look at me with shock until they realize what I'm doing. Nonni and Fern are both terrified as they shuffle on the forest floor. I motion for them to be quiet and to stay low, hiding behind a large fallen tree.

Anna and Genevieve follow my lead, helping Tom, Teresa, and Javier hide too. Then the three of us find a large tree to gather behind.

"We need to get as many as we can before they reach us," I whisper.

I somersault across the forest floor, away from the rest of the group. *You can do this, Lila. You have to do this.*

I conjure up the courage and honor that fills me as I protect this precious group of people who trust in me. I push down the anger I feel, willing it not to turn my magic into something unstable.

I pull my hands from my chest and push them forward with as much power as I can. The light that surges from me knocks one of the Necromancers down with a shout. *That's it, Lila. Keep going.*

Out of the corner of my eye, I see Anna and Genevieve do the same. We are far apart now, all targeting the Necromancers from different angles.

Within a few minutes, I let hope wash over me as we knock Jaquelin's henchmen down one by one. Anna, Genevieve, and I work in perfect unison. Once we cannot see or hear any others, we hoist the other members of our group up and start running.

We don't get far before Genevieve, Nonni, Javier, and Teresa have guns pointed at their heads.

"Stop!" A gunman's voice shouts. "I command you to surrender on behalf of Amaryllis Headquarters."

Nobody moves an inch.

"Now!"

"How do we know if you're really from Headquarters?" Genevieve demands.

"Get on the ground now!" The voice answers. "Don't try anything stupid!"

"You don't understand," I plead as I lower myself to the ground with my hands up in the air. "There are Necromancers from the rebel group chasing us. We're not safe here."

"Lila?" My favorite voice calls out.

I push myself up to my knees, unable to believe it until I can see him, feel him.

As soon as his wide eyes meet mine, he is unstoppable. He barrels into me, pulling me into the tightest embrace of my life. I'm not sure how we remain standing after the amount of force that I just got hit with.

"You came." I can barely get the words out of my breathless chest.

"Of course I did," Ryker says fiercely. He pulls back and looks at me, searching my person for any sign of injury. "Are you okay?"

"Ryker, we are not safe here, we have to get everyone out-" I plead frantically.

"Let's go." Ryker looks around behind me as he extends his hand in the way they came from. My body immediately obeys his command.

I recognize two of the other gunmen as Rachel and Connor. Rachel squeezes my hand briefly before making her way back to Connor's side. It takes her a minute to pull Connor's gaze back to her, the panic on his face melting away as soon as his staring at me gets interrupted. "Stay with me, Con," I hear Rachel say. I wish I had time to dissect it.

The fourth gunman, the one who yells, is unfamiliar to me. I'll have to ask later.

"All due respect, but where the hell are we following you to?" Genevieve asks Gunman #4 as we pick up our pace.

He tilts his head at her, eyebrows furrowed- or at least they appear to be under the dim night sky. "Back to Headquarters," he half-shouts back.

"So, what, we're going to run the whole way there?" I wonder how either of them have the breath to speak right now. I'm in the best shape of my life and I'm still struggling for air.

"There's a portal up ahead," Ryker puts a painless end to the conversation. The sound of his voice almost pushes me over the edge. I've missed him so much.

Something sounds from behind. Just before I can turn to find the source, Ryker yells over my shoulder to keep going.

My legs obey him despite all odds. Some force bigger than me- perhaps the strong desire to keep these families together- drives me forward. On borrowed air.

My small group of Necromancer friends continues running to who-knows-where as the Soldiers take turns shooting towards our assailants.

I see the unnamed one go down first. Fern follows shortly after. A burst of energy and light crashes on the floor next to me, some of its rays stinging into my calves. We need to gain some ground before we all end up dead.

"Genevieve!" I scream.

I'm grateful she knows what I mean. We both jump forward at the same time. I roll my body back behind the largest tree I can find. It's not quite thick enough to cover my entire body but it will have to do.

The Soldiers are scrambling. Shouts of desperation and pleas of salvation.

Five Necromancers. We only have to stop five more. I can no longer see Ryker or Anna. Or anyone else for that matter.

I can't determine who is screaming, either. This forest can't take much more chaos. I hit another one with my magic and they fall down. Four left.

Genevieve takes out another. Three. Tom runs past Genevieve and I and I'm relieved to see him alive.

"Get down!" I yell as I position myself for another shot.

I've lost sight of the last three. *Where are you?*

"Ryker!" Connor's thunderous voice rolls through the trees. I follow his gaze to Ryker leaning against a tree, holding his chest with a pained expression. My heart sinks.

There are few of us left and my head is spinning.

Anna shakes me, hard. "Lila!"

My ears are ringing as I watch my nightmares unravel before me.

"Lila!" I finally meet her eyes. "We need you! This is your purpose, Lila! You are the strongest one here!"

Before I can make sense of it, Anna and Genevieve grab both of my hands. Bright chords of light flow through them and into my hands. It causes a sensation of both intense power and incredible pain throughout my being.

What happens next is orchestrated purely by electricity. I watch myself become someone, some*thing* else entirely.

My body simply turns into a conduit of energy. The magic of all my ancestors joins together with mine, Anna's, and Genevieve's. I recognize at this moment that I am completely unstoppable.

Within seconds, every one of our attackers is laid flat on the now-barren ground. There were more of them than I had thought. Nature tells me to keep my distance from any of my friends.

The enchantment I spill over my fallen peers travels like an angelic tune. Trails of light flow from me to Ryker, Fern, and the unnamed Soldier. Then, everything disappears.

THIRTY-EIGHT

Ryker

We're Romeo and Juliet. Too willing to sacrifice ourselves. First Lila, then myself, then Lila again.

I witness as she transforms from her beautiful self to a majestic being, destroying every force that goes against her, and bringing life back to the dead. She then crumples into herself, dropping from the air like a bird hitting a glass window.

It hurts too much. I want to go to her, but I'm fading too quickly.

I wish I could say I passed out from blood loss and woke up happy and healthy in the Infirmary, but that wouldn't be close to the truth.

We still had to run to find Lorenzo to portal us back home. Unfortunately, I didn't sleep through the excruciating event like some of the others. I was painfully in and out of consciousness as Rachel wobbled me through the thick forest.

The Necromancers split their efforts between their injured- Lila and an older man, both unconscious. Liam was barely hanging onto life so Connor had to carry him entirely. That left Rachel with me.

Eventually, we made it to Lorenzo and were each able to portal to Headquarters. Now, half of us lay handcuffed to Infirmary beds while the other half are locked in cells.

I requested that Liam and I be placed together, separate from the others, and eventually the Infirmary staff allowed it. I couldn't stand being so close to her lifeless body. They assured me she'll have a full recovery, but I can't forgive her for putting me in this position.

Liam is healing slowly, but the medics are confident he will have a full recovery after some time. As of now, he's in some kind of medically-induced coma, supposedly lasting three or so days.

I have a pretty gnarly wound spreading from my left shoulder to my sternum that, when undressed, resembles raw meat. Though I guess technically it is.

Every five to ten hours, a Headquarters Necromancer comes by to do some kind of magic healing to our wounds. It is agonizing. If I couldn't immediately see the benefits, I'd be sure they were just torturing us.

We're lucky, though, because any ordinary human would take months to heal, while we will only have to deal with these injuries for mere days.

The physical ones, anyway.

After about two days- I think- of being in the Infirmary, Connor is released from detainment and is granted visiting privileges.

"Hey, Ryk." Connor forces a soft tone, probably for the first time in his life. He stands awkwardly between both beds.

"It's good to see you," I reassure him. "I'm glad they finally let you out. How's Rachel?"

"We're all cleared. Except for…" Connor shoots me a regretful look. "Lila has been taken to the Penitentiary until the Council holds a Tribunal."

He braces himself for an eruption on my behalf. But I knew this was coming. When Lila left us, I knew there would be consequences. She should've known too. And if she didn't, it's her fault for leaving without giving me the chance to warn her.

"Are you okay?" It's obvious that my detachment concerns him more than whatever reaction he was expecting.

I contemplate his question before answering as honestly as I can. "Yes, I think I'll be fine." But I involuntarily shift my gaze to my hands, closed in my lap.

"I bet she'd really appreciate your support-"

"She can stand up for herself, Connor. She doesn't want my help." There's a finality to my words that he doesn't seem in the mood to contend. "Have they given you any updates about Liam?"

He deserts his planned conversation and surrenders to the change in topic. "They said he should be waking up either today or tomorrow. He may have some memory loss. He'll have a hard time doing anything by himself for a little while. But he's alive and doing well."

Both of us are looking at Liam as we speak, willing him to wake up already. The medics aren't sure if he can hear us or not but I spend most of my day talking to him.

"We're all going to be alright," I tell Connor and Liam assuredly. I appreciate it when Connor nods his head in agreement.

Finally, the medics take Liam out of his coma. It's a faster process than I would've guessed.

He's awake and doing better than he should be. Connor stepped out to get the three of us food. In his absence, I've been filling Liam in on how the rescue mission ended and where everyone is now.

He's hung up on the fact that I haven't seen Lila yet.

"You're such an asshole," Liam declares.

I throw a pillow at him with my good arm.

He pretends to be hurt by it, but he's laughing. "Don't you have to be nice to me, now that I'm disabled?"

I scowl. "You're no more disabled than I am."

"Well, either way, you're an asshole."

I throw my hands up defensively. "Why am I an asshole?"

"Because you sat and moped about her for weeks, trying to get her back. Then you find her, hug her like your life depends on it.

You fight like hell to get her back, and then ignore her when you get back to safety. Making you," he shrugs before adding, "an asshole."

"I'm injured, you moron," I defend. We both know it's an excuse. "I can't really barge in her Tribunal-"

Liam scoffs. "I didn't realize you were such a scaredy cat." He gives me a dirty look.

"Scared?"

Something changes in Liam's sarcastic demeanor when he says "Look, I'm not going to make you say it, man. But we both know you're going to regret it if you don't go make things right with Lila."

Connor comes back into the room then, holding three bags of greasy food. I would pay money to have seen the Infirmary staff's faces when he walked in with them.

We goof off as we eat together and catch up. I can't remember the last time the three of us hung out like this. It's refreshing.

When Connor leaves, I finally get the courage to go see Lila. I don't know why I feel so weird about him knowing how I feel about her. Liam assured me that Connor is well aware. But in case he's not, I spare him.

It's truly nonsensical. He doesn't need protection and he probably won't think twice about it. Regardless, I'm not ready to confess my feelings about the girl that repeatedly gets murdered in his nightmares.

He does seem to be coping better now. Being a part of saving her may have been the best thing for him. He still sleeps at the Institution, but at least now it's his choice.

Rachel came in about half an hour ago to let us know Lila had been cleared. Connor was relieved and Liam had raised an eyebrow as if to say "now or never."

So here I go.

Her bedroom door is open when I arrive. It's alarming and I almost rush in to see if she's okay.

Then I hear her and Rachel talking. I should have assumed Rachel would come straight here. Still undetected, I decide to return later.

Until I hear my name.

"-Ryker would love to see you. You should go visit him."

"Why do you say that?" Lila sounds caught off guard by Rachel's statement.

"It's obvious there's something going on between the two of you."

"What? Did he say that?" She sounds offended at the idea.

"He didn't have to."

"We are just friends. We've gotten close over the past several months-"

"Really close," Rachel gives her one more push.

"Rachel! It really isn't like that!"

"Lila, he was a mess after you left. He threatened just about everyone to find you. If you don't feel that way about him, you should probably tell him before he commits murder for you."

She sighs. "Okay, I'll talk to him."

I don't stick around for the rest of the conversation. I've heard more than enough.

THIRTY-NINE

Lila

Two guards bring me to the center of a spacious room that appears to be made completely of concrete. It's cold, in a disturbing type of way. The type that gives you goosebumps and a shiver down your spine.

The guards turn and walk out the same door we came.

"Wait-" I make an attempt to move. But I'm frozen in place, unable to follow them out.

It takes minutes for my eyes to adjust and for me to realize I'm not alone. There is a column of light surrounding me, making it difficult for me to see the dark shadows that circle me from afar.

"Hello?"

The silence is deafening as I wait impatiently for a response.

"Lila Moreau," a thundering voice calls. *I've never been called by that last name before.* "You have been summoned to appear in front of this Council to determine the legitimacy of the charges brought against you. At this time, you have been charged with Treason against Amaryllis. How do you plead?"

I swallow the lump in my throat. "Not guilty. I did not betray Amaryllis, despite the many times you have betrayed me-"

"Enough," the voice commands. They must be using magic, because I'm no longer able to speak. "Let the investigation commence."

The column of light increases in luminosity until everything becomes white. It's just on this side of relaxing, given I have an ache throbbing through my head.

The feeling is similar to that of a portal, like parts of me are being sucked through space and time. I'm loopy and tired when they finish whatever this is and pull me back to consciousness.

I'm standing in the center of the large room again, the column of light dimming until I can barely see the circle of people in the distance.

"What happened?" I croak. I'm relieved when the words are heard by the Council.

"Lila Moreau, our investigation of your memories-" *what?!-* "has determined your fate. Though you did willfully interact with known members of a terrorist group, we did not find any evidence to prove you guilty of Treason. As of now, you are released from your charges. If new evidence surfaces, a new case will be opened and an investigation will be performed accordingly. Do you understand the rulings of this Tribunal?"

The firm voice is now music to my ears. I have to fight back the tears of relief that threaten to spill over my eyelids. "Yes, I understand."

The two guards from before re-enter the room and guide me out the large doors. Once we're back in the hall, one of them removes the bracelets on my wrists. They both offer me small nods of their heads, as if to say "congratulations."

My head is foggy as I float through the halls, trying to remember the direction to return back to the Living Quarters. A large part of me expected to spend the rest of my life incarcerated.

I hold my breath as I pass Ryker's room and unlock my own. It's silly, I know he's not in there. He's still in the Infirmary with the other injured Soldier. Now that I'm free, I need to go see him. But I need to organize my thoughts first, process everything that's happened in the last few weeks.

A shower. I need a long, warm, therapeutic shower.

❖❖❖

Someone knocks enthusiastically on my door. A fraction of a second after I crack it open, Rachel explodes on the other side. She smacks the door open and throws herself onto me, nearly knocking me to the floor.

"You're free!" she squeals, giggling like a girl who found her lost puppy.

I hug her tightly. "Thank you for everything." Again, I find myself choking back tears.

She pulls back to look at me and I notice her wet face. "I love you, Lila. I'm sorry for everything you've been through. I should've been more there for you-"

"I love you, too," I cut her off with another tight hug. She cries softly into my hair.

When she's finally able to take a deep breath, we both pull back and take a seat on my bed. We both have to wipe our faces of tears.

"So, tell me everything!"

"Well, they searched my memories, I guess. So they saw that I was not working with the rebel group and released me from the Treason charges."

"Wow," Rachel exhales. "So, what now?"

I laugh breathily. "I have no idea."

"We should throw a party."

"Do you know anything about my friends?"

Her eyes darken. "They're still in the Infirmary. The older man hasn't woken up yet. It's not looking good. The family is with them but they aren't letting anyone else in. The others are awaiting their Tribunals."

My head bobs slowly on my shoulders as I take in the information. "So Fern is unconscious but still alive, and Nonni and Tom are with him in the Infirmary. The others are in cells awaiting Tribunals," I repeat.

"Yes."

"So everyone is safe?"

Rachel nods. "For now, everyone is safe."

"Anna is in a cell?"

"Yes."

"Right." I grimace. "Everything is going to be okay. Am I allowed to be in there with her?"

Rachel looks at me apologetically. "No, I'm sorry."

"Okay." I adjust my position on the bed, overtly aware that Rachel is watching me carefully. "What about…" I can't bring myself to finish the question.

Rachel sees right through me anyway. She's known me for long enough. "He's still recovering, but he's okay. His brother, Liam, just woke up from a medically induced coma."

My heart skips a beat. "Liam?"

"Yeah. He was the Soldier that went down."

"Oh, I didn't know."

"They're going to be fine, Lila." Rachel rubs my arm. "I didn't really ask how Liam was, I was busy bragging that you were set free. You should go meet him." Her lips spread into a big toothy grin. "And I'm sure Ryker would love to see you. You should go visit him."

How am I supposed to face him now? Ryker and his brother are injured because of me. "Why do you say that?"

"It's obvious there's something going on between the two of you."

"What? Did he say that?" I wince inside, *that sounded way too defensive, Lila.*

A shy smile crosses Rachel's face. "He didn't have to."

Crap! I try to cover my panic. "We are just friends. We've gotten close over the past several months-"

"Really close." She wiggles her eyebrows at me.

"Rachel! It really isn't like that!"

"Lila, he was a mess after you left. He threatened just about everyone to find you. If you don't feel that way about him, you should probably tell him before he commits murder for you."

I sigh. "Okay, I'll talk to him."

She rolls her eyes. "You are a hopeless liar."

"We wanted to keep it to ourselves. He said if anyone found out, they'd take him off my case!"

Rachel squeals again. "Yay! I knew it, I knew it, I knew it!"

"Shh," I hush her with a breathless laugh. "Who else knows?"

She beams. "Liam was the first to find out, I think. Connor is still kind of in denial. He thinks Ryker's love for you is unrequited." *Love*. The word leaves her mouth so casually, but the weight of it sinks to the bottom of my stomach.

"That's funny," I brush her off.

"Yeah, well, now I can force him to accept the truth." She sits up victoriously.

"What about you?" I turn the investigation around. "Any love interests? Are you pining for Connor *and* Ben now?"

She punches my arm. "Take that back!"

We laugh for what feels like hours. The most effective therapy.

The first thing that passed through my head when I heard Liam had woken up was relief. Dread was a close second, though.

"I regret to inform you all of some information I came across during my time away." I can almost swear Ryker flinches at the last words. He's only looked at me once since I walked into their room at the Infirmary.

Liam and Connor both meet my eyes with looks of pity that make this conversation even more difficult.

"There isn't an easy way to say it, so I'm just going to put it all out there." I exhale a shaky breath and fix my gaze on my fidgeting hands. "I met a woman, Anna Moreau, who was introduced to me as my mother. Anna told me that she and my father joined the rebel group under false pretenses that the group would help them find their daughter.

"When they found out it was the same rebel group of Necromancers that had taken me as a child-" my voice catches and I have to swallow hard. "My parents, specifically my father, Robert, fought against them. Unfortunately, he suffered the consequence of death." Tears begin to fall from my eyes. Luckily, I am looking down, so they fall straight to the floor, hopefully unnoticeable to my audience.

"Anna then informed me there were others that were fighting alongside my father, Agents from Headquarters that were trying to eliminate the rebel group." I look up now. I'm surprised to see understanding in Connor and Liam's eyes. Ryker's expression does not match his brothers' but he is finally looking at me. In between silent sobs, I finally get the names out. "Eloise and Andrew Jordan."

FORTY

Ryker

"What the hell?" The rage sits me straight up. My shoulder throbs from the abrupt movement but I'll have to deal with it later. "You're lying-"

"Ryker," Connor interrupts my rampage. He turns to face Lila, softening his tone. "Lila, would you please excuse us?" She squeezes her flooded eyes shut and makes to exit. "We'll find you later." I glimpse the nod of her head before the door closes behind her.

Connor and Liam share a glance before focusing on me.

"She's lying," I deny. What else can I do?

"She's not, bro," Liam responds solemnly. He rubs the back of his neck with an open palm. He's been awake for a few hours and he's already moving better than I am. "Shit, man. We should have told you earlier-"

"Told me what? We can't trust her, she's been lying-"

"Ryker." Connor steps in. "She's not a liar. What she told you is true. She obviously didn't know we knew."

"Our parents died in a train accident-"

"They didn't, Ryk. We just panicked when you asked how they died. You were too young to understand-"

"Bullshit!"

"We would've had to explain what happened to Connor and Lila and the rebel groups that were kidnapping and killing children close to your age-"

I cut Liam off, desperate for answers. "And it never came up again? I've known about Lila for *years*."

They both wince at my tone.

"You're absolutely right, bro. We should have told you sooner. But that's our bad, don't take it out on Lila. She told you immediately."

I shake my head, unable to comprehend it all. "She's got her own lies to own up to."

"What-" Connor starts, but I don't let him finish.

"Why were they involved? They should have been retired."

"It was a matter of Treason, Ryk. There was a Traitor within Headquarters, so they pulled in agents that they could trust. The Jordan family was one of them."

Neither of my brothers stop me when I storm out of the room.

There was little that could have prepared me for the Council's visit. It was short, with little room for discussion. They showed up at my bedroom door and announced that I was chosen for a mission. They mentioned it would be surveillance. I agreed as soon as they said they would be sending me away from Headquarters.

Precisely after I accepted, they informed me that Miss Moreau would be joining me. That it was crucial we work together, with our unique experience and skills. I made a weak attempt at getting out of it, but the Council made it clear it wasn't optional.

I switched on my Soldier switch and packed mine and Lila's gear. Luckily, we traveled by portal, so I didn't have to sit in a vehicle with her for hours.

We arrived just before sunset, giving me enough time to set up our respective tents and explain basic information to Lila before we each turned in for the night.

Clearly, she didn't listen to the debrief before deployment, because she didn't bring warm enough clothing.

"I can hear your teeth chattering from here," I tell her, aggravated at her for no reason at all. Well, other than the fact that I'm stuck here with an unprepared Lila.

"I-I'm f-fine!" Lila attempts to sound enthusiastic. It only irritates me further. She's so relentless, most likely freezing on purpose so I'll show her mercy.

"Can't you make a heater with your magic or something?" I mutter.

The sound of shivering is the only response I get.

"Did you die of hypothermia?"

Nothing but shivering.

I heave a sigh as I sit up from my less than luxurious spot on the ground. I push myself up onto all fours so I can crawl out of my tent. The closer I get, the louder the sound of Lila freezing to death becomes.

Pulling back her tent door, I hear "W-w-what are y-you d-d-doing?"

I roll my eyes, though I'm unsure she can see it in the darkness of the tent. Without saying anything, I lay beside her, unwrap her from the nest of blankets she's created, and pull her to me. A small gasp escapes her mouth but she makes no attempt to fend me off.

We lay in an awkward embrace for mere seconds before her shivering starts to let up. She shuffles even closer, nuzzling her head into my chest. My arms naturally circle her upper body, stroking her cold skin and clothes with my hands.

Finally, she takes a successful deep breath.

"Thank you," she whispers, untucking her head an inch or two. I'm not ready to acknowledge that I'm pressed up against Lila. I especially refuse to indulge the idea that we may spend the entire night like this.

Lila doesn't bring it up either. We stay like this, listening to each other's breath in the otherwise silent night. My wondering if I should return to my own tent gets interrupted by Lila's voice.

"Ryker?" I'm decidedly unprepared for whatever she has to say. I briefly consider ignoring her altogether.

"Hmm?"

"You don't have to stay with me," she mumbles against my chest.

I can feel myself stiffen under her words. "Oh." I must've misread the situation. I begin to pull myself away from her but she surprises me by speaking again.

"No." Lila shakes her head, though I'm not sure at what. "I didn't mean-" she sighs. "I'm not kicking you out. I know I'm not your favorite person right now, and I don't want to make you uncomfortable..." she trails off.

Unfortunately, this might be the most comfortable I've been in a long time. Not that I'd admit it. "If I leave, you'll keep me awake with your excessive shaking and chattering."

Lila lets out a small laugh and the warmth of it brushes my chin. *Ignore it, Ryker.*

Lila shifts under me. "Ryker?"

Deep breath. "Yeah?"

"I'm really sorry." She says it as if she's testing the waters. Like there is more she wants to say, but she doesn't want to push her luck. It doesn't matter, though, because I don't want to hear it.

"Shh. Go to sleep." I force a nonabrasive tone.

She sucks in a breath and I don't feel her exhale before I drift off.

Of course, I don't sleep well. We fall asleep facing each other. At some point in the never-ending night, Lila is spooning me.

The first thing I notice is how nice it feels to have her wrapped around me, her arm gripping across my abdomen. That is, until I notice the subtle shivering that plagues her from head to toe.

I twist us both around until we have switched spoon positions. I pull her chilly back to my torso, encircling her arms and legs with my own.

Lila whimpers as she shakes. I push the hair out of her face and whisper in her ear, "shh."

She continues to tremble and my right hand instinctively comes up to stroke her arm and shoulder. She flinches under my fingers and I pause until she scoots further into my embrace. I can't tell if it's a conscious decision or a survival skill.

Hours pass before I'm woken up again. This time, Lila is sitting upright. I'm about to ask her what she's doing when she puts a hand over my mouth. It's still dark but I can see the outline of her finger touching her lips, encouraging me to stay quiet.

I sit up, too, and notice a noise coming from outside our tent. An abnormal clicking sound echoes through our cloth shelter. I move to investigate and Lila squeezes my thigh hard.

What is it? I try to ask with my eyes.

Nothing good, she seems to say, her eyes intense as she decides how to proceed. I realize now that she has one hand extended toward the makeshift door, palm open and… sparkling?

She isn't looking at me, despite my attempts to communicate silently with her. I have to touch her before she turns her attention back to me. I throw my hands up in frustration.

Instead of responding, she pushes my hands down to my lap. I'm about to lose my patience when she squeezes my hand, wanting to reassure me.

The physical stuff has always been easy between us, maybe even too natural. But despite the comfort of her touch, and that our survival depends on it, I remind myself that this part of our relationship is over.

I remove my hand from her grasp, not at all intending to offend her, but it does anyway. Rejection crosses her face in the blink of an eye. She recovers quickly, though, bringing her other hand up to strengthen her magic.

Before too long, the noise disappears completely and Lila's hands drop to her sides. Her shoulders slump as her entire body goes limp. I barely have time to catch her before she falls to the ground.

"Lila!" I shout a little too loud. She's unresponsive. I check for a pulse and after poking around her neck, I find one. She's alive. She must have been using more magic than I realized.

Seeing her like this does something weird to my stomach. It brings back the memory of her collapsing in the forest, escaping from the Necromancers who took her away from me.

I had just gotten her back and all of a sudden I was losing her again. And now… Now, nothing is right with us. It hasn't been the same since she went with Jaquelin. At the end of the day, she left me. And I know she's got a lot to process, but she hasn't asked me to be a part of it. She doesn't need me anymore.

As soon as the sun starts to brighten the morning sky, I make my way out of the tent. We came here to track magic, after all. And whatever was surrounding us earlier most likely had to do with Necromancy.

Dawn in the forest is foggy and surreal. I'm not going to be able to track whatever was just out here without Lila's help. Instead, I look for any clue that will lead us to the rebel group.

After walking around aimlessly for about half an hour, I scale a tree. It takes longer than I'd like to admit to get to the top, but I make it. I keep watch until Lila wakes up, since I can't trust myself to stay close to her without doing something humiliating.

FORTY-ONE

Lila

I startle awake, alone under a small cloth habitat. I blink hard while the events of the last several days play through my head. I fall back to the ground out of embarrassment from last night, guilt from the last conversation I had with Ryker before the mission, and exhaustion from using so much magic.

Next, I remember the reason I used magic.

"Ryker?" I call, but no answer.

I probably need to be quiet but I'm beyond all reason now.

"Ryker!" I stumble into his tent. It's empty. *Oh no, no, no, no.*

I stumble around the campsite (if you can call two wimpy tents in the middle of a forest a campsite) sweeping the woods for any sign of-

"Lila?" I hear Ryker call out. "Up here." I find him at the top of an imposing tree. A sigh of relief escapes my mouth.

"Sorry, I didn't mean to scare you-"

"It's fine." I wave my hand in the air. Surely that's not the most humiliating thing I've done today, so I let myself off the hook. *Food. You need food.*

Rummaging through my backpack doesn't help much. There are like twenty protein bars, a handful of dried fruit packets, and five or so bottles of water. Ryker must've been the one to pack.

My stomach growls and I relent, unwrap one of the protein bars, and bite into it. It does little to please my tastebuds. Hopefully it's more filling than it is delicious.

"Hey." Ryker opens the tent slightly with his long, manly fingers. "I just wanted to get a good lookout position while you came to. Sorry I wasn't here when you woke up."

My heart skips a beat and I have to remind it that Ryker has moved on. I briefly wonder if there is someone else, if that's the reason he hasn't wanted to see me since I got back to Headquarters, but I immediately suppress it. I know he's upset about his parents.

Fortunately, my unpredictable mouth stays shut during my inner monologue.

"Can I have one?" He points to the bar in my hand. Doesn't he have his own backpack?

I bite my tongue and hand one to him with a bottle of water.

"How are you feeling?"

Why is he acting so nice? Did I wake up in an alternate reality wherein *I'm* mad at *Ryker*, and not the other way around?

"Um," I stutter as I clear my head. "I'm okay. My head hurts."

"You should drink some water."

"Yeah. I will, thanks." It's almost as if the conversation itself falls asleep. There is an odd tension between us and not knowing why is going to eat at me.

Ryker grimaces. "Well, I was thinking I'd keep a lookout from up there. I'm not really sure what we're looking for, but figure it can't hurt to have eyes in the sky."

"Good idea." I swallow audibly. "What should I do?"

He blinks as though he doesn't have an answer. "Well, it might be a good idea to record the events of this morning."

A blank stare.

"With the sounds and whatever magic thing you did." He looks at me expectantly.

The ghost of a smile appears on his lips as it finally dawns on me. *He's not talking about sleeping together, you antisocial lunatic!* I attempt a recovery. "Right, of course." I clear my throat. "Is there somewhere in particular I should write it out?"

This time, I'm positive he is biting back a laugh. A chuckle, at the very least. "There's a notebook in the backpack, or you can put it on your device. There won't be a signal, but there should be an offline section you can use."

I force an awkward, dry smile up in his direction. "Great. Thanks."

As soon as he's out of the tent and several steps away, I facepalm.

Before long, I've written everything I can remember about this morning, post snuggling with Ryker.

Peeking out the tent's opening, I see Ryker still up in his tree. It's going to be a long day. I flip to the back of the notebook and sketch the creatures that were here.

In my imagination, they are gnome-sized ogres that click instead of grunt as they walk through the impossibly large forest.

Before I know it, I'm drawing the inside of the tent as well. Ryker's sleepy body draped around my own in the confines of my simple habitation.

"Lila," he calls, snapping me out of it.

I close the notebook and tuck it back into my backpack before stepping into the sunlight. "Yeah?"

"Can you feel which way they went?"

Right. I should definitely be able to do that. But how? "Uh, sure! I'll see what I can do."

Meandering doesn't do much to stimulate my magic radars, so I end up sitting on the ground. Shouldn't I be able to channel energy from the earth or something?

Palms flat on the earth, I focus on my breathing. I have to remind myself what Ryker once taught me about meditation. What Lorenzo and Anna taught me about energy. I tune in to the nature all around me, to the magic that lingers everywhere.

Inhale. Exhale. Inhale. My fingers tickle with electricity. Exhale. A jolt shoots from my fingers up to my chest. Inhale. The clicking sound echoes through my ears. I would panic, but somehow I know I'm hearing the past.

The cloud that's been shading the sun dissipates and the warmth of the rays resting on me fills me with energy. My eyes pop open and the scene unfolds before me.

The creatures are larger than I had imagined, more similar to goblins. They don't communicate with words. Instead, they click and hiss and gargle as they use their exceptional sense of smell to track their targets.

I guess Jaquelin finally figured out that her blindly obedient servants won't be returning.

The path of the gnome ogre goblins is ultimately revealed and I point in their direction. "This way!" I search for Ryker in the tree.

The sky is a shade or two darker now and grasp how long I must've been sitting there.

"Excellent. I'll keep an eye out. So far, I haven't seen anything out of the ordinary."

A few more hours pass and Ryker abandons his post on the tree, now a reasonable distance from me so we can discuss our predicament.

"They were sent by the rebels to track us."

He regards me tacitly.

"The gnome ogre goblins. They were sent here to-"

My description causes his hard exterior to crack. "The *what*?" he asks in disbelief.

The amount of emotion he shows catches me off guard.

"Well, I don't know what they're called!" He bursts into laughter and- it's nice. I can't remember the last time I heard him laugh. "Well, do you?"

He cackles more, clutching his abdomen.

"You're such a smartass." I want to storm off, but he grabs my wrist.

I stay put but refuse to give him the satisfaction of looking him in the eyes while he mocks me mercilessly.

"I'm-" he snickers- "s-sorry!" He spits out, attempting to compose himself.

"Screw you." I'm grateful he can't see the smile I'm trying to wipe off my face.

His roaring settles to a slight chuckle and then comes to a stop, only a lingering smile left to show for it. "Anyway," he circles back. He walks around until he's standing in front of me again, still holding on to my wrist. "How do you know they're tracking us?"

I shake my head. "I don't know how, but during my vision thing, I just knew they were looking for us. I felt it in the morning, too. That's why I masked us."

"What does that mean?" His brows furrow.

"Well, I hid us behind my magic."

The wrinkle between his eyes deepens and his fingers drop my wrist at last. "You did? That sounds like a lot of work. Is that why you passed out?"

Heat rushes to my face. "I guess so."

Ryker's expression softens and I see something unrecognizable in his eyes. He opens and then closes his mouth. Then he drops the conversation all together, apparently, because he walks away without another word.

I follow him with my eyes and freeze when he starts taking his tent down. "What are you…"

"Combining the tents," he says matter of factly.

"Yes, I see that." I swallow hard. "But why?"

"It's almost dark. We don't know what's out here or its powers. We should take shelter."

"We *had* shelters-"

Ryker spins on his heel, pressing pause on his fort-making to glare at me. "Lila, do not make this any more difficult than it needs to be." There is a finality to his words that I'd better not challenge.

I sit quietly as he finishes. When he does, he holds his hand out in the way that only Ryker does, demanding I follow his direction.

I'm no longer as intimidated by him as I once was, but I do wish we could go back to how things were before I left. Before I returned and gave him the most devastating news of his life.

He'll hate me forever for it. There isn't much I can do about it, I know. But I'll be damned if I don't at least try.

As soon as he sits down on the floor of our shared space, I pounce.

"Look, I'm sorry. I'm truly very sorry about what happened to your parents. I'm sorry I was the one to tell you. I'm sorry-"

Ryker scoffs. I blink, but his demeanor remains. I didn't imagine the disgust because it's still there.

"I'm not asking you to forgive me, Ryker, I just want you to know how *sorry* I am."

Another scoff. Is there something wrong with my ears? But no. "Are you serious?" There is so much heat behind his words that I'm momentarily afraid to continue.

Then I can't hold myself back any longer. "Of course I am! Do you think I *wanted* to be the reason for the death of your parents?"

I'm almost sure I see his face twitch at my inquisition. "Lila," his voice changes now, a raw twist to his words "is that really what you think of me?"

"You have every right to be upset." I have to break the intense eye contact he's giving me.

"I was upset. I felt betrayed. My brothers already knew, Lila. They kept the reason for my parents' death a secret from me my whole life. Unfortunately, you took the brunt of it, but I was never upset at you for telling me the truth."

A tear falls down my face and I brush it away forcefully. I don't want him to pity me and he always bends over backwards when I cry. Or at least, he used to. "I didn't know they knew."

"You didn't," he reassures. "I didn't believe you. But after you left, they told me it was true, that they didn't know how to tell me…" he trails off.

"I'm so sorry." I wipe away another tear, turning my face away to avoid him seeing.

"I know you are. I'm not angry with you for telling me."

This makes me inspect him carefully. "But you are angry with me."

A muscle jumps in his tight jaw.

"Why, then?"

He's silent for a long minute, his eyes piercing into my soul. "We should get some rest."

An unsolicited noise escapes my mouth. "I doubt your girlfriend would appreciate us sleeping together." It comes out before I can stop it. What's worse is that he doesn't deny it.

"Well, I don't appreciate you keeping me up all night."

"I'll use magic to keep myself warm."

"You need to save your energy for when those-" he pauses like he might use my term for them, but then thinks better of it, as if it might bring too much happiness to the conversation- "things come back."

I huff and lay on the floor, pulling the blanket over me.

FORTY-TWO

Ryker

Lila tries to hide her trembling under the mound of blankets- to no avail. I can still see it in the faint light of the night. Is the moon really that bright?

She's so stubborn. She has been for as long as I've known her, but was it always this obnoxious?

"Just get over here."

"No!" she raises her voice. Only one of us is going to make it out of this mission alive. The other will be murdered by me.

"Lila."

"Leave me alone!"

It's the last straw for me. I push my hand under the blankets and pull her until she is pressed against me. She kicks and pushes to get away. She's almost successful and I have to tighten my grip on her. A dull ache throbs in my shoulder as I do.

"Stop squirming!"

She doesn't. Instead, she lands a blow to my shin and I swear under my breath. Lila's body goes still.

Even so, I keep my arms locked around her. She's taking rapid, shallow breaths and her heartbeat pulses through her skin.

I want to flip her around, to peer into her soul. To know why she mentioned me having a girlfriend. I want to know how it's possible that she thinks I could have moved on. Maybe she has. She lost interest and expects me to have done the same.

I want to yell at her. Tell her that she messed me up completely. I want to fight with her, laugh with her, soothe her when she cries five times a day. But she doesn't want any of it. At the end of it all, her indifference is what's going to kill me.

I force myself to let go of her. It's selfish to hold her like this and I certainly can't do it against her will.

The sound of leaves swaying in the chilly night breeze fills the space between us. The separation leaves me feeling empty.

Hours pass like this. Several cold, miserable, lonely hours. That's how it feels anyway. I can't bring myself to move further from Lila to check my device.

She starts shivering again, albeit sporadically.

"Lila," I urge. "Please let me warm you up."

"I don't want-" she cuts off her sentence but then doesn't continue. Did I mishear?

"I can't sleep knowing you're freezing."

She must've waited until she stopped shivering to speak, because when she says "I don't want to give you any more reason to hate me," it comes out clear and crisp.

I sigh, not sure how else to convince her. "I don't hate you, Lila. That's always been my problem."

She hesitates before turning around. The green in her eyes is barely visible here. "Why are you so angry with me?"

"Because of what you said."

Her dark eyebrows pinch together. "About your parents?"

"No." It comes out as a groan. "I came to see you. After your Tribunal."

Her eyes widen, making the white parts glow brighter under the moon lighting.

"I heard you talking to Rachel. I heard what you said." She's a statue now, unsure of the unsaid. "That you're not interested in me as more than a friend. I know I may not necessarily have the right to be mad about it, but it sucks. For me."

A delicate smile inches its way onto her face. Is she… mocking me? "You didn't listen past that, did you?"

"I left as fast as I could."

"Ryker, that's why you're upset with me? You think I'm not interested? You missed the most important part of that conversation, you dork."

My face must show my confusion.

"I didn't know that everyone knew. You told me not to tell anyone."

Shit. Did I really not think of that?

"It didn't matter anyway. Rachel called me on it and I told her the truth. That's when I found out that apparently everyone knows." She gives me a pointed look.

She has no idea how invested I am. Will she leave again if she finds out? "I didn't tell anyone."

"Sounds like you didn't have to." Though I can't see it in this lighting, Lila sounds as if she's blushing. "I'm not going to lie, I got my hopes up when Rachel told me. I needed to see you so badly. But Liam had already woken up by the time I…" she doesn't finish the sentence. "I had to tell you about your parents. After that, well, I was pretty sure you'd never speak to me again."

My eyes squeeze shut as I contemplate what an asshole I am.

"It scares me, Ryker. It's scary how much I want you, and even scarier how much I seem to need you."

I open my eyes, unwilling to miss any part of this conversation. "It seems to me like you don't need anyone."

She forces out a halfhearted chuckle. "That's not true at all. How could you even think that?"

"Because you left!" The words that have been bouncing around in my head have finally been said out loud. Even without getting a response, I feel a weight has lifted from my shoulders.

Her eyes immediately drop. Though I feel lighter, the tension between us gets heavier with every passing minute. "She *took* me, Ryker."

I have nothing to say so I wait for Lila to speak again.

"I didn't want to leave you, Ryker. Lorenzo's message was really vague and I couldn't put you in danger-"

"Lila," I cut her off. "Please don't feed me that bullshit. My literal job is putting myself in danger to protect you."

Her eyes close and she swallows hard. "But *I* couldn't let anything happen to you. I just," she sighs. "I thought I was strong enough to handle it without anyone getting hurt."

"Obviously, you were," I say flatly.

"I didn't mean to leave you hanging. I didn't have time to think of all the consequences. But there wasn't much choice in the matter, Ryker. My only choice was to go with her alone or for you to attack her right in Lorenzo's office. Do you really think that would have been better?"

"I wouldn't have attacked her," I negate.

"You would have tried to reason with her. But she wasn't going to listen. She had to get me out of there to fulfill the Legacy. She never would have backed down. You and Lorenzo and probably Rachel would've gotten hurt, maybe killed, and Jaquelin still would have taken me."

That's… something I did not consider.

"There are a million ways it could've gone terribly, and I wanted to limit the repercussions."

"That makes sense. I would've done the same," I admit.

She looks up at me then, hopeful. "So you didn't meet someone else?" I don't answer immediately and she panics. "I mean, just since you said that you're mad that I left and-"

"Didn't even cross my mind." I put her out of her misery.

A soft intake of breath provokes movement on my part. But I can't. Not yet. I will not succumb first. "Will you be able to forgive me?"

Ideas about Lila making it up to me fill my mind. *Don't be an ass*, I think to myself. "I do forgive you."

A shiver shoots up Lila's spine with impeccable timing. *Do not touch her unless she asks you to.*

"Ryker?" Her voice interrupts the one bouncing around my head.

"Yes, Lila?"

"Will we ever go back to how things were?"

"No." Too much has happened, everything is different. We're both different people than we were a few weeks ago. "We'll have to learn how to move forward with how things are."

She's relieved. "Will you ever kiss me again?"

My heart takes it upon itself to pump extra blood through my veins. "I don't think I should."

"Why not?"

"To 'limit repercussions.'" I throw her words back at her. I mean it, though. It would be nearly impossible to pick myself up again the next time.

"You think I'm going to leave again?" Can she read my thoughts?

"Aren't you?"

Lila sighs. She sounds sad, like she lost whatever hope she had only seconds ago. "You don't feel that way about me anymore, do you?"

Hell yes I do. "We were supposed to be honest with each other. If we don't have that, then why bother?"

Lila sits up now, fighting the shaking that her body immediately takes on once the blanket falls from her shoulders. It takes everything in me not to reach out and wrap myself around her.

"The only thing that I can do to truly show you how much you mean to me is to stay. I will stay with you here or follow you elsewhere. If you'll have me, Ryker Jordan, I'll patiently wait for your trust. I will show you every minute of every day how important you are to me."

FORTY-THREE

Lila

He's not going to touch me. Maybe he doesn't want to. In that case, I can't touch him either.

Should I lay down? How am I supposed to sleep after all that?

"Okay," Ryker says quietly.

'Okay'? What does that even mean? He doesn't say anything else. I return to my position on the floor, covering my chilly skin with multiple blankets. Instead of facing Ryker, I lay on my back and stare up at the cloth that hangs overhead. "Okay."

Ryker chuckles softly. Before I can get a good look at him, he's pulling me to himself. "Get over here," he demands playfully. Bolts of electricity shoot through my body at every point of contact.

We're pressed up against each other, his body heating every part of me, eliminating any chills that lingered. His hands linger on my waist as he looks down at me. Our faces are an inch apart and Ryker's shallow breaths warm my frigid nose.

My stomach churns, my body tingles, my head spins. It's been far too long since I've had him touch me like this. We touched last night, sure, but it was obligatory and unromantic.

This, on the other hand, is passionate and reciprocated. I'm nervous, unsure if my heart is still beating.

My voice quivers but I need to tell him again, I need him to understand. "You can trust me, Ryker."

He nods slowly, holding my eyes firmly with his. His heart is strong in his chest, possibly beating for the both of us.

My fingers shake as I put my hand on his cheek. Somehow, his stare intensifies even more. There is so much left unsaid, and so much communicated without the need for words.

Time stretches as we peer into each other's eyes. Neither of us wants to take the next step, to put everything on the line. We both need it too much. But how much clearer can I be? Meanwhile Ryker has said very little. I have more to lose than he does.

"I trust you, too." These must be the words he was waiting for because as soon as I whisper them, Ryker can't close our gap fast enough.

His mouth is hungry. His lips are hard against mine, desperate for connection. I push back, giving him what he needs, what we both need.

At first, we're stiff. My eyes flutter open as Ryker twists me away from him. I worry that he's trying to let me go. He doesn't, though.

Instead, he rolls until he's almost on top of me, putting his weight in one of his strong, veiny arms. The other wraps around my lower back, keeping me close. He breaks our kiss for a second to look me deep in the eyes.

Then his gaze drops to my chest and below, making me blush. "Are you- is this okay?" He's breathless.

"Yes," I answer, overly enthusiastic. He lets out a breath of relief and lowers himself to me.

I don't wait for him this time, though. I pull him down and kiss him as best I can. The pressure of his body is exhilarating.

A small hum comes from his throat and I can no longer help myself. I reach my hand to his back and feel his muscles through his shirt. Why does he still have a shirt on?

I slip my hands under his shirt and feel his warm skin against my palms. It must inspire him, because he does the same, his large hand holding my bare hip ever so gently.

It's the purest kind of connection, something sweet and delicious and passionate without the pressure of *more*. We kiss for... well, I have no idea how long.

Eventually, though, we just embrace each other. The air is fresher, the sounds of nature outside more soothing than they seemed earlier.

My head is on one side of Ryker's chest while his opposite- injured- arm draws circles on my back. "Does this hurt your shoulder?"

"I've never felt so little pain in my life." He kisses the top of my head.

I'm grateful he can't see the stupid smile I have plastered across my face.

The rise and fall of his chest begins to slow and his fingers squeeze me, twitching, as he falls asleep. It doesn't take much longer for me to follow.

The brightness seeping through the threads of the tent is what ultimately wakes me up.

I sit up quickly when I don't feel Ryker next to me. There's a wildflower on the floor next to me, with a piece of paper- I gasp

It's the picture I drew of Ryker and I sleeping together. If I had a mirror, the reflection staring back at me would most certainly have crimson cheeks right now.

"Ryker?" I call out.

I hear rustling outside and I smile wide. Just before I pull the cloth back, I feel a jolt of something that stops me dead in my tracks. A Necromancer is on the other side of this tent.

Too many thoughts bombard me. *Who is here and how did they find us? Where is Ryker?*

I dig through the blankets until I reach earth and calm myself, summoning the energy the same way I did yesterday. I call upon nature, my ancestors, Necromancy itself to help me.

I write a note to Headquarters and create a small portal, just big enough to push the paper through.

Then, I muster up my courage and step into the sunlight.

"Hello, Jaquelin. Fara. Long time no see."

They sneer victoriously. Jaquelin is the first to speak. "Lila, Lila, Lila. Why do you have to make everything so difficult?"

"You got yourself in this mess, Jaquelin. You should've known better than to follow a man like Roman. Kidnapping, manipulation, threats, it's just pathetic."

Fara's snicker is cut short by the snap of Jaquelin's fingers. "You're going to finish what we started and take the barrier down."

I laugh, probably harder than necessary. "Are you that delusional?"

On Jaquelin's command, Fara drags something into my line of sight. *Ryker.* He's unconscious but appears to be otherwise unharmed.

They think they have me figured out. "What do you want with him?"

"To ensure you do your part. As long as you take down the barrier, we'll let him go."

"And you want me to take your word for it? Ignore the fact that, once the barrier is down, you'll create half-breeds that listen to your every command. You want me to believe that you'll never use that power against anyone I care about?"

"You don't have much of a choice now, do you?" Fara chimes in.

"Don't talk to me, puppet. Jaquelin and I will work together alone." I'm proud of myself for sounding firm.

"Very well," Jaquelin responds thoughtfully.

Fara is quick to react. "What?"

Jaquelin shoots her a sharp look and she backs down.

"So what exactly do I need to do?" Other than get away with conning the leader of a powerful group of Necromancers, that is.

Ryker wakes up while Jaquelin is explaining the ritual needed to break the bonds of the barrier. He's mostly out of earshot, but I still hear him swear a few times and call my name.

"May I?"

Jaquelin looks back and forth between the two of us and then dismisses me with a wave of her hand.

Ryker visibly calms down as I approach him. I want to reach out and touch him, and maybe he even expects me to, but I have to appear somewhat indifferent if this is going to work.

"Why aren't you tied up?" he asks.

How is that his first question? "Ryker, I need you to stay calm." I have to choose my words carefully since Fara is obviously eavesdropping. "Promise?"

He glares at me. I'll take it as a maybe.

"They have captured you as… motivation. They want me to destroy the barrier. If I don't, they'll kill you and then probably take me and blah blah blah."

Ryker's expression almost makes me laugh. He's annoyed. It's relatable. "And you're considering it?"

"What choice do I have?"

"You can't take the barrier down, Lila!"

"They're going to kill you!"

"Then I'm dead either way. And that kind of magic is going to kill you or at the very least wipe you out completely. Then you'll be vulnerable to them or half-breeds or anything else."

I kneel down and cup his face with both hands. "You've been taking care of me for long enough. I think it's my turn." His lips soften as I press a kiss to them. "Trust me," I whisper in his ear, barely loud enough for even him to hear.

He gives me a puzzled look. I rub his worry lines away with my thumb just as Fara reaches her breaking point.

"That's enough." She pulls my arm aggressively.

I glare at her as I get up from off the ground. I steal one last glance at Ryker before I turn my full attention back to Jaquelin and her evil plan to dominate the world.

"Why exactly do you want this, anyway?"

She looks at me the way I would look at a talking frog. Like the words she's hearing are inconceivable. "To lead us out of oppression. Maybe you get special treatment from the Soldiers and the Council, but the rest of us are left hanging out to dry."

"Aren't you part of Headquarters? I mean, before you put this target on your back? Didn't they choose you to represent Necromancers? Why wouldn't you use that to make a real difference?"

"There's no power in that role. It's an illusion."

"Really? Or are you just seeking revenge and domination? It seems to me like you were chosen by the Council. They trusted you to lead Necromancers in Amaryllis. You could have helped Headquarters understand what Necromancers go through, what they need to thrive. You could have taught Soldiers about Necromancy so they don't fear it. But you wasted it all. And for what- power? Control?"

Jaquelin's eyes light with fire. "You have no idea what you're talking about!"

"I know more than you could possibly imagine."

She squints her eyes at me briefly. Within seconds, she relaxes her face, moving on from the conversation. "It's almost time. You need to get prepared."

"What exactly is the plan? Are you going to sacrifice yourselves to the cause?" I mock.

Jaquelin doesn't appreciate it. "You will draw on our powers until the barrier shows movement. Once we know it's working, we'll portal Ryker to a safe distance and be on our way."

FORTY-FOUR

Ryker

She is so beautiful. I've known it for as long as I can remember. But seeing her like this, a conduit of pure light and magic, is a whole different experience. It's such a privilege to witness her taking on the world. I just wish it were under better circumstances. I'll have to ask her to show off for me the next time we are alone.

It's kind of hard to imagine right now. Being alone, that is. Fara and Jaquelin are in between us, both linked by a stream of light to each side of Lila. I am a bit too far to have heard the whole plan, but I believe Lila is pulling power from the two of them in order to complete the spell that will tear down the barrier.

I don't appreciate being left out of the loop, but Lila told me to trust her and I do. And I have nobody to blame but myself for being in this position. I had my guard down this morning and I fell straight into the trap that Jaquelin had set for me.

There is a column of light emanating from Lila, shooting high up into the sky. I can only imagine it means that the spell on the barrier is working. I try to keep calm, but the sudden change in Lila's expression puts a pit in my stomach.

"Eyes on me," I shout as loud as I can. But I know that look. I'm losing her. "Baby, look at me," I'm almost begging now.

Fara and Jaquelin are in some sort of trance due to the ritual, and don't notice that Lila is passing out. She's never done this much magic before and we don't know the consequences it could have.

She's drawing on their magic too. So maybe, if I'm lucky, they'll lose consciousness at the same time as her and I can get myself out of these stupid chains.

"Lila!"

Her eyes flutter closed and there's a split second before her limp body falls to the forest floor. *Please let this be the last time I have to witness it.*

The barrier halts its shimmering overhead. I'm immediately released from whatever magical restraints Fara had put on me.

"No!" Jaquelin screeches. I guess she's not going to faint. Wonderful. Now I have to come up with a Plan B.

I stay very still, trying not to draw any attention to myself. I have no weapons and there are two very powerful Necromancers that would love to end my life. Fortunately, it seems they've forgotten that I'm here. They must not have been able to hear me yelling.

"No! It has to be you!" Jaquelin is screaming down at Lila's collapsed figure. I wonder briefly if this is why Headquarters has been finding dead Necromancers around Amaryllis.

Fara rushes to Jaquelin's side and then hurries to check Lila's neck for a heartbeat. Something happens to my organs when she shakes her head 'no'. *Please be wrong.*

"Ahhhh!" Jaquelin roars, kicking and throwing any object in her vicinity.

They have to be wrong. I have to get her out of here. She has to be okay. She had a plan, right? *I trust you, Lila.*

While watching the rebel group's last attempt to rule the world unravel, something catches my attention. The forest feels different, less charged. An epiphany comes to mind and what better time than the present to prove my theory?

I gather the limited resources that surround me: a medium-sized stick and a somewhat-pointed rock. I roll myself slowly until I'm positioned behind a small boulder.

Jaquelin is pacing and I wait until she's about a meter from me before I lunge at her from behind. She falls hard to the ground with the force of my body weight.

We wrestle in the dirt for several seconds before I'm confident that my theory is true. Jaquelin and Fara lost their magic- at least temporarily. And I'm going to capitalize on it.

Fara jumps to her boss's aide, clawing at my back and shoulders to get me off of her. I'd be humiliated to go into battle with these two. They are pathetic without magic.

With one solid sweep of the legs, Fara is on the ground. Jaquelin seems to have more combat training out of the two of them, and I can't pin her down. I'm still wrestling her when footsteps approach.

"Surrender yourselves to Amaryllis Headquarters! Put your hands in the air!"

I quickly release Jaquelin from my grasp and rush to Lila's side. I haven't even looked toward the Soldiers, and hope they know who I am.

Just like Fara said, there is no pulse on Lila's neck. I try to resuscitate her, but someone- Lorenzo- stops me.

"Let me take her-"

"No!"

"Ryker, I know what she needs. Let me take her."

He's given me no reason not to trust him. Lila trusted him and he helped save her and get her back to Headquarters. "Fine. I'm coming with you."

"Ryker," Lorenzo sighs. "You have to go with the Soldiers."

"What are you talking about?"

"A few of them will take Jaquelin and Fara back to the Penitentiary. The rest are combing through the forest until they find the remaining Necromancers. We can't risk them appointing a new leader. The Council will pick through Jaquelin's memories of information but we can't wait for that. You need to help. Make sure this group is eliminated and won't bother us again."

More Soldiers than I expected are marching through the trees, walking past us swiftly. Jaquelin and Fara are already gone.

"How did they know we needed help?"

Lorenzo's eyes glisten. "Lila sent a note to Headquarters through a very small portal. It set off an alarm and then we found the location of the portal, we found her note that you were both in immediate danger with Necromancers."

I look at her admirably. I wonder if she has any idea how incredible I think she is. Why didn't I tell her when I had the chance?

"Ryk!" Rachel hugs me tight. Connor lingers behind her.

"Hey guys."

Rachel gasps as she sees Lila slumped in my arms. "What happened?"

"She'll be alright, Rach. Lorenzo was just about to take her home and work his magic on her." I point in Lorenzo's direction with my chin and he takes the hint. I kiss Lila's forehead quickly and lay her gently in his arms. "Are you guys looking for the rest of the Necromancers?"

They nod. Rachel still isn't at ease. Connor doesn't look calm either, but I can tell he's trying to.

"I'm coming with you."

Nothing could have prepared me for the tragedy that the forest held. There were bodies everywhere, surrounding the Rebel Necromancy building. Men, women, and children alike. I've never witnessed anything so devastating.

As we stand in the middle of what appears to be an ambush, there is a weighty moment, mourning the lives that were taken. One Soldier takes a knee, and the rest of us follow.

Eventually, we have to keep moving. We stand and it seems we all turn on autopilot in order to finish the mission ahead of us. Now, though, we have a different purpose. Not only are we protecting our families, we are looking for revenge for the fallen families here.

The hairs on my neck stand straight up as we make our way through the dim hallways of the building. The few bodies that scatter the building are found in rooms. I wonder if the ambush started from inside the building or out.

We've almost cleared the whole building when Rachel squeezes my shoulder. It doesn't take me long to hear the reason behind her bizarre expression: muffled sniffling.

I use hand signals to communicate with her and Connor, creating a formation to locate the sound. I don't know how I became the leader of this small group. Nevertheless, they follow behind me, making me the one to call the shots.

There is only one door near us that the sniffling could be coming from. We move in quietly to the dark room, turning on our flashlights, which illuminates a set of desks and chairs, along with a second door.

Once we confirm the classroom is clear, we close in on the door. Whoever is on the other side must see our lights, because the sniffles come to a stop.

My heartbeat drums in my ears as my hand closes around the doorknob. When I open it, I'm met with several pairs of eyes. Someone gasps- it might even be me, but there's no time to find out. The classroom closet is full of children. Orphans. Children whose parents were murdered.

"Oh my-" Rachel chokes up.

I don't want the children to worry, so I move in front of her and talk over her voice. "Hi, hello." I holster my weapon, removing the light and shine it on my own face. "I'm Ryker. Is everyone okay?"

Their faces are all wet except one boy. He's the first to speak. "We're not hurt. The teacher told us to hide in here quietly," he says matter-of-factly. He's the tough one, the glue keeping everyone together. I'm so proud of him- not that I have any right to be.

"You all did a great job," I say soothingly. I'm sure anyone else would be better at this than I am, but Rachel is biting back sobs and Connor is a giant. "It's time to leave now, okay?"

The brave boy nods his head in understanding.

I quickly count the children- nine- and rack my brain for a way to get them out of here without seeing anything.

"Would you all like to play a game?" I try to keep my voice light, but there is a lot depending on their ability to follow simple instructions. Once a few of them agree, I continue. "We're going to pick you up and run really fast through the forest. The fun part is that you all have to keep your eyes closed super tight. Do you think you can do that?"

The boy with dry eyes answers valiantly. "Yes!"

I face Rachel and Connor, searching for the same amount of enthusiasm. It seems my tone has helped Rachel regroup and Connor is always ready. I'd be lying if I didn't say that him holding a small Necromancer child and running through a forest of death didn't concern me, but the determination in his eye reassures me. And we're out of options.

"Okay, then. Ready, set, close your eyes!"

FORTY-FIVE

Lila

Air, I need *air*. I can't *breathe*!

"You're okay, honey. You're okay, I got you."

Someone is holding my hand. My panting is loud to my own ears. What is going on? "Ryker?" I try to whisper. Nothing comes out.

But it's not Ryker. Anna is by my side, stroking my forearm with her free hand. "You're okay, sweetheart. Take your time."

She helps me sit up slowly. I'm in my bedroom at Headquarters. With Anna. How strange.

"What-" I struggle to find my voice. Is there cotton in my throat? I don't know why there would be but I can't catch my breath.

"Shh, it's alright. You performed a pretty hefty spell, Lila. It wiped you out, using up all of your *available* magic." She puts emphasis on the word. I guess we'll discuss that part later. "You did it, though. You tricked Jaquelin and Fara long enough for the Soldiers to arrive. They are in the Penitentiary, awaiting Tribunals."

"What about Ryker? Is he…" I trail off.

"The Soldier that was with you? He's perfectly fine. You did a great job of protecting him and the barrier, honey. I always knew you were special, but I'm just grateful to be able to witness it. You're so much more magical than I ever could've imagined." A tear runs down her face and I'm unsure how to react.

This must be how Ryker felt every time I cried. Except he wasn't related to me by blood and I didn't cry single tears. I bawled like a baby several times a day.

I squeeze Anna's hand to comfort her. "I don't know if I'm a very good daughter."

My words surprise us both and I almost regret opening my mouth until Anna smiles. "I don't know if I'm a very good mother."

I grin, relieved that she seems as nervous as I feel about our acquaintance.

"We can take it slow. I want to be as involved in your life as you'll let me. But I know you probably don't need me anymore, so whatever you want to give me, I'll graciously accept."

I clear my throat before I respond. I'm not even sure she's expecting me to, but I have a lot to say. "When I was younger, I always dreamed of what it would be like to meet my family. At some point, I figured it'd never happen. Then, I met people like Rachel and Ryker, people who I could trust and who believed in me. When Jaquelin told me that my parents were dead, I was sad that I'd never meet them, but part of me knew that I already had a family. Amaryllis is a part of me now. The people I've met here are my family." I pause, unsure how to proceed.

"The most important thing I've learned in the last several months is that relationships make us stronger. I used to think that friends, family, and lovers only made us more vulnerable, easier to be hurt. I had a hard time letting people in. But I know now how silly that is. Love can make us vulnerable, sure, but there isn't much to fight for without it. I don't need you to raise me or teach me how to braid my hair. I know how to drive and shave my legs. But I still *need* you. We'll figure out a rhythm that works for us."

Anna cries and tells me she's proud of me. Which, in turn, makes me cry. We embrace silently, enjoying the simplicity of each other's company.

"What about Genevieve and the others? How's Fern?"

Anna runs her hands through my hair as she answers. "Fern is still unconscious. The medics are pretty sure he'll never wake up. But Nonni and Tom are doing alright. Genevieve, Teresa, and Javier are good. They are working with the Council and the Soldiers to find the rest of the rebel group. I was with them until Lorenzo brought you back."

"And Lorenzo? How's he?"

"Better than ever. Sounds like he may be getting a promotion, actually." She smirks at me.

Someone knocks on the door and Anna doesn't hesitate to get up and open it.

"Hi Anna," a familiar voice says.

"Hi, Dear."

"I was just coming to check on-" Rachel lets out yelp as her eyes fall on mine. "I'm so glad you're okay!" Anna moves out of the way so Rachel can throw herself onto me.

Why was she worried about my well-being? Ryker and Anna should be the only ones who know what happened, right?

Undecided about what to ask first, I end up asking "Where've you been?" I'm not even sure why, but I'm immediately glad I did.

"With the rest of the Soldiers rummaging through the forest for rebels and everything." Her voice changes when she says it, as if the casual choice of words does no justice to the mission.

"Did you see-" I'm interrupted by another knock at the door.

Anna opens it again, revealing Connor this time. I try to push down the panic that begins to rise in my chest each time the person at the door isn't Ryker. Where is he? If he really is okay then why isn't he here?

"Hey, Anna." Does everyone know my mother? Ryker and I were only gone for three days.

"Lila, I'm so glad to see you doing better. I was wondering if now might be a good time to chat?" He sounds regretful. Of what, I'm not sure. Maybe because it's a full house. He probably didn't expect other people to be here. Maybe he's just embarrassed.

A few flashes of him trying to kill me fly through my head but I shake them off. "Sure."

"Rachel?" His voice is so tender when he says her name, reminding me of the moment they shared in the forest. "Would you mind staying in here with us? In case…" He doesn't finish and doesn't need to. Rachel puts a reassuring hand on his arm in response.

It's heartbreaking that he has to ask, though I'm grateful he did. I don't want either of us to be in that situation again.

"I'll be back in a bit," Anna excuses herself.

There is a bit of an awkward silence as I wait for Connor to start speaking. I start to wonder if I should begin, but, thankfully, he beats me to it.

"I know we spoke briefly about my parents a couple of days ago but I didn't really get to say everything I wanted to before you got assigned to your mission and well," he swallows audibly in between words, "I just want to apologize to you."

"Connor," I start, but I'm not sure what else to say.

"No, Lila. I know it's uncomfortable for so many reasons, but I just need to tell you. I'm so sorry. I'm sorry for how Headquarters has treated you. I'm sorry for the lack of control you've had over your life up to now, because of us. I'm sorry about your dad, and all the time you lost with your mom. I'm so sorry that you didn't grow up with magic, without knowing how incredible you are. I'm sorry for my part in it."

I'm at a loss for words. I wasn't expecting that much out of this huge man. He has an intimidating exterior. Surely I should've known he has a big heart, but I'm not sure how I would have. This is our first real conversation, after all.

"And I'm *very* sorry for trying to kill you," he adds.

The three of us laugh then, and I'm grateful for the break in tension.

"Thank you." My voice is more sappy than I anticipated. "But you don't really need my forgiveness. Your family has done more for me than anyone else in my whole life. Starting with you. You have saved me more than once, so trying to kill me really just balances the playing field for me to pay you back." I give him my most genuine smile.

"I'm not really sure that's how it works," Connor says uncomfortably. "But thank you anyway. I just don't want you to feel nervous around me. I bet we'll be seeing a lot of each other."

The way he smirks when he says it makes me blush. Where is his brother, anyway? I'm so tired of not having him by my side. "I hope so."

"Let's go do something together!" Rachel jumps in.

I look at her apologetically. "As much as I would love to, I'm still feeling pretty tired. I think I might rest for a bit longer."

"Totally! Sorry, of course you should rest. We'll come check on you later." She gives me a gentle hug.

Connor nods his head in my direction and then they both walk out the door, leaving me to drift off.

FORTY-SIX

Ryker

Once the kids are in Headquarters custody, The Council pulls me into a meeting to discuss how they were found and how to proceed.

It was difficult to hear their testimonies of what happened at the Roman and Jaquelin's Necromancer Homebase. Afterward, the Council shared that rumors had spread about the Enchantress escaping. The Necromancers found out that Roman was still alive, that he and Jaquelin were planning to sacrifice their people to drop the Veil that surrounds Amaryllis.

This caused an uprising within the community. According to the information the Council got from Jaquelin, Roman had them all killed. It's a lot to take on, but I'm grateful to be on this side of things. We got to save children. And now we can help rehabilitate them. We have the chance to do right by them, to amend the wrong we've done to the person that means most to me.

"The only person truly qualified to rehabilitate them is Lila Moreau. She's been through what they just went through. She'll understand them and help them develop healthy habits and thoughts regarding magic, Amaryllis, and Headquarters. Lorenzo is also a strong candidate for their training."

Several Council members hum while they consider my proposal. The others remain stone faced.

"This will be taken into consideration, Soldier. Thank you for your input."

I recognize that they're dismissing me, but I can't go without adding, "You won't regret choosing her. Trust me."

Because nobody could ever regret putting their faith into someone like her.

It's the most I can do to not sprint to Lila's room. Before I arrive, I run into Rachel and Connor.

"She's resting," Rachel says regretfully.

I briefly consider barging into her room anyway out of desperation to see her, but ultimately think better of it.

"How'd she seem?"

"She's good. Just a little tired, I guess." Rachel shrugs like she's also disappointed by Lila's exhaustion.

"Right."

"Have you heard about the event they're having in town?"

"No. What event?"

"Some Soldiers were just talking about some big party at Amaryllis. A celebration that the Enchantress is back-" Rachel wiggles her eyebrows- "and that the rebel group is no longer dominating the Necromancers."

"Wow," I marvel. "I can't remember the last time Amaryllis celebrated anything."

"And they're celebrating your girlfriend! What are the odds? You have to take her!"

I look to Connor for help but he only shrugs.

"If she's as tired as you said, then I don't think she'll be doing anything."

"Don't be that guy, Ryk," Connor finally adds to the conversation.

"What 'guy'? Rach just said that Lila's exhausted," I argue.

"Do you know nothing about women? Of course she's going to want to go with her man. Otherwise, we're taking her," he challenges.

"Isn't it going to be, like, formal, or whatever?"

They both catch on to my embarrassment. Rachel responds first, a little too enthusiastically. "We're going shopping!"

Any attempt at a protest is completely ignored by her. Connor laughs obnoxiously as Rachel drags me out of the building.

"Has anyone considered that *I* might also be tired?"

She rolls her eyes and pulls me toward the train station. "You are not going to be tired when you see Lila in her dress tonight."

"Dress?"

"I'll pick one out for her. You'll love it." She winks at me.

She's right. I definitely won't be thinking about anything other than Lila in a dress for the remainder of the day.

Rachel and Lila get ready in the next room while I get my tux on. The last time I dressed this nice was at my parents' funeral. That was also probably the last big gathering I attended that didn't involve training Soldiers.

I fumble with my bow tie as I imagine what Lila will look like. It feels like forever has passed since I last saw her. I'm baffled by how much I miss her. My parents have been gone for a long time and my brothers aren't always around so I've never really been the homesick type. But I crave Lila when she's not in my immediate vicinity.

Rachel wouldn't let me see the dresses she got for herself and Lila. The anticipation is killing me. I've only seen her wear tee shirts with jeans and the Soldier uniform. Unless you count the towel I saw her in just weeks ago. She could wear that and my jaw would still hit the floor.

When I leave my room, I'm greeted by a woman.

"Hi," she says softly. She looks vaguely familiar. "I'm Anna. You must be a Jordan?"

"Yes, ma'am. I'm Ryker Jordan. Did you know my parents?" I usually dread this conversation, but she's not as hungry for validation as other acquaintances of the Jordans.

"Yes, I did. I'm Anna Moreau." Her eyes darken.

Anna Moreau. The woman my parents died for. Lila's mother. "Oh, wow. It's nice to meet you." I reach my hand out to her.

She takes it, albeit hesitantly. "Likewise. It's a pleasure to meet Lila's other family members." It's a bit of an odd thing to say. Please let this be a figure of speech and not a confession. Please tell me Lila and I are *not* related.

"How do you mean?"

"My Lila said that she'd welcome me into the family she's gained along the way. The name Ryker was mentioned along with Rachel. I don't know her very well as an adult, but I can tell you mean quite a lot to her." Anna squeezes both of my hands with hers.

I'm at a loss for words, so I squeeze back. I can't believe I'm one of the first things Lila talked to her long-lost mother about. Learning it makes waiting to see her even more agonizing.

"I bet you're both so happy to have found each other," I say finally.

"It wouldn't have been possible without the sacrifices of the entire Jordan family. I will never be able to repay your family."

Before I can respond, Liam and Connor come around the corner.

"Ryker! Don't you look dapper? Who are you trying to impress, huh?" Liam teases.

"I'm going to go see how the girls are doing. Have a wonderful night." Anna squeezes my hands once more and then quickly disappears behind Lila's bedroom door. I wonder if she's nervous about being surrounded by the three Jordan boys or if she truly wants to help the girls. Maybe it's a little of both.

Something about the moment makes me pull both of my brothers into a bear hug. I can feel them look at each other around my head. It's not a routine gesture. Nevertheless, they hug me back and I'm grateful.

We're spared the awkward after-hug conversation by the opening of Lila's bedroom door. I whip around faster than I'd like to admit and both boys perk up at the sight of Rachel.

She's wearing a long shiny red dress that fits her well.

"You look beautiful, Rach." I pull her into a hug as well and can only imagine the look she's shooting my brothers behind my back.

"You too!" She's smiling wide as she steps back.

My cheeks flush as I notice the way Connor is looking at her. How long has *that* been going on? We're going to have to discuss it later, though, because the door is opening again.

Lila puts an end to my impatience as she steps into the corridor. Wow. She's wearing a long black dress covered in beads. It has thin straps and a v-neck that lays perfectly on her chest.

I'm already breathless, but when she turns to close her door, I notice that the back of her dress dips down, exposing half of her back. Her hair is down and curlier than ever.

As she turns back to face me, my heart hits a new record of beats per minute. She's wearing makeup for the first time in a long time. Most importantly, though, she looks incredibly happy and free.

"What's wrong?" Lila asks nervously.

I shake my head as I search for the right words. "Absolutely nothing." It comes out barely more than a whisper.

A smile that could brighten the deepest parts of the universe stretches across her face.

"Okay, okay. Let's go party!" Rachel interrupts.

Her and my brothers turn around and start toward the stairs. I take the opportunity to kiss Lila. I catch her gasp with my lips.

As soon as I can pull away, I whisper in her ear ,"You are magical. I think I'm addicted to you."

She giggles and I fall a little further.

"We have to go before I lose it," I admit against my own will. She nods innocently and I take her hand, pulling her towards the others.

"One last stop," Liam announces.

Lila and I share a glance as we come to a stop a few doors away from our rooms.

Liam holds the door open as one of the Necromancers from the forest steps out in a gold dress.

"Genevieve!" Lila squeals. They wrap each other in a tight embrace, bringing a smile to my face. I'm glad that Lila is making friends here.

The first train at the station is completely full. Lila stays perfectly close as we wait passively for the next one.

I don't realize how crowded the station has become until we're boarding. People shuffle in left and right, not so subtly pushing their way into the car.

I take a seat and pull Lila onto my lap, encompassing her in my arms. She smells fantastic. "I can't wait to dance with you all night long."

FORTY-SEVEN

Lila

Ryker keeps hold of me all night, as if he's worried I'd drift away. I've never felt so precious. The way he holds me and looks at me melts my insides.

Occasionally, I wonder if I should be embarrassed by his very public displays of affection, but I can't bring myself to do anything other than bathe in it. I do what I can to reciprocate, but my feeble attempts do little to compare.

In no universe is my looping my arm through his, or my laying on his chest while we dance making him feel even a fraction of what I feel when he pulls me close or whispers in my ear.

Ryker leads every dance, a given since I know nothing about how to move my body. We slow dance to every song that the orchestra plays.

I've never been to such an elegant event. The building is what I imagine a castle to be. The walls and ceilings are laced with beautiful gold details. Every room is exceptionally well-lit with chandeliers and candles alike.

There are servers walking about the room with hors d'oeuvres and skinny glasses filled with sparkly and bubbly drinks. I don't know if life here in Amaryllis will ever stop feeling like a dream.

"Are you enjoying yourself?" Ryker whispers in my ear. His breath sends shivers up my spine- again.

"For the first time in a long time." I tighten my grip on his shoulders. "All because of you."

"That's sweet, but not true at all. You are responsible for how far you've come. People will try your whole life to take away your successes, Lila. Don't let them. You are so incredible." His eyes are deep and sincere.

"But you, Rachel, your brothers, and your parents are the reason I was able to get this far. You were the catalyst of my evolution. In more ways than one."

His eyes glimmer then. I plant a soft kiss on his tan lips.

"Ryker?"

"Yes, Lila?"

"Aren't we going to be in trouble with the Council if people recognize us? I mean, I know that our close friends already know, but the rest of Headquarters doesn't. Won't they take you off my case if they see us like this?"

Ryker chuckles quietly. Or maybe he chuckles at regular volume but the music and dancing around us drowns it out. "What case, Lila? You're the Enchantress. You're above all of us. You don't need any bodyguards anymore."

A jolt of excitement shoots through me-

"Ow!" Ryker shivers.

I guess it wasn't just excitement after all. "Sorry," I say sheepishly.

He laughs as he picks me up and spins me around in a tight circle. I giggle shamelessly until he sets me back down. "You want to go somewhere else?"

"Yes." I should be embarrassed about how eager I sound, but something about Ryker's demeanor convinces me I don't need to be.

Ryker hand lingers on the small of my back as we say goodbye to Rachel, Connor, Liam, and Genevieve, who I now realize have met up with Ben and his friends.

Ryker buys us gelato at a small shop on the way to the train station. The park we stop at to eat is simple and quaint. It is very quiet outside the city, as I'm sure most people in Amaryllis are either at the party or working at Headquarters.

The park has beautiful lights that string from tree to tree. It's not dark, per se, but I can still see the stars up above.

"What a magical night," I marvel.

I feel Ryker's eyes on me. "Unbelievable."

I lean into him and he wraps an arm around me.

"Lila?"

"Yeah?" I say into his chest.

"Will you tell me what happened to you? With Jaquelin and Fara?"

I sit up and search his face. I wonder where the question is coming from. "Of course. You know how Lorenzo and I were talking about storing magic?"

He nods but remains silent.

"Well, I learned more about it when I was with the Necromancers. Jaquelin accidentally told me a little bit about it- how the Necromancers that night in the forest were pulling from the magic that I had been absorbing since childhood. That information, along with the textbook Lorenzo had left me, I had started to form a hypothesis.

"When I woke up on our mission and you weren't there, I sensed magic outside the tent. I thought it was as good a time as any to test out my theory. I was able to hide the magic I had stored inside of me over the last few weeks. That way, when they forced me to perform the ritual to destroy the barrier, I wouldn't have enough power."

Ryker contemplates my words carefully. "I thought you died."

My heart aches at his tone. "I'm so sorry, Ryker. We didn't exactly have time to debrief. I wanted to tell you-"

"Shh," he hushes me and places a kiss on the top of my head as he pulls me back to his chest. "I know. You did exactly what you needed to get us both out of there alive. I just can't bear seeing you so… lifeless."

I shudder at the thought. I too have seen Ryker barely clinging to life. It's been my motivation and my nightmare. "We're safe now." I hug him tightly. He squeezes back but doesn't say a word. "Let's go home."

We're both quiet on the way home. The train ride seems longer than ever. The car is sprinkled with other people, but the friction between Ryker and us couldn't be subdued by anything at this point.

We walk hand in hand, wrapped around each other up to our floor of the Living Quarters. When we get to the door of my room, Ryker turns to me. His face is serious as he makes his decision.

I let him struggle for a minute, but then let him off the hook, pointing to my door. "Anna is sleeping in here."

His demeanor changes immediately. "Remind me to thank her later." Ryker picks me up and carries me the few steps to his door, unlocking the door faster than I've ever been able to manage.

He sets me down softly and puts his hands on either side of my face. His eyes widen as they bore into my soul.

Finally, he lowers his face to mine. His lips are soft and warm as they press gently into mine. He takes his time with it, savoring every moment, and I'm so grateful for it.

He draws back, causing my eyes to fling open. He smiles victoriously as they do. "Do you want to change into something else? This dress can't be comfortable."

Seriously, that's what he's thinking about right now? Although now that he mentions it… "Actually, yes. And I'd love a bathroom break."

He pecks me on the mouth and then walks into his closet. He pulls out two pairs of pants and two shirts. "Socks?"

"Nah."

"Here," he says casually, as if this is the most peaceful he's ever been. Somehow it calms my nerves about the fact that we're about to spend the night together. It isn't the first time, and I hope it won't be the last.

I kiss him once more before I close the bathroom door behind me. I give myself a few seconds to silently scream into the mirror about the whole situation. That we defeated Jaquelin and the rebels. Over finding my mom. About everything to do with Ryker and him wanting me and touching me and kissing me.

Then I finally get a grip and realize I can't get out of my dress. Rachel had to zip me up. I facepalm and sigh. "Ryker?"

"Yeah?" he calls from the other side of the door.

"Can you help me?"

There's a moment of hesitation from his side before he asks, "You want me to come in there?"

I roll my eyes and open the door. I should've known that would break one of his rules. His eyes fall over my whole body as he takes in the fact that I'm still dressed.

"I can't get out of this dress by myself. You're going to have to undo the back."

He swallows hard and it makes the butterflies in my stomach go mad. "Okay."

I spin around and move my hair out of the way. A small gasp comes from behind me and I glance at Ryker from the mirror.

He moves closer and brushes his fingers across my back. "Connor has scars like this on his chest."

I forget about them unless someone points them out to me. Nobody could ever tell me why I had them, but foster parents, kids in locker rooms, and roommates always asked about them. "I don't know what they're from."

"I do." Ryker continues to graze them with his fingertips. I turn around quickly. "They're from that night in the forest with Connor. You know when I found you and Anna and everyone in the forest? The Necromancers were kind of shooting magic or whatever, do you remember?"

I nod to show I'm following along.

"That's what happened in the forest when Connor met you. You'd have to ask him for the details, but one of the bolts hit you in the back."

I reach to see it in my reflection but can't get a good look.

"What's wrong?"

"I've just never actually seen the scars. People have asked, but I assumed it was something that happened as a baby and I was too young to remember."

Ryker exits the room, rifles around in his jacket and returns with his device. "Turn around."

I do as he says.

He takes a picture of my back and then leans over to show it to me. White marks stretch across the top of my back, forming a star-like shape. "Woah," I mumble.

"Just one more thing that proves how strong you are." Ryker leans down and presses his lips to the spot. I watch in the mirror as he straightens and begins unzipping my dress.

His eyes gloss over as he works the zipper down to the base of my spine. I can hear his uneven breath as he meets my eyes in the mirror. He begs me to either ask him to continue or dismiss him.

"Thank you."

He doesn't move a muscle. I wish I knew what he was thinking.

"Ryker? You can wait outside. I'll be there in just a minute, okay?"

He nods excessively then, and hurries out of the bathroom, making sure to close the door tightly behind him.

FORTY-EIGHT

Ryker

I didn't expect her to look even more beautiful once she changed. But seeing her wear my clothes does something to my lungs. It's not that the clothes are spectacular. In fact, they're plain black and baggy on her tiny figure. But seeing her in them means that I can let myself pretend she's mine.

"What do you think?" she asks, spinning around. What an impossible question.

"I think I'm never going to let you leave this room."

My blunt answer surprises her. Maybe because I wasn't so confident just minutes ago while I undid her dress. But I've regained control. I can't wait to sleep by her side all night long.

"Get over here." My voice is raspy and tired. I wish I wasn't so exhausted, but it's probably for the better.

"Should I turn the light off?" She asks hesitantly.

"Sure."

Lila flips the light switch before hopping onto the bed. She sprawls out on top of me with an innocent smile. Holding her like this is so much better than our night in the stake out. We're both much more relaxed and content on being solely present with each other.

I let out a laugh and pull her to me as she smothers my face in tiny kisses. She ultimately lands on my lips and I surrender to her touch.

We kiss for a while- long enough to both need rehab, probably- and then we shuffle until we find a comfortable position in my small bed.

I squiggle on her back with my fingers as we wait for sleep to consume us both. Lila drifts off first, giving me time to catch up on my thoughts.

My life changed when Lila came into it. Connor's mission all those years ago was a turning point for our family. My parents then followed, keeping an eye on Lila's parents. I wonder if they had made the connection by then that Anna and her husband were looking for the same little girl that their son had been fighting reality with every time he closed his eyes.

Maybe that's why they sacrificed everything. Then, years later, I took a job with the intention of making Connor proud. Little did I know, this girl would not only bring my family together, she would save Amaryllis and everything that's been built here.

I can't think of a better cause for my parents to have chosen to fight for.

Someday, I'll have the words to express these thoughts to Lila and maybe even to my brothers. Until then, I want my actions to express the things I can't say.

"Tonight, and every other night that you let me-" I kiss the top of Lila's head- "I'll be right here."

EPILOGUE

"Turn it off," Lila groans as the alarm sounds. It happens every morning, so you'd think she'd be used to it by now.

Ryker rolls in the bed. "It's *your* alarm, Lila."

Her face scrunches as she attempts to open her eyes.

Ryker laughs under his breath and reaches over her, turning the alarm off. On his way back to his side of the bed, he pulls Lila tight against his chest and kisses her several times on the face.

"Today's the big day, Grumpypants."

Lila finally gets her eyes open. "What are you talking about?"

"Your pupils are receiving their Aegis ceremonies and moving on to Necromancy school." He strokes her face soothingly. No matter how grumpy she gets, he's still glad he gets to wake up next to her everyday.

Lila sits straight up in the bed when the words finally sink in. It makes Ryker laugh.

"Oh my goodness!" Lila exclaims. She leans over to kiss Ryker. "Thank you, thank you, thank you!"

Ryker pulls her into a tight hug and rolls her over his body to the other side of the bed so she can get down. Lila releases his mouth and his body follows suit.

She jumps off the bed and rushes to get ready.

Four out of nine children have reached the age of ten, meaning they are due for the Aegis ceremony to protect them from evil magic. Ryker, Lila, Lorenzo, and Finch stand in as the family members and friends of the children.

The ceremonies are magical and each child gets their own. Lila marvels at the experience, as she never had the opportunity to attend her own ceremony.

Even though there are four of them, and they're virtually the same, she tears up with each one. Ryker squeezes her hand lovingly.

When it's all said and done, the two of them take the four children out to a special lunch to celebrate their advancement.

"So we can't come to your classes anymore, Miss Moreau?"

"You're too advanced now!" She tries to sound cheerful. "However, you will be moving to Miss Genevieve's class, and she is a good friend of mine. She's excellent at Necromancy and has so much to teach you all. You will love it."

Her words comfort the four Necromancers in training. There is a mutual love and respect between the pupils and their teacher. Ryker has a soft spot for them too, being the one to find them in such devastating circumstances. But he's not nearly as expressive.

Once they finish their meal, Lila and Ryker walk the children over to their new classroom in Amaryllis, and say their goodbyes.

Genevieve is there to receive them and show them around. She confirms she'll get them back to housing in a few hours, releasing Lila and Ryker from responsibility.

Their train ride back to Headquarters is silent and heavy. Ryker can tell that Lila is on the brink of a meltdown, and anything could set her off.

Once they arrive, Ryker subtly guides a wandering Lila up to their shared room, sitting her on the bed.

He takes off his shoes, then hers, and takes a seat next to her. Lila starts crying as soon as her head meets Ryker's chest. He lets her sob as he runs his fingertips up and down her spine.

The patience and grace Ryker continuously shows Lila makes her cry even more. There's no reason she should be this lucky.

"I should be happy for them," she cries.

"You *are* happy for them, sweetheart. It's just hard to let go sometimes." His voice soothes her almost as much as his touch.

"I'm so proud of them, though."

"They know. Everyone in Amaryllis knows precisely how you feel about them. And how they feel about you." Ryker presses a kiss to the top of her head.

Lila sighs. "Will I ever be the one doing the comforting while you cry on my chest?"

"I don't know about the crying part, but I'll gladly take any opportunity to lay on your chest." Ryker smirks.

The comment makes Lila laugh, just as he hoped.

"We've got to meet up with Rachel, Genevieve, and the boys soon," Lila reminds Ryker.

"We have some time."

This makes both of them laugh as they fall back onto their bed.

Ryker is the first to wake up, not surprisingly. He quietly moves about the room, getting ready for this evening. He gets dressed and fixes his hair.

Lila starts to shuffle in the bed. Ryker grabs the last item from his sock drawer and then walks over to his sleepy woman.

He kisses her, first on the nose, then the lips, and followed by both cheeks. "It's almost time to go to dinner, sweetheart."

Lila's face scrunches again as she opens her eyes. "Good morning, handsome." Her eyes widen. "Wait, is that what you're wearing?"

"Yeah, why? What's wrong?"

"Ryker, I don't have anything that nice!"

He smirks at her. "Yes you do."

"No," she argues. "I'm not wearing that dress."

"But it's my *favorite* dress in the world."

"Ryker! It is way too fancy for dinner with your brothers."

"First of all, no it's not. Second, look at me. I look handsome as hell. And third, it's a nice restaurant!"

Lila rolls her eyes and hops off the bed, making her way to the closet. She groans as she pulls the dress from its spot. She glares at Ryker up until the bathroom door is closed.

She uses the restroom, brushes her teeth, and washes her face before she attempts to get the dress on. It slips on easier than she thought it would. Certainly her body has changed in the last couple years.

"Ryker," she calls flatly.

"Yes?" His voice sounds condescending and Lila rolls her eyes again.

"I need you to zip me up."

Ryker takes no time to enter the bathroom. His eyes light up when he sees her in that dress. It takes him back to that first night they truly spent together.

"I doubt it'll even fit."

"It had better," Ryker says breathlessly. It's been a while since he's been so blown away by her and it sends butterflies through her stomach.

Ryker works the zipper up Lila's back without much effort. He presses his lips to her scar and they both reminisce. They meet each other's eyes in the mirror and time seems to slow.

In one swift movement, Ryker spins Lila around and lifts her onto the bathroom counter. He leans his forehead against hers in anticipation.

"You're going to rip it," Lila whispers.

"That would be *awful*."

Lila giggles and closes the gap between them. Literal sparks fly as their lips touch. It drives Ryker even crazier. He holds Lila's waist firmly against his own.

They find a pace, moving in perfect unison.

"Knock knock!" A voice calls from the hallway.

It takes Lila and Ryker several seconds to notice and then several more to pull away from each other.

"Time to go," Ryker sighs. But he's not disappointed. He'll have all night with her.

Lila swipes on some mascara and throws her hair into a curly bun that sits at the base of her skull. "Let's do it."

❖❖❖

Dinner is lovely. The atmosphere is warm and the food is exquisite. Their group is definitely the best dressed in the restaurant, but Lila was relieved to see Rachel wearing her red dress.

It's almost sad that none of them had needed a nice outfit since the party in Amaryllis, but it makes the night all the more nostalgic.

Ryker tries to remain calm as the night goes on, not wanting to let the surprise get ruined. His brothers do an excellent job at keeping Lila distracted.

When all the food is gone and paid for, the group separates.

"We're going to get gelato. You two want anything?" Rachel asks Ryker and Lila. Right on schedule.

"Nah," Ryker says nonchalantly. "Lila wants one though."

It makes Lila beam. "Raspberry, please!"

"Okay, we'll be back in a bit."

Lila and Ryker walk hand in hand through the near-vacant city streets.

"Wait," Lila gasps. "Isn't this-" She runs into the park. Ryker follows close behind. "Isn't this the park we came to after the party?"

Lila gasps again as she spins around and finds Ryker on one knee, his hands holding a small wooden box with gold lines decorating the outside.

"Lila Moreau," Ryker says shakily. "There is absolutely nothing that could have prepared me for you. I never imagined I would feel so many things for one person. You're absolutely magical. You've uprooted my entire life in the best possible way. You make me want to be so much better and I can't fathom spending another day without you."

"Are you… asking me to marry you?"

"If you could keep your questions until the end, I'd really appreciate it."

"Right, sorry." She covers her mouth.

Ryker opens the dainty box, revealing a delicate golden ring. "We don't really marry the same way, here in Amaryllis. But there's a binding ceremony that is pretty similar. So, yeah. I'd like to know if you'd like to be with me forever. What do you say?"

There is a moment of silence between Ryker's question and Lila's answer. He starts to panic, wondering if maybe she thinks it's too soon, when she interrupts his thoughts with a screech.

"Yes! Yes, yes yes! I love you, Ryker Jordan." She jumps onto him suddenly, giving him barely enough time to catch her before she smacks the pavement.

"I love you too, Lila."

The two embrace on the park floor, completely oblivious to the evil that surrounds them.

Acknowledgements

It constantly blows my mind how many people I have in my life that unconditionally love and support me. This story has taken a lot of time, sweat, and tears. I hope you enjoyed it.

Reader, thank you for reading my book. It means a lot that you spent time reading something that I created. It was hard and surreal to release my work for anyone to read. It's vulnerable and anxiety inducing. So, thank you for giving me a shot! I hope to have more for you soon.

Justin, thank you for being the first person I thought of. At that point, this book was just a crazy and spontaneous idea. Thank you for giving me enough faith in it to keep going. You've always been on my side and I'm more grateful than you know.

Kara, I could never thank you enough for being my biggest cheerleader in everything I do. I respect your taste in books, so it means the world to me that you actually liked my book. Thank you for giving it a chance. Thank you for pushing through several rough drafts. I apologize for the whiplash you had to endure between drafts, ideas, and my emotional roller coaster. I wish I could promise it will never happen again, but you know how I am. I love you, sis.

Adam, thank you for your wonderful feedback. Thank you for being someone I could trust with this part of myself. Thank you for your honesty and the time you probably didn't know you were signing up for. You're so awesome and I appreciate your role in my life.

Jaret, thank you for holding me, consoling me, and letting me talk your ear off at every inconvenience. Thank you for never getting tired of my ideas. Thank you for appreciating my intense need to create, despite the mess it tends to cause. I'll write a book about our love story someday and read it on repeat. I love you.

Family, thanks for supporting me in this journey. Many of you know about it now, but only a few of you have had to deal with the ups and downs. Thank you for being you. Thanks for pushing me forward without having any clue what this novel entailed. I hope you liked it. Thanks for being proud of me even if you didn't.

About the Author

CASSANDRA RIOS was born and raised in the U.S.A., where she currently lives with her beloved family.

She is a book and movie lover, especially when they include romance. In her opinion, stories are a wonderful way to learn lessons and have experiences that we otherwise wouldn't get the chance to.